NORTH SHORE PUBLIC LIBRARY
3 0651 00239 0213

W9-BRM-805

Gingerbread Cookie Murder

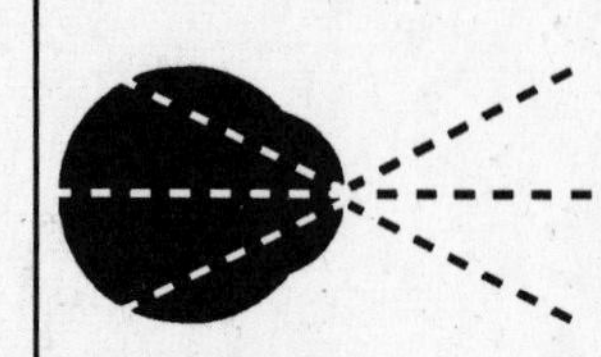

This Large Print Book carries the Seal of Approval of N.A.V.H.

GINGERBREAD COOKIE MURDER

JOANNE FLUKE
LAURA LEVINE
LESLIE MEIER

THORNDIKE PRESS
A part of Gale, Cengage Learning

Detroit • New York • San Francisco • New Haven, Conn • Waterville, Maine • London

Thorndike Press, a part of Gale, Cengage Learning.

Thorndike Press® Large Print Mystery.
The text of this Large Print edition is unabridged.
Other aspects of the book may vary from the original edition.
Set in 16 pt. Plantin.

LIBRARY OF CONGRESS CATALOGING-IN-PUBLICATION DATA

Fluke, Joanne, 1943–
Gingerbread cookie murder / by Joanne Fluke, Laura Levine, Leslie Meier.
p. cm. — (Thorndike Press large print mystery)
ISBN-13: 978-1-4104-2998-8 (hardcover)
ISBN-10: 1-4104-2998-9 (hardcover)
1. Detective and mystery stories, American. 2. Christmas stories, American. 3. Large type books. I. Levine, Laura, 1943– Dangers of gingerbread cookies. II. Meier, Leslie. Gingerbread cookies and gunshots. III. Title.
PS3556.L685G56 2010
813'.54—dc22 2010027944

Published in 2010 by arrangement with Kensington Books, an imprint of Kensington Publishing Corp.

Printed in the United States of America
1 2 3 4 5 6 7 14 13 12 11 10

Gingerbread Cookie Murder

Joanne Fluke

A big thank you to Kathy Allen for testing lots of Hannah's recipes. And thanks to John and Kathy's friends for critiquing them.

Chapter One

Twenty-four reindeer burned to a crisp and it was all her fault! Hannah Swensen pulled the smoking cookie sheets from her oven and dumped the contents in the kitchen wastebasket. She should have known she'd never hear her stove timer over Ernie Kusak's deafening Christmas music.

To bake, or not to bake. Hannah pondered the decision for several seconds. She'd left work early to come home to bake, and if she quit now, she'd have to get up very early tomorrow to finish the cookies she'd promised to deliver to her niece Tracey's first grade class in time for their morning snack. On the other hand, she'd probably burn several more herds of reindeer unless she stood with her ear to the oven. And Tracey had promised her classmates that Aunt Hannah's gingerbread reindeer cookies were the best cookies in the whole world.

"Later," she said with a sigh, covering the

ing bowl with plastic wrap and sliding it to the refrigerator. The cookies could wait. Earplugs, however, could not.

Hannah hurried to her bedroom, pulled out the top drawer of her dresser, and took out a small plastic pouch. The last time she'd worn earplugs was when she'd watched her business partner, Lisa, compete in a pistol match. Ernie's music was certainly as loud as a gunshot, and that meant they ought to work just fine.

The earplugs were the squeezable kind and fairly comfortable, but even after she'd put them in place, she could still hear the refrain of *I Saw Mommy Kissing Santa Claus* quite clearly. They didn't completely drown out the racket, but they did make it bearable.

Hannah was about to turn to go back into the living room, when she spotted a lump under the covers of her bed. Her feline roommate had also made an effort to escape the musical assault.

"Smart boy!" she complimented the twenty-three pound, orange and white cat who cohabited her condo. It was clear that Moishe shared her opinion of Ernie's music, because he'd tunneled under a quilt, two blankets, a sheet, and a feather pillow.

At least it wasn't the same song, over and

over. *Have a Holly Jolly Christmas* had
blaring away when Hannah had come ho
from The Cookie Jar, her bakery and coffe
shop in town. The previous evening she'd
been subjected to the strains of *We Wish You a Merry Christmas* when she'd climbed up the stairs to her second-floor home. The night before that it had been a dozen verses of *The Twelve Days of Christmas.* Twice. There was nothing wrong with Christmas music. Hannah *loved* Christmas music. But this was way too early, a whole month before Christmas, and Ernie turned it up way too loud. Lisa had suggested that Ernie might have a hearing problem, and Hannah agreed. If Ernie had no hearing loss now, he was bound to have one before the holiday season was over!

Hannah gave a little sigh. She'd done her best to solve the problem today when Ernie had come into The Cookie Jar for coffee. With unprecedented tact for one who had none to speak of, Hannah had asked him very nicely if he would please lower the volume of the music. Ernie had agreed immediately, promising to reduce the decibels right after his kids came home from school and saw the newest addition to his Christmas display. Hannah had been so grateful, she'd given him a dozen gingerbread Santa kies to seal their bargain.

Everyone in Lake Eden, Minnesota, had reeled in shock when Ernie Kusak had divorced his wife Lorna in June. As far as the founders of the Lake Eden gossip hotline knew, the Kusak marriage was rock solid. They didn't have financial worries. Lorna worked as a legal secretary for Howie Levine, Lake Eden's most popular lawyer, and Ernie made good money as the manager and head driver for Cyril Murphy's Shamrock Limousine Service. The couple had two teenage children who earned high grades in school and appeared happy and well adjusted. Their son, Christopher, was a senior at Jordan High and their daughter, Lindsay, was a junior. Lorna had never complained to any of the local women about Ernie, and on the infrequent occasions that Ernie had time off and joined the crowd in the back room at Hal and Rose's Cafe to play a hand of poker, he had nothing critical to say about Lorna. No one was sure why their twenty-year marriage had suddenly dissolved, and neither Lorna nor Ernie was talking.

Once the Kusak divorce was final, Hannah's sister, Andrea, had sold their house to Gary Jenkins, one of Ernie's coworkers, who wanted to move from a neighboring town and reduce his commute time. She'd found a condo in Hannah's complex for Lorna to buy with her share of the proceeds, and Gary had invited Ernie to live in what had formerly been Ernie's own basement bedroom. He'd been living there for four months when fortune smiled on him and he purchased the winning ticket in the Super-Six Lottery with a jackpot of over eight million dollars.

The lottery changed Ernie's life. When he moved out of his old basement and used some of his newly found riches to buy a condo in Hannah's complex, speculation ran wild that Ernie had come to his senses and was attempting to get back into Lorna's good graces. But Lorna wasn't convinced she wanted to re-marry Ernie, even though he was now a wealthy man.

Hannah was the first to admit that establishing a college fund for Chris and Lindsay was a good first step toward restoring Lorna's affections. Buying both kids new cars, however, was a bit much. Of course the kids liked to hang out at Dad's condo with their friends. Ernie had equipped it with the newest video games, there were always cold drinks and snack foods on hand, and Ernie had programmed the takeout number for Bertanelli's Pizza on his phone.

A giant-screen television in the media room was set up to receive first-run movies and sports events via satellite, and Chris and Lindsay's friends were always welcome. According to Lorna, the only part of the three-bedroom condo that Ernie had set aside for his own pleasure was the master bedroom. That said, Lorna had snapped her mouth shut and refused to say anything further.

Even though now, with her earplugs in place, Ernie's music was borderline tolerable, Hannah supposed a member of the homeowners' association should go down and caution Ernie again. But Ernie had promised her he'd turn down the volume right after his kids came home from school. Perhaps they'd had a late afternoon activity at Jordan High and they weren't home yet.

Hannah glanced out the window that overlooked the grounds as she left her bedroom. The wind had tossed the fresh snow that had fallen during the day, rearranging it in long ridges that buried the winter plants and formed irregular hillocks on the ground. Now that evening was fast approaching, the plush blanket of snow was imprinted with Dali-esque shadows of trees and buildings, as if she were viewing it through an ancient, wavy glass. The light level was different, too. It seemed to be a lot brighter than it should be for this time of night and it appeared to be . . . green!

Hannah flicked off her bedroom light for a better look. The light reflecting against the bank of snow was definitely green, a bright Kelly green. But wait . . . it had just changed color! Now it was red, as red as a stoplight, and as she watched, it changed again to flashing yellow. What on earth was going on? The Northern Lights had never been this brilliant before!

Puzzled, Hannah headed back down the hall to see if the scene was the same from her guest room window. Yes, the snow that had gathered in clumps against the bushes was also reflecting the changing colors. The simple solution was to go outside to see if she could figure out what was happening, but she had another piece of business to accomplish first.

As she passed by her desk in the living room, Hannah picked up the list of condo board members that was propped up against her computer keyboard. The other residents would be coming home from work soon and she had to find a board member to give Ernie another warning. He'd been cooperative when board members had warned him in the past and there was no reason to think he wouldn't cooperate tonight. Music this loud was simply unacceptable. She could hear every word of *We Three Kings* right through the same earplugs that had effectively blocked out the sound of gunshots the last time she'd worn them.

The president of the homeowners' association was the logical choice to call. It was Sue Plotnik, Hannah's downstairs neighbor, and she occupied the unit across from Ernie's. Unfortunately, or perhaps fortunately for them, the Plotnik family had left this morning for Sue's parents' house in Wisconsin.

The next name on the list was the vice president, but he wasn't home when Hannah called him. Neither was the secretary nor the treasurer. That left three members-at-large and they didn't answer her calls either.

There was only one name left on the list. It was hers. She'd been elected to the board last week to fill a vacancy left by a member who'd moved. Since no one else was available, *she* had to go downstairs and ask Ernie to turn down the music.

Going out in the Minnesota winter, even just running down the stairs to knock on a neighbor's door, required donning survival gear. Hannah put on her parka and zipped it up, jammed a ski cap over her unruly masses of red curls, and pulled on her snow boots. Once she'd thrust her hands into fur-lined gloves, she opened the door and stepped out onto the frigid landing.

And there she stopped. And stared. The mystery of the colored, flashing lights she'd seen reflected on the snow outside her windows was solved.

It was well below zero and Hannah's breath steamed out in clouds of white vapor, but she didn't notice. Her gaze was fixed on the sky above, where penguins in Santa hats were cavorting wildly with polar bears shaking tambourines.

As Hannah watched, mesmerized, an infinite line of elves on ice skates wound around the unlikely couples, carrying gaily wrapped packages that looked much too large for them to handle. Every motion, every turn, every swooping swirl was carefully synchronized with Ernie's Christmas music.

It took a few moments for Hannah to recover her power of speech. When she did, she uttered a phrase she'd never use around her young nieces. Not only had Ernie installed a theater quality sound system to play his music at a deafening level, but he'd also just added a spectacular laser display as a showcase.

Hannah stamped her feet to restore mobility. They felt like square blocks of ice. Standing here staring at Ernie's exhibition wouldn't solve the noise problem. She headed down the stairs, turned at the bottom, and clumped past Sue and Phil's darkened condo. Ernie had the unit on the other side of the staircase and she glanced up at the condo immediately above his. Only the kitchen light on the table was burning and Hannah was familiar with Clara and Marguerite's habits. When that light was on and the rest of the condo was dark, the Hollenbeck sisters were not at home.

There was a drum roll from overhead and Hannah glanced up at the sky. Good heavens! Here came flying snowmen holding sleigh bells just as the music segued into *Jingle Bells!* Hannah tore her eyes away from the sight and concentrated on keeping her footing on the icy walkway. She reached Ernie's door without incident and rang the buzzer several times.

Nothing, absolutely nothing happened. That didn't surprise Hannah. She doubted that Ernie could hear the buzzer with all this racket going on. She tried again several times, and even used the ornamental knocker on the outside of the door. When that had no effect, she resorted to pounding on the door with her gloved fists.

After several moments, she stopped. It was no use. The old-fashioned globe lights that dotted the grounds of the complex clicked on and Hannah shivered. Night had fallen and it was bitterly cold. The wind whipped around the corner of the building and threatened to blow off her ski cap. Strands of hair not covered by the stretchy knit fabric were transformed into miniature whips that flayed at her cheeks. Her feet had lost all feeling and her teeth were chattering faster than the wind-up denture toy Norman Rhodes, one of the men she dated, kept in the kids' corner of the Rhodes Dental Clinic.

She'd make one last attempt and then she'd go home. Hannah pressed the buzzer repeatedly with her right hand and beat a volley of thumps on the door with her left. When there was no response before her arms tired, she convinced herself that Ernie wasn't home and turned to retrace her steps. As she passed the grated ground-level openings that let air and light into the underground garage, she noticed that Ernie's new Ferrari was parked in his spot. Dragging her icy legs up the stairs, Hannah decided that there were only two conclusions to draw from this new piece of information: Either Ernie was home and hadn't heard her, or Ernie had left with someone else.

A welcome blast of heat greeted her as she opened her condo door and she took a big gulp of the non-frozen air. She'd done her duty as a board member, even though it hadn't worked. She tossed her parka on the couch and glanced at the phone on the end table to see if she'd missed any calls. The red light wasn't blinking and that meant no one had called. That was good. She probably couldn't have heard the message if she'd played it back anyway.

Hannah was about to go off to the kitchen to pour herself a steaming cup of coffee when she had an idea. There was one last way she could try to contact Ernie. She could call him and if she let the phone ring long enough and he was home, he might hear it, especially if a relatively quiet Christmas song came on.

The moment she thought of it, Hannah kicked off her boots, sat down on the couch, and reached for the phone. She was just in time. The current song ended and a softer transition to another Christmas carol began to play. And then, just as she was about to pluck the phone from the cradle, it rang.

"Hello?" she said, just as the first bars of *Go Tell It on the Mountain,* sung by an extremely powerful soprano, began battering her eardrums.

"Hannah? Are you there?"

"Hold on!" she shouted, doing battle with the soprano by racing to the laundry room and banging the door shut behind her. The noise, muffled by four interior walls, abated somewhat and she turned back to the phone. "I'm here," she said.

The voice answered again, but she couldn't make out the words. Had she suffered permanent hearing loss? She reached up to touch her ear and her fingertips encountered a foreign object. For a moment, she was puzzled, but then she remembered that her earplugs were still in place. "Hold on," she said again. "I have to take out my earplugs."

A moment later she was back on the line. "Norman?" she asked. "Is that you?"

"It's me. Why do you have your music turned up so loud? And what was that about earplugs?"

"It's not my music. It's coming from Ernie Kusak's place. And my earplugs are preventive medicine for hearing loss."

"Poor Moishe!" Norman sounded very sympathetic. "His hearing is even more acute than yours."

"I know. I'm sure it hurts his ears. He's hiding under the covers on my bed and he never does that."

"I'd better come over and get him right away," Norman said, and that made Hannah smile. When it came to her, it was a case of *Love me, love my cat.* And Norman loved her cat almost as much as he loved his own cat. "Moishe can stay with Cuddles while we go out for dinner. It's nice and quiet at my place. Can you be ready in twenty minutes?"

"Yes," Hannah said quickly. It was Norman to the rescue once again. She just hoped that things wouldn't change once his new business partner and former fiancée, Beverly Thorndike, moved to Lake Eden in January. Norman had sworn that nothing would change between them, but Hannah wasn't so sure. Even though Norman had done his best to convince her that his relationship with Beverly was strictly business, Hannah just couldn't believe it was that simple. Beverly and Norman had been engaged for over a year. Was it possible to completely turn off the loving feelings that they must have had for each other? Or would those feelings return when they were together all day at the Rhodes Dental Clinic?

"Hannah?"

Hannah came back to the present with a jolt as she realized Norman had asked her a question. This was not the time to worry about what might and might not happen between Norman and Beverly. "Sorry," she apologized. "What did you say?"

"I asked you if you could put on Moishe's harness and leash before I get there."

"I'll try, but he may not want to come out from under the covers."

"I can't blame him for that. I can barely hear you over the music. Just have everything handy and I'll hook him up when I get there."

"Will do," Hannah promised. "If you don't have earplugs, stick some cotton in your ears before you get out of your car. And don't bother to ring the doorbell. If Ernie's music is still on, I probably won't hear it anyway."

"Do you want me to bang on the door?"

"Don't bother. That might not work either. I'll be watching for you to come up the stairs and I'll let you in."

Gingerbread Cookies

DO NOT preheat oven —
This dough must chill overnight.

Sally makes these for the Christmas buffet at The Lake Eden Inn.

1 cup softened, salted butter ***(2 sticks, 1/2 pound, 8 ounces)***
1 cup white ***(granulated)*** sugar
1/2 cup hot strong coffee
2/3 cup dark molasses
1 teaspoon baking soda
1 teaspoon salt
2 and 1/2 teaspoons ground ginger
1/2 teaspoon ground cloves ***(I'm not fond of cloves so I leave this out)***
1 teaspoon cinnamon
4 and 3/4 cups all-purpose flour ***(don't sift it — pack it down in the cup when you measure it)***

In a large bowl, mix the softened butter with the white sugar.

Add the half-cup of hot strong coffee and then stir in the dark molasses.

Mix in the baking soda, salt, ground ginger, ground cloves, and cinnamon. Stir well.

Add the flour in half-cup increments, mixing after each addition. Give everything a final stir and then cover your bowl with plastic wrap and store it in the refrigerator overnight.

In the morning when you're ready to bake, preheat the oven to 375 degrees F., rack in the middle position.

Divide the dough into four parts for ease in rolling. Roll out the first part of the dough on a floured board. If you plan to use gingerbread men or reindeer-shaped cookie cutters, roll your dough out to 1/4 inch thick. ***(Arms and legs tend to snap off when you frost them if they're rolled too thin.)*** Otherwise roll your dough out to 1/8 inch thick.

Dip the cookie cutters in flour and cut out cookies, getting as many as you can from the sheet of dough. Use a metal spatula to remove the cookies from the rest of the sheet of dough and place them on an UNGREASED cookie sheet. Leave at least an inch and a half between cookies.

Once you've cut out your cookies, there will be leftover dough. You can gather it into a ball, re-flour the board, and re-roll it. ***(I've done this up to three times — the fourth time the dough got too stiff to roll well.)***

If you want to use colored sugar or sprinkles to decorate, put it on now, before baking and press it down just a bit with your fingers or with the spatula. If you'd rather frost the cookies, wait until they're baked and completely cooled.

Bake 1/4 inch thick cookies at 375 degrees F. for 10 to 12 minutes. Leave them on the sheet for a minute or two and then transfer them to a wire rack to complete cooling.

Bake 1/8 inch thick cookies at 375 degrees F. for 8 to 10 minutes. Leave them on the cookie sheet for a minute or two and then transfer them to a wire rack to complete cooling.

If You Hate to Roll Out Cookies:

You don't absolutely have to roll out these cookies. Take your dough out of the refrigerator, preheat the oven to 350 degrees F., and get out a nice sturdy teaspoon. ***(We use a 2-teaspoon scooper at The Cookie Jar.)***

Put approximately a half-cup of white sugar in a bowl. You'll be making dough balls and rolling the cookies in the sugar before placing them on the baking sheet.

Lightly grease your cookie sheet or spray it with Pam or another nonstick cooking spray.

Scoop out some cookie dough and make dough balls about the size of walnuts with your fingers. Roll the balls in the sugar and then place them on the cookie sheet, 12 to a standard-size sheet.

Flatten the dough balls with the smooth bottom of a drinking glass, the blade of a metal spatula, or your impeccably clean hands. Make sure they're no thicker than 1/4 inch.

Bake the cookies at 350 degrees F., for no more than 8 minutes. ***(You don't want them as hard as rocks.)*** Remove them from the oven, let them cool on the sheet for a minute, and then transfer them to a wire rack to cool completely.

You can frost all three types of these cookies if you wish, even the ones that were made from dough balls dipped in sugar. You can use your own favorite frosting, or the Cookie Icing recipe below:

Cookie Icing:

2 cups sifted confectioners sugar ***(powdered sugar)***
1/8 teaspoon salt
1/2 teaspoon vanilla ***(or other flavoring)***
1/4 cup cream

Mix up icing, adding a little more cream if it's too thick and a little more powdered sugar if it's too thin.

If you'd like to frost the cookies in different colors, divide the icing and put it in several small bowls. Add drops of the desired food coloring to each bowl.

Use a frosting knife, or use a brush to "paint" the cookies you've baked.

Yield: 3 to 4 dozen cookies made with small cookie cutters, 2 to 3 dozen cookies made with large cookie cutters, 8 to 10 dozen dough ball cookies.

mother, Carrie, was in the lead with her new husband, Earl Flensburg. Following them was Hannah's mother, Delores. She was dressed in an outfit that only Delores could pull off, a formfitting red wool suit with black braid outlining the collar and cuffs. With her and quite obviously her companion for the evening was a handsome older man.

"Who's that man with your mother?" Norman asked.

"Gary Jenkins. He bought Lorna and Ernie's house."

"I don't think I've met him."

"I have, but just once. Andrea introduced us. Gary used to be a standby driver for Ernie at Shamrock Limos, but after Ernie won the lottery and quit, Cyril promoted him to Ernie's old position. Mother's been helping him furnish the house. It's Craftsman style and Granny's Attic carries quite a few Craftsman pieces."

"I don't think he's *just* a client."

Hannah watched as her mother smiled up at Gary Jenkins. It was definitely a thousand-watt smile, and that meant Norman was right.

"Mother's been dating a lot lately," she confided. "Andrea and Michelle think that as long as she's playing the field, there's nothing to worry about."

"They're probably right." Norman thought about it for a minute. "I hope she's not on some sort of quest to get married again, now that my mother did. Your mother might feel left out."

Hannah thought about that for a moment. "I don't think that's it," she said. "Mother spends more time with Carrie now that she's married than she did before. And she's always liked Earl. They went to school together."

"Do you think your mother could be having some sort of midlife crisis?"

"Not unless she lives to be a hundred and twenty!"

The moment the words left her mouth, Hannah knew she'd made a mistake. She'd promised her mother never to divulge her true age. The only reason Hannah knew was that she'd helped her mother with legal matters after her dad had died. Her sisters knew that Delores was older than she claimed to be, but they had no idea how much older. Several of her mother's former classmates knew, but they weren't talking. It was one thing to gossip, but quite another to bring the wrath of Delores down on their heads!

"Are you telling me that your mother's actually . . . ?"

"Stop!" Hannah interrupted him with a firm hand on his arm. "I'm going to pretend I said nothing. And *you're* going to pretend I said nothing."

"Are you trying to tell me that if I thought I heard you say something that related to your mother's age, it could present a real danger to our health and well-being?"

Hannah gave a nod. Norman caught on fast

"Okay. All I can say is, there must be a lot of ambient noise in here because I didn't hear a single word you said."

They saw it before they even turned off the highway, a chorus line of reindeer wearing Santa hats and capes, standing on their hind feet and kicking to the beat of *Have Yourself a Merry Little Christmas.*

"Are those . . . ?"

"Reindeer Rockettes," Hannah answered before he could finish his question. "Ernie's not home yet and the laser show's still playing. I saw this part before you came to pick me up."

Norman left his window rolled all the way up until they came to the gated entrance. Then he took Hannah's gate card, lowered the window quickly, and slid the card into the slot to lift the wooden arm. Once they were inside the complex, lights flashed behind them and they both turned around to look.

"It's Mike," Hannah said, recognizing Mike Kingston's cruiser. She gave a little wave to acknowledge the other Lake Eden bachelor she occasionally dated, and they drove on with Mike following them.

Once Norman had pulled into Hannah's extra parking spot and Mike had parked directly behind them, Norman poked cotton in his ears and Hannah re-inserted her earplugs. Then they got out of Norman's sedan to greet Mike.

"Someone from the complex called you?" Hannah shouted her question.

"Yeah. Seventeen complaints so far. What's the number?"

"What number?"

"The unit number. Where does Ernie live?"

"Downstairs kitty-corner from me. I'll show you."

"You don't have to show me. Just give me the unit number. I've got the code for the breaker box."

"You can cut off his electricity?" Norman leaned closer to be heard.

"Sure. I'll kill the lights and that'll kill the music. And then I'll go in and read Ernie the riot act."

"Good idea. Ernie's in unit forty-nine." Hannah led Mike to the breaker box and he punched in the code. Once the box was open, he threw several switches and blessed silence ensued.

"What a relief!" Hannah gasped, removing her earplugs with a flourish. "Thank you, Mike."

"You're welcome."

"So now you're going to go talk to Ernie?" Norman asked him.

"Yeah. I need to make sure this sort of thing doesn't happen again." Mike turned to Hannah. "How's Moishe? This must have freaked him out."

"It did. He tunneled under my blankets until Norman came to pick him up." Hannah turned to Norman. "I guess I could drive to your house and bring him home now that Mike's turned off Ernie's music."

"Oh, let him stay. He looked so comfortable on the couch with Cuddles. I've got a short day tomorrow. Doc Bennett is coming in to do Bertie Straub's whitening at two and he'll take over for the rest of the day. I can bring Moishe home right after that."

"Seems to me you've had quite a few short days lately." Mike gave Norman a friendly slap on the back. "Are you sure there's enough work for that new partner of yours?"

"Beverly? Oh, there's enough work for her. Doc Bennett wants to cut back on his hours and Bev's agreed to free me up for more of what I want to do."

Hannah held her breath, hoping that Mike would pose the question and she wouldn't have to do it. But Mike didn't. "What *do* you really want to do?" she finally asked Norman.

"Paint." Norman looked slightly embarrassed as he turned to face Mike. "It was Hannah's idea. I used to paint and I gave it up when I became a dentist. Hannah reminded me that there was more to life than just work and she told me I shouldn't give up my dream. So when Beverly needed to sign on somewhere as a dentist, I snapped her up to give me more free time."

"Good for you!" Mike said, nodding in approval.

"Right," Hannah echoed, although she wished she hadn't told Norman not to give up his dream if that was the real reason he'd hired Beverly Thorndike. Now Norman's former fiancé was coming to Lake Eden and Hannah felt almost as if it were *her* fault!

"So when is she coming?" Mike asked.

"Not until January fifteenth. She's still under contract at another clinic and they won't let her go early. But that's okay. I can wait."

So can I! Hannah thought, although she didn't say it.

"You're going to stay here, aren't you?" Mike asked. "I mean, you're not going to go off to Paris and live in a garret or something like that, are you?"

Norman laughed. "Nope. This is my home and I plan to stay here. I might travel a bit, though. Mother and Earl really loved Rome when they were there on their honeymoon."

"Minnesota has beautiful places, too," Mike said, echoing Hannah's thoughts. "You don't have to travel to foreign countries to find things to paint. Take that pine tree in your front yard, the one that's just to the right of the driveway. That's the prettiest pine tree I ever saw."

Norman clapped Mike on the shoulder. "I agree. And that's why I bought the place."

"No kidding?"

"No kidding."

Hannah stared at her two boyfriends who were grinning at each other. Every once in a while, she wished they'd get out of their mutual admiration society. It wasn't that she wanted them to fight over her. At least she didn't think she did. But did they really have to be such good buddies?

"What's that?" Mike asked, pointing to the carryout container in Hannah's hand.

"Chocolate mousse from Sally. I gave her the recipe and she always sends an extra dish home with me."

"Oh, boy!" Mike looked as if he were about to drool. "If I leave off Ernie's electricity for the next week, do you suppose you might give me that chocolate mousse?"

"I might just do that," Hannah said, and then she handed it over. "Now let's go and beard Ernie in his den. Right after you read him your riot act, I want to have some choice words with him for breaking his promise to me and upsetting Moishe!"

HANNAH'S FAVORITE CHOCOLATE MOUSSE

3 one-ounce squares unsweetened chocolate
2 Tablespoons cold salted butter (1/4 stick, 1/8 cup, 1 ounce)
4 egg whites ***(save three of the yolks in a bowl for later)***
1/4 teaspoon cream of tartar
3 Tablespoons water
1/3 cup white ***(granulated)*** sugar
3 egg yolks ***(use the leftover yolk to add to scrambled eggs in the morning)***
1/4 cup white ***(granulated)*** sugar

1 Tablespoon flavored liqueur or prepared strong coffee ***

*** ***You can use 2 teaspoons vanilla extract if you don't want to use liqueur or coffee.***

Hannah's Note: The eggs are not cooked in this recipe. If you have concerns about raw eggs and food safety, use pasteurized eggs.

Take out a one-cup glass measuring cup. Cut or break the squares of unsweetened chocolate in two and add them to the cup. Add the 2 Tablespoons of butter.

Microwave the chocolate and butter for 1 minute on HIGH. Stir. If the chocolate isn't melted, heat it for an additional 20 seconds. Stir. If that still doesn't do it, heat it in 20-second intervals until you can stir it smooth.

Set the chocolate aside on the counter to cool a bit.

In a bowl with an electric mixer, or a whisk if you're feeling energetic, beat the 4 egg whites with the 1/4 teaspoon of cream of tartar. Beat them until they form soft peaks when you turn off the mixer and test them by dipping in a spoon.

Put the 3 Tablespoons water and the 1/3 cup sugar in a small microwave-safe cup. Heat it on HIGH until it boils. ***(This should***

take about 40 seconds.) Use potholders to remove the cup from the microwave. It may be hot!

In a thin stream, slowly pour the hot water and sugar mixture into the mixing bowl with the egg whites, beating continuously until they're incorporated. Transfer the contents of the mixing bowl to another bowl. Rinse out the mixing bowl and dry it. It doesn't have to be impeccably clean because it's all going to end up in the same bowl before long.

Put the 1/4 cup white sugar in the mixing bowl you rinsed, along with the 3 egg yolks. Beat them for one minute. Turn off the mixer.

Cup your hands around the chocolate and butter mixture that's cooling on the counter. If the mixture is not so hot it'll cook the egg yolks, give it a stir, turn the mixer on again, and add it to your egg yolks and sugar. If it's too hot, just wait a minute or two until it's cool enough.

Once the chocolate mixture has been added, mix in your choice of flavored liqueur, coffee, or vanilla extract.

Remove the bowl from the mixer. You're going to finish this by hand.

With a spatula or wooden spoon, fold the egg white mixture into your bowl, stirring

word was running through both of their minds. *Slay-dar.* That was the word Mike had coined for her uncanny propensity for finding dead bodies. It was true that she always seemed to know when something was about to go terribly wrong, especially when it involved a murder victim, but Hannah didn't put much stock in ESP, or signs from the beyond, or anything of that ilk. She preferred to believe that she was just unlucky enough to stumble across almost every casualty of foul play in Lake Eden and the surrounding area for the past three years.

"Don't pay any attention to me," she said, even though chills were now running up and down her spine. "Ernie's probably still out with his friend and he forgot he left the music and light show playing."

"Right," Norman said, not sounding convinced.

"Too bad I don't have a key," Mike said, placing his hands flat against the door and giving it a test push. "This looks like a solid oak door."

"I have a key!" a female voice called out, and a split second later Lorna Kusak came around the corner. She was a short, curly-haired brunette in her mid-forties and she looked mad enough to kill.

"Lorna." Hannah hurried toward her and took her arm, hoping to defuse some of the anger she could read on the older woman's face. "You shouldn't be out here without a coat."

"I know, but I wanted to get to Ernie the second he got home. And I know he's home because he finally shut off that awful music."

"I shut off the electricity to Ernie's unit," Mike told her. "That's why the music stopped."

"Well, thank goodness you did! That idiot ex-husband of mine left his music on practically all night and my phone never stopped ringing. For some reason, people thought I had a key and I could get in to shut it off."

"But didn't you say you had a key?" Mike asked.

"Yes. I do. But I'm not *supposed* to have a key and I didn't dare admit it to anybody. Ernie doesn't have a key to my place and I don't have a key to his place. It's part of our divorce settlement."

"But you *do* have a key," Mike repeated.

"Of course I do. I just don't want Ernie to find out about it, that's all. And the kids aren't home from the mall yet, or I could have sent them down to turn off the music and saved you a trip out here."

"So the key you have belongs to one of

the kids?" Mike asked.

"No, it's mine. Ernie gave the kids keys and one day when Lindsay forgot hers on top of her dresser, I had it duplicated. I know I shouldn't have done it, but you just never know with teenagers. Ernie's never been good about chaperoning the kids. Sometimes he goes off to have a beer with one of his buddies and leaves the kids and their friends unsupervised. That's a recipe for trouble . . . you know?"

"You're right," Mike said, holding out his gloved hand for the key. "I don't see any reason to tell anybody you've got the key. And I'll make sure you get it back right away."

"Oh, good." Lorna looked very relieved as she handed it over. "If Ernie asks, you can pretend you picked the lock or something, can't you?"

"Sure. That won't be a problem." Mike turned to Norman. "Why don't you take Lorna back to her condo so she can warm up? It's too cold to be out here without a coat. I'll let myself in, take a quick look around to make sure everything's okay, and then I'll send Hannah over with Lorna's key."

"How about you?" Hannah asked Mike.

"I'm staying at Ernie's place until he gets

home. We're going to have a heart-to-heart about decibel levels and noise abatement. And while we're at it, we might even discuss the folly of leaving teenagers unsupervised."

Mike continued to ask questions about the frequency of Ernie's loud music as they walked Lorna and Norman to the bend in the walkway. There they parted ways. Lorna and Norman went around the corner of the building, and Mike turned to Hannah. "Wait here. I'll go check out Ernie's place and be right back."

"Not on your life," Hannah said, dogging his heels as he began to retrace his steps to Ernie's condo.

In the few seconds it took them to get back to Ernie's door, Mike turned around twice. Each time Hannah met his questioning look with a firm shake of her head. She wasn't staying outside in the cold while Mike went in to check things out. No sirree-bob! She'd heard a lot of gossip about Ernie's fun-and-games condo and she wasn't about to miss the chance to see it for herself!

Hannah leaned forward as Mike unlocked the front door and pushed it open. The inside of Ernie's condo smelled like beer and gingerbread. For a moment she was puzzled, but then she remembered that she'd bribed Ernie to turn off the music by giving him a dozen gingerbread cookies. The beer didn't need explaining. Everybody in Lake Eden knew that beer was Ernie's libation of choice.

There was another scent under the others, something unpleasantly metallic. The smell made Hannah think of the word *effluvium.* It was such a pretty word for something akin to decomposing garbage. Everyone except bachelors seemed to know that kitchen garbage cans that weren't emptied daily tended to foster mini science experiments of the odiferous variety.

The smell of garbage or whatever it was began to fade slightly as they stepped deeper into the living room. Hannah could tell it was the living room because Ernie's condo was an exact reversal of hers.

"Ah-ha!" Mike said, crossing the room and shining his flashlight on the wall opposite the living room windows.

"Ah-ha what?" Hannah asked him.

"I found the controls for the music and the light show. I'll shut everything down now and then I'll run down to the garage and turn Ernie's electricity back on."

By the light shining in the window from the old-fashioned globe streetlamps that dotted the walkways, Hannah could see Ernie's floor-to-ceiling entertainment center. It was massive, covering the entire wall. The comparable wall in Hannah's condo sheltered her television and stereo, a full-sized desk, a standing lamp, Moishe's Kitty Kondo, two bookcases that held at least a hundred hardcover books apiece, and a bright orange beanbag chair she'd been meaning to give to the Helping Hands Thrift Shop.

"Got it," Mike said, sounding very satisfied with himself. "I found the switch and turned off the sound system."

"How about the laser show?"

"I'm not positive, but I think that's off too. I'm going down to the garage to turn on the power, and I want you to move over here by this table lamp. If it doesn't light up on its own, you can turn it on once I throw the breaker."

Duh! Hannah thought to herself and bit back a grin. She was certainly capable of figuring out how to turn on a lamp by herself. But that wasn't the right attitude to have, not with a man like Mike. She told herself she liked it when he took care of her. It made her feel fragile and feminine. At the same time, she *didn't* like it when he took care of her because that meant she wasn't strong and independent.

"Enough," Hannah said to herself, probably startling any dust mites lurking under Ernie's furniture. And then there was a low humming noise followed by a fan clicking on. Warm air blew out of the vents and Hannah knew that Mike was throwing the breakers to turn Ernie's electricity back on. The furnace was working and she heard a noise from the kitchen, the tinkling sound of ice dropping down from an ice maker. Hannah glanced toward the doorway and that was when she realized that there was light reflecting against the kitchen wall.

The light was dim and had a yellow cast. Hannah immediately identified it for what it was, the little light that glows when a refrigerator door is open. Totally disregarding Mike's instructions to stay put until he got back, Hannah got to her feet and headed for the kitchen, intending to shut the refrigerator door before Ernie lost any of his perishables.

But there was another perishable, one she wasn't happy about discovering. Her beautifully decorated gingerbread Santa cookies were crumbled and scattered on the tiled kitchen floor. The cookies were labor intensive. It wasn't the mixing and the baking. That was the easy part. It was Lisa's hand decorating that took time and considerable talent.

Her glance shifted to the refrigerator and she got another shock. There was a foot sticking out behind the refrigerator door. The foot was wearing a dark blue tennis shoe with silver laces, just like the ones Ernie Kusak had been wearing when he'd come into The Cookie Jar this afternoon.

This was bad. This was very bad. And there was more.

Hannah stood in the kitchen doorway staring at the pool of ketchup that had leaked out under the open refrigerator door. Of course it wasn't ketchup. She *knew* it wasn't ketchup. But pretending it was ketchup kept her from thinking about what it really was. And if she thought about that, she'd turn on her heel, run down the stairs to the garage, and throw herself into Mike's protective arms. If her trembling legs would hold her. And she wasn't sure they would.

A moment passed, perhaps two. Time flew when you were having fun. But this wasn't fun. It was quite the opposite. She heard the sound of a door opening and then closing again. And then someone came up behind her.

"Hannah?" It was Mike's voice. "Why are

you just standing in the doorway like . . . uh-oh!"

"Is it . . . ?" Hannah realized that she couldn't speak the name for fear her ketchup dream would dissolve.

Mike squeezed past her to take several steps into the room. Hannah shut her eyes so she wouldn't have to watch him, but she knew the drill and she couldn't help imagining it playing out against her closed eyelids. First Mike would feel for a pulse. Then he would assess the injuries making special note of the position of the body and any nearby items that could possibly be construed as evidence. He would touch nothing. When he was through, he would step back, attempting to retrace his own footsteps and rejoin her. And he would be through with his initial survey right about . . .

"Hannah?"

Mike's voice was very close to her ear and Hannah gave a ghost of a smile. Her imagined timeframe had been perfect. "Yes?" she replied, still not opening her eyes.

"It's Ernie," he said, removing all doubt. "He's been dead for a while. Doc'll be able to tell us how long, but my guess is the middle of the afternoon."

Hannah's eyes flew open. There was no

need to pretend any longer. Ernie was dead. "He was putting my cookies in the refrigerator. And they don't need to be refrigerated. Isn't that ironic . . . or something like that?"

"Yeah," Mike said, stepping back and taking her arm. "Let's go, Hannah. There's nothing more we can do here."

Hannah let Mike take her arm and steer her to the front door. "I wonder if he got to have one."

"One what?"

"One cookie. I'd like to think that Ernie got to eat at least one before they all dropped on the floor."

Chapter Four

Hannah stopped as they rounded the corner. "What are you going to tell Lorna?"

"That we found Ernie's body and we're going to treat it like a homicide. Don't worry. I won't go into detail."

"I didn't think you would. It's just that they were married for years and it's bound to be a shock."

"I imagine it will be. I'd like it if you'd come along. It might make things easier for her."

"Of course I will. Poor Lorna. I know she was mad at Ernie, but I think she still loved him."

Mike nodded, but he didn't offer a comment. Hannah knew what that meant. When it came to solving crimes, the detective always looked hardest at members of the victim's immediate family. Perhaps Lorna was no longer a member of Ernie's immediate family, but she would be a suspect nonetheless. "If I'm going with you, you'll have to wait a second. I'm going to run up to my place to get some chocolate cookies."

"Why? This isn't exactly a social call."

"I know that. And that's why we need the cookies. Lorna might want a dose of endorphins after she hears the bad news." Hannah was about to start up the stairs to her condo when Mike called her back. "Yes?" she asked, turning toward him.

"How many chocolate cookies do you have?"

"A lot. I made a triple batch of Double Chocolate Drop Cookies for Mother's Christmas cookie exchange. I've got over twenty dozen."

"And how many does your mother need?"

"Ten dozen."

"That means you have ten dozen extra."

"Eight dozen. You're forgetting the two dozen I'm taking to Lorna and the kids."

"Okay, but that still leaves eight dozen."

"Not really. I was planning to freeze the rest and give them away when I visit people for Christmas."

"Don't do that. They won't be nearly as good once they've been frozen and thawed."

Hannah turned to give him a sharp look. "How do you know what they'll be like after they've been frozen?"

"I'm guessing, but I bet I'm right. Things are always better fresh. It would be a real pity to freeze all those cookies when you could do a really good deed with them."

"What good deed?" Hannah asked, her eyes narrowing slightly.

"Let's say you could make somebody's night a lot nicer, several somebodies in fact."

"And just who would these people be?"

"They're people who answer the call of duty any time of day or night. They perform tasks that aren't pleasant, but someone has to do them, and these people do them without complaint. I think people like that deserve a couple of your delicious cookies, don't you?"

Hannah thought she knew, but she asked the question anyway. "Are you talking about the crime-scene guys?"

"Yes. They're on the way. And Lonnie should be here any minute to secure the crime scene for me. Then there's Doc Knight and his orderlies. They're coming out here, too."

"And what you're telling me is you want me to feed everyone who works the crime scene?"

"Yeah, pretty much. I was just thinking that it surely would be nice if you could put on a big pot of coffee and give them a few homemade cookies for coming out on a cold night like this."

Hannah laughed. She couldn't help it. Mike sounded like a kid begging for treats.

"So will you?" Mike pressed his advantage.

"Okay," she said, heading up the stairs to her condo. What Mike didn't realize was that feeding the experts who worked the crime scene was definitely to her advantage. He thought he'd conned her into serving coffee and cookies, but she planned to turn the tables on him. Inviting the crime-scene experts up for refreshments would give her the chance to ask questions and to listen as they talked among themselves. Her invisible waitress trick would work beautifully. No one would even notice her as she refilled coffee cups and fetched more cookies for them. She could even serve something more substantial, a real night lunch that would take them longer to eat. She'd make out a shopping list for Norman and ask him to drive out to the Quick Stop for her while she went with Mike to talk to Lorna. Sean and Don, the twin brothers who owned the convenience store just off the highway, would have everything she'd need. And when Norman came back with the groceries, he could stay and help her gather intelligence about Ernie's murder.

■ ■ ■ ■

Of course it wasn't easy, but it wasn't as bad as Hannah had expected. Lorna didn't scream, or become hysterical, or even cry after Mike told her that Ernie was dead. Instead she gave a deep sigh and said, "Oh, dear. I was afraid that would happen."

Hannah bit the inside of her cheek to keep from speaking, and reminded herself that this was not her interview. Mike was running this show. And then, because Mike was slow to ask the next question, she jumped in anyway. "Why's that, Lorna?"

"Everybody was mad at Ernie for some reason or other, including me." Lorna looked over at Mike. "I suppose that makes me a suspect, doesn't it?"

"It could. Why were you mad at him?"

"For lots of reasons, but tonight it was that music. I told you, the phone never stopped ringing with complaints. I try to be a good neighbor. I don't disturb anybody, I don't drive too fast in the complex, and I make sure the kids don't act up at the recreation center or the pool. Everyone liked me until Ernie moved in and started causing trouble. Now they all blame me, and nobody seems to understand that I didn't ask Ernie to move in here. I wish they could understand that I don't like it any more than they do!"

"Of course you don't," Hannah soothed, moving the plate of cookies closer. "It's terrible to be blamed for something you didn't do. Have another cookie. The chocolate will help you calm down."

Mike's eyes flicked to Hannah's and she could almost hear the message in their depths. *Stop trying to calm her down. Most people tell the truth when they're upset.* Hannah didn't like it, but she supposed he had a point. She just hoped that Lorna had an iron-clad alibi.

"So you were mad about Ernie's loud music because your neighbors blamed you?" Mike asked.

"That's only part of it. You know how when you get mad, you just want to bash someone's head in?"

"Sure," Mike said. "I think everybody's felt like that at one time or another."

Somehow, Hannah managed to keep her mouth closed and her expression neutral. Even though Lorna wasn't a close friend, Hannah's every instinct was to warn her. You didn't tell a cop that you wanted to bash your ex-husband's head in right after someone had killed him by doing exactly that!

"Well, I'm not proud of it, but I've always had a bit of a temper, and that's the way I felt tonight. I think a lot of it was the frustration."

"Frustration?" Mike asked.

"I was so frustrated, I was practically beside myself," Lorna explained, digging the pit she'd excavated for herself another few feet deeper. "I had work to do and I was on a deadline. And there was no way I could concentrate with all that racket coming from Ernie's unit, not to mention the flashing lights in the sky."

"The laser show?" Mike asked, and Hannah knew it wasn't really a question, but a way to encourage Lorna to keep talking.

"That's right. My computer's in the bedroom and my desk is opposite the window. The kids and I keep our computers in the bedrooms so we won't disturb each other when I'm working at home, or they're doing homework. The reflection of those lights was so bright on my screen, I couldn't even see the words I was typing!"

"You said you were on a deadline?" Mike followed up on Lorna's earlier comment.

"Yes, for Howie. He has papers to file at the courthouse in the morning and I haven't finished them yet. How could I possibly finish typing and proofreading with *Jingle Bell Rock* blaring in my ears, my computer screen reflecting dancing penguins and skating snowmen, and the phone ringing every other second?"

"I can understand why you couldn't concentrate," Mike told her with one of his friendliest smiles. "And I can also understand how mad you must have been at Ernie. How about your neighbors? They weren't exactly happy with him either, were they?"

"Heavens no! They were all really upset."

"Was there anyone who was more upset than the others?" Mike asked, giving Hannah a look that warned her not to interfere.

Lorna thought about that for a moment. "Yes. Steve Gilman's already had a couple of run-ins with Ernie, and I think tonight was the last straw. Steve told me that if the music wasn't off when it was time to put his grandson to bed, he was going to march over there and . . ." As Hannah watched, Lorna began to blush. "I'm not going to tell you exactly what Steve said. It was pretty descriptive. All three Gilman brothers were career marines, you know."

"When is his grandson's bedtime?"

"Seven-thirty. He said little Stevie gets

really cranky if he stays up past his bedtime." Lorna stopped and began to frown. "But the music wasn't off by seven-thirty. It was after nine when I saw you standing outside Ernie's door and ran down the stairs with the key."

"You're right. And that means I have to ask you for a judgment call. Do you think Steve might have been so mad he decided to take action?"

"You mean . . . ?" Lorna gave a little shudder when Mike nodded. "Oh, no! I don't think Steve could possibly . . . I mean, I know he was in the marines and all, but I don't think he'd actually . . ."

Mike reached out to pat her shoulder. "You're probably right. As a matter of fact, I'm almost sure you are. But I find it helps to write down absolutely everyone who had any kind of motive to want the victim dead."

"Well that lets me out then!" Lorna said, reaching for another of Hannah's cookies. "I was mad at Ernie and I wanted him gone from here and out of my life, but I *certainly* didn't want him dead!"

"But I got the impression that you disliked him. You didn't dislike him then?"

"You bet I disliked him. I *hated* Ernie Kusak! He treated me like his maid even though I worked as hard as he did. And I earned more money than he did, too. Ernie was a slacker. He did his darnedest to spoil our kids and turn them into freeloaders. And he had absolutely no respect for women, which you would know if you lived in my condo and could see the parade of trash that waltzed in and out of his place!"

She's fashioning a noose for herself, Hannah thought, wishing Lorna would stop listing all the reasons she might have killed Ernie. And then just because she couldn't resist, she asked, "If you hated him that much, why did you marry him?"

"I loved him." Lorna gave a rueful laugh. "Blame innocence. Blame inexperience. Blame the fates for all I care. Take a look at me. I'm not a beautiful woman. I wasn't, even back then. That's why I was flattered out of my mind when Ernie paid attention to me in high school. I thought our life together would be a Disney movie."

"Disney movie?"

Mike looked so confused, Hannah stepped in. "Lorna's talking about romantic movies like *Cinderella, Sleeping Beauty,* and *Lady and the Tramp,* movies that contain a never-ending succession of hearts and flowers, gorgeous fairytale couples, and cute little animals popping up here and there to sing darling songs about living in bliss forever."

Lorna blinked. And then she shot Hannah an appreciative glance. "I've got to get to know you better," she said, and then she turned back to Mike. "It's like Hannah said. That's what happened. And once I found out Ernie had married me for my willingness to wait on him, my facility for keeping a good job so that I could support his credit card habit, and my ability to mother his children, the romance faded."

"But . . ." Mike glanced at Hannah and then back at Lorna. "But you said you didn't want him dead."

"I didn't. But that wasn't because I still had feelings for him. It was the money and that was all it was. Ernie was going to pay college expenses for our kids. Goodness knows I can't afford it. Since we've been divorced I've saved some, but not enough. Ernie was willing to pay it all and let them choose their own colleges. That's worth a lot to me. That's worth being civil to him even when my neighbors give me grief about him. It's worth putting up with his attempts to spoil our kids and destroy any inroads I've made on the value of the work ethic. It's even worth putting up with his attempt to shame me with the procession of gorgeous, plastic-enhanced women that saunter past here nightly on their way to his place."

Lorna took a moment to compose herself and then she looked up at Mike again. "Maybe I would have killed Ernie if the timing was right. He gave me plenty of reasons to want him gone, but the timing *wasn't* right. Chris graduates this coming June and he wants to be a doctor. That means four years of undergrad, heaven only knows how many years of medical school, and then an internship or a specialty, or whatever. It's going to be years before Chris can support himself. Lindsay's easier. She wants to go into fashion design, but she agrees she should get some kind of practical degree just in case she doesn't make an instant splash on the runway with her line of clothing."

"So what you're saying is that you couldn't kill Ernie without jeopardizing your children's future?" Hannah phrased her comment in the form of a question and waited for Lorna to respond.

"That's exactly right." Lorna seemed pleased that someone had understood. She gave Hannah a quick smile before she turned to Mike again.

"But didn't Ernie establish a college fund or a trust, or anything like that for his children?" Mike asked her.

"No. I think he liked holding the children's future over my head. If I didn't cooperate, Ernie wouldn't cooperate either. It was a way of re-establishing control over me. There was no end to the things Ernie wanted me to do for him."

"What sorts of things?" Hannah asked.

"Little things. Little irritating things, like asking me to come over and iron a shirt for him because he was expecting company, or put a pot roast in his oven so he could feed it to his buddies when they came over to play poker. Nothing too bad, you know, just the sort of things you might ask a housekeeper to do."

"And you felt you had to do these things?" Mike asked her.

"Yes. I *knew* I had to do those things. Ernie could be nasty if he was crossed and that was the last thing I wanted. And now somebody has cheated my children out of their future by killing Ernie. If I'd known that this was going to happen, I would have run right down there and offed him myself!"

DOUBLE CHOCOLATE DROP COOKIES

Do not preheat the oven yet.
The cookie dough must chill for at least an hour before baking.

3/4 cup softened salted butter ***(1 and 1/2 sticks, 6 ounces)***
2 cups brown sugar ***(pack it down when you measure it)***
2 eggs
1/4 cup vegetable oil
1 cup sour cream
1/2 cup whipping cream or half and half
2 teaspoons vanilla extract
1 teaspoon baking soda
1/2 teaspoon salt
1 cup unsweetened cocoa powder ***(pack it down in the cup when you measure it and then level it off with a table knife)***
2 and 1/2 cups all-purpose flour ***(pack it down in the cup when you measure it and then level it off with a table knife)***
2 cups semi-sweet ***(regular)*** chocolate chips

In the bowl of an electric mixer combine the softened butter, brown sugar, eggs, and vegetable oil. Beat them together until the mixture is light and fluffy.

Add the sour cream and the whipping cream. Mix until they're incorporated.

Mix in the vanilla, baking soda, and salt.

Add the unsweetened cocoa powder and mix at LOW SPEED until it's incorporated. ***(If you try to add the cocoa powder at high speed, it'll fly out in a cloud all over your kitchen — don't ask how I know this.)***

Working at LOW SPEED, add the flour in 1/2 cup increments, mixing after each addition. ***(This time you could get a cloud of flour if your mixer speed is too high.)***

When all the flour has been incorporated, take the bowl from the mixer and stir in the chocolate chips by hand.

Cover your mixing bowl with plastic wrap and refrigerate it for an hour. Overnight is fine, too.

When you're ready to bake, preheat your oven to 350 degrees F., rack in the middle position.

Cover your cookie sheets with parchment paper. You can spray the parchment paper with Pam or another nonstick baking spray if you like, but you don't really have to. If you don't have parchment paper or baking paper, just grease your cookie sheets or spray them with Pam. You may have to let the cookies cool for 3 minutes or so after they're baked so that they won't fall apart when you remove them, but it beats slogging through the snow to the store to buy baking supplies.

Drop the cookie dough by teaspoonfuls onto the cookie sheets, 12 to a standard-size sheet. ***(Lisa and I use a 2-teaspoon disher at The Cookie Jar.)***

Bake the cookies at 350 degrees F. for 8 to 10 minutes. ***(Mine took 9 minutes.)*** They should bake until they're "set" but not dry. You can test them by lightly touching one cookie on the top. If your finger doesn't come away with sticky dough on it, your cookies are ready to come out of the oven.

Remove the cookie sheet to a wire rack and let the cookies cool on the sheet for 2 minutes. Then lift the cookie sheet and pull the parchment with the cookies off onto the wire rack. Leave them on the parchment paper until they're completely cool.

Hannah's Note: You can eat these cookies just as they are, dust them with powdered sugar to pretty them up, or — if you're craving a chocolate overload — frost them with the Chocolate Fudge Frosting (recipe below) and decorate them with a pecan half on top while the frosting's still soft.

Chocolate Fudge Frosting

2 cups semi-sweet chocolate chips ***(a 12-ounce package)***

14-ounce can sweetened condensed milk ***(NOT evaporated milk)***

1 pecan half to decorate the top of each cookie***

*** ***You can also use something with a Christmas theme to decorate your cookie. I've used red and green M&Ms, a sprinkling of crushed candy canes, or any small soft Christmas-themed candy. If you make these for other holidays, let your imagination run wild in the candy aisle!***

If you use a double boiler for this frosting, it's foolproof. You can also make it in a heavy saucepan over low to medium heat on the stovetop, but you'll have to stir it constantly with a wooden spoon or a heat-resistant spatula to keep it from scorching.

Fill the bottom part of the double boiler with water. Make sure the water doesn't touch the underside of the top when you put the two parts together.

Put the chocolate chips in the top of the double boiler and set it over the bottom. Place the double boiler on the stovetop at medium heat. Stir occasionally until the chocolate chips are melted.

Stir in the can of sweetened condensed milk and cook approximately 2 minutes, stirring constantly, until the frosting is shiny and of spreading consistency.

Work fast to frost every cookie and plunk on the decoration you've chosen. If your frosting hardens up before you're through frosting the cookies, you can always reheat it over low heat until it's spreadable again.

Hannah's Note: Two Christmases ago, Mother took Old-Fashioned Sugar Cookies to her cookie exchange. The ladies loved them, but I got calls from every single one of them asking if I'd make sure Delores brought Double Chocolate Drop Cookies topped with Chocolate Fudge Frosting the next year.

Chapter Five

It was ten minutes before eleven at night when Hannah took the fresh steno pad out of her silverware drawer and made another note. She'd designated the notebook as Ernie Kusak's murder book and it already contained several lines of information she'd learned concerning his death. One of the crime-scene technicians had found a pink flower petal on the kitchen floor and identified it as a hybrid poinsettia. Since there was no poinsettia plant in Ernie's condo, it was possible that the killer had brought the petal in with him. That led to speculation that Ernie's killer had gained access by pretending to deliver the plant to Ernie and then taken it with him when he'd left.

Doc Knight had described the blow to Ernie's head and hypothesized that it was delivered by a man who was taller than Ernie. The angle of the blow told him that. Of course it was also possible that the killer was a tall, athletic woman. Doc wasn't willing to rule on that.

The choice of murder weapons was interesting to Hannah. The killing blow had been delivered with a water pitcher that had shattered into chards in the process. One of the crime-scene technicians had identified the spot where the water pitcher had been stored by matching the base of the pitcher to the ring in the dust on the top of Ernie's refrigerator. Hannah found the use of the water pitcher intriguing since there were two other kitchen items equally heavy and closer to hand than the top of a refrigerator that was a foot taller than the average man. She'd noticed a marble rolling pin on the counter, and a heavy cast-iron frying pan on the stovetop. Either one would have been much more convenient to grab and also easier to wield. The selection of murder weapon made Hannah wonder if it had been deliberately chosen. Perhaps the water pitcher meant something of significance to Ernie's killer. Then again, it could have been a random choice.

The timer dinged just as Hannah finished her note about the two ashtrays, one next to Ernie's chair and the other on the coffee table by the couch. Both had been filled with pistachio shells. Although Doc Knight hadn't confirmed it yet, the crime-scene investigators were sure that Ernie had been eating them since the red dye in the shells had stained his fingertips. Hannah took this theory even further. She speculated that Ernie's killer had visited with him for a while, at least long enough to fill an ashtray with pistachio shells.

Six beer bottles had been found at the scene. Mike and Lonnie were in the living room talking about it, and Hannah could hear every word. There were no fingerprints on three beer bottles that had been consumed by Ernie's guest. That led Mike to believe that Ernie's guest and his killer were one and the same. As Mike had put it, there was no reason to wipe off your fingerprints if you hadn't done anything wrong.

The Game-Day Oven Burgers smelled marvelous as Hannah pulled them from the oven. They were always part of the game-day buffets that Sally and Dick Laughlin put out at the Lake Eden Inn during football season. Dick and Sally's friend, Rick Fine, had given them the recipe and it was one of Hannah's favorite and delicious quick meals.

There were two more dishes that made up Hannah's night lunch. She'd also made Oven Bean Hotdish and a big bowl of

Smokin' Willie's Crispy Crunchy Coleslaw. With Double Chocolate Drop Cookies for dessert, and plenty of hot coffee, it all added up to a sizeable meal. It also took time to eat and that was one of the reasons Hannah had gone all out. The more time the crime-scene principals spent eating and drinking in her living room, the more time there was to discuss what they'd learned about Ernie's murder.

"At least you got some prints from that bathroom window," Lonnie said as Hannah carried everything in on a tray and set it down on her dining room table.

"Good ones, too," one of the crime scene experts commented. "If he's in the system, we'll get a hit."

"How long will it take to find out?" Norman asked him.

"A while. They're always backed up. Too many budget cuts, you know? If it was a hate crime it'd get priority, but it's not."

"Come help yourselves," Hannah told them, and then she sealed her lips. She recognized the special distinction that set a *hate crime* apart from a regular crime, but the phrase still irked her. It was just another example of the liberties people were taking with the English language. As far as she was concerned, Ernie's murder *was* a hate crime. Someone had hated him enough to bash his head in and deliberately end his life.

Once her guests had filled their plates and were eating hungrily, Hannah put on a second pot of coffee and waited for the conversation to begin again. It did once the food was gone and everyone was munching on cookies and sipping a final cup of coffee.

"That was one heck of a blow," Doc Knight said, and then he turned to Hannah. "These cookies hit the spot, Hannah."

"Glad to hear it," Hannah replied, hoping that Doc wouldn't go into so much detail it would cause indigestion. She wasn't terribly worried about Doc's orderlies, or the crime-scene guys. They were accustomed to viewing the aftermath of violent death and had grown inured to it. Her concern was for her own stomach, which had tightened uncomfortably when Doc had mentioned the killing blow.

"What's your estimate on time of death?" Mike asked Doc.

"Judging from the degree of morbidity and internal organ temperature, I'd ballpark it any time between three in the afternoon and eight at night. I might be able to narrow it down a little more once I complete the autopsy, but that's all I can tell you for now."

"I can narrow it down," Hannah told them. "I know it's not before four."

Mike swiveled toward her. "How do you know that?"

"Ernie came into The Cookie Jar at three and he didn't leave until almost three-thirty. It takes at least a half-hour to drive out here from town."

"Did he seem upset when you saw him?" Lonnie asked her.

"Not really. We talked about his music and I asked him to make sure he didn't turn it up too loud. He said he'd turn it down the minute the kids got home from school, and I gave him a dozen cookies because he was so nice about it."

"Santa cookies?" one of the crime-scene investigators asked.

"Yes. I should have known something was wrong when the music was so loud. Ernie's always complied with homeowners' association warnings before."

Mike turned to Lonnie. "I need you and Rick to find out what time the kids were supposed to come home from school. Their mother said they went straight from school to the mall to do some Christmas shopping with their friends. I want to know which friends went with them and precisely where they went."

"You don't think Ernie's own kids would . . . ?" Hannah let the question hang there without finishing it. The concept Mike was suggesting was horrible.

"I don't think anything. I eliminate possibilities." Mike gave her a stern look. "Come to think about it, *you* came home early and *you* were right here during the time period."

"But you don't think that I . . . ?"

"I told you," Mike interrupted her. "I'm eliminating possibilities. Do you have an alibi?"

"Not unless someone saw me go down and pound on Ernie's door. I was trying to get him to turn down the music. That's possible, I guess, but nobody else in our building was here at the time. Most people in our complex work regular hours and they weren't home yet."

"I picked her up at six-thirty," Norman offered. "She's got me as an alibi after that. We went out to dinner at the Lake Eden Inn."

Mike jotted that down and then he turned to Hannah again. "Save some time for me tomorrow. I'll drop by The Cookie Jar in the morning to take your statement. I need to know exactly what happened when you knocked on Ernie's door. I also need to talk to anybody who was in the coffee shop when Ernie walked in, including Lisa."

"Okay," Hannah agreed, "but why?"

"Because you may have been some of the last people to see Ernie alive."

GAME-DAY OVEN BURGERS

Preheat oven to 350 degrees F., rack in the middle position.

1 pound lean ground sirloin
1 packet ***(1/2 box)*** Lipton Dry Onion soup ***(I used Beefy Onion)***
1 egg, beaten
2 Tablespoons of your favorite burger flavoring: ketchup, Worcestershire, steak sauce, hot sauce, or whatever ***(I used A.-1. Steak Sauce)***
1/4 cup bread crumbs***
4 Kaiser Rolls, *unsliced*

*** ***If you don't have bread crumbs, you don't have to run right out and buy them. You can substitute a scant 1/4 cup cracker crumbs or matzo meal.***

Put the meat in a large bowl. Add the onion soup and mix it up with your fingers.

Whip up the egg in a glass with a fork and add it to your bowl. Squish everything around with your fingers.

Add 2 Tablespoons of your favorite burger flavoring and mix that in.

Sprinkle on the bread crumbs and mix them in just as evenly as you can. They'll soak up some of the egg and the meat juices.

Take 4 *unsliced* Kaiser Rolls and carve out the insides. Be very careful that you don't make a hole in the bottom. Try to leave at least a quarter-inch of bread around the inside of the roll and on the bottom.

Hannah's 1st Note: There are two ways to prepare your Kaiser Rolls. One way is to pick out the insides until it resembles a little bread bowl. The other way is to cut a thin slice off the top of the roll, set it aside, and then pick out the bread inside until it resembles a little bread bowl. If you choose to get rid of the top, your burger will look brown and delicious. If you choose to pack your meat mixture inside and then clamp on the lid, your burger won't brown as much. This method, however, has the added advantage of allowing you to take off the top after it's baked and add extras like lettuce, pickles, and sliced tomato before clamping the top

back on again.

You decide. They're delicious both ways.

Spoon about 1/4 cup of the meat mixture into each hollow Kaiser Roll. One pound of lean ground sirloin should fill 4 Kaiser Rolls.

If you're afraid the juices are going to leak out the bottom and run all over your oven, bake the rolls in a disposable aluminum pan with sides or in a cake pan lined with foil.

Bake the Oven Burgers at 350 degrees F. for 45 minutes. Serve warm. If you'd like to add cheese, take them out of the oven 5 minutes early, put on a piece of cheese, and stick them back in again for the remaining 5 minutes.

Hannah's 2nd Note: If you can't find Kaiser Rolls, any round bakery roll that's not too soft will work. Make sure your rolls are over 2 and 1/2 inches high, ***unsliced,*** **and the size of a large hamburger bun. I've even used unsliced hamburger buns from grocery stores that have bakeries. I haven't tried this recipe with commercial hamburger buns** ***(the kind you find in the bread aisle),*** **but instinct tells me they'll be too soft and the juices from the hamburger will probably leak out.**

Hannah's 3rd Note: I usually serve these Game-Day Oven Burgers with Smokin' Willie's Crispy Crunchy Coleslaw and Oven Bean Hotdish.

SMOKIN' WILLIE'S CRISPY CRUNCHY COLESLAW

5 cups shredded green cabbage

5 cups shredded purple ***(red)*** cabbage

1 cup shredded carrots

1/2 cup chopped green onion ***(you can use up to 2 inches of the stem)***

1/2 cup white ***(granulated)*** sugar

1 cup mayonnaise ***(I use Hellmann's — it's called Best Foods west of the Rockies — you can use any brand you like, but don't use salad dressing!)***

2 Tablespoons red wine or cider vinegar ***(I used raspberry vinegar and it was great!)***

1/4 cup salted shelled sunflower seeds

Hannah's Note: If you bought whole cabbage, finely shred it. If you're pressed for time, buy the cabbage already shredded in the grocery store. The same applies to the shredded carrots. You can shred them yourself or buy them already shredded.

Measure out the cabbages and the carrots

and toss them together in a large bowl.

Clean and chop the green onions. ***(To clean them, just slice off the base of the white end, peel back the first layer of skin and pull it back as far as you can. You can use up to 2 inches of the green stem. After that, it gets tough and difficult to chop.)***

Add the green onions to your bowl.

Take out a smaller bowl or a 2-quart measuring cup to hold your coleslaw dressing.

In the small bowl combine the sugar, mayonnaise, and vinegar. Mix it with a rubber spatula or whisk it until it's smooth. If you like freshly ground black pepper, you can grind some now and stir it in.

Pour the dressing you just made over the cabbage mixture in the bowl. Toss the coleslaw, or stir it with a spoon or spatula until it's coated with the dressing.

Refrigerate until ready to serve. Then give a final stir, turn out in a pretty salad bowl, and sprinkle the salted shelled sunflower seeds on top.

OVEN BEAN HOTDISH

Preheat oven to 350 degrees F., rack in the middle position.

Grease or spray a 3-quart casserole dish with Pam or another nonstick cooking spray. You can also use a disposable half-size steam table pan, but be sure to place it on a cookie sheet to support the bottom. This dish is heavy and the pan may buckle if you don't support it.

1/4 cup bacon bits ***(I used Hormel)***
2 Tablespoons salted butter ***(1/4 stick, 1 ounce)***
1/2 cup brown sugar ***(pack it down when you measure it)***
1/2 teaspoon garlic powder
1/2 cup cider vinegar
1 Tablespoon prepared mustard ***(I used Dijon)***
1 teaspoon salt
1/4 cup dried chopped onion
2 fifteen-ounce cans butter beans ***(or white beans if you can't find butter beans)***
1-pound can ***(16 ounces)*** black-eyed peas
1-pound can ***(16 ounces)*** red kidney beans
1-pound can ***(16 ounces)*** baked beans ***(I used B&M)***

1/2 cup grated cheddar or mozzarella cheese

In a frying pan on the stove, heat the bacon bits in the butter. Let them cook for a minute.

Stir in the brown sugar, garlic powder, and vinegar. Let them cook for a minute.

Add the prepared mustard, salt, and dried chopped onion. Let that cook for a minute.

Stir everything. Then cover the pan and let it cook on simmer for 10 minutes.

While your sauce is simmering, drain the butter beans, black-eyed peas, and red kidney beans. Dump them in the bottom of your prepared casserole or steam table pan. Add the can of baked beans and mix them in.

Drizzle the sauce over the beans and stir it all up so everything is mixed and evenly distributed.

If the casserole dish has a cover, put it on. If it doesn't, cover the top with foil.

Bake the casserole at 350 degrees F. for 50 minutes. Carefully take off the cover and sprinkle the grated cheese on top. Return the casserole to the oven and bake it, *uncovered,* for an additional ten minutes.

Chapter Six

That's precisely when Hannah saw the dim yellow light spilling out of the kitchen doorway. Lisa's dramatic storyteller's voice floated into the kitchen from the coffee shop. Andrea and Hannah were in the kitchen at The Cookie Jar and they'd left the swinging restaurant-style door slightly ajar so that they could hear Lisa's embellishments. Hannah's young partner had reached the critical point in her narrative, the moment when Hannah discovered Ernie's body.

There was a collective gasp from Lisa's audience. She had a packed house, standing room only, and every single customer at the counter and tables had purchased at least two cookies and a cup of coffee or tea. The Cookie Jar would make an incredible profit today thanks to Hannah's propensity for finding dead bodies. It was entirely possible that their bank deposit tonight would exceed the deposit they'd made the day after she'd found the last murder victim. And thinking like that actually made Hannah wonder if murder could be good for the economy!

The light drew our Hannah like a moth to a flame. She moved to the kitchen doorway as if she were being pulled forward by a force she could not resist. And there, in the doorway, she stopped to simply stare at the horrific sight that met her eyes, the spectacle that turned her tip-over-tail.

"Tip-over-tail?" Andrea repeated, turning to her older sister with a frown.

"It means discombobulated," Hannah explained to her sister. "Lisa must have reread Mother's Regency novel." She placed a plate of cookies on the work station and took the stool across from her sister. "I want to know what you think about these cookies. My friend Sally Hayes sent the recipe."

Andrea reached for a cookie and took a bite. "They're great! Coconut and cranberries are a good combination. What do you call them?"

"Chewy Coconut Cranberry Cookies."

"That fits. It's kind of catchy, too. But these aren't the cookies I'm taking to Tracey's classroom, are they?"

"No. Tracey gets my gingerbread reindeer cookies. I baked them this morning and Lisa decorated them. They're in that box on the counter."

"Oh, good. She's been telling everyone that you make the best reindeer cookies in the world. But I wouldn't mind taking some of these coconut cranberry cookies for myself. I really like them." Andrea stopped and looked down at her purse. "Did I just hear *All You Need Is Love?*"

"Either that or we're having a joint auditory hallucination. It's not a radio. It didn't sound good enough for that. It was tinny, more like a . . . maybe like a cell phone ringtone?"

"You're right! That's exactly what it sounded like, but *All You Need Is Love* isn't one of my ringtones. How about you?"

"It isn't me. I don't have my cell phone with me today. It's at home in the charger. But someone's phone rang and it sounded like it was coming from your purse."

"Oh, no!" Andrea gave a little groan and dove into her purse with both hands. As Hannah watched she came up with not one, but *two* cell phones.

"They both look like yours," Hannah pointed out the obvious. The two cell phones were exactly alike.

"That's because Mother and I are on the family plan. I got a new phone with all sorts of totally great apps like unlimited Internet access, and maps with GPS and driving directions, and free e-mail, and even a bar-code scanner that tells me the cheapest place to buy whatever it is I scan. And I didn't lose any of the features I had on my old cell phone. They all transferred over, including my contacts and voice mail. And since I paid for my upgrade, that entitled Mother to get the same phone for half price. If you were on our plan, you could have gotten one, too."

"But I like my cell phone. I don't need anything fancy. All I ever do is make calls and answer calls."

"But how about if you were lost in the woods and you needed to find a way out? You could use the GPS map feature."

"I could also call the forest ranger's office and he'd come out and get me."

"Okay. That's true. But say you want to look something up on the Internet. You can't do that with your phone."

"Sure I can. All I have to do is call you and you can use your unlimited Internet access to look it up for me."

"But . . ." Andrea stopped and gave an exasperated sigh. "Arguing with you is impossible!"

"That's true. So how did you get Mother's phone?"

"She dropped by the office when she left Granny's Attic last night to show me the neat old whiskey jug she found for Gary."

"Gary Jenkins?"

"Yes, he collects them. He had shelves built for them in his kitchen. Mother says he has over two hundred whiskey jugs and he's always on the lookout for more."

"Mother forgot to take her phone when she left your office?" Hannah guessed, since she still hadn't heard how Andrea had come by their mother's phone.

"That's right. She got a call, pulled it out of her purse to look at the display, and let the call go to voice mail. She must have forgotten to put the phone back in her purse."

"You thought Mother's phone was yours and you stuck it in your purse before you left your office?"

"That's exactly how it happened. I didn't realize I had both phones until just now."

"Do you know which phone is yours and which phone is Mother's?"

The question had barely escaped Hannah's lips when their mother's phone rang again and the first five bars of *All You Need Is Love* began to play. Andrea glanced down at the display and frowned. "I wonder who this is. It's our area code and the number is three, five, six, eighteen, twenty-four."

Hannah shrugged. "Doesn't ring a bell with me."

"Oh, well. They'll probably call again. I'd better run up to Granny's Attic and give back Mother's phone. If she missed it, she's probably frantic."

"She uses it that much?" Hannah was surprised. She'd seldom seen Delores place a call or answer one.

"Not really, but she wants it in case of emergencies. Don't you remember when Dad bought her first cell phone? She was one of the first people in Lake Eden to have one. And Mother had the family plan way back then. She's been rolling over her unused minutes for practically forever. As a matter of fact, let me see how many rollover minutes she has. If there's enough, I could ask her to lend me some."

Hannah watched as Andrea tapped the phone screen and sent various commands into the electronic ether. Then the answer to her sister's question must have appeared because Andrea gave a low whistle. "*That* many! Wow!"

"*How* many?"

"Close to a million and they haven't even added in the minutes for this month yet. Mother hardly ever uses her phone."

"Close to a million minutes!" Hannah repeated it almost reverently. "That means Mother could talk on her phone a full eight hours a day for the next . . . That's just not right, Andrea!"

"What's not right?"

"There's something wrong with the system when a person's rollover minutes exceed their life expectancy."

Andrea thought about that for a minute and then she sighed. "Don't think about it. It's just too depressing. Have one of your cookies, Hannah."

Hannah did and both sisters were quietly munching when they heard Lisa's voice again.

Of course Hannah would love to be here herself, but she wanted me to tell you all about it, Lisa's words floated into the kitchen. *You see, she'd really want to answer your questions since you're her friends, but . . . well . . . she can't. She's not supposed to say anything about it and we're getting around that rule by having me tell you. Now you won't say anything to anybody . . . right?*

There was a veritable chorus of *Right, Of course not!* and *Never!* And while the chorus was still assuring Lisa that they wouldn't say a word, Andrea spoke up. "Lisa's really good at this, isn't she?"

"Yes. The nice thing is that she enjoys it, and it saves me from answering all those questions. Everyone always wants to ask me about the crime scene and I was so shocked when I found Ernie's body, I really didn't notice much detail. That's why I asked you if you could get a look at any of the crime-scene photos."

"I know. And here they are." Andrea reached into her briefcase-sized purse and pulled out a large manila envelope. "I scanned them into my computer after Bill came home last night and printed them out this morning after Bill left for work. Please don't spread them out on the worktable. You know how squeamish I am."

"I do." Hannah paged through the scans of the photos. The ones of the body were in glorious color and she could understand why Andrea didn't want to see those, but there were also photos of perfectly ordinary things. "Is it okay if I lay out the photos that don't have Ernie's body in them?" she asked her sister.

"That's fine. Those don't bother me at all. Besides, I'm kind of interested in what Ernie did to decorate his condo. I haven't seen it since I sold it to him."

One by one Hannah positioned the photos. The two sisters stared at them for a few minutes and then Andrea shrugged. "I'm not impressed with his decorating skills," she said.

"Neither am I. With all that money, you'd think he would have hired someone to . . . look at that!"

"Look at what?" Andrea leaned closer.

"That framed lottery ticket on the wall of the guest bathroom. It must be the winning ticket, but I thought you had to turn it in."

"You do, but Ernie probably took a photo of it before he handed it over. That's what I'd do if I ever won the lottery. I'd want to frame it and put it on my wall."

"Can you read the numbers?" Hannah asked, leaning forward for a better view.

"Some of them. There's a three and a five and a six. And then there's . . . I think that's an eighteen. And I'm almost positive the next one's a twenty-four. And the last number is thirty-one. No, wait! It's thirty-seven. See that little line on the top? It's thirty-seven for sure."

"Can I write on this?" Hannah asked, and when Andrea nodded, she jotted down the numbers. "Three, five, six, eighteen, twenty-four, and . . . Wait a second!"

"What?"

"That's the number that called Mother's phone, isn't it?"

"You mean the *All You Need Is Love* caller?"

"Yes. Check on it, Andrea. It could be important."

"How?"

"I don't know, but it's too weird to be a coincidence. That phone number's got to tie in with Ernie somehow."

Andrea pulled up the missed call display and handed the phone to Hannah. "You're right. But we don't know whose number it is."

"Only one way to find out." Hannah held out the phone. "Call it and find out."

"Why do I always have to be the one to make the phone calls?" Andrea grumbled, but she plucked the phone from Hannah's outstretched hand.

"That's because you're so good at it. Go ahead. Just make up something and find out who it is."

CHEWY COCONUT CRANBERRY COOKIES (AND/OR CHEWY COCONUT CHOCOLATE CHIP COOKIES)

Preheat oven to 350 degrees F., rack in the middle position.

1 and 1/2 cups melted salted butter ***(3 sticks, 12 ounces, 3/4 pound)***

1 and 1/2 cups white ***(granulated)*** sugar

1 and 1/2 cups brown sugar ***(pack it down in the cup when you measure it)***

1 and 1/2 teaspoons baking powder

1 and 1/2 teaspoons baking soda

1/2 teaspoon salt

2 teaspoons vanilla extract

3 large eggs, beaten ***(just whip them up in a glass with a fork)***

3 cups quick cooking oatmeal ***(I used Quaker Oats Quick-1 Minute)***

3 cups all-purpose flour ***(pack it down in the cup when you measure it)***

3 cups sweetened dried cranberries ***(I used Craisins)***

3 cups flaked coconut*** ***(pack it down in the cup when you measure it)***

*** ***I always measure out my flaked coconut and then I use the food processor***

with the steel blade to chop it up a little finer. That way, it doesn't get stuck between your teeth. You can also measure it, lay it out on a cutting board, and chop it in finer pieces with a sharp knife.

Hannah's 1st Note: This is easier with an electric mixer, but you can also do it by hand.

Melt the butter in a small microwave-safe bowl ***(I use a quart glass measuring cup)*** for 2 minutes on HIGH in the microwave. Let it sit for one minute, stir, and if it's not melted, microwave it for an additional 30 seconds.

Take the melted butter out of the microwave and set it on the counter to cool.

In a large bowl combine the white sugar and the brown sugar.

Add the baking powder, baking soda, salt, and vanilla extract. Stir it in well.

Add the beaten eggs and stir until the mixture is light and fluffy.

Cup your hands around the bowl with the butter. If it's cool enough so it won't cook the eggs, add it slowly to your bowl, beating all the while. Mix until it's thoroughly incorporated.

Add the quick cooking oatmeal in one-cup increments, ***(just eyeball it — you don't have to be exact),*** mixing it in completely before adding the next increment.

Hannah's 2nd Note: The reason for adding dry ingredients like oatmeal and flour in increments is so they won't spill over the sides of the bowl when you stir them in. It seems like more work, but believe me, cleaning flour off the counter and floor isn't any fun!

Add the flour in one-cup increments, mixing it in completely before adding the next increment.

Mix in the sweetened, dried cranberries, adding them slowly to your bowl. Mix until they're evenly distributed.

Hannah's 3rd Note: If you're using an electric mixer, you may want to finish the rest of the mixing by hand. Coconut tends to stick to the beaters.

Mix in the coconut. Stir until it's thoroughly incorporated. ***(This dough may get quite stiff — if your arm is getting sore from stirring, just get in there with your impeccably clean hands and mix it up with your fingers.)***

Spray your cookie sheets with Pam or another nonstick cooking spray, or line them with parchment paper. ***(I used silicon-coated parchment baking paper.)***

Drop the cookie dough by mounded teaspoonfuls onto baking sheets. ***(I used a***

2-teaspoon scooper and that was just the right size.) Bake no more than 12 cookies per standard-size sheet.

Press the cookies down a bit with the blade of a spatula or the palm of your impeccably clean hand. They do spread out a bit in the oven, but not too much.

Bake at 350 degrees F. for 8 to 10 minutes or until nicely browned on top.

Cool on the cookie sheet for 2 minutes and then remove the cookies to a wire rack to cool completely.

Yield: Approximately 10 dozen delicious cookies.

Hannah's 4th Note: You can make two totally different types of cookies from one batch. Here's how:

Divide your dough into 2 equal parts before you add the cranberries or coconut.

Add one and a half cups sweetened dried cranberries and one and a half cups coconut to the first part of your dough. Stir them in. Bake according to the above directions. This will yield 5 dozen Chewy Coconut Cranberry Cookies.

Add 1 and 1/2 cups of miniature chocolate chips and one and a half cups coconut to the other half of the dough.

Stir them in. Bake according to the above directions. This will yield 5 dozen Chewy Coconut Chocolate Chip Cookies.

You can also add a cup of chopped nuts to either half (or both if you wish for an even chewier texture.)

Chapter Seven

"What's wrong?" Hannah asked, staring at her sister's shocked expression.

"Shhh!" Andrea warned, and then she turned back to the phone. "Hi, Gary," she said. "It's Andrea Todd. Mother mentioned that you collected old whiskey jugs and I wondered if you wanted to check out the basement of the Rock Tavern. We're listing it next week, and Al and I are doing a walk-through of the building this weekend."

Hannah gave her sister the high sign. She didn't know if the excuse Andrea had given was true, but it certainly was plausible.

There was a pause and then Andrea spoke again. "Sure. I'll let you know what time and you can meet us there. I just thought that since it's been a tavern all these years, there might be some old whiskey jugs in the basement."

"Gary Jenkins?" Hannah asked when Andrea hung up.

"That's right. And Mother downloaded *All You Need Is Love* for his ringtone. It must be getting serious, Hannah."

"Maybe, but that's not my main concern right now. I want to know why Ernie used Gary's cell phone number on his lottery ticket."

Andrea shrugged. "Well, you can't ask Ernie, so I guess you'll have to ask Gary if he knows."

"That's exactly what I'll do." Hannah got up and crossed the room to the kitchen window. "I've got something else for you to taste. They ought to be cool enough to cut by now." She opened the window, retrieved a cake pan, and carried it to the counter. "We made more Double Chocolate Drop Cookies this morning and we had one batch of dough left over. I experimented with it and made these cookie bars."

"I wish I could be that creative!" Andrea said with a sigh.

"Oh, you are," Hannah told her. "That story you fed Gary about looking for whiskey jugs in the basement of the Rock Tavern was very creative."

"Well, I had to say something. I'm the one who called him, after all. So I just said the first thing that came to my head."

"It was brilliant. It sounded totally believable. Is it true?"

"Not exactly, but it might be true eventually. I'm meeting with the owners of the property next week to see if they'll list with us."

Hannah cut several of the cold cookie bars and placed them on a little plate for Andrea. "I need you to taste these and tell me two things."

"What two things do you want to know?"

"First tell me if they're good enough to serve to my customers. And then try to think of a good name for them."

"I can do that." Andrea watched as Hannah carried the plate of cookie bars to the workstation. "Why did you put the pan on the ledge outside the window when you could have put them in your walk-in cooler?"

"I wanted them to cool off in a hurry and it's over fifty degrees colder outside than it is in my walk-in cooler."

"I guess that makes sense. But if you wanted them to cool off really fast, why didn't you put them in your freezer?"

"Because it's only thirty degrees in my freezer and it's ten below zero outside. You do the math."

"Okay, okay. I get it. But it's crazy. It shouldn't be forty degrees warmer inside your freezer than it is outside your back door."

"You're forgetting that we live in the frozen northland, the home of ice and snow."

Andrea laughed. "That's true. You win. If you want to put cookie bars outside the window, I'm not going to stop you. But what would the board of health say?"

"They'd inspect the packaging to make sure I'd wrapped the pan properly, and I don't think they'd cite me. Besides, if I'd put these in my cooler or freezer, they wouldn't be cold enough for you to test."

"Oh. Well. That sheds a whole new light on it." Andrea laughed as she reached for a cookie bar and took a bite. "Mmmm!"

"Was that *Mmmm* as in *good,* or *Mmmm* as in *I'm not sure?*"

"It was *Mmmm* as in fantastic."

"So I can serve them to my customers?"

"Yes, if you charge them enough. I love that combination of caramel and chocolate. It's just super."

"So do I. What do you think I should call them?"

"Magic Chocolate Caramel Cookie Bars."

"The caramel and chocolate parts make sense to me. They're two of the main ingredients. But why do you want to call them *magic?*"

"Because everyone's going to love these and it'll be exactly like one of Herb's magic tricks. Just have Lisa take some out to the coffee shop and see how fast they disappear."

It was almost three in the afternoon when Hannah took the last sheets of cookies out of the oven and slid them onto shelves on the baker's rack to cool. She could hear the din of voices and the clink of spoons in coffee mugs as customers sipped hot beverages and enjoyed the treats she'd spent most of the day baking.

The kitchen was where Hannah wanted to be and the coffee shop was where Lisa preferred to be. Everything worked out to suit them both. One relished telling the story of how Hannah had found Ernie's body and the other just wanted to hide out so she wouldn't have to answer any questions.

Marge Beeseman, Lisa's mother-in-law, hurried into the kitchen. She smiled when she saw the full baker's racks. "Oh, good. We're almost out. Those cookie bars were a big hit. Lisa charged over a dollar apiece for them and Jack said nobody even blinked when he rang them up."

"Over a dollar!" Hannah breathed, just shaking her head. She probably would have charged fifty cents. Now that Lisa was setting the prices, they were doing much better than they ever had before. That made Hannah grateful all over again.

"What are these?" Marge asked, as she took two pans of baked cookies from the cooling racks and transferred them to one of the display cookie jars.

"Molasses Crackles. And the cookies below them are Lisa's White Chocolate Supremes."

"And these?" Marge pointed to several shelves on the second baker's rack.

"Red Velvet Cookies."

"Perfect!" Marge removed several from a pan and transferred them to a plate. "I'm giving these to Jack. He was just talking about them this morning and he said he wishes Ellie could come back to bake them. He's talking about her a lot more now. I can tell he really misses her."

Tears sprang to Hannah's eyes. She knew that although Jack Herman had forgotten some things because of the disease that was ravaging his brain, Alzheimer's could never erase Lisa's father's memories of the wonderful woman he'd married so many years ago.

There was a swishing sound as Marge took another pan from the rack and that was when Hannah realized what Marge had told her. Jack was with Marge now, and he was talking about Ellie much more. When Marge had moved in with Jack and given Lisa and her son Herb the Beeseman family home for a wedding present, she'd assumed the role of Jack's caretaker. They were caregiver and patient. That was clear to see. But there was clearly deep affection between them. Hannah would venture to say that Jack loved Marge and Marge also loved Jack. It was bound to hurt Marge when Jack talked about his dead wife with such obvious love and devotion.

"I'm sorry, Marge," Hannah said quickly. "That must be very difficult for you."

"It's no problem at all. They come right off the sheets, Hannah. Just watch." Marge tipped the cookie sheet and the cookies slid off into the display jar. "See?"

"Not that. I meant that it must be difficult when Jack talks about Ellie and says he misses her."

"It's sweet of you to be concerned for my feelings, but that's not a problem either." Marge came over to pat Hannah on the shoulder. "You see, Jack married the love of his life, and so did I when I married Herb's father. We were both happy and content. And both of us were very much in love. Jack didn't stop loving his wife when she died, just like I didn't stop loving my husband when he died. All that love's still there and so are the memories. We were all friends and that makes it even better. Remembering friends no longer with us is a way of keeping them alive in our hearts."

Hannah just sat there for a moment after Marge left the kitchen. She'd just learned something she hoped she'd remember for the rest of her life. She thought about what a generous and genuinely nice person Marge was until a knock on the door interrupted her thoughts.

It was Norman. Hannah let him into her warm kitchen and got him a hot cup of coffee with two Magic Chocolate Caramel Cookie Bars.

"Mmmm!" Norman said when he tasted one. Since that was an echo of Andrea's earlier comment, Hannah was pleased.

"Not too sticky and chewy?" she asked.

"Not at all. It's good for my business."

Hannah stared at him for a moment. She wasn't sure if he was joking or not until he laughed.

"Just kidding. They're perfect," he told her. "Have you found out any more about

Ernie's murder?"

While Norman ate cookie bars and drank his coffee, Hannah filled him in on the events of the morning. "Would you like to go with me to talk to Gary Jenkins?" she asked.

"Sure, but there's something we ought to do first. You need to talk to Marsha Gilman. I just finished cleaning Barbara Donnelly's teeth and she told me Mike arrested Steve on suspicion of murder early this afternoon."

Hannah's mouth dropped open she was so surprised. She didn't doubt what Norman was telling her. Barbara was Bill's secretary and she knew what was going on in the Winnetka County Sheriff's Station. But why hadn't Mike, or Bill, or even Barbara herself called her?

"It's not official yet, but Barbara always knows what's going on. She said Steve had a couple of altercations with Ernie in the past."

"That's what Lorna said when Mike and I talked to her last night. But she didn't think that Steve could have killed Ernie. What evidence do they have that he did it?"

"Barbara said a neighbor saw Steve leaving Ernie's apartment last night. And according to Barbara, Steve's fingerprints came up in the registry when they ran them."

"So fast?" Hannah was amazed. "Does that mean Steve's been in trouble with the police before?"

"No, it means that Steve was in the Marine Corps. Barbara says that a lot of times the files get lost or are never recorded, but this time the system worked."

"That's bad news for Steve if he didn't do it."

"That's exactly what Barbara said. She knows Steve and Marsha pretty well and she doesn't think he could have done it. Barbara wants you to go out to see Marsha. She's already talked to Marsha, so Marsha knows you're coming to help her. Barbara wants you to help prove that Steve is innocent."

"That's a tall order, but I'll do my best," Hannah promised. "Does Barbara want anything else?"

"Yes. She wants you to never tell Bill his secretary interfered with the course of an official murder investigation."

Magic Chocolate Caramel Cookie Bars

Preheat oven to 350 degrees F., rack in the middle position.

Line a 9-inch by 13-inch cake pan with heavy-duty aluminum foil. Make sure the foil is large enough to leave little "ears" of foil sticking out on at least two sides. ***(This is for later, when you'll lift the bars out of the pan.)*** Spray the foil with Pam or another nonstick cooking spray. That way you won't get your cake pan dirty and you'll be able to lift the bars right out of the pan to cut them when they're cool.

3/4 cup softened salted butter ***(1 and 1/2 sticks, 6 ounces)***
2 cups brown sugar ***(pack it down when you measure it)***
2 eggs
1/4 cup vegetable oil
1 cup sour cream
1/2 cup whipping cream or half-and-half
2 teaspoons vanilla extract
1 teaspoon baking soda
1/2 teaspoon salt
1 cup unsweetened cocoa powder ***(pack it down in the cup when you measure it***

and then level it off with a table knife)

3 cups all-purpose flour ***(pack it down in the cup when you measure it and then level it off with a table knife)***

2 cups semi-sweet ***(regular)*** chocolate chips

2 cups miniature marshmallows

1 cup chopped salted nuts ***(I used cashews)***

14-ounce jar caramel ice cream topping ***(I used Smuckers)***

1/2 cup all-purpose flour ***(yes, more flour — pack it down in the cup when you measure it)***

In the bowl of an electric mixer combine the softened butter, brown sugar, eggs, and vegetable oil. Beat them together until the mixture is light and fluffy.

Add the sour cream and the whipping cream. Mix until they're incorporated.

Mix in the vanilla, baking soda, and salt.

Add the unsweetened cocoa powder and mix at LOW SPEED until it's incorporated. ***(If you try to add the cocoa powder at high speed, it'll fly out in a cloud all over your kitchen — don't ask how I know this.)***

Working at LOW SPEED, add the flour in half-cup increments, mixing after each addition. ***(This time you could get a cloud of flour if your mixer speed is too high.)***

When all the flour has been incorporated,

take the bowl from the mixer and stir in the chocolate chips by hand.

Spread the mixture out in the prepared baking pan, patting it down with the palms of your impeccably clean hands until it's smooth.

Sprinkle on the 2 cups of miniature marshmallows.

Sprinkle the cup of salted chopped nuts on top of the marshmallows.

In the bottom of your work bowl, mix the jar of caramel ice cream topping and the 1/2 cup all-purpose flour. Continue to stir until the mixture is smooth and without lumps.

Drizzle the caramel mixture on top as evenly as possible.

Bake at 350 degrees F. for 25 minutes.

Cool completely in the baking pan on a wire rack, and then refrigerate. These bars must be chilled for at least two hours before you cut them.

When the bars have chilled for two hours or more, lift the foil from the cake pan and place the bars on a flat surface. Cut them into brownie-sized pieces and carefully peel them from the foil.

Arrange the Magic Chocolate Caramel Cookie Bars on a serving plate, cover them with foil or plastic wrap, and return them to the refrigerator.

Serve these bars chilled and store the leftovers ***(there probably won't be any)*** in the refrigerator. They'll get too sticky if you leave them out on the counter.

Yield: Approximately 48 squares, depending on how generous you are when you cut them.

Hannah's Note: Have an extra pot of coffee ready to go when you serve these cookie bars. They're very rich and folks will need strong coffee to cut the sweetness.

Mother wants me to frost these bars with chocolate frosting. She's even more of a chocoholic than I am!

Chapter Eight

"No music," Hannah said as they turned in at the entrance to her condo complex. "It's so quiet, it's almost . . . sad."

"Sad, but easier on the ears," Norman said, trying for a lighter tone as he reached out to squeeze her hand.

"I know you're right, but one of our most colorful neighbors is gone. Ernie could be a real pain and I certainly can sympathize with Lorna for putting up with him all those years, but at least he was never boring."

"Is that a compliment, or faint praise?"

"I'm not sure. All I know is that Ernie's death creates a void and I can't help but wonder if anything will fill it." Hannah stopped and gave an embarrassed little laugh. "I'm being maudlin. You shouldn't take me seriously. It's probably lack of sleep."

"I *always* take you seriously," Norman said, waiting a few seconds and then adding, "even when you're slightly deranged."

That snapped Hannah right out of her over-sentimental mood and caused her to sputter with laughter. "Bless you," she said, wiping her eyes on the cashmere scarf her mother had given her for Christmas several years ago. "You always seem to know what I need."

"My mission in life," Norman declared, turning to her with a look that was half-teasing, half-serious before he pulled into the underground garage and parked in her spot.

A cold wind was blowing as they emerged from the underground garage and walked down the curving sidewalk to Marsha and Steve's unit. The wind had teeth that nipped at their noses and cheeks as they walked along the cold concrete walkway and made them shiver and wish they were inside a nice warm home with a roaring fire in the fireplace and a hot cup of coffee or cocoa at the ready.

As they approached their destination, the light over the door flicked on and Hannah wondered if Marsha had been watching for them. Norman rang the doorbell and Steve's wife opened the door immediately, confirming Hannah's speculation.

"Please come in," Marsha said, leading

the way into the neat, tidy living room and gesturing toward the couch. Hannah noticed that Marsha's eyes were red-rimmed, the evidence of recent tears. "I have coffee ready if you'd like some."

"I'd love some," Hannah said, knowing that all difficult conversations went better with coffee and chocolate. "And I brought you some fudge I made this afternoon. I was hoping you'd try it and tell me what you think of it."

"I'd love to. Fudge is one of my very favorite things," Marsha said with a smile as she went off to the kitchen to fetch the coffee.

Ten minutes later they were sipping coffee and eating the fudge that Hannah had made at The Cookie Jar. Bertie Straub had named it when Hannah had brought it to the anniversary of her fifteenth year of business at the Cut 'n Curl and Hannah had called it Goodie Fudge ever since.

"Marshmallows, raisins, and . . . what else is in here?" Marsha asked, reaching for her second piece.

"Some chopped, salted pecans. It gives it that buttery flavor."

"It's chocolate heaven," Norman said, earning a smile from Hannah.

"It certainly is!" Marsha took another bite

and then she sighed. "Do you two think you can help Steve? Barbara told me to ask you. I know Steve didn't do it, but I'm the only one."

"Of course we'll do our best to help him," Hannah promised and then she glanced at Norman. She'd included him without even asking. Norman gave a nod to signify that what she'd promised was fine with him and Hannah continued. "You said you knew Steve didn't kill Ernie. How do you know that?"

"I know because I'm his wife and I've been his wife for over thirty years. We don't have any secrets from each other and I believe what he told me when he came back from Ernie's condo."

Hannah and Norman exchanged glances. "Which is . . . ?" Norman asked and they waited to hear what Steve had told Marsha.

"Let me start from the beginning. Steve and Ernie had a history. They'd had words in the past. Ernie didn't like Steve telling him what to do, and Steve didn't like Ernie breaking the homeowners' association rules. The music was the final straw because we were taking care of our grandson, little Stevie, for a couple of days while our son and daughter-in-law went to her sister's wedding. Little Stevie was a handful, I can tell you that!"

"Where is he now?" Hannah asked the obvious question.

"He went home with his parents this morning. I'm just glad they didn't come to take Steve away until after everyone had left!"

"We already know that Steve called Lorna yesterday to see if she could shut off the music," Hannah told her.

"And Lorna said she couldn't do anything because she didn't have a key. The kids did, but they weren't home and Lorna had already tried pounding on Ernie's door with no success. Steve said he didn't blame Lorna. He knew that there was nothing Lorna could do if she couldn't get in and Ernie wouldn't answer the door. But Steve did say that if Ernie hadn't turned down the music by little Stevie's bedtime, he was going to march down there and . . . and clean Ernie's clock."

The hesitation in Marsha's voice told Hannah that Steve had used a stronger phrase. That didn't really matter. What mattered was what happened next.

"Steve waited until it was time to put little Stevie to bed and then he carried out his threat. The music was still blaring away, so he put on his coat and boots and went out to confront Ernie." Marsha stopped and swallowed hard. "It was how he looked when he came back that told me something was horribly wrong."

Hannah waited and so did Norman. Marsha would tell them in her own time.

"Steve's face was pasty white, almost gray, and his hands were shaking. He didn't say anything. He just looked at me like the pictures you see of shell-shocked veterans with their vacant eyes. I tried to snap him out of it. I said, *What did Ernie say when you asked him to turn down the music?* And Steve said, *Nothing.* I couldn't believe someone as contrary as Ernie would say nothing at all, so I asked him again. And Steve said, *Ernie didn't say anything at all. He was dead when I got there.*"

"So Steve said Ernie was dead when he got to Ernie's condo?" Norman asked, just to make it perfectly clear.

"That's what he told me. You see, Steve got really mad when he pounded on Ernie's door and Ernie didn't answer so he decided to go inside on his own. He went in through the guest bathroom window. Ernie's unit is just like ours with the glass louvers in the bathroom window. They're easy to remove from the outside if you know what you're doing."

"And Steve knew what he was doing?" Hannah asked.

"Yes. He did the same thing at our place only last week. We locked ourselves out and Steve went in through our guest bathroom window so he could open the front door and let me in. You're lucky you're on the second floor, Hannah. Anybody who's in the least bit athletic can get into a ground floor condo."

Hannah didn't comment, but she was glad she'd chosen an upstairs unit. There were probably several ways to get inside her condo, but she really didn't want to know what they were.

"So that's how Steve's fingerprints got on the louvers in the bathroom window?" Norman asked.

"That's right. Steve figured Ernie wasn't home and he broke in so he could shut off Ernie's music. Then he was going to come right back out again, but he noticed a light on in the kitchen and he stepped inside. There was Ernie, on the floor behind the refrigerator door, and Steve said he was deader than a mackerel."

"Did he touch Ernie to make sure he was dead?" Hannah asked, wondering if Steve had left fingerprints in the kitchen, too.

"I asked him that and he said he didn't

have to touch Ernie, that he'd seen enough guys with their heads bashed in to know if they were dead or alive. He said there was no question that Ernie was dead."

"What did Steve do next?" Norman asked her.

"He came home. He said he was too rattled to go back through the bathroom window, so he just opened the front door and got out as quick as he could. And he totally forgot to shut off the music, which was the reason he went in there in the first place."

"Did you suggest that Steve call nine-one-one and report that Ernie was dead?" Hannah asked her.

"Of course I did, but Steve wouldn't do it. And he talked me out of it when I said I would. He convinced me that the police would blame him for Ernie's murder. And it turns out that Steve was right. They *do* blame him!"

"Did you tell the police everything you told us?" Norman asked her.

"Of course I did, but nobody ever believes the wife. They probably thought I was making up a story to protect Steve, but that's not true! He didn't do it! I know he didn't!"

"There's only one more thing we need to know," Hannah said in her best soothing voice. "There were six beer bottles sitting in the living room, three by Ernie's chair, and three by another chair. Steve didn't have a couple of beers at Ernie's house, did he?"

Marsha looked shocked. "Of course not! You don't drink beer with a man you're mad at. And you certainly don't sit down and have a beer after you've just found him dead on the kitchen floor!"

"Do you know how long Steve was gone?" Hannah pulled out her steno pad and prepared to write down the time.

"Yes. I was walking with little Stevie over my shoulder, rubbing his back and trying to get him to drop off to sleep. I kept passing the grandfather clock in the living room and glancing at the time. Steve left at seven forty and he was back here by the time the clock chimed eight."

Norman calculated quickly. "So Steve was gone exactly twenty minutes?"

"That's right. Twenty minutes isn't long enough to kill anybody!"

It was enough time to commit a murder, but Hannah didn't say that. And they took their leave after promising, once again, to do their best to clear Steve. Hannah didn't speak until they were well out of earshot, halfway down the curving walkway toward her condo.

"I need to feed Moishe and then I have to go out to the sheriff's station to talk to Bill and Mike. Would you like to come along?"

"I don't see why not. We can always pick up a pizza at Bertanelli's if you're hungry."

"That sounds good to me."

Norman followed Hannah up the stairs to her condo and prepared to catch the orange and white cat that was in the habit of hurtling himself into their arms.

"I'm glad you're coming," Hannah said, reaching in her purse for her keys. "It's always better when we do it together."

"That's only because you know I'll drive and my car has a better heater than your cookie truck."

"That's true, but it's not the only reason. I think we do a really good job when we question people together."

"Thanks." Norman braced himself as Hannah opened the door. He caught Moishe in mid-leap, carried him inside, and placed him on his favorite perch on the back of the living room couch. "You're planning on questioning Mike and Bill?" he asked.

"You bet! I want to find out how they can possibly believe that Steve Gilman broke into Ernie's condo, slammed down three beers with him in rapid succession, and then murdered him and hurried home, all in twenty minutes."

Hannah had just delivered Moishe's food bowl, the one with the picture of Garfield silk-screened on the bottom, when the phone rang. While her feline roommate dined on a mixed grill of salmon bits and tuna flakes canned by his favorite brand of gourmet cat food, she crossed the kitchen to answer the call.

"Hannah! I'm so glad I caught you!" a familiar voice said.

"Lorna?"

"That's right. I'm so excited I forgot to say it was me. Have you heard the news? It's just wonderful!"

"What news?"

"Howie just called to tell me the details of Ernie's will! And I didn't even know he had one! Can you run over for a minute? I just hate to talk about things this important on the phone. I guess it's because I've been a legal secretary for so many years and we have to be so careful about what we say."

"Let me check with Norman," Hannah said, glancing into the living room and receiving a nod from Norman. He knew who was calling. Hannah had used Lorna's name. And his nod meant that a slight detour was fine with him before they left for the sheriff's station. "It's okay with him," she told Lorna. "We'll be there in less than five minutes."

The wind had picked up force by the time they left the condo and Hannah was glad Norman had insisted that she wear her long parka. Earlier in the day, her parka jacket had been perfectly adequate, but the temperature had dropped and now the wind chill was definitely a factor.

Little flakes of snow pelted against her cheeks as they hurried down the walkway to Lorna's place. Hannah pulled up her hood and let the fur shield her from the snowstorm that seemed to be brewing.

Lorna must have been watching for them because she opened the front door before they had a chance to ring the doorbell. "Come in," she said. "Oh, I'm just so happy that Ernie had a will! I was almost positive he hadn't make any provisions for us at all."

"Us?" Norman queried, asking the question a split second before Hannah could ask it.

"I mean the kids. I don't need anything from Ernie. I've got a good job, I own this condo, and I have some money in the bank. I can take care of myself."

"So what did Howie tell you about Ernie's will?" Hannah asked.

"He said Ernie left half of his estate to the kids. The lottery money's been earning interest all this time and it still amounts to almost eight million dollars. The kids get four million in trust for them. Ernie made Howie the trustee and instructed him to pay all the kids' expenses."

"And Ernie left you the other four million?"

Lorna laughed. "Absolutely not. It goes to Ernie's friend Gary Jenkins."

Hannah exchanged startled glances with Norman. And then she asked, "Does Gary know?"

"No. Ernie told Howie that he didn't want Gary to know until after he was dead."

"Why?" Hannah was puzzled.

"Howie asked him that and Ernie said he wanted it to be a big surprise. Besides, he felt he owed Gary something because Gary bought our house and let Ernie live in the basement bedroom for free until Ernie lucked out and won the lottery."

"Does Gary know he's about to become a millionaire?" Norman asked.

"No, Howie said he'd tell Gary in the morning, right after he took a copy of the will down to the sheriff's station."

"Does that mean Howie thinks there's something in the will that might relate to

Ernie's murder?" Hannah leaned forward. This could be a new twist on the case.

"Not at all, but Ernie's death is a homicide and they need to know exactly what's in the will. There are a couple of much smaller bequests and the authorities might like to check those out."

"Did Howie tell you about those?" Hannah took out her steno pad and jotted down several notes while she waited for the answer.

"Yes. Howie read the entire will to me. There's a thousand-dollar bequest to Terrence Brown. He's another of Ernie's coworkers. And Ernie left Cyril Murphy ten thousand dollars and an apology for quitting right after he won the lottery and leaving Cyril in the lurch."

"Any more?" Hannah asked when Lorna paused.

"Just one. Ernie left twenty thousand dollars to me with a note that said I should finally get myself a nice engagement ring."

"Do you know why he did that?" Norman asked.

"He might have felt guilty he never bought me one," Lorna answered. "Or . . ." her expression softened, "maybe Ernie really did love me after all."

GOODIE FUDGE

1 cup golden raisins ***(or any other dried fruit that you prefer, cut in raisin-sized pieces)******

2 cups miniature marshmallows ***(I used Kraft Jet-Puffed)***

1 cup chopped salted pecans ***(measure after chopping)***

3/4 cup powdered ***(confectioners)*** sugar ***(pack it down in the cup when you measure it)***

1/2 cup salted butter ***(1 stick, 4 ounces, 1/4 pound)***

1/2 cup white corn syrup ***(I used Karo)***

12-ounce package semi-sweet chocolate chips ***(2 cups)***

2 teaspoons vanilla extract

***** I've used dried cherries, chopped dried apricots, and dried peaches in this fudge. They were all delicious and I think I'll try dried blueberries next. Lisa makes it with chopped dried pineapple for Herb because he loves pineapple.**

Prepare your pan. Line a 9-inch by 13-inch cake pan with heavy-duty aluminum foil. Make sure you tuck the foil into the corners and leave a flap all the way around the sides. ***(The reason you do this is for easy removal once the fudge has set.)***

Spray the foil with Pam or another non-stick cooking spray.

Sprinkle the raisins ***(or the other cut-up dried fruit you've used)*** over the bottom of the foil-lined cake pan.

Sprinkle the miniature marshmallows over the fruit.

Sprinkle the chopped pecans over that. Set the pan near the stovetop and get ready to make your fudge.

Measure out the powdered sugar and place it in a bowl near the stove. You need it handy because you're going to add it all at once.

Melt the butter together with the corn syrup in a medium-sized saucepan over low heat.

Add the chocolate chips and stir constantly until they're melted and smooth.

Remove the saucepan from the heat and add the vanilla. Be careful because it may sputter.

Stir in the powdered sugar all at once and continue stirring until the mixture in the pan is smooth.

Working quickly, spoon (***or just pour if you can***) the fudge you've made out of the saucepan and into the cake pan.

Spread the fudge out as evenly as you can and stick it into the refrigerator to cool.

Once the fudge has hardened, pull the foil with the fudge from your still-clean cake pan. Pull the foil down the sides and cut your Goodie Fudge into bite-sized pieces. Store in a cool place.

Yield: 48 or more bite-sized pieces, depending on how large your bite is.

CHAPTER NINE

"Come on, Hannah," Bill said, leaning forward over the round conference table in his office. "You know I can't discuss the official investigation with you."

Norman glanced over at Hannah. It was exactly what she'd predicted Bill would say when they'd gone over the facts they'd learned on the way to the sheriff's station. Neither one of them was going to mention Ernie's will. Howie could take in his copy tomorrow morning. They'd concentrate instead on punching holes in the case that Mike and Bill had built up against Steve.

"You don't have to discuss the official investigation with me," Hannah told them. "All you have to do is explain what possessed you to charge Steve Gilman with murder."

"It's simple," Mike said, reaching out for another piece of the pizza Hannah and Norman had brought with them. "The evidence was there. Steve's fingerprints are all over the place."

"Not on the beer bottles," Norman pointed out, earning an approving glance from Hannah.

"That's because he wiped them off." Bill leaned back and took another sip of the coffee Hannah had insisted on bringing with them. She knew the pot at the Winnetka County Sheriff's Station hadn't been washed since the Saturday cleaning crew had come in. Bertanelli's brew was bound to be better than anything made in the squad room.

"Okay, let's say he wiped them off," Hannah agreed readily. "But that means you think Steve was calm and collected enough to realize that his fingerprints were on the beer bottles and he had the presence of mind to wipe them off."

"Exactly right," Bill said with a nod.

"If Steve really was that calm and collected, wouldn't he also wipe his fingerprints from the bathroom window and the inside of the front doorknob? You're saying he wiped off some, but he left others for you to find. That doesn't make sense."

Bill gave her what Hannah construed as a very patronizing look. "It doesn't have to make sense. You're forgetting that not everything killers do makes sense. Emotions are heightened. Judgment takes a backseat."

"All right. I'll accept that," Hannah told him, conceding the point. "But I don't think that the clock can take a backseat."

"What clock?" Mike asked.

"The clock that's ticking away the time and measuring how long Steve was at the crime scene. We just talked to Marsha Gilman and she said that Steve left his house at seven forty. And he came back when the clock was striking eight. That's only twenty minutes."

"Twenty minutes is long enough to commit violent murder," Mike pointed out. "Mr. Gilman was in a rage when he left his place. He admits that. He also admits that he broke into Ernie's condo. That wouldn't take long for a man who knew exactly how to do it. Once inside, Mr. Gilman confronted the victim and killed him. I don't see any inconsistency there. The timeframe works."

"No, it doesn't work. You're forgetting the beer bottles. You're trying to convince me that Steve left his house in a killing rage, broke into Ernie's place, slammed down three beers with the man he hated, bashed in Ernie's head right after he'd drained the last beer, wiped down the bottles so he wouldn't leave any fingerprints, and then went home, all in twenty minutes."

There was silence for a moment and then Bill sighed. "When you put it like that, I've got to admit that it sounds a little implausible. But I don't doubt that's what happened. It's the only scenario that fits."

"No, it isn't. What if someone else drank those three beers with Ernie?" Norman proposed. "What if that happened earlier in the afternoon, before Steve arrived on the scene?"

Bill shook his head. "But it *didn't* happen earlier. If someone else drank those beers with Ernie, Steve wouldn't have had a reason to wipe the prints from the bottles."

"Exactly!" Hannah began to smile. Bill had made her point. "There'd be *no* reason for Steve to wipe off those prints because his fingerprints weren't on the beer bottles in the first place. The murderer shared three sociable beers with Ernie. And then something set him off and he killed Ernie. He left, but not before he wiped his prints off the beer bottles."

There was another full minute of silence and Hannah could tell she'd made her point. Both Mike and Bill were considering the possibility that someone else, some friend who'd shared three beers with Ernie, had killed him.

"No," Mike said at last. "You're assuming that Mrs. Gilman is telling the truth about the time. You can't assume that since the only other witness to the time Mr. Gilman left his house and the time he returned is a two-year-old child."

Bill didn't look happy, but he nodded. "Mike's right. The circumstantial evidence is there and it's a proven fact that Steve Gilman had altercations with the victim in the past. It's also true that Steve Gilman taught several hand-to-hand combat courses during his last three years in the Marine Corps."

"He's our man," Mike insisted. "He had the motive, means and opportunity. All you have is conjecture and that's not enough."

"I'm sorry, Hannah." Bill reached out to pat her hand. "I know you've solved murder cases in the past. We really do appreciate your efforts to help, but this time you're dead wrong."

"What's that?" Norman asked as Hannah reached into the tote bag she'd tossed into his backseat.

"T.C.B. Fruitcake for Gary. I made a batch a couple of weeks ago and this is the last one I have."

"Fruitcake?" Norman began to frown.

"Does Gary like it? Or are you planning to torture him for information by making him eat it?"

Hannah gave him a stern look, but she couldn't hold in her laughter for long. Once she'd composed herself again, she said, "Marge got the recipe from a friend of hers and T.C.B. stands for This Can't Be. The full name is This Can't Be Fruitcake and that's because it's so good."

"*Fruitcake* and *good* are mutually exclusive. I really hate citron."

"There isn't any citron. Marge's friend Nancy uses dried fruit instead. This one has dried peaches and pineapple."

"What else is in there?"

"Raisins, nuts, and crushed graham crackers."

"That's beginning to sound okay."

"It is, and I forgot to tell you about the coconut. That's in there, too."

"I never thought I'd say this, but what you described actually sounds like a good fruitcake."

As they approached Gary's front door, Norman turned to Hannah. "Are you going to mention Ernie's will?"

"I was debating that before, but now I think I will. Bill and Mike were really condescending. They didn't even consider that they could be wrong about Steve. They just dismissed our ideas as immaterial."

"So you're going to tell Gary and get the jump on them?"

"You bet I am! I know Gary hasn't heard yet and I want to get his initial reaction."

"There's going to be you-know-what to pay when Mike and Bill find out what you've done. I may have to bail you out of jail."

"You'd do that for me?"

"Of course I would. It's a cinch they're not going to solve this case, not when they think they already have the killer behind bars. You have to find Ernie's real killer and you can't do that in jail."

"Then you'd bail me out to see that justice was done?"

"That's part of it. And also for the safety of the community. After all, there's a killer on the loose."

"For the safety of the community," Hannah repeated, not sure if she was pleased with Norman's answer.

"There's another reason too, but it's personal."

Hannah began to feel much better. She was sure that Norman was about to say something about how he'd miss her, or perhaps even tell her that he loved her and didn't want them to spend time apart. "What's your personal reason?" she asked, her smile all ready to emerge.

"I need you to make another batch of that T.C.B. Fruitcake so you can give me one for Christmas."

The minute Gary opened the door, it was pretty obvious they'd caught him working. There were splatters of green paint on his sweatshirt and several dabs of what looked like mahogany stain on his white painter's pants.

"Sorry," Hannah apologized, handing him the fruitcake, which was tied with a red and green bow. "I brought you something for the holiday season."

"Thanks!" Gary seemed pleased at this unexpected generosity. "It's Hannah, isn't it? And Dr. Rhodes?"

"Hannah," she confirmed it.

"And Norman. I'm only Dr. Rhodes at the clinic."

"Well . . . thank you very much." Gary looked down at the package he was holding. "What is it?"

"Fruitcake, but it's not really fruitcake. It's more like candy. Just keep it in the refrigerator until you cut it. And use a strong knife with a long flat blade."

"Like a chef's knife?" Gary asked.

"That'll do just fine. Do you have a minute, Gary? There's something I need to tell you."

"Sure. Come on into the living room. I don't have my couch yet, but I have chairs. Your mother's looking for just the right furniture for me." Gary led the way into the living room, which was only partially decorated. "If you want beer, I've got some Cold Spring John Henry and some Moonlight Ale. Or a mixed drink? I stocked the bar right after I bought this place."

"I'll take a John Henry, thanks," Norman said. "No need for a glass."

"Do you have any diet drinks?" Hannah asked when Gary turned to her.

"Diet Coke, Diet Pepsi, and diet ginger ale."

"I'd love a diet ginger ale," Hannah said, naming her mother's favorite diet drink.

"Like mother, like daughter," Gary said with a grin, heading off to get their drinks.

The built-in bar covered one whole wall and Gary ducked behind it to open the refrigerator. Hannah caught a glimpse of Perrier-Jouet, her mother's favorite champagne, before the door closed again. Diet ginger ale and Perrier-Jouet. It was clear

Gary stocked her mother's favorites. Perhaps this relationship was more serious than she'd thought.

Once the drinks had been served, Gary turned to Hannah. "Are you here to ask me about my intentions toward your mother?"

"No!" Hannah gave a little laugh. "That's not it at all. It's just that I have news for you."

"I hope it's better than the last news I got!" Gary took a swig on his beer directly from the bottle. "When I got home from dinner with your mother, Lorna called me to tell me that Ernie was dead."

"You were good friends?" Norman asked.

"Friends and drinking buddies. That's why I've got a case of Aspen Meadow Black and Tan on ice. It was Ernie's favorite beer." Gary's expression hardened and he turned to Hannah. "Have they arrested anybody yet?"

"Yes. One of Ernie's neighbors is in custody. The police think he did it."

"Well, I'm glad they caught him. It was a terrible thing, just a terrible thing. Ernie had his faults, but he was a good guy at heart."

A golden opportunity had presented itself and Hannah took it. "Yes, he *was* a good guy, especially to his friends. That's what I came to tell you. You won't get the official word until tomorrow, so please don't tell anyone I told you, but Ernie left you four million dollars in his will."

"Whoa!" Gary held out his arms as if to ward off a blow. His hands began to tremble and beer sloshed out of his bottle onto an area rug that looked very expensive to Hannah.

"Gary? Are you okay?" Hannah was concerned when she saw how pale his face was.

"I'm . . . okay," Gary said, and his voice was shaking. He made a move to set down his beer bottle, missed the edge of the coffee table and tried again. This time he made it and he turned to Hannah. "Did you just say what I thought you said?"

"I did. Ernie left four million dollars to you in his will."

"But why? I didn't do much for Ernie. Sure, I let him stay in his old basement bedroom, but any friend would do that. And I always had a cold beer for him, but that's what friends do. Why would Ernie leave me all that money?"

"I don't know," Hannah said, realizing that Gary was still in shock. "I was hoping you'd know."

"Well, I don't. It's just . . . incredible!" Gary picked up his beer bottle again and took a big swallow.

"Are you happy about it?" Norman asked him.

"Well . . . sure! Who *wouldn't* be happy about all that money?"

"Then you'll accept it?" Hannah asked.

"You betcha! I'd be a fool to turn down big money like that." Gary stopped speaking and looked thoughtful. And then he said, "I'm going to split it with Lorna and his kids. That's only right. Ernie loved his kids and he wanted them to go to college and everything."

"Ernie provided for his children," Norman told him. "He put another four million into a trust fund for them and named Howie Levine as executor. Lorna and the kids will be fine."

Gary took another drink from his beer. "I'm having a lot of trouble believing this. Are you sure you're right?"

"I'm sure," Hannah said, watching carefully. She was certain that he was still reeling from the shock of the news she'd given him, and she decided to ask him about his cell phone number while he was still off balance. "Do you have any idea why Ernie chose your cell phone number on his winning lottery ticket?"

"*My* number?"

"That's right. He choose those numbers when he bought the ticket."

"I don't know unless . . ." Gary stopped speaking and looked confused. "Sometimes I forget my own cell phone number. I mean, I never call myself. But I know Ernie's number because I call him so often. Maybe Ernie was like me. He couldn't remember his own number, so he wrote down my number. Or maybe Ernie didn't choose any numbers at all. Maybe he just bought a Quick Pick and let the machine choose for him."

"Those are two good possibilities," Hannah said. "There was one other number on the ticket. It's thirty-seven. Does thirty-seven mean anything to you?"

Gary thought about that for a moment. "Not really. It's one inch over a yard. You know that one if you play football. I can't count how many times we came up just an inch or two shy of a first down. And . . . wasn't there some airplane lost in thirty-seven?"

"Amelia Earhart's plane," Norman answered him. "She flew solo across the Atlantic in nineteen thirty-two and in nineteen thirty-seven, she was lost over the Pacific on an around-the-world flight."

"Do you think Ernie knew that?" Hannah

asked him.

"I don't think so. Ernie wasn't into history. Just give me a second and let me think about it."

Gary picked up his beer again and took another drink. Hannah noticed that his color was coming back and his hands had stopped shaking.

"It's not a limo number," Gary told them. "We don't have that many. And it's not any part of Ernie's new address or the address of this house. The only thing I can think of is maybe something really good happened to Ernie the year he turned thirty-seven. And that's why he used that number."

"Do you have any idea what that *something really good* might be?" Hannah asked him.

Gary shook his head. "Sorry. I don't have a clue. I didn't meet Ernie until he was in his forties and I don't remember him talking about anything really important in his past. Maybe you should ask Lorna. She might know."

"Good idea." Hannah finished her drink and stood up. "Thanks for all your help, Gary. And congratulations on your good fortune."

Gary rose to his feet and shook hands with both of them. "Thanks," he said. "It's a mixed bag, you know? I'm happy about all that money. Don't get me wrong there. It's just too bad that my buddy had to die for me to get it."

T.C.B. FRUITCAKE (THIS CAN'T BE FRUITCAKE)

Hannah's 1st Note: Marge's friend Nancy makes this every Christmas in small, tea bread pans. She loves to watch people's faces when she tells them that it's fruitcake. Nancy says most people hesitate before they reach out to take it. Nancy waits until they do and then she tells them it's not regular fruitcake, that it's more like candy with all the good stuff including marshmallows, graham crackers, dried fruit, nuts, and coconut.

Prepare your pans. You'll need 8 baby loaf pans. ***(My pans are stamped** 5 3/4 × 3 × 2 **1/8 on the bottom.)*** Line each pan with a piece of plastic wrap that's large enough to overlap the sides and cover the top of the pan when your T.C.B. Fruitcake is inside. Set the pans aside.

Use a **very large** mixing bowl to make this delicious Christmas treat. If you don't have one, go out and buy a big, disposable, foil turkey roaster and use that. While you're at it, pick up a pair of food service gloves, or even the type of gloves ladies used to put on to wash dishes by hand. You'll be mixing everything with your hands and things will get a little sticky.

Spray your very large mixing bowl or foil turkey roaster with Pam or another nonstick cooking spray.

Measure out all the ingredients except the evaporated milk and the salt, and set them out on your counter. ***(I measured mine and put them in individual 2-gallon plastic food storage bags — I'm lazy and didn't want to wash an extra 6 bowls.)*** Nancy says it's best to pre-measure. Then you won't have to stop once you start adding ingredients. Everything will be ready and the mixing process will go lickety-split.

3/4 cup canned evaporated milk ***(not sweetened condensed milk, not regular milk from the refrigerator, not anything except canned evaporated milk)***
1 pound miniature marshmallows ***(that's roughly 10 cups — I used Kraft Jet-Puffed)***
1 pound crushed graham crackers ***(you can crush your own or buy graham cracker***

crumbs — one pound is approximately 4 cups)

1/2 teaspoon salt

1 pound seedless raisins ***(Nancy uses a combination of red, black, golden, and jumbo raisins — my store wasn't that well stocked and I ended up using only golden)***

1 pound mixed dried fruit of your choice ***(check the weight on the labels and add it up — Nancy's used dried cherries, blueberries, Craisins, and apricots, all cut into small raisin-sized pieces)***

4 cups of roughly cut unsalted nuts of your choice ***(I used pecans)***

4 ounces shredded or flaked coconut ***(if you chop this into smaller pieces, everyone will like it better)***

red and green candied cherries to decorate the tops

Scald the milk in a large-size saucepan. This just means that you should heat it almost to boiling over medium-high, stirring constantly so that it won't burn. When it starts to bubble around the edges of the pan, pull it off the heat and turn off the burner.

Working as fast as you can, add the marshmallows to the hot milk, give a rapid stir, and quickly put a lid on the saucepan. Set your oven timer for 5 minutes. The marshmallows should be melted by then. Don't lift the lid and peek. Your goal is to keep the heat in so that the marshmallows will melt.

Place the graham cracker crumbs into the very large mixing bowl or turkey roaster. Add the salt and mix them up.

This would be a good time to check to see if you've measured all the other ingredients. You'll still have a couple of minutes before the stove timer rings.

When your timer dings, check the milk and marshmallow mixture. It should be melted. If it isn't and you can't stir it smooth, return it to the burner you used to scald the milk and turn it on LOW. Stir constantly until the marshmallows and milk make a smooth mixture.

Using a heat-resistant flexible spatula or a wooden spoon, stir the marshmallow mixture into the mixing bowl with the graham cracker crumbs and the salt. Continue to stir until everything is moistened.

Here's where things get sticky. It's time to don those rubber or food service gloves you remembered to buy at the store. ***(Just in case you forgot, you can always butter your hands, or spray them with Pam or another nonstick cooking spray. This will***

keep the sticky stuff from sticking to your fingers.)

Add the rest of the ingredients ***(the raisins, the chopped dried fruit, the chopped nuts, and the coconut)*** in rapid succession and then get in there with both hands to mix it all up.

When everything is mixed, press the mixture into your lined loaf pans. Make sure your T.C.B. Fruitcakes are pressed down all the way into the corners and are fairly flat on top. Decorate the tops with the candied cherries. Then cover them with the excess plastic wrap.

As an extra safeguard, wrap each pan with another layer of plastic wrap and then refrigerate the pans.

Nancy says these fruitcakes can be eaten or presented as gifts right after they're thoroughly chilled. They store well for months in an air-tight container in the refrigerator.

To wrap a T.C.B. Fruitcake for a gift, tip the loaf right out of the pan. It will be already covered with plastic wrap, but you can wrap it with another layer or use Christmas wrapping paper. Dress it up with a stick-on bow if you want to be fancy. And don't forget to tell your happy recipient that it should be kept refrigerated.

Serve T.C.B. Fruitcake well chilled. Use a good, heavy-duty knife to cut it into bite-size pieces and everyone will agree it's very rich and good.

Hannah's 2nd Note: If you don't have baby loaf pans, Nancy says you can press the whole mixture into a 9-inch by 13-inch cake pan lined with plastic wrap. (Don't forget to make the piece of plastic wrap long enough to also cover the top.) Once the mixture is thoroughly chilled, you can remove the fruitcake from the pan, wrap it in another layer of plastic wrap, and return it to the refrigerator. To serve, cut it into brownie-sized pieces. It doesn't look like fruitcake that way, but it's equally good!

Hannah's 3rd Note: Mother thinks I ought to add some miniature chocolate chips to the mixture. I told her I wasn't sure that would work because unbaked, chilled chocolate chips are hard and they might spoil the texture. Of course that didn't stop Mother. Her next suggestion was to melt 2 cups of chocolate chips and add them to the bowl right after I stirred in the marshmallow and milk mixture. I think that'll probably work and I'll try it next Christmas. For

a non-dessert maker, Mother has some pretty good ideas.

Chapter Ten

Neither one of them spoke much on the drive to The Cookie Jar to pick up Hannah's truck. The moment they'd gotten on the road, Hannah had called Lorna Kusak on Norman's cell phone and asked her about the number thirty-seven. The number meant nothing to Lorna and, as far as she knew, nothing significant had happened to Ernie when he was thirty seven. It was another strikeout, but Hannah couldn't help but feel that the last number on Ernie's winning ticket was the clue that would catch Ernie's killer.

Norman pulled up next to the candy-apple red Suburban with the gold letters advertising Hannah's business on both doors. "You're going to bake, aren't you?" he asked her.

"Yes. I'm still thinking about all the new facts I learned today and my mind is racing. If I went straight home, I couldn't sleep anyway."

"And you always think better when you're baking," Norman added.

"Right," Hannah said with a smile. Norman knew her very well.

"It's already ten and I know you're tired. You did all that cooking for the crime-scene techs last night. Is there any way I can help you?"

Hannah was about to say no, that baking relaxed her and she was used to working by herself. Then she reconsidered. "Yes," she said.

"Great. I'm pretty good at following a recipe. I learned from an expert."

Hannah smiled again. She knew Norman was referring to the times they'd baked together. "Baking's not the problem, Norman. I really need you to do something else for me, something I can't do down at The Cookie Jar."

"Sure. What is it?"

"It's something Gary said. He seemed to think that if you chose your own numbers to play in the lottery, the chances of winning were just the same as if you let a machine pick them for you."

"Gary's right."

"Really?" Hannah was surprised. "I always thought that your chances were better when you let the machine choose for you."

"It doesn't matter which way you do it. The chances are still the same. What matters is the method the lottery uses to pick the winning numbers."

"You mean the little numbered balls that spin around and come out a little door?"

"Yes. If everything's on the up and up, that's entirely random. When the balls start spinning, each number has an equal chance of slipping out of the drum. It could be someone's favorite number or one that's been chosen by the lottery machine."

"Then you're telling me that it's not really rare that five numbers from Gary's telephone number came up on the winning ticket."

"Wrong. I think it's *very* rare. I also think that it's rare Gary didn't have any unusable digits in his cell phone number."

"Unusable?"

"Unusable as far as the lottery's concerned. For instance, my cell phone number has two sevens in it, so my number could never come up. Once ball number seven falls out of the drum, it can't get back in to fall again."

"I see. And Gary didn't have any repeating numbers?"

"That's right. What I'd have to do is run

the probability on how many people have five and only five lottery-acceptable numbers for their cell phones."

"Would that be difficult?"

"I don't know. It all hinges on how I set up the equation on the computer. I'm sure I can find an Internet site that figures probability."

"Then you'll do it?"

"Of course I will. You know I'll do anything I can to help you."

"Thanks, Norman." Hannah snuggled up and placed a kiss on his cheek. "I guess I'm obsessing about those lottery numbers. It just bothers me that the winning ticket had Gary's cell phone number."

"It bothers me, too. You'd think that if anyone would play those numbers, it would be Gary himself."

After she'd washed her hands and tied on an apron, Hannah made coffee. Then she began to gather the ingredients for Hannah's Best Butterscotch Cookies. She needed twenty dozen by ten o'clock the next morning for the Lake Eden Chamber of Commerce holiday brunch.

The recipe was already on her kitchen clipboard. Hannah read through it once and that was when she noticed the note on the bottom in Lisa's handwriting. It read, *Submitted this recipe in Hannah's name to the National Cookie Day Contest, cash prize twenty-five thousand dollars.*

Hannah stood there for a moment in shock and then she sighed deeply. Lisa had made a terrible error by submitting the recipe, but it was a natural mistake. She'd assumed that because Hannah's name was on the recipe, it was one of her own. But it wasn't. She'd gotten the recipe from her favorite English Literature professor in college, Dr. Hannah Albertson.

Hannah considered the problem that loomed over her head. She couldn't claim a recipe that belonged to someone else! Dr. Albertson had told her that it was an original, that her favorite flavor was butterscotch and she'd experimented with it over the entire course of her teaching career. The recipe she gave Hannah was the one that was most successful, the one she'd put her own spin on, the cookie that everyone loved best. She had to call the contest officials first thing in the morning and correct the mistake.

The sound of the mixer was soothing. Hannah mixed the softened butter, cream cheese, and sugar together, gradually increasing the speed until they were light and fluffy. She added the eggs, one at a time, and mixed them in before she put in the vanilla extract and the baking soda. Once those were incorporated, she added the flour, one cup at a time, and took the bowl from the mixer.

It took a little muscle to stir in the butterscotch chips and even more muscle to add the white chocolate chips. She was just stirring in the chopped cashews when she had a frightening thought. What if she *hadn't* seen Lisa's note on the recipe? What if she'd won the contest and collected the twenty-five thousand dollars? Dr. Albertson would be outraged that Hannah had stolen *her* recipe and the cash prize that should have gone to her! If that happened, Hannah wouldn't really blame Dr. Albertson if she drove all the way to Lake Eden and practically killed her!

Killed her. Killed her for a stolen recipe and the money it earned. The words scrolled through Hannah's mind, and she set the bowl down on the stainless steel surface of the workstation with a heavy thump. She was pretty sure that Dr. Albertson wouldn't actually *kill* her for twenty-five thousand dollars, but what if the amount were larger? Much larger, even life-changing?

Are you talking about eight million dollars?

the niggling little voice in Hannah's head said, *the eight million dollars Ernie Kusak won with his lottery ticket?*

As Hannah thought it over, little tingles of excitement ran up and down her back. The pieces were beginning to fall into place and that meant she was on the right track. What if Ernie's winning ticket really wasn't his ticket? What if the winning numbers belonged to someone else, someone who'd given Ernie money and asked him to pick up a ticket? If that someone found out that Ernie had kept *his* ticket and pocketed eight million dollars, he could be mad enough to kill Ernie!

The next question to consider was how could that someone, the person who rightfully owned that winning ticket, find out that Ernie had stolen it? Hannah got another cup of coffee, covered her work bowl with plastic wrap, and placed it in the walk-in cooler. The answer came the minute she sat down again. Ernie had a framed photo of his winning ticket hanging in the guest bathroom.

Everything fit! Ernie's guest that fateful afternoon could have been the rightful owner of the winning ticket. The empty beer bottles proved that he'd downed three beers with Ernie and he would have had to visit the restroom eventually. When he did, he'd see *his* personal numbers on the photo of the winning ticket! Was that grounds for murder? You bet! And now Hannah was pretty sure she knew the identity of Ernie's killer. It just had to be Gary Jenkins. The circumstantial evidence was stacking up against him. His cell phone number was listed on the winning ticket, and he'd been the largest beneficiary in Ernie's will. The will, itself, practically proved that Ernie felt guilty for what he'd done . . . didn't it? She had to call Mike and Bill right away and tell them to arrest Gary Jenkins.

But they wouldn't do it. As they'd told her earlier when she'd tried to clear Steve Gilman, everything was conjecture and you couldn't convict on conjecture. There had to be hard evidence. Hannah needed to find a piece of evidence that would prove that Gary murdered Ernie. She'd already tied five winning numbers to Gary. If she tied that last number on the winning lottery ticket to him, would it be enough to convince Bill and Mike?

Hannah racked her brain to try to think of the next step. If Gary was the killer, he certainly wasn't about to admit that he knew anything about the number thirty-seven. She needed another resource, someone who knew him very well, someone who . . .

"Mother!" Hannah gasped, jumping up and racing for the phone. Delores might know something about Gary and the number thirty-seven. She'd certainly spent enough time with him!

But Delores wasn't home. The phone rang ten times and then her mother's answering machine picked up. *This is Delores,* it told Hannah in a cheerful, up-beat voice. *If I'm not here, I'm somewhere else. If it's a workday, you can try Granny's Attic. If it's not, you'll just have to try to track me down.*

Hannah hung up without leaving a message. Instead, she tried her mother's cell phone. She was switched immediately to voice mail and got another recorded message. It was time to try Andrea. Her sister might know where their mother was.

One glance at the clock told Hannah it was too late to call the Todd household, but Hannah punched in the number anyway. Andrea answered on the first ring and she sounded wide awake.

"It's Hannah," Hannah told her, probably unnecessarily since Andrea was bound to recognize her voice. "Do you know where Mother is?"

"She's not home?"

"No. I called there. And I tried her cell phone, but it went straight to voice mail."

"Hold on a second. I've got an idea." Andrea put the phone down with a soft little bump. Then Hannah heard the sound of footfalls receding and then returning much faster than they'd left.

"I'm back." Andrea was slightly breathless when she picked up the phone again. "Mother's at Gary's house. She parked on the street right in front. I think that's a little brazen, don't you?"

Instantly, an image of the old pickup truck Bill had owned when Andrea was in high school crossed the screen of Hannah's mind. She'd walked past it on her way to pick up the morning paper and spotted her sister and Bill inside, sleeping in each other's arms. She'd tapped on the window to wake them so that Andrea could get inside before their parents woke up. It was clear that Andrea had forgotten that incident, but Hannah hadn't.

"What do you think we should do?" Andrea asked. "I don't like the idea of Mother over there alone with him at this time of night."

"Me neither," Hannah said, but for an entirely different reason. "Don't worry, Andrea. I'll drive over and just happen to drop in. I have to talk to Mother about something anyway."

It was a bit uncomfortable when Hannah arrived at Gary's house, and that would be an understatement in anyone's book. Gary and Delores were having champagne in the living room and there was a plate of cut T.C.B. Fruitcake that had only one piece left. It was clear that Hannah was interrupting their evening.

"I'm sorry to barge in like this," Hannah said as Gary led her into the living room. "I just dropped something off at Andrea's house and I spotted Mother's car. I came over on impulse to say congratulations to you again."

"What did you drop off, dear?" Delores asked.

Hannah thought fast. She needed to let her mother know that this wasn't a social visit and that all was not well. "Andrea called and asked for my recipe for *coq au vin.*"

"She did?"

If this hadn't been so serious, Hannah would have laughed. Her mother looked shocked beyond all belief. "Andrea wants to make it tomorrow night for Bill."

"Oh. I see." Delores gave a slight nod and

Hannah knew her mother had caught on that something was up. Delores didn't know what, but Hannah's heads-up had worked.

"We've been celebrating Gary's good fortune," Delores told Hannah. "Isn't it wonderful? No one deserves a windfall more than Gary."

"Thanks, Dolo," Gary said, smiling at her.

Hannah waited for the other shoe to drop. She knew from past experience that her mother hated to be called *Dolo,* but Delores just smiled back. "Aren't you going to offer my daughter a glass of champagne?" she asked Gary.

"Of course I am." Gary hefted the bottle. "But I think this one's just about gone."

"But you *do* have more, don't you, Gary?"

"Sure. It's in the refrigerator. I'll get it."

"No, I'll get it." Hannah waved him back down in his chair. "I'm the party crasher here. It's only right that I do the work." And that said, she swooped up their champagne flutes and ducked behind the built-in bar before Gary could protest.

HANNAH'S BEST BUTTERSCOTCH COOKIES

Preheat oven to 325 degrees F., rack in the middle position.

3/4 cup ***(1 and 1/2 sticks, 6 ounces)*** salted butter, softened
6 ounces cream cheese, softened ***(that's 3/4 of an 8-ounce package)***
3/4 cup white ***(granulated)*** sugar
3/4 cup brown sugar
2 teaspoons vanilla extract
1 teaspoon baking soda
2 large eggs
3 cups flour ***(pack it down in the cup when you measure it)***
1 cup ***(6 ounces)*** butterscotch chips
1 cup ***(6 ounces)*** white chocolate chips
1 and 1/2 cups chopped, salted cashews ***(measure BEFORE chopping)***

Hannah's Note: You can use an electric mixer for this recipe, or you can do it by hand. It's your choice.

In a large bowl, mix the softened butter, softened cream cheese, white sugar and brown sugar together until they're light and fluffy.

Mix in the vanilla, and the baking soda.

Add the eggs, one at a time, mixing after each addition.

Add the flour in one-cup increments, mixing after each addition.

Take the bowl out of the mixer. You'll have to mix in the last three ingredients by hand.

Add the butterscotch chips to your bowl and stir them in.

Add the white chocolate chips to your bowl and mix thoroughly.

Add the chopped salted cashews and mix well.

Drop the dough by mounded teaspoonfuls onto an UNGREASED cookie sheet, 12 cookies to a standard-sized sheet. ***(You can also cover your cookie sheets with parchment paper or baking paper if you have it.)***

Flatten the cookies a bit with the blade of a spatula or the palm of your impeccably clean hand. They'll spread out a little more in the oven, but not a lot.

Bake Hannah's Best Butterscotch Cookies at 325 degrees F. for 8 to 10 minutes or until nicely golden on top.

Let the cookies cool for two minutes on the cookie sheet and then remove them to a wire rack to cool completely.

Yield: Approximately 7 dozen delicious cookies

Chapter Eleven

Hannah took a bottle of Perrier-Jouet from the refrigerator behind the bar. She also removed two cans of diet ginger ale. She opened the champagne bottle with a barely discernible pop, something a caterer learns how to do early in his or her career, and filled Gary's glass. Once she'd taken it to him, she filled two champagne flutes with diet ginger ale, delivering one to her mother and taking the other for herself.

"Thank you, dear," her mother said, admiring the bubbles. She took a sip, gave a ladylike little cough, and stared hard at her daughter. Hannah shook her head slightly and Delores turned away and began to talk about the simply marvelous antique furniture that she was having reupholstered for his den.

Conversation flowed as Delores and Hannah sipped their ginger ale and Gary drank his glass of champagne. Hannah jumped up to refill it from the bottle on the bar. They drank and talked for what seemed like forever to Hannah until the opportunity she'd been awaiting arrived.

"Excuse me," Gary said. "I'll be back in a couple of minutes. You ladies will be all right, won't you?" And then, without waiting for an answer, he walked oh-so-carefully down the hall.

"What's going on?" Delores asked the minute he was out of earshot.

We may be sitting here drinking with Ernie's killer, that's what's wrong! her mind provided the answer, but Hannah didn't say that. There was no sense in alarming her mother until she was sure. "How well do you know Gary, Mother?"

"I know him . . . very well."

"Good," Hannah said, before her mother could ask another question. "Do you happen to know if the number thirty-seven means anything special to him?"

"Thirty-seven? Why yes, dear. I believe that was his number when he played quarterback on his high school football team in Ohio. He comes from Columbus, you know."

"Are you sure it was thirty-seven?"

Delores hesitated a moment. "I'm not positive, but we can find out. There's an action photo Gary had framed and it's in his home office. We can go take a peek if you'd like. Gary won't mind."

Hannah followed as her mother led the way to Gary's office. Gary was nowhere in sight and she hoped they could be back in the living room before he returned.

Delores flicked on the light and pointed to the framed photo on the wall. "There's Gary and he's throwing a pass," she said.

Hannah's heart hammered hard as she stepped closer for a better look. Gary's back was to the camera and his jersey sported the number thirty-seven. This was no longer conjecture. Even Mike and Bill had to agree with that. Six lottery numbers out of six ought to be proof enough for them.

"What is it, dear?" Delores asked. "You look terribly upset."

"I am. Gary killed Ernie and that picture's the proof." Hannah grabbed her mother's arm. "Let's go! Quick!"

"You're not going anywhere, either one of you," Gary ordered, standing in the doorway with a pistol.

Ruger. Forty-four mag. Hannah's mind reeled off the stats. She'd shot a pistol just like the one Gary was pointing at them the last time she went out to the shooting range with Lisa and Herb. But recognizing the gun didn't do anything except identify what might very well become their murder weapon. She had to do something to get that gun away from Gary . . . but what?

And then Delores spoke in the sultriest voice Hannah had ever heard. "Come on, Gary. You know I don't like guns."

"I know, Dolo . . . but she figured it out. You kept bragging about what a good detective she was and you were right. I *did* kill Ernie. And now . . ." Gary shook his head as if he didn't want to speak the words. "And now I have to kill you."

"Because we know?" Hannah asked, wondering if she could jump him and wrestle the gun away.

"Yes. I really don't want to do it, but I want my money. He stole my winning lottery ticket and I want my money!"

"I don't blame you one bit," Delores said, still in the same sultry voice. "But you wouldn't kill a lady without letting her have one more glass of champagne . . . would you?"

"Well . . ."

Gary was torn. Hannah could see it on his face. All she could do was hope that the beer he'd had with them earlier and the champagne he'd consumed with Delores had impaired his judgment.

"Okay," he said at last. "But just you, Dolo. She's got to . . ."

"Wait!" Hannah stepped in before Gary could utter the fateful words. "I think I deserve a final glass of champagne, too. After all, I brought you that wonderful fruitcake. And it was good, wasn't it?"

Gary cocked his head and looked a bit confused. After a long silence, he finally said, "Yeah, it was good. And I guess you're right, Let's go to the living room. But no funny stuff. I'm right behind you with this gun."

As they walked down the hallway followed by Ernie's killer, Hannah knew that time was her friend. If she was here longer than an hour and Andrea noticed, she'd send Bill over to see what was going on. Of course Bill might not be home. And Andrea could come over by herself. That was an eventuality to be avoided by all costs.

"I guess I don't blame you for killing Ernie," Hannah said as they headed to the living room. "He stole that money from you by taking your lottery ticket and claiming it for his own."

"That's right. And you know what really burns me? I didn't know it until I saw that framed ticket in his bathroom."

"How did Ernie get your ticket?" Delores

asked him, catching on to what Hannah was trying to do.

"We were out the night before the drawing and I had to drive a client to the Cities in the morning. It was an all day job. He had a couple of TV interviews and he hired me to stick around until they were over. I figured I wouldn't have time to slip out to buy a lottery ticket and Ernie said to give him my numbers and he'd buy it for me."

"So he bought a ticket using your numbers?" Delores asked.

"He did, but that's not what he told me. He said he was really busy and didn't have time to buy any tickets at all."

"And you believed him?" Hannah asked, hoping she sounded sympathetic.

"That's right. I believed him right up until yesterday. Ernie always came to my place. He told me he liked to visit his old house. But yesterday I dropped in to see him at his condo. We had a couple of beers, all friendly like, and then I went to the bathroom. I saw his framed lottery ticket on the wall and I realized that his winning numbers were really mine!"

"He cheated you," Delores said, stepping into the living room and heading straight for the bar. "I need a clean glass. You don't mind, do you, Gar?"

Gary swallowed hard and Hannah guessed that the nickname her mother had used was a term of affection. "I don't mind," he said. "But Dolo . . . I really hate to . . ."

"Don't think about it," Delores said, reaching for the glasses. "How about you, Gar? Do you want another glass?"

"I don't need one right now," Gary said, and Hannah noticed that he was beginning to slur his words slightly. Was it possible he'd miss even if he shot at them at point-blank range?

"Are you sure you don't want one?" Delores asked again, picking up the champagne bottle and moving out from behind the bar. "Here's your glass. I'll just fill it and . . ."

As Hannah watched, her mother wheeled around and executed one of the best moves she'd ever seen. Delores held the champagne bottle with one hand, handed the glass to Gary with the other, and then swung the bottle into the side of Gary's head with a resounding clunk.

The pistol dropped to the floor and Hannah dove for it. Gary went down like a felled tree. The champagne bottle bounced once and then hit the edge of the brick fireplace and shattered into pieces.

"That was just great, Mother!" Hannah

said, jumping onto Gary's back to pin Ernie's killer, who appeared to be unconscious, down on the hardwood floor. "Find something we can use to tie him up. And then call Bill and Mike. He killed Ernie. You heard him admit it. You're a hero, Mother! You caught the killer!"

Delores moved, but her steps were in slow motion. She grabbed the first thing handy, an electrical cord on the table, and helped Hannah secure Gary's hands behind his back. Then she pulled out her cell phone and called Andrea while Hannah kept watch over Gary to make sure he stayed immobile.

It all happened very fast once Bill and Mike arrived. They listened to Delores and Hannah's account of what had happened, clamped on the handcuffs, and prepared to carry Gary out to the cruiser.

Once Mike and Bill had left, Delores sank down in a chair. "Do you realize that this is the second drastic mistake I've made when it comes to men?"

There was a tone in her mother's voice that made Hannah turn and observe her closely. Vibrant only minutes before, Delores now looked old and defeated. Hannah had never seen her that way and it worried her. "Come on, Mother," she said. "Anyone can make a mistake when it comes to men."

"Yes, but *twice?*" Delores shivered slightly. "I seem to have a knack for choosing killers."

Hannah thought fast. What Delores had said was true, but saying that would only make her feel worse. There must be some way to restore her self-confidence. She just had to think of it.

"That was one heck of a swing," Hannah said at last. "I've never seen anyone wield a champagne bottle like that before."

"That's because I've always wanted to christen a ship." Delores gave a slight smile. "Julie Andrews looked so good when she christened that Holland America cruise ship. And Dame Judi Dench was very impressive when she did the honors for Carnival Legend. Then there's Queen Elizabeth. I'll never forget that picture of her in the paper when she christened the Queen Mary."

"Well, you did it better than any of them. They christened ships, but they didn't knock out a killer."

Delores thought about that for a moment and then she smiled. "You're right, dear. I caught him in exactly the right spot and I knocked him out cold. That was pretty good, wasn't it?"

"It was great."

"There's only one thing that really bothers me about it, Hannah."

"What's that?" Hannah asked, hoping her mother wasn't going to say she'd wanted to marry Gary, or something equally depressing.

"I smashed the bottle. And I love those bottles with the little flowers all over them. I save them and use them for vases. They're just perfect when my lilac trees come into bloom."

Hannah reached out to give her mother a hug. Like most Minnesotans, they weren't overtly demonstrative, but they'd both been through a lot tonight.

"I'll buy you another bottle of champagne just like the one you broke," Hannah promised. And then, after a moment's thought, she revised her promise. "Come to think of it, you did Bill and Mike a big favor. They were about to charge the wrong man with murder. And Steve Gilman owes you a huge vote of thanks. I'm going to talk to all three of them and we'll *each* buy you a bottle for Christmas."

GINGERBREAD COOKIE MURDER RECIPE INDEX

BAKING CONVERSION CHART

These conversions are approximate, but they'll work just fine for Hannah Swensen's recipes.

VOLUME:

U.S.	*Metric*
1/2 teaspoon	2 milliliters
1 teaspoon	5 milliliters
1 Tablespoon	15 milliliters
1/4 cup	50 milliliters
1/3 cup	75 milliliters
1/2 cup	125 milliliters
3/4 cup	175 milliliters
1 cup	1/4 liter

WEIGHT:

U.S.	*Metric*
1 ounce	28 grams
1 pound	454 grams

OVEN TEMPERATURE:

Degrees Fahrenheit	325 degrees F.
Degrees Centigrade	165 degrees C.
British (Regulo) Gas Mark	3
Degrees Fahrenheit	350 degrees F.
Degrees Centigrade	175 degrees C.
British (Regulo) Gas Mark	4
Degrees Fahrenheit	375 degrees F.
Degrees Centigrade	190 degrees C.
British (Regulo) Gas Mark	5

Note: Hannah's rectangular sheet cake pan, 9 inches by 13 inches, is approximately 23 centimeters by 32.5 centimeters.

■ ■ ■ ■

The Dangers of Gingerbread Cookies

Laura Levine

■ ■ ■ ■

ACKNOWLEDGMENTS

Thanks to my technical advisors, Michele Serchuk, Frank Mula, and Gloria Carbone Mitchell. And to Gina DiNardo (for half her name), and Melissa Mason (for her snappy holiday greeting).

CHAPTER ONE

Christmas with my parents is always a mixed bag.

On the one hand, Tampa Vistas is a lovely retirement community, replete with clubhouse, swimming pool, and Metamucil on tap. And I get to spend two whole weeks in Florida, lying around the pool, soaking up the sun, and occasionally nibbling on a Christmas cookie or three. On the other hand, I am normally clad at said pool in a Fashion Don't capri pants set (compliments of my mother, a confirmed home shopping addict), listening to the palm fronds rustling and my parents driving each other nuts.

So it was with decidedly conflicted emotions that I stepped out into the baggage claim area of Tampa International Airport.

"Jaine, sweetheart!"

I looked over and saw my mom waving at me, clad in one of her ubiquitous capri sets, this one adorned with a sequined palm tree on her ample chest. Mom tips the height chart at five feet one and one-quarter inches (she insists on counting that quarter of an inch), so her capri pants were practically slacks.

"It's so good to see you, honey!"

She wrapped me in a warm embrace, smelling, as she always did, of Jean Naté. And the minute I felt her powdery cheek against mine, all the minuses of my annual Christmas trip to Florida faded away.

It was good to be back.

"Oh, my!" Mom said. "You're looking cuter than ever!"

This was not addressed to me, but to my cat, Prozac, who had accompanied me on the flight from Los Angeles, a hair-raising tale in itself, sure to turn up in a future edition of *When Bad Things Happen to Good People.*

"Where's Daddy?" I asked, looking around.

"Oh, that man is driving me crazy."

Nothing new there. Sometimes I think my parents vowed to love, honor, and aggravate each other till death do them part.

Mom vented her latest frustrations on the drive home.

"You won't believe this, sweetheart," she said, narrowly sideswiping a BMW with her

Camry, "but your father ordered a Christmas tree from an infomercial!"

Of course I'd believe it. While Mom is hooked on the shopping channel, my father is an infomercial junkie. He'd buy bottled air if he saw it advertised on TV.

"He said he was tired of ordinary Christmas trees. He wanted something new and exciting. So he ordered a god-awful gold monstrosity of a tree. It was supposed to come weeks ago but first showed up this afternoon. He's home putting it together as we speak. Did you ever hear of anything so silly? A gold Christmas tree! That's like having a rubber chicken on Thanksgiving!"

Her rant was interrupted just then by a piteous moan from the cat carrier, which I'd set down in front of me.

"Darling Zoloft looks uncomfortable, sweetheart. Why don't you let her out?"

"Her name is Prozac, Mom, and she's got plenty of room in there."

I was not feeling particularly loving toward my kitty at that moment. In spite of a tranquilizer strong enough to fell King Kong, she'd spent a good portion of the trip across country howling at the top of her lungs, silenced only by the kitty treats I fed her every other minute.

By the time we landed in Tampa, even the

screaming toddler in front of us was shooting me dirty looks.

"And besides, if I let her out, she'll head straight for the accelerator. Trust me, you don't want her loose in your car."

"Don't be silly, Jaine. I can tell just by looking at her that Zoloft is a perfect little lady."

And then, in the middle of the highway, Mom reached over and flipped open the carrier door. I braced myself for imminent death, certain Prozac would be doing the merengue around the pedals, causing Mom to lose control of the car and go crashing into the nearest gasoline tanker.

But much to my surprise, Prozac stepped out daintily from her carrier and jumped into my lap, where she curled up into an obedient little ball.

"What did I tell you?" Mom said. "A perfect little lady."

Prozac looked up at me with what I swear was a smirk on her face.

Sure have her fooled, don't I?

"How's my little Lambchop?"

Daddy untangled his long legs from a sea of gold tinsel branches and smothered me in a big bear hug.

Unlike Mom, Daddy is tall and skinny (if

you don't count his tummy paunch), Jeff to her Mutt. Back when he was in school, he was known as Curly for his thick brown ringlets — curls that I inherited and that for Daddy are now a distant memory.

"Hank Austen!" Mom said, hands on her hips. "I can't believe I've been gone all this time and you still haven't put together the tree."

"The instructions seem to be in Chinese," he said, squinting through his bifocals at a flimsy instruction manual. "Either that or ancient Egyptian hieroglyphics. Anyhow, it's a minor setback. I'll tackle it again tomorrow and have this magnificent tree assembled in no time.

"Look, Lambchop!" He pointed to the gold mess at his feet. "It's got lights and ornaments already built in. So we don't have to bother decorating the tree."

"But I like decorating the tree," Mom muttered.

By now she'd whipped out the Dustbuster and was doing battle with the stray pieces of gold tinsel molting on the living room carpet.

"And check this out," Daddy said, his enthusiasm un-dampened. "It's got a revolving stand, so the Christmas tree will spin around."

"Great," Mom moaned. "We get to see how hideous it is from every angle."

I have to admit, it was pretty repulsive. Even Prozac, who normally attacks Christmas trees with all the fury of a cranky Hun, took one sniff and walked away in disgust.

"Thank heavens we're having Christmas dinner at Aunt Clara and Uncle Ed's," Mom sighed. "At least the relatives won't have to look at it."

"Let's not argue over the tree, Claudia," Daddy said. "Not when our little Lambchop is home."

And indeed a temporary truce was struck while we settled down in the kitchen for a midnight snack. True, it was only nine p.m., but that's practically midnight, Tampa Vistas Time.

"You hungry, sweetheart?" Mom asked.

Indeed I was, after the packet of stale peanuts a sullen flight attendant had hurled at me on the plane.

In no time, Mom whipped up some turkey and avocado sandwiches, tossing a big hunk of turkey to Prozac, who had been tailing her adoringly from the moment she approached the refrigerator.

"Mom, please don't feed her human food. She'll never go back to cat food if you do."

"Oh, just this once, honey. How can I say

no to such a darling kitty?"

Prozac shot me a triumphant look.

I had her at "meow."

We spent the next hour or so catching up on family gossip, after which my parents turned in for the night.

As I watched them head down the hallway to their bedroom, Daddy's arm around Mom's waist, I marveled as I always did at how much they cared for each other in spite of their ongoing skirmishes.

I was in the guest bedroom, unpacking, when Mom toddled in wearing her Lanz nightie.

"I almost forgot to tell you the exciting news about the holiday play."

Every year the gang at Tampa Vistas puts on a holiday-themed play, a mind-numbing affair that gives new meaning to the words *general anesthesia.*

Mercifully, I'd been able to doze through most of last year's production of *A Christmas Carol,* featuring the world's only Tiny Tim with liver spots.

"This year it's an original play called *The Gingerbread Cookie That Saved Christmas.* And you'll never guess who wrote it! Edna Lindstrom!"

I blinked in surprise. Mom's good friend and next-door neighbor, Edna Lindstrom, was a dithery woman who spent most of her time knitting afghans and tea cozies — positively the last person on the planet I'd think capable of writing a play.

"Seeing as you're a Hollywood writer and all, Edna wants you to take a look at it."

Somehow my parents labor under the delusion that, because I live in L.A., I am a big-time Hollywood writer. No matter how often I tell them that I write freelance ads for a living, they insist on believing that I am a big cheese in la-la land.

"But, Mom, I don't write plays. I write toilet bowl ads."

(It's true, I'm afraid. My biggest client is Toiletmasters Plumbers, serving the greater Los Angeles area since 1989.)

"Toilet bowl ads. Plays. It's all the same. You're still a professional writer. That's why Edna wants your opinion. Maybe you can throw in a line here and there. I told her you'd be happy to. You don't mind, do you, honey?"

Oh, dear. This didn't bode well. I'd read my share of amateur plays, and I figured I was in for some rocky reading.

What I didn't count on, of course, was the corpse that came with the final curtain.

CHAPTER TWO

I woke up the next morning to my favorite alarm clock — the tantalizing smell of sausage frying. Wasting no time, I sprang out of bed and trotted off to the kitchen.

There I found Daddy in his robe and slippers, reading the newspaper. Mom sat across from him in their red vinyl banquette, her hair still in curlers. Completing this cozy family tableau was Prozac, nestled on Mom's lap, scarfing down a plate of sausage slices.

Prying her pink nose away from the plate, she gazed up at me in ecstasy.

We gotta come here more often!

"Don't eat so fast, Zoloft, darling," Mom cooed, "or you'll get a tummy ache."

"I thought you weren't going to feed her any more human food."

Mom shot me a sheepish smile.

"Oh, honey. How can one little sausage hurt?"

Trust me. By the end of the week, she'd be feeding her caviar from Limoges china.

With an irritated sigh, I helped myself to a plate of sausage and eggs. Which, I must admit, was quite yummy. I would've gone back for seconds on the sausage, but thanks to Prozac, there weren't any.

So instead I helped myself to a piece of Christmas fudge from the refrigerator.

Every holiday season Mom buys a box of chocolate pecan fudge, working on the theory that if we each have one piece of fudge for dessert at night, we will be less likely to pig out on Christmas cookies.

That's the theory, anyway.

In fact, my parents have been known to go through three boxes of fudge before the Thanksgiving dishes have been put away.

"Fudge for breakfast?" Mom tsked in disapproval. "Jaine, how could you?"

"Easy," I said, handing her a piece.

After lingering over coffee and fudge, Mom and I did the dishes and got dressed for my parents' favorite holiday activity:

Showing me off to their neighbors.

"Jaine is a famous Hollywood writer!"

We were making the rounds at the clubhouse pool, and Daddy, playing fast and loose with the truth, was singing my praises to a pleasant sixtysomething couple.

"Yes," Mom chimed in. "She wrote 'In a Rush to Flush? Call Toiletmasters!' "

The couple, who'd been in the middle of a game of Scrabble, looked up from their tiles with forced smiles.

"How nice," the woman said. "Our son is a Rhodes scholar PhD."

"Working with refugee victims in Rwanda," her husband threw in.

"That's nice, too, I guess," Daddy said, whisking me away.

"Those people are such braggarts," he grumbled. "Never stop yapping about that son of theirs. So the kid is a Rhodes Scholar humanitarian. Big deal."

It was still fairly early in the morning, so pickings were slim in the Showing Off Jaine Department. Just a handful of people at the pool area, all of whom had already been subjected to the highlights of my résumé.

Over by the edge of the pool a stunning young redhead in a tank top and leggings was leading a water aerobics class. About a half a dozen Tampa Vistas ladies were in the water, kicking away with gusto. I admired them for their discipline, their dedication, and — most of all — their willingness to appear in public in a bathing suit. I personally think that if God had meant us to wear bathing suits, She would have never invented cellulite.

I watched as the gals went through their paces, surprised my parents didn't interrupt them to reel off my credits.

But thank heavens they refrained. They were about to give up and call a halt to my PR tour when Mom's eyes lit up.

"Oh, look! It's Edna. With Preston McCay!"

Sure enough, I saw my mom's buddy Edna Lindstrom strolling out onto the pool deck, arm in arm with a dashing, silver-haired dude dressed head to toe in tennis whites.

"Isn't he handsome?" Mom asked, following my gaze. "Retired plastic surgeon, just moved here a few weeks ago from Cleveland. All the ladies are crazy about him!"

"Aw, he's not so hot," Daddy pouted.

"You're just jealous, Hank, because he beat you out for the lead in Edna's play."

"That ridiculous play?" Daddy snorted in disdain.

"Shh!" Mom nudged him. "They're coming over."

Indeed, Edna was approaching with Dr. Suave at her side.

"Jaine, dear," she said, pecking me on the cheek. "How nice to see you! And how cute you look."

I've put off telling you this for as long as possible, but I'm afraid I was clad — compliments of Mom — in a hot pink capri set, the focal point of which was a sequin-studded flamingo pulsating on my chest.

"And this is my friend Dr. McCay," Edna said, showing him off like a prize heifer at a country fair.

"Please, call me Preston." He beamed me a mouthful of perfectly capped teeth.

Mom was right. He certainly was a handsome guy, the kind of silver-haired cutie you see eating corn on the cob in Poligrip commercials. And with his chiseled nose and remarkably wrinkle-free face, I'd bet my bottom Pop-Tart he'd been under the knife once or twice himself.

"Preston's talked me into a game of shuffleboard," Edna said, glowing with pleasure. "We really shouldn't, not with the play opening tomorrow night."

"A break will do us good!" Now Preston beamed his smile at her.

Somehow Edna managed to tear herself away from its high wattage and turned back to me.

"I'm counting on you to drop by our dress rehearsal, Jaine, to give us your professional opinion."

"Jaine's a famous Hollywood writer," Daddy informed Dr. Suave, right on cue. "She wrote 'In a Rush to Flush? Call Toiletmasters!' "

"And 'Just a Shade Better' for Ackerman's Awnings," Mom added for good measure.

Any day now they'd be taking their act on the road.

"Very impressive," Preston said, an amused glint in his eye.

"Well, toodle-oo." Edna hooked her arm in Preston's, and together they headed over to the shuffleboard court.

"Aren't they a darling couple?" Mom asked as they walked away.

Frankly, I thought they were a tad mismatched. Edna Lindstrom was a short, pigeon-like woman whose spindly legs seemed to buckle under the weight of her massive chest. Not exactly arm candy. Never in a million years would I picture her with Dr. Suave.

"Don't tell a soul," Mom said, lowering her voice to a whisper, "but Preston has asked Edna to marry him! Isn't that the most exciting news ever?"

"Big whoop." Daddy stifled a yawn.

"Hank Austen, you're awful. Edna's been very lonely ever since Ralph died, and I, for one, think it's wonderful she's found love.

And what a charming man. I just adore the way he dresses in tennis whites."

"I could dress in white, too," Daddy huffed, "if I wanted to look like a Good Humor man."

"C'mon," I said, determined to break up this "discussion" before it escalated any further. "Let's go stretch out and catch some sun."

"You gals go ahead," Daddy said. "I see Doc Wilkins. He owes me a rematch at Ping-Pong."

"Must you?" Mom sighed. "You two always wind up fighting."

"Don't be silly, Claudia. Doc and I may disagree, but we never fight."

Mom rolled her eyes as he trotted off to the Ping-Pong tables.

Minutes later Mom and I and my sequined flamingo were stretched out on lounge chairs. The water aerobics class had broken up and it was quiet around the pool. All I heard was the rhythmic splash of a swimmer doing his laps and Mom turning the pages of an abandoned *People* magazine. I was just on the brink of a delightful midmorning nap when I was jolted from my reverie by a bloodcurdling yowl.

"My eye! My eye!"

With a stab of fear, I realized it was coming from the Ping-Pong tables. Oh, dear. What if Daddy was hurt?

Daddy, however, was not the injured party, as Mom and I discovered when we went racing to his side. Standing there, holding his eye in pain, was a skinny, hawk-nosed guy who looked to be somewhere in his seventies. I couldn't help but notice a very bad toupee on his two-toned head.

"You aimed that ball at my eye on purpose!" he shouted at Daddy.

"I did not!"

"Did so! You were steamed because I was winning."

"That's the most ridiculous thing I ever heard," Daddy sputtered. "I just happen to have a strong serve."

"Now, Doc." Mom stepped between them. "Hank would never purposely hurt you."

I had to agree with her there. Daddy doesn't have a mean bone in his body.

"If *you* say so, Claudia," the guy grudgingly conceded, shooting Daddy a dirty look with his good eye.

"Here, let me have a look at that." Preston McCay came trotting up to our happy little party. "I'm a doctor. A plastic surgeon. Well, I used to be. Just retired last year. Had one of the most successful practices in the metropolitan Cleveland area, if I do say so myself."

Something told me he *did* say so. Constantly.

"Clyde is a doctor, too," Mom said, playing hostess. "Preston McCay, meet Dr. Clyde Wilkins. Although everybody calls him Doc."

"Clyde Wilkins, the cardiologist?" Preston asked.

"Right," Doc said absently, touching his wound and wincing.

Preston's eyes lit up.

"The keynote speaker at the AMA convention back in '92!" Preston shot his finger at him like a gun. "I never forget a face."

Doc forced a pained smile.

"Perhaps you heard my talk on the ten-minute tummy tuck?"

"Afraid I missed that one," Doc replied, with more than a hint of irritation in his voice.

With his rapidly swelling shiner, he was clearly in no mood to stroll down memory lane.

"Well, let's have a look at that eye," Preston said, getting the hint. He leaned in to get a better look at the area around Doc's eye, which seemed pretty red and raw to me. "No doubt about it," Preston said. "Periorbital hematoma."

"Oh, heavens, no!" Mom gasped. "Will he have to be hospitalized?"

"Not quite. A periorbital hematoma is doctor talk for a black eye."

"A black eye? That's still terrible!" She nudged Daddy in the ribs and hissed, "Apologize, Hank!"

"I don't see why I have to apologize. Anyone can see it was an accident. And besides, he should've stepped out of the way when he saw the ball coming."

"Hank Austen, you're impossible!"

She wasn't getting any arguments from anybody on that one.

"I can't believe you wouldn't apologize to Doc!" Mom sputtered as we walked back home. "You gave that poor man a black eye!"

"Who says I gave him a black eye?" Daddy countered. "It wasn't black, was it?"

"Well, it will be. That's what Preston said."

"Of course he'd say that. He's just sticking up for another doctor. These doctors always stick together."

"See what I have to put up with, honey?" Mom sighed, turning to me.

I mumbled something incoherent, opting to stay out of the war zone.

Insisting he had nothing to apologize for,

Daddy spent the rest of the walk home detailing the many ways in which Doc Wilkins cheated at Ping-Pong.

"I need something to calm my nerves," Mom said when we finally walked in the front door.

I was right behind her when she cracked open the fudge.

Chapter Three

Every once in a while you see a play that's so moving, so exhilarating, and so beautifully written, you understand why Broadway tickets go for two hundred bucks a pop.

Alas, *The Gingerbread Cookie That Saved Christmas* was not one of them.

A shameless rip-off of both *A Christmas Carol* and *Peter Pan,* the tortured plot involved a gingerbread man who comes to life and helps a lonely older woman discover her many blessings.

I showed up at the clubhouse theater that night after dinner, blissfully unaware of the snorefest ahead of me.

"There you are, Jaine!" Edna said as I came down the aisle. "Let me introduce you to everyone. Of course, you already know Preston."

There onstage was her fiancé, Dr. Preston McCay, in what was supposed to be a gingerbread man costume, but what looked more like a molting bear with a human head. As Edna would later explain to me, Preston's dialogue could not be heard through the costume's head, so they opted instead for facial make-up.

He now waved to me with his gingerbread paw.

"And this is our leading lady, Laurette Kendall."

I exchanged hellos with a cool blonde seated onstage in a rocking chair. She looked to me like the kind of gal who'd spent most of her life sipping daiquiris at the country club.

"And this is our director, Gloria Di Nardo."

An imposing steamboat of a woman clad in a flowery caftan and matching turban got up from where she was sitting in the first row and swept over to me. As she headed up the aisle, I could see there was a lot of Gloria under that caftan.

"Delighted, my dear." She took my hand in hers, her fingers sparkling with cubic zirconias. "Edna tells me you toil in the fields of Hollywood. I myself come from a long and illustrious theatrical background. I played all the big parts. Lady Macbeth. Ophelia. Edna Turnblad. Indeed, I was the toast of the Secaucus, New Jersey, dinner theater circuit!"

I tried my best to look impressed.

"So tell me, dear, what have you written?"

"In a Rush to Flush? Call Toiletmasters!" Edna piped up.

Gloria's smile froze.

"You mean you write *TV commercials?*"

"It wasn't exactly a TV commercial," I said. "But it did appear on bus stops all over Los Angeles."

"How lovely for you, dear," she said with a dismissive wave of her zirconias, then sashayed back to her seat.

If you ask me, she had a lot of nerve being so uppity, what with that Secaucus Dinner Theater credit.

"Okay, everybody," she called out. "Let's take it from the top."

Edna and I settled down next to each other a few rows behind Gloria as Preston scooted offstage and what passed for action began.

The play opened with Laurette's character on the phone with her ungrateful daughter, who was abandoning her at Christmas. Next to me, Edna, the proud playwright, was mouthing the lines as Laurette spoke them.

Her phone call concluded, Laurette hung up and reached out to a plate on an end table. But whatever she was looking for wasn't there.

"Gloria," she called out into the audience, "the cookies are missing."

At which point Preston came stomping out from the wings.

"For crying out loud," he snapped. "Can't Raymond get anything right? Where the hell is he, anyway?"

"Calm down, hon," Gloria said, taking out her cell phone. "I'll get him."

Raymond, Edna informed me, was the play's prop master / stage manager / lighting director. As well as the chief handyman at Tampa Vistas.

"Such a sweet fellow," Edna said. "And such a hard worker."

Gloria soon had him on the line.

"Raymond, dearest," she trilled, "we're missing our gingerbread man cookies."

Minutes later a short, wiry man in jeans and a work shirt came running down the aisle with a bunch of plaster of Paris prop cookies.

"Sorry," he said as he bounded up the steps to the stage. "A couple of them were chipped, so I brought them to the shop last night to paint them." Although he spoke with a Spanish accent, he seemed to have an excellent command of the English language. "And then, this morning, there was an emergency with the lawn sprinklers, so I didn't have time to bring them back."

Apparently this explanation did not satisfy Preston.

"We can't stand around waiting because you screwed up. Do your job, man. Put those cookies on that plate."

Raymond flushed, clearly upset at being reamed out in front of the others.

"Now!" Preston added with a snap of his fingers.

Raymond dropped the cookies on the plate and walked over to Preston, his fists balled in angry knots.

"Don't snap your fingers at me, senor."

Preston, unaccustomed to back talk, blinked in surprise. "Who the hell do you think you're talking to?"

"An arrogant son of a bitch [pronounced *beetch*]. Just because you're a doctor, you think the world has to bow to you. Well, you're not the only professional around here, senor. Back in Cuba," he said, his chest puffed with pride, "I was an electrical engineer."

"You're not in Cuba anymore, buddy," Preston sneered, "so I'll snap my fingers whenever I want."

To prove his point, he snapped them again.

"Here's what you can do with your fingers, senor."

And with that, Raymond displayed a most insulting middle finger of his own. "I don't have to put up with disrespect from a *bastardo* like you."

"No, you certainly won't," Preston said, eyes narrowed most unpleasantly. "Because the minute this play is over, I intend to have you fired."

Raymond muttered a few words in Spanish, which I'm guessing did not mean "lovely chatting with you" and stalked out of the auditorium.

The rest of us just sat there in awkward silence.

"You have to take a firm hand with these people," Preston said before striding back into the wings.

Yikes. I sure would've hated to be a nurse in *his* office.

If only the rest of the play had been half as dramatic as the little scene between Preston and Raymond. But, no. It was, as already noted, a snorefest of monumental proportions.

To make matters worse, it took ages for it to come limping to a close. Mainly because Gloria was constantly interrupting to give

Laurette directions.

— More pathos, darling. I want to feel pathos oozing from every pore!

— Projection! They need to hear you in the back row.

— Joy! I'm not seeing joy in your eyes!

"How am I doing?" Preston would ask with each interruption.

"Wonderful, sweetheart," Gloria repeatedly assured him, with flirtatious pats on the arm.

It looked like Edna wasn't the only one smitten with Dr. Suave.

Eventually the cavalcade of clichés came to a halt. Having gotten Laurette's character to stop and smell the roses, see the sunny side of life, and look for silver linings, the gingerbread man — copping a gag from his good buddy Peter Pan — flew off into the night.

Literally.

Somehow Raymond had rigged a wire and pulley system and grudgingly returned to operate it, so that Preston's molting bear with a human head was able to soar up, up, and away offstage.

When it was all over, Edna turned to me eagerly.

"So what do you think?"

Time to put on my tap shoes.

"I've never seen anything like it."

And for that, I was profoundly grateful.

"Guess what, everybody!" Edna called out to the others. "Jaine loves it!"

"Oh, good," Gloria said, with just a touch more sarcasm than was called for. "Now we can open as planned."

But Edna, on cloud nine, was oblivious to Gloria's barb.

"I know!" she said. "Let's all go to The Cheesecake Factory to celebrate!"

"What a wonderful idea!" seconded Gloria, who had clearly packed away a cheesecake or two in her day.

"Yes, that sounds like fun," Laurette agreed.

"You'll be coming, too, Preston, won't you?" Edna asked her fiancé.

"I don't think so, gals."

Edna's face fell.

"I wish I could," he said, "but I'm beat. I want to go straight home and get into bed."

A disappointed sigh from Gloria, who looked like she wanted to hop right in there with him.

Now that they knew Preston wasn't going to join them, Gloria and Edna didn't seem all that enthused about going out for a snack. But having made such a fuss, they were stuck.

And I, never one to turn down a piece of cheesecake, agreed to join them.

As it turned out, we never did get our cheesecake.

When we got to The Cheesecake Factory, there was a line out the door, and none of us felt like waiting.

So we drove over to a nearby Chinese restaurant, one of those funky retro joints with paper lanterns, private booths, and MSG on tap.

Since the four of us were obviously not hot-date material, the hostess led us past the romantic private booths, cordoned off from view by silk curtains, and seated us at a table in the middle of the room.

At first I'd been disappointed with our change of culinary plans. But the minute I walked in the restaurant and saw a guy biting into a crisp, greasy egg roll, my taste buds sprang into action.

We ordered egg rolls and spareribs and steamed dumplings to share. And when the food showed up, we dug in with gusto, abandoning chopsticks to eat the stuff with our fingers. Well, Edna, Gloria, and I ate with our fingers.

Laurette sat ramrod straight, eyeing her egg roll as if it were a creature from an alien planet, finally cutting it into bite-sized pieces with her knife and fork.

Edna, on an MSG high, seemed to have gotten over the disappointment of Preston's no-show. She and Gloria chattered enthusiastically about the opening of *The Gingerbread Cookie That Saved Christmas,* even talking about the possibility of taking it on the Florida dinner theater circuit.

"Wouldn't that be something!" Edna said, eyes glowing.

"It's a natural for dinner theater," Gloria said with a wave of her sparerib. "The kind of uplifting play that leaves people with a very special feeling."

Namely, heartburn.

Even Laurette joined in their fantasy, wondering if they could possibly do a performance or two in her hometown of St. Louis.

While the others were lost in their delusions of dinner theater grandeur, I remained grounded in reality and focused on my chow.

"Please pass the plum sauce," I asked Edna as I reached for a sparerib.

"Good heavens, no!" she gasped, suddenly going pale.

"Okay, then. How about the soy sauce?"

But then I realized she wasn't talking to

me. No, she was staring straight ahead at one of the private booths where a waiter had opened the curtain to serve dinner. I followed her gaze, and I, too, gasped in surprise.

There, in the booth, was her fiancé, Preston McCay, the same Preston who'd said he was going straight home to bed.

It looked like he was headed for bed, all right. But not alone.

Sitting across from him, gazing at him google-eyed, was the gorgeous redhead I'd seen earlier that day, teaching water aerobics at the Tampa Vistas pool.

Now she and Preston sat holding hands over the steamed rice.

"This can't be happening," Edna said, red-faced with anger. "He's engaged to me!"

"To you?" Gloria sputtered. "He's engaged to me!"

"And me!" Laurette said, shoving the rest of her egg roll straight in her mouth.

Laurette, too?

Holy Moses. You could've knocked me over with a pupu platter.

Then, before I knew it, Edna grabbed the sparerib out of my hand and hurled it across the room at Preston, hitting him on his forehead, somewhere around his brow lift.

As much as I hated to lose that sparerib,

the guy had it coming.

"Calm down, ladies," Preston was saying.

Edna, Gloria, and Laurette had gathered around his booth in an angry circle. I stood behind them, unwilling to miss a beat of the action.

"I never actually asked any of you to marry me."

"That's not true!" Edna cried. "You said that someday you wanted to get married."

"That's what you told me!" Gloria said.

"And me!" From Laurette.

"I'm sorry if you made an incorrect assumption, ladies. I do want to get married. Just not to any of you. The object of my affections is my darling Ginny."

The young redhead grinned in triumph.

She was a looker, all right, with startling green eyes and — unlike her rivals in romance — not a wrinkle in sight.

"Show them your ring, babe," Preston urged.

Ginny flashed a rock the size of a sugar cube.

Preston was old enough to be her very old father, but Ginny didn't seem to mind. Nor did she care that he'd been romancing three other women on the side. You didn't have to be a rocket scientist to figure out that all she wanted was to get her hooks on a retired plastic surgeon.

"But what about all the casseroles I cooked you?" Edna wailed.

"And all the Lean Cuisines I defrosted?" Laurette wanted to know.

"And all the goddamn Glenlivet you guzzled up?" Gloria growled.

"All quite delicious," Preston assured them. "Except those Lean Cuisines, Laurette. You could've done better."

Laurette looked like she wanted to bean him with another sparerib.

"But I do appreciate all the good times we shared," Preston said, ever the diplomat. "Now if you'll excuse Ginny and me, our food is getting cold."

And with that, he snapped the curtain closed.

CHAPTER FOUR

Prozac woke me at the crack of dawn the next morning, clawing my chest for her breakfast.

With a bleary eye, I checked the time on the clock radio my parents have owned since Marconi was in diapers.

Oh, groan. Only 6:02. And this was supposed to be my vacation.

"Just five more minutes, Pro," I begged.

But she showed me no mercy.

Hauling myself out of bed, I staggered to the kitchen and opened a can of Luscious Lamb Guts, a delicacy that usually sends Prozac into a feeding frenzy. But not today.

She took one sniff and looked up at me, outraged.

Wait a minute. This isn't Farmer John's Premium Grade A Sausage.

"No, it isn't. It's cat food. You'll eat it and like it, young lady."

Oh, yeah?

She shot me a defiant glare and began yowling at the top of her lungs.

Seconds later Mom came running into the kitchen, her nightie billowing out behind her.

By now Prozac was in full throttle Sarah Bernhardt mode, chewing the scenery for all it was worth.

"What on earth have you done to this poor cat?" Mom said, scooping the little monster up in her arms.

"Me! You're the one who's spoiled her rotten. Now she won't eat her cat food."

"There, there, Zoloft," Mom cooed. "How about if Grandma makes you some nice Canadian bacon?"

Prozac looked up at her with huge orphan eyes.

Extra lean, please.

Throwing up my arms in defeat, I left the lovebirds in the kitchen and stomped back to bed. I tried to sleep, but it was no use. From the kitchen, I could hear Mom crooning a lullaby to Prozac, the same lullaby she used to sing to me when I was a kid. Of all the nerve! Singing her *our* lullaby!

Oh, well. I might as well make good use of the extra morning hours Prozac had foisted upon me and go for a nice calorie-burning walk. Frankly, I could use the exercise after all that Chinese food I'd scarfed down last night.

So I threw on some sweats and, feeling quite noble, set out on my calorie-burning expedition.

As I walked past the cookie-cutter houses of Tampa Vistas, all painted in various shades of beige, I thought back to the scene at the Chinese restaurant last night.

I simply could not get over the monumental gall of Preston. Imagine! Dating four women at once! The man made Don Juan look like a Trappist monk.

I could still see the faces of his poor jiltees — Edna, Gloria, and Laurette — as they registered first shock, then disbelief, then downright fury.

Lord, those gals had been angry. Lucky for Preston, we'd been out in public. Otherwise I think they might have strung him up by his boxers.

By now I'd reached the clubhouse, where I saw Raymond, the handyman, letting himself into the building. Edna was right about him. He certainly was a hard worker. Here it was, only six thirty, and already he was on the job.

"Hey, Raymond!" I called out.

He looked up, startled at first, but then seeing it was me, smiled brightly.

"Buenos días, señorita."

It was really disgraceful the way Preston had reamed into him last night. All because of a few prop cookies. Preston McCay was clearly a jerk of the highest order, and if you ask me, his jilted girlfriends were well rid of him.

Wishing Raymond a very buenos días of his own, I waved good-bye and continued on past the clubhouse.

You'll be happy to know I put in a full mile before coming back home.

Okay, so it wasn't exactly a mile. It was six and a half blocks. But it was six and a half blocks more than I usually walk before breakfast. I could practically feel the pounds melting away. And this, I decided, would be the beginning of a whole new eating regimen. Just because it was Christmas didn't mean I had to mainline calories.

Indeed, I made up my mind to have a sensible low-fat breakfast of toast and coffee. Not a smidgeon more.

Yeah, right. Five minutes later I was at my parents' breakfast nook, shoveling Canadian bacon and eggs in my mouth at the speed of light.

Mom was sitting across from me, with Prozac in her lap, alternately stroking and scratching her. The little princess was in cat heaven, purring like a buzz saw.

"She loves it when you scratch behind her ears," Mom informed me, as if I hadn't been scratching her royal highness behind the ears for the past umpteen years.

"She'll keep you doing this for hours if you let her," I said. "Possibly days."

Prozac glared at me through slitted eyes.

Hey, mind your own beeswax, willya?

"That's okay," Mom said. "I don't mind. Anything for my precious angel."

Good heavens, where's a barf bag when you needed one?

Lucky for me, I've got a cast-iron stomach. I was just reaching for some jam for my toast when Daddy's voice rang out from the living room.

"Come quick, everybody, and see the Christmas tree!"

Daddy had been working on it all last night and now he'd finally managed to assemble it.

Mom reluctantly put Prozac down and hurried into the living room. Grabbing a piece of toast for the road, I scooted after her.

"Doesn't it look great?" Daddy stood there in his robe and pajamas, holding a screwdriver and beaming with pride.

"But, Hank." Mom blinked, puzzled.

"Where's the top of the tree?"

Indeed, the top quarter of the hideous orange tree seemed to be missing.

"I guess they forgot to include it," Daddy conceded.

"For heaven's sake, Hank. It looks ridiculous."

"Yeah," I said. "Like a Christmas tree with a Mohawk."

"Don't be silly, girls. Anybody can have a tree with a pointy top. Ours makes a statement."

"Yes," Mom snapped, "it's saying, 'Return me this instant and demand your money back!' "

Daddy chose to ignore this dollop of sarcasm.

"Just wait'll you see it rotate. It's amazing! All I have to do is click the remote."

"Ta-da!" he said, clicking the remote with a flourish.

It was amazing, all right.

We watched, openmouthed, as the tree jerked to a start, rotated a grand total of two inches, and then promptly toppled over.

"Oh, for heaven's sake!"

Mom groaned in dismay at the orange mess on her carpet.

Then she turned on her heel and stalked off to the kitchen.

When I heard the refrigerator door open, I knew exactly what she was looking for.

"Oh, no!" she wailed. "Who ate the last piece of fudge?"

Whatever you do, don't tell her it was me.

Chapter Five

"I don't see why I have to go to this stupid play."

We'd just finished dinner (meat loaf and mashed potatoes — seconds on the potatoes — totally ashamed of myself), and now Daddy was putting up a stink about going to the world premiere of *The Gingerbread Cookie That Saved Christmas.*

"We're going to the play," Mom said, with exaggerated patience, "because Edna Lindstrom is our good friend and we have to stand by her in her hour of need."

Mom had been on the phone with Edna all afternoon, rehashing the disastrous scene at the Chinese restaurant.

"Frankly, it serves Edna right," Daddy said.

"What on earth do you mean?"

"If she'd given me the lead in her play, she never would've fallen in love with that bum Preston McCay in the first place."

"If that isn't the silliest thing I ever heard," Mom said, getting up to clear the dishes. "Just get dressed, Hank. Wear your good sports jacket, and please try not to fall asleep during the show."

Reluctantly, Daddy stomped off to get dressed.

A half hour later we found him waiting for us, pouting, at the front door.

"What on earth is that *thing* around your neck?" Mom asked, staring at a bright red Christmas tree tie, dotted with tiny blinking lightbulbs.

"It's my Christmas tree tie. It came free with the revolving Christmas tree."

"You don't really intend to wear that thing in public, do you?"

Daddy dug in his heels.

"Yes, I do!"

"Okay, okay," Mom sighed, glancing at the gold monster in our living room. "At least *this* tree works."

Next, we trotted off to pick up Edna, who slid in beside me in the backseat of the Camry, sniffling into a hankie sodden with tears.

"This was supposed to be the happiest night of my life," she said as we rode over to the clubhouse. "And now it's ruined. I feel like turning around and going right back home."

"It works for me!" Daddy said.

"We'll do no such thing," Mom piped up.

Somehow Mom managed to get Edna and Daddy into the theater and settled down in their seats.

Neither one of them was happy about it.

"I should've never come," Edna sighed, her ample bosom heaving.

"But, Edna," Mom said, "you can't miss the opening of your own play."

"Yes, I can," she cried. "Preston's ruined it for me. That horrible man." Another sniffle into her hankie. "I wish he were dead."

"Edna, please. People can hear you."

It was true. People around us were turning to look at her.

"I don't care. I still wish he were dead. I wish *I* were dead. I can't remember when I've been this miserable."

"I realize it's painful now, honey," Mom said, patting her hand, "but in a few weeks you'll forget all about it. Isn't that right, Hank?"

But Daddy, who is famous for napping in the theater, was already beginning to doze off.

"Isn't that right, Hank?" Mom repeated, with an elbow jab to Daddy's ribs.

"Isn't what right?" Daddy asked, jolted into consciousness.

"That in a few weeks Edna won't remember any of this."

"In a few weeks? Hey, at our age, she'll be lucky if she remembers it by next Tuesday."

"That's not helping!" Mom snapped.

"Hank's right," Edna said, tears welling in her eyes. "I'm an old woman. Way too old for romance."

The very thought sent her sobbing into her hankie.

"Now look what you've done!" Mom hissed.

"*You're* the one who insisted I come here!" Daddy hissed right back.

"Face it," Edna was saying. "My love life is over. I may as well just accept the fact that I'm going to be one of those pathetic women who sit home alone talking to their cats. No offense, Jaine, darling."

I smiled weakly, determined to spend next Christmas back in L.A., cleaning my closets and nuking a Hungry-Man dinner. It had to be more fun than this.

"This whole evening is a disaster," Edna moaned. "Gloria invited theater critics from all the local newspapers and TV stations. And not one of them replied! Except for that kid from the *Tampa High Bugle.*"

Indeed Gloria was sitting in the row in front of us with a skinny adolescent in a Tampa High sweatshirt. The earnest lad was busy scribbling notes as Gloria yammered on about the time she wowed Secaucus with her Blanche DuBois.

"Tennessee Williams's hairdresser came to the show and said he'd never seen a better Blanche!"

The kid actually looked impressed.

"Omigosh," Mom gasped. "Look who's here!"

We turned and saw Doc Wilkins coming down the aisle. By now his eye had turned a bilious shade of purple. Several people stopped him to offer their condolences.

"Oh, Hank," Mom said, her own eyes wide with pity. "Look what you've done to the poor man."

"So he's got a black eye. Big deal. My bunion is killing me, and you don't hear me complaining."

"How can you be so insensitive?"

"I wouldn't be surprised if he's faking the whole thing," Daddy huffed, "just to get the sympathy vote. I'll bet that black eye is nothing but make-up."

"Hank Austen, you're impossible. The man is seriously injured and it's all your fault."

"Why is everything always *my* fault?"

"Because nine times out of ten, it is."

Mom waved feebly at Doc Wilkins, and he was gracious enough to wave back.

"Somehow we've got to make it up to him. In the meanwhile," she whispered as the overhead lights began to dim, "turn off your tie. We can't have the silly thing blinking throughout the performance."

"I am not turning off my tie! It's not bothering anybody."

At which point, an announcement came on over the loudspeaker:

"Welcome to the Tampa Vistas Community Theater production of *The Gingerbread Cookie That Saved Christmas.* At this time the management would like to ask everyone to please turn off all cell phones, pagers, and Christmas tree ties."

Honestly, if it weren't for Mom, Daddy would've been kicked out of Tampa Vistas ages ago.

Edna's play had undergone no magical transformation since the last time I'd seen it. It was still the same cavalcade of clichés, the same shameless rip-off of Dickens and *Peter Pan.*

On the plus side, our leading lady, Laurette, gave a most unusual performance.

Instead of the kindly older woman Edna had intended her to be, Laurette was a raging harridan, Medusa in a rocking chair, delivering her lines to Preston with undisguised venom.

Of course, none of it made sense.

The audience just sat there, scratching their heads, as Laurette snarled at the gingerbread man who was supposedly changing her life for the better.

Like I said, a most unusual performance. Not unusual enough, I'm afraid, to keep Daddy from falling into a coma-like sleep, his snores periodically echoing in the theater.

Mom and I took turns nudging him awake.

At last the play limped to a close, and the gingerbread man was about to fly off into the night.

"How can I ever thank you?" Laurette snarled at Preston, who still looked more like a molting bear with a human head than any gingerbread man I'd ever seen.

He smiled at her, the same condescending smile he'd been beaming at the Chinese restaurant.

"Just remember to see the glass half full."

"Yeah, right," she said, looking for all the world like she wanted to sock him in his gingerbread jaw. “Do you really have to go?”

“Yes, dear lady. I hate to leave you, but that’s the way the cookie crumbles! Ha-ha!”

With the faint sound of Raymond’s pulley cranking in the background, Preston took off into the rafters.

And then the unthinkable happened.

Before our horrified eyes, the cable suddenly snapped, and Preston came crashing back down again.

A collective gasp arose from the crowd as his body landed onstage with a most sickening thud.

Then everyone just sat there in shock, dead silent.

Everybody except for Daddy, of course.

He was snoring louder than ever.

CHAPTER SIX

Preston still had a pulse when Doc Wilkins ran up onstage and checked it. But alas, he also had a broken neck. By the time the EMT guys showed up, he'd bit the dust.

It was all over the news the next morning. The media pundits were calling it *The Gingerbread Man Murder,* the police having ruled out accidental death. And if Edna thought she had troubles before, it was nothing compared to what she faced now.

"I'm going to be arrested any minute!" she wailed when Mom and I stopped by to visit her after breakfast.

We sat across from her on her sensible plaid sofa, the kind that doesn't show the dirt. Poor Edna looked awful, her face drained of color, her helmet-head curls sticking out in unruly clumps.

"But that's absurd!" Mom said. "Why on earth would the police arrest you?"

"Because they think I killed Preston! They

showed up on my doorstep early this morning, before I even had a chance to get dressed. I never had dealings with police in my life, not even a driving ticket, and there I was, in my ratty old bathrobe, practically being accused of murder! I was so humiliated, I thought I'd die."

"What did they say?" I asked.

"They told me that the wire on the pulley that was holding Preston had been tampered with, probably with some sort of wire cutter. Then they wanted to know my whereabouts the night before last and all day yesterday. They think I'm the one who tampered with the wire!"

"Oh, dear," Mom clucked.

"But I was nowhere near the clubhouse. Gloria wanted to have a final run-through of the play yesterday, but Laurette refused to be onstage with Preston one more minute than was absolutely necessary. And, of course, I didn't want to go, either. I never wanted to see that horrible man as long as I lived. But I certainly didn't kill him!"

Her eyes welled with tears.

"Of course you didn't, darling." Mom jumped up and put her arm around her.

"So the theater was empty all day yesterday?" I asked, still wondering why the cops had focused their attention on Edna.

"As far as I know, yes."

"Then anybody could have wandered in and done it."

"Oh, no. Not anybody. The theater is always locked. Only people with keys can get in."

"Who had keys?"

"The maintenance men. And all of us involved in the production. Preston, Gloria, Laurette, and me. We all got master keys to the clubhouse facilities so we could rehearse after hours if need be."

"But if you *all* had keys, why do the police think you did it?"

"Because they heard about how I threw that sparerib at Preston in the Chinese restaurant, and how I said last night that I wished he were dead."

"People around here have such big mouths," Mom clucked in disapproval.

I had no doubt that the Tampa Vistas rumor mill had gone into overdrive, naming Edna Lindstrom as its Most Likely Murder Suspect.

"When I went to jazzercise class this morning," Edna sniffled, "all the women were looking at me funny. It was horrible. Just horrible!

"I came home and tried to calm my nerves with some knitting," she said, pointing to an unfinished sweater in a knitting basket at her feet, "but I gave up after I dropped fourteen stitches."

"Now, Edna," Mom said, "I'm sure everything is going to be all right."

But I could see she was almost as worried as Edna.

Normally I would have offered to snoop around and investigate for Edna. Solving murders happens to be a hobby of mine. A dangerous one, I know, but one that keeps me busy in between toilet bowl ads.

But there was no way I could offer to help. Not with Mom in the room. I've spent years keeping my part-time hobby a secret from my parents. They'd have double coronaries if they knew their precious daughter was trotting around, sniffing out killers.

And yet I couldn't just sit back and do nothing. Lord knows how long Edna would linger under a cloud of suspicion. Maybe I could unearth something that would speed up the process and lead the cops to the killer.

I made up my mind to start poking around.

I just wouldn't tell my parents about it. No need to drive them crazy. They had each other for that.

■ ■ ■ ■

Mom begged Edna to join us for lunch, but she refused.

"Honestly, Claudia," she said, "I couldn't eat a thing."

Why the heck couldn't I ever feel like that? I wondered, yearning to swipe a candy cane from Edna's tree.

"I'll come back the minute we're through," Mom assured her, "and keep you company."

"Would you?" Edna's eyes shone with gratitude.

"Of course, sweetheart. In the meanwhile, don't get up. We'll see ourselves out."

Edna nodded and absently picked up her knitting.

"Oh, drat!" we heard her exclaim as we headed for the front door. "Dropped another one."

Back home Daddy was busy hurling curses at the rotating Christmas tree, which still refused to rotate.

"You won't believe this, Hank," Mom told him, "but the police think Edna Lindstrom killed Preston!"

"I'd believe it," Daddy said, crawling out from under the tree.

"Hank Austen, how can you say such a thing?"

"You saw how angry Edna was last night. She said she wished Preston was dead."

"You don't seriously think she killed him."

"Anything's possible. Why, just the other day I saw a show on TV about a minister who murdered his brother-in-law and stuffed his body in the church organ."

"I wish you'd stop watching those gruesome shows," Mom sighed and trotted off to the kitchen to fix lunch. Which turned out to be tuna salad sandwiches for us and Bumble Bee straight from the can for the Princess.

"Would you like some more, sweetheart?" Mom asked when we were through.

Needless to say, she was not talking to me or Daddy, but to Prozac, who was staring up at her with her patented Starving Orphan eyes.

After feeding her little darling some more premium albacore, Mom at last turned her attention to me.

"Jaine, honey, I wanted us to spend the day together, but I can't possibly leave Edna alone. You don't mind, do you, if I go back and keep her company?"

"Of course not, Mom. I'm sure I'll find something to do."

And indeed I would.

The minute she was gone, I got Gloria and Laurette's contact information from Mom's address book. Lest you forget, Edna wasn't the only one with a motive to kill Preston. Gloria and Laurette were also charter members of the I Hate Preston Club. I needed to talk to them and see what they'd been up to.

But first, I wanted to pay a little visit to Raymond, the handyman. He was, after all, the most obvious suspect, the one person who had easiest access to the pulley wire. I remembered his angry exchange with Preston, and Preston's threat to have him fired.

Jobs weren't that easy to come by these days, especially for a Cuban refugee. Had Raymond bumped off the duplicitous doctor to save his gig at Tampa Vistas?

I intended to find out.

There was no sign of Raymond in the clubhouse, so I headed out to the pool area, where a bunch of ladies in capris and matching T-shirts — clearly the outfit of choice at Tampa Vistas — were playing cards under a shaded umbrella.

As I approached their table, I heard one of them saying, "And then Edna threw a whole Peking Duck at him. Right there in the Chinese restaurant!"

See, class? That's how rumors get started.

"Excuse me," I said, stepping under the umbrella. "I was wondering if any of you have seen Raymond."

One of the gals, whose bouffant curls were an alarming shade of blue, squinted up at me through harlequin glasses.

"You're Hank Austen's daughter, aren't you?"

"Yes, I am."

"Poor thing," she said, leading the others in a chorus of tsk-tsks.

Daddy obviously had a bit of a reputation at Tampa Vistas.

"About Raymond," I repeated, "have you seen him?"

"Why?" Ms. Harlequin asked. "What has Hank broken now?" She turned to her pals with a guffaw. "Remember the time he set his own BBQ on fire?"

The other gals giggled at the memory.

"My father hasn't broken anything," I said, feeling a rush of indignation.

It's one thing for me and Mom to complain about Daddy. It's not okay for anybody else.

"So have you seen Raymond?" I asked for the third time, forcing a stiff smile.

"I thought I saw him heading over to the

maintenance building," one of the gigglers piped up.

"Where would that be?"

"Over there, behind those bushes."

I followed a path leading to a no-frills box of a building next to the clubhouse, shielded from view by a wall of shrubbery.

The giggler was right. Raymond was there when I knocked on the door.

"Come in," he called out.

His office was a jumble of tools and plywood. Raymond was seated behind a battered desk, tinkering with some kind of motor. Off to the side of his desk I noticed the prop gingerbread cookies from Edna's play.

"Ms. Austen," Raymond greeted me with a smile. He sat ramrod straight in his chair, his black hair combed so the rake marks still showed, his work shirt impeccably clean. "What are you doing here?"

I debated whether to tell him that I was investigating Preston's murder. I doubted he'd go blabbing to my parents. Then again, maybe he had a big mouth. Best not to risk it.

"Actually, Raymond," I fibbed, "I'm lost. I was looking for the Tampa Vistas Café."

"That's on the other side of the clubhouse," he said, "past the Ping-Pong tables."

"Silly me. I've got absolutely no sense of direction."

"Tampa Vistas is a big place," he said. "It's confusing at first."

He smiled again, clearly expecting me to be on my way.

Not about to happen.

"Oh, wow." I picked up one of the plaster of Paris cookies from his desk. "I still can't get over what happened to Dr. McCay last night."

At the mention of Preston's name, Raymond's face turned to stone.

"The police think it's murder," I said.

"I'm not surprised. Dr. McCay was the kind of man who makes enemies in life."

Enemies like Raymond.

"Such arrogance," he said, shaking his head. "I hate to think of how he must have treated his poor patients. The man, he had no *corazón*. No heart. I heard how he cheated on all those poor ladies. Edna and Laurette and Gloria."

"Do you think any of them could have done it?"

"Quien sabe?" He shrugged, spritzing the motor he'd been working on with some WD-40. "It's hard to know what people are capable of."

"The police questioned Edna this morning. She's terribly upset."

"Poor lady," he said, giving the motor another spritz.

"I suppose they must've questioned you, too."

He looked up sharply.

"Why do you say that?"

"Only because you were in charge of the pulley."

"Yes, I was. But I asked Manuel, one of the other maintenance men, to help me backstage. He was with me all night and has already sworn to the police that I in no way tampered with the wire on the pulley."

"What a lucky break you asked him, huh?"

It was perfectly possible, of course, that Manuel had lied to the cops to give his amigo an alibi. And even if Raymond hadn't tampered with the cable during the performance, who's to say he hadn't messed with it earlier in the day?

Raymond put down the WD-40 and shot me a penetrating look.

"What are you doing here, senorita?"

"What do you mean?" I blinked in feigned innocence.

"C'mon. I know you weren't really looking for that café."

"No," I admitted, "I wasn't."

"So what do you want?"

"The cops think Edna might have killed Preston. I'm convinced she didn't, and I'm trying to help her out."

"You some kind of private eye?"

"As a matter of fact, I am," I said, wishing I'd opted to wear something a bit more noirish than my Frosty the Snowman T-shirt.

"And you think I killed Dr. McCay?"

"Well, he did threaten to have you fired."

At that, he threw back his head and laughed.

"You think I'd kill for this executive-level job?" He waved dismissively at the equipment in the cluttered room. "Please, senorita. I am a resourceful man. I fought my way out of Cuba. A man like me can always find work."

Then he spoke slowly, enunciating every word, to drive home his point.

"I didn't kill Dr. McCay. I didn't like him, but I didn't kill him."

"Then what," I asked, "were you doing at the clubhouse yesterday at six-thirty in the morning?"

"Fixing a leak in the men's room," he said, arms clamped defiantly across his chest.

But I had only his word for that, didn't I?

For all I knew, he was in the Tampa Vistas Theater, hard at work fraying a wire for the grand opening of *The Gingerbread Cookie That Saved Christmas.*

Chapter Seven

Next stop, Gloria Di Nardo.

I headed up the path to her town house, rehearsing my excuse for stopping by. I certainly hoped I'd have better luck fooling her than I had with Raymond.

She came to the door, swathed in a caftan, a tall glass of iced tea in her hand.

"Jaine, sweetie!" she exclaimed, waving me inside. *"Entrez, ma chérie!"*

I followed her to a living room straight out of a New Orleans bordello, with gold-flocked walls, Victorian furniture, and a slew of Tiffany-style lighting fixtures. Practically every inch of wall space was taken up with framed posters from the Secaucus Dinner Theater, featuring Gloria as — among others — Anna Christie, Hedda Gabler, and the world's oldest Juliet. Rounding out her homage to herself was a mantel crammed with still more theatrical photos of Gloria. I was surprised the small Christmas tree in the corner didn't have Gloria ornaments dangling from its branches.

"Can I get you something to drink, darling?" she asked, waving her drink in front of me.

One whiff, and I realized it was not, as I'd thought, iced tea, but booze.

"A wee bit of bourbon, perhaps?"

Something told me this was not her first glass. No wonder she'd greeted me with such enthusiasm.

"No, thanks." I managed a faint smile. "I'm fine."

"To what do I owe the pleasure?" she asked, leading me to a seat on a velvet sofa festooned with throw pillows.

Time for my little deception.

"Edna asked me to stop by. She found this brush in her car and thought it might be yours."

I reached into my purse and took out my good tortoiseshell hairbrush. Of course it wasn't hers, but I thought it was a damn clever excuse to explain my presence in her shrine to her past performances.

So you can imagine my surprise when, after examining its natural boar bristles, she grabbed the brush out of my hand and said, "Yes, it's mine, all right. Thanks so much."

The nerve of that woman! A Svengali-like

saleswoman at Bloomie's had convinced me to part with thirty-five bucks for that brush. And now Gloria had practically stolen it. Clearly the woman had a mere passing acquaintance with the concept of ethics.

But there was nothing I could do about it. So I launched into the investigative portion of my visit.

"Poor Edna," I sighed. "She's so upset. The police came to question her this morning."

"Is that so?" Gloria said, totally uninterested in Edna's plight. "Say, I was just looking through some old photos from my days in Secaucus."

Indeed there was a ginormous photo album splayed out on the faux antique coffee table in front of us.

"Would you be interested in taking a wee peek at it?"

And before I could answer, she'd plopped down beside me on the sofa, showing me her darn album.

I spent the next forty-five minutes strolling down memory lane with Gloria, reliving every nanosecond of her theatrical past, replete with yellowing reviews from the *Secaucus Sentinel.* Most of which were raves.

According to the *Sentinel* theater critic, a gentleman named Vincent Santini, Gloria had been "incandescent," "glowing," "magnificent," and "awe-inspiring" in her various roles.

"What terrific reviews," I said.

"They are, aren't they?" Gloria beamed. "Mr. Santini was such a discerning critic and never once lost his objectivity, in spite of our relationship."

"Your relationship?"

"Oh, Vinnie was my brother-in-law. But like I say, he was totally impartial. Until he and my sister got divorced. Then he lost all sense of perspective.

"I sure do miss the Great White Way of Secaucus," she said, getting up and heading over to a gilded cabinet against the wall.

She opened it to reveal a humungous jug of Jack Daniel's.

"Sure you won't have a drink?" she asked, topping hers off.

"No," I assured her. "I'm fine."

"Frankly," she confided, "it's been quite a comedown being stuck here in the sticks. I thought I had a chance to revive my career with *Gingerbread Cookie.* You should have seen the play when Edna first brought it to me. What a mess. But I worked my magic and made it shine! I thought it would be my big break, my return to the big time. Oh, well." She sighed, plopping down on the sofa. "There's always next Christmas."

I wasn't so sure about that. Not if she kept mainlining Jack Daniel's.

We finished looking through the final several thousand pictures in her album.

"Wasn't that fun?" she asked when the torture was over. "How about I go get Volume II?"

No frigging way was I sitting through Volume II. Not even for Edna.

"It's been fascinating," I said, popping up from my perch among the throw pillows, "but I really must be going."

What a bust this visit had turned out to be. Annoyed at myself for having wasted so much time, I was determined not to leave without lobbing her a question or two.

"Such a shame about Dr. McCay," I said as she walked me to the door.

"Good riddance to bad rubbish," she snapped, showing no qualms about speaking ill of the dead.

"I don't suppose you have any idea who frayed the wire?"

"Word on the street is it's Edna. She should've never thrown that sparerib at him. Not that I blame her. Preston was a ghastly toad of a man. A cheating piece of slime.

"That's the story of my life," she sighed, draping herself against the wall in a gesture straight out of the Dame Edna School of Acting. "I keep falling for the rats.

"But what goes around comes around," she added, perking up. "Every single guy who ever did me dirty wound up paying the price. Take my first husband. He left me to marry some bimbo ballroom dancer and then drowned in a boating accident on their honeymoon. The director who fired me from a summer stock production of *Uncle Vanya?* Killed in a freak car crash. And the critic who trashed my Desdemona? Fell down a flight of stairs.

"Yep," she said, polishing off the rest of her bourbon in a single gulp. "Bad karma always gets 'em in the end."

Gloria sure had a lot of dead bodies littering her past.

And what I couldn't help wondering as I left her place was: Did all that bad karma get a little help from Gloria?

"Ta-da!"

Daddy stood next to his topless Christmas tree, beaming.

He'd finally gotten the darn thing to stand upright, and now he clutched the remote in his hand, eager to send it spinning.

He and I were both waiting for Mom, who was in the kitchen, whipping up a meat loaf for Edna.

"Claudia!" he called out. "Hurry it up, willya?"

At last Mom came into the living room, with Prozac in her arms.

I swear, that cat had walked a grand total of three steps since she got here; Mom had been toting her everywhere between snacks.

"You know, Mom," I said, eyeing my pampered princess, "all four of her legs work. She *can* walk."

"Oh, but Zoloft likes being carried, don't you, precious?"

Prozac graced her with a yawn.

Now you may scratch me behind my ears.

"Okay, people," Daddy said. "Can we forget about the cat for a minute and focus on the tree?"

He clicked the remote and his topless tree began rotating. Miraculously it remained upright.

"How on earth did you manage to fix it?" Mom asked.

"It wasn't easy, but I finally figured out a way. I nailed the stand to the floor."

"You what???" Mom's eyes bulged with disbelief.

"I nailed the stand to the floor."

"You put holes in our good carpet?"

"They're small holes. You'll hardly notice them."

"Oh, Hank!" she sputtered. "How could you?"

Prozac, the little toady, swished an indignant tail in his direction.

"Dear Lord," Mom said, heading back to the kitchen, "grant me the strength — and the fudge — to get through all this."

I was about to trot after her (after all, she'd said the magic *F* word) when Daddy stopped me.

"Not so fast, Lambchop," he said, blocking my path.

"What's up, Daddy?"

"That's what I'd like to know."

He shot me a penetrating look.

Uh-oh. He couldn't possibly have found out about my investigation, could he?

"What do you mean, Daddy?" I asked, aiming for a look of surprised innocence.

"I saw you copying those addresses from Mom's address book. And I saw you going into Gloria Di Nardo's town house."

"Oh, that," I said with an airy wave. "I was just returning something Gloria left in Edna's car. And I copied those addresses because I wanted to send some of Mom's friends Christmas cards. We sort of bonded over Edna's play."

"Now, Lambchop," Daddy said, wagging an admonishing finger, "I can always tell when you're fibbing."

"I'm not fibbing," I lied.

"Then how do you explain this?" he asked, whipping a crumpled piece of paper from his pocket.

" 'My Suspects,' " he read, " 'By Jaine Austen.' "

"Where did you get that?"

"Prozac was playing with it."

I often write out a list of my suspects when I'm working a case. It helps clarify my thoughts. This one, before it got soaked in cat spit, went something like this:

Raymond, the Handyman: *Preston had threatened to have him fired. Did Raymond tamper with the wire to save his job?*

Gloria Di Nardo & Laurette Kendall: *Both dumped by Preston. Both had access to the pulley wire. Either could've frayed it in a fit of rage.*

Ginny Knight, aerobics instructor hottie: *No obvious motive. No access to the cable.*

(The only reason I put her on the list is because I never trust a woman with a 24-inch waist.)

"I repeat," Daddy said, summoning the sternest look in his repertoire. "What're you up to?"

Fresh out of lies, I broke down and told him the truth, that I was investigating Preston's death, hoping to get Edna off the hook for murder.

Daddy's eyes widened in dismay.

"But you can't go running after a killer, Lambchop. You could get hurt."

"I've never been hurt before."

(Well, not much, anyway.)

"Before? You mean you've done this before?"

Oh, drat. I hadn't meant for that to slip out.

"Maybe once or twice," I confessed, underestimating just a tad.

"Your mom would have a coronary if she ever found out."

"So let's not tell her, okay?"

"Of course not. And as far as this investigation is concerned . . ."

I fully expected him to call it to a halt, but much to my surprise, he announced, "I'm coming with you."

"Huh?"

"I've always wanted to be a private eye!"

Inwardly I groaned. You've seen Daddy in action. No way was I going to make any progress with him by my side.

"I'm sorry, Daddy, but I work alone."

Off his disappointed pout, I added, "And

besides, if you come with me, Mom is sure to find out. I'll be far less conspicuous working by myself."

"You have a point there," he admitted. "But I'm still not happy about the idea of you running around chasing a killer."

"But we can't let Edna be arrested for a crime she didn't commit!"

"Who says she didn't do it?"

"Oh, please. Edna's not the murdering kind."

"Well, somebody out there is," he said, "and I don't want you to be Victim #2."

"Honest, Daddy, I know what I'm doing. I promise I'll be extremely careful."

Once again, I expected him to nix the whole project, but again he surprised me when he said, albeit with a reluctant sigh, "Okay, but I expect you home by nine o'clock every night."

"It's a deal," I conceded, the world's first P.I. with a curfew.

Chapter Eight

Laurette Kendall lived in a ranch-style house framed by a tidy jungle of hibiscus, bougainvillea, and bird-of-paradise.

She was out front when I showed up the next day, in a wide-brimmed straw hat and gardening gloves, hacking away at her bougainvillea. Nearby a plastic Santa basked in the warm Florida sun.

"Hi, Laurette!" I called out.

"Oh, hello, Jaine."

She looked up at me questioningly.

Contrary to what I'd told Daddy, we hadn't exactly bonded the other night at the Chinese restaurant. In fact, I don't think she'd said more than seven words to me. Those words being, "You've got plum sauce on your chin."

So I'm sure she was wondering what I was doing there.

Time for my all-purpose, handy dandy excuse.

"Edna asked me to stop by," I said. "She found this comb in her car and thought it might be yours."

Having learned my lesson, I took a very cheap comb from my purse and showed it to her.

I'm happy to report Laurette had a few more scruples than Gloria. Or else she just didn't want a very cheap comb.

"Not mine," she said, eyeing the comb briefly and then returning to her bougainvillea.

My cue to leave.

But I plodded ahead, anyway.

"What a shame about Dr. McCay, huh?" I said.

At the mention of Preston's name, her back stiffened, and she stopped whacking.

"A terrible shame." Her cool gray eyes met mine. "He deceived us all, but still, he certainly didn't deserve to die."

Talk about the voice of reason. If a guy had cheated on me the way Preston had cheated on Laurette, I'd be carrying a healthy grudge — and perhaps a voodoo doll — for at least a year or three.

She was little Ms. Rational, all right.

And yet, I couldn't help remembering the venom with which she'd delivered her lines the night of the play. Underneath that calm exterior lurked a temper. Of that I was certain.

"I don't suppose you saw anybody near the pulley that night."

"Everybody was near the pulley that night," she shrugged. "Me, Raymond, Manuel, Ginny . . ."

My ears perked up.

"Ginny Knight was backstage?"

"Yes, she stopped by to wish Preston good luck." She wrinkled her country club nose in disgust. "And probably for a quickie, if I know her type."

Well, how do you like that? The grieving fiancée had been backstage the night of the murder, within tampering distance of the wire.

Not that I could see any obvious motive for Ginny to kill Preston, not when she had everything to gain by marrying him.

But one never knows, does one?

I hurried over to the clubhouse to look for Ginny, but she was gone for the day. Checking the water aerobics schedule posted on the bulletin board, I saw she was teaching a class at 10 a.m. the next day.

I made up my mind to be there.

Back home I found my parents in the den, Mom glued to the shopping channel, Daddy doing the crossword puzzle.

"Dammit!" Daddy said. "They made another mistake in the puzzle today. They left out another box."

Whenever Daddy's answers are wrong, he's convinced it's the newspaper's fault.

"So where have you been, sweetheart?" Mom asked, tearing herself away from a tanzanite and iolite "showstopper" cocktail ring — only $59.95, plus shipping and handling.

"Just hanging out at the clubhouse."

Not a total lie. Technically, I had been there.

"Well, put on something pretty. Edna's gone off for a doctor's appointment, and I want to treat you to a gals' lunch. Just the two of us."

"What about me?" Daddy asked. "Can't I come, too?"

"No, you can't come," Mom said, still miffed over those holes in their carpet. "It's girls only."

"Well, what am I supposed to eat?"

"There's tuna salad and mayo in the refrigerator. And bread in the bread box. You'll think of something."

"Oh, all right," he pouted.

"C'mon, sweetheart," Mom said, hooking her arm in mine. "Let's get dressed. Why don't you wear that cute flamingo capri set I bought you?"

By now I was resigned to the fact that I would be spending the rest of my vacation with a sequined animal plastered across my chest.

About an hour or so later Mom and I were seated across from each other on the deck of a charming bay-view restaurant, scarfing down chopped veggie salads. (Okay, Mom was eating a salad. I had the hamburger steak, with mashed potatoes. And onion rings, if you must know.)

At the table next to us, a trio of middle-aged women were taking a break from their Christmas shopping, soothing their shop-worn nerves with chardonnays.

"It's a zoo out there," we heard one of them say.

Mom smiled smugly.

She'd finished her shopping some time in March.

"That's the wonderful thing about buying from TV," she nodded sagely. "No hassles at the mall."

I, on the other hand, specialize in mall hassles.

Like Daddy, I am a procrastinator of the highest order and save my gift list for zero hour, when the malls are filled with pawed-over merchandise and zombie shoppers stumbling around like extras from *Dawn of the Dead.*

"So how is Edna doing?" I asked, eager to avoid a lecture on the wonders of TV retailing.

"Poor thing," Mom sighed. "She's thinking of moving in with her son and his family back in Minneapolis. She says she can't show her face in Tampa Vistas anymore." She pecked at her salad listlessly. "If only there were some way we could help her."

I suddenly wondered if I should tell her about my investigation. Just to ease her mind. Maybe she'd be okay with it.

"Look, Mom . . . ," I started to say as I buttered a roll.

"Be careful you don't cut yourself with that butter knife!" Mom cried, her eyes wide with concern.

Scratch that confession. If Mom was afraid of me handling a butter knife, she'd never let me go chasing after a killer.

"What were you about to say, honey?"

"Um. What do you think Daddy would like for Christmas?"

"You're all he wants for Christmas, sweetheart. And that goes for me, too."

"Yes, I know, but you're getting actual gifts. Like it or not."

"Well, Daddy could always use another sports shirt. I saw the nicest one on the shopping channel the other day. If you pay for express delivery, you could get it in time for Christmas. Of course, the express delivery is almost as much as the shirt, so I'm not sure it's worth it."

"I think I'll pick up something at the mall."

"Just remember to take along hand sanitizer," she warned. "Those places are hotbeds of germs."

"What about you, Mom? What would you like?"

"Really, honey, I don't need a thing."

She says this every year.

"Okay, so you don't need anything. But what do you *want?* What do you really, really want?"

"Grandchildren."

She says that every year, too.

"What do you want that I can get in the mall?"

"Seriously, Jaine, I don't see why you can't marry Lance. He's such a lovely fellow."

Lance, for those of you who don't already know, is my neighbor back in Los Angeles, a devilishly attractive Neiman Marcus shoe salesman.

"Why can't I marry him? First, because

he hasn't asked me. And second, because he's gay."

"Oh, please," Mom said with an airy wave. "That's just a phase. I'm sure he'll get over it, once he marries you and starts having my grandbabies."

(Note to Gay Activists: Please do not write angry letters to Mom. She means well.)

"So," I said, getting back to the topic at hand, "what do you want for Christmas?"

"How about a nice pot holder?"

"Surely you can do better than that, Mom. Something fun. Something exciting."

"A set of pot holders?"

"Something you'd never buy yourself."

"I know! Monogrammed pot holders!"

I was beginning to think it would be easier just to give her a grandchild.

Chapter Nine

The rest of the day passed uneventfully. Daddy had run into a new snafu with his revolving Christmas tree. When he switched on the tree's built-in lights, the tree wouldn't turn. And when the tree was turning, the lights wouldn't go on.

The house echoed with colorful curses all afternoon as he wrestled with his problem.

Meanwhile, I was busy wrestling with the murder.

As far as I knew, any one of my suspects could have done it. Gloria, Laurette, and Raymond all had keys to the theater. They all could have gone in and tampered with the wire. It was unattended from the time dress rehearsal ended until right before the opening performance. And although Ginny Knight didn't have a key like the others, she was seen backstage during the performance.

As H. Poirot and S. Holmes would be the first to tell you, crime-solving is a grueling business. A person can work up a real appetite sifting through suspects.

Especially if that person is moi.

Around about midnight, I was stretched out in bed, Prozac snoring on my belly, no doubt dreaming of the zillion-dollar-a-pound baby lamb chops Mom had fixed her for dinner. I was lying there, trying to figure out why Ginny Knight might have wanted to kill Preston, when I got a sudden urge to rendezvous with my good buddies Ben & Jerry.

Gently dislodging Sleeping Beauty from her perch, I tiptoed down the hallway to the kitchen, careful not to wake my parents, who had gone to sleep after the evening news.

Alas, when I checked the freezer, all I found was some appalling low-fat ice milk.

Of course, there was always the Christmas fudge. But I'd already met my Minimum Lifetime Requirement of fudge. And besides, I was in an ice cream kind of mood.

So I threw on a raincoat over my I ♡ MY CAT nightshirt. And, grabbing the keys to Mom's car from the table in the foyer, I headed out on a Chunky Monkey run.

The local supermarket was fairly deserted at that time of night, just a dozen or so cars in the parking lot.

Inside, under the market's harsh fluorescent glare, night owls and midnight snackers wandered the aisles.

Wasting no time, I made a beeline for the ice cream case and spotted my beloved Chunky Monkey. As I reached for it, I got the feeling someone was watching me.

But when I turned around, no one was there. Just me and Ben and Jerry.

I took my booty to the express lane, where I was irritated to see a lady pulling up with a cart jammed full of groceries. Even more irritating, the bored checker started ringing up her sale. A recent graduate of Slacker U., he said nothing to his customer about her flagrant disregard of the express lane rules.

I looked over at the other available checker, but her line was snaking back toward the aisles.

With a sigh, I got behind the rule breaker. A line began to form behind me as the checker continued to ring up her purchases at the speed of slow-running molasses.

Once again, I got the feeling someone was watching me. I turned around, but none of the people in line behind me — most of them cursing the Express Lane Scofflaw — seemed the least bit interested in yours truly.

Several centuries later I made it to the

register and paid for my ice cream. By now I could've churned my own.

Back outside, in the dim light of the parking lot, I was heading for Mom's Camry when I heard footsteps behind me. This time there was no denying it.

Someone was following me.

A frisson of fear slid down my back. Could it possibly be the killer? Had one of my suspects panicked at my questions and decided to put an end to them with another murder?

I reached in my purse and grabbed my travel-size can of hair spray, which I have found works almost as well as Mace in disabling an assailant.

Clutching my Aqua Net, I whirled around and saw a guy in a windbreaker and baseball cap. At least I thought it was a guy. It was hard to tell in this crummy light. And he had the visor of the cap pulled down low over his face, so I couldn't make out his features.

Was it Raymond? I wondered. Or Laurette disguised as a man? Or maybe a hit man, hired by the killer to bump me off?

Whoever it was took a step toward me. Springing to action, I blasted my Aqua Net. I only hoped it would work, what with his darn visor in the way.

Suddenly I heard:

"Lambchop! What're you doing?"

"Daddy? Is that you?"

"Of course it's me," he said, hiking up his cap. "Who else do you know who calls you Lambchop?"

"What on earth are you doing here? You almost gave me a heart attack."

"You didn't really think I was going to let you track a killer all by yourself, did you?"

"Daddy, I told you I'd be okay."

"Sorry, but I couldn't take any chances with my little Lambchop."

"How long have you been following me?" I asked.

"Except for today's lunch with Mom, I haven't let you out of my sight."

Good heavens! He'd been tailing me all this time, and I hadn't even noticed.

(Note to Self: Do not give up day job.)

(Note to Self, Part II: Get day job.)

"And might I remind you, young lady," he said with a stern finger wag, "that you broke your curfew?"

"But I wasn't out detecting! I was buying ice cream."

"What kind?"

"Chunky Monkey."

"In that case," he grinned, "all is forgiven."

Chapter Ten

A Chunky Monkey hangover is not a pretty thing. I woke up the next morning with a whole new generation of cellulite clinging to my thighs.

After downing several cups of coffee in the vain hopes that caffeine would somehow cancel the calories I'd scarfed down the night before, I set out for the pool to question Ginny Knight.

She was in the middle of her aerobics class when I got there, calling out instructions to the dozen or so ladies bobbing in the turquoise water. In her body-hugging sweats, she was quite the poster girl for physical fitness — every square molecule of her bod toned and tanned to perfection.

It was hard not to gaze in awe at her abs of steel peeking out from between the top of her sweatpants and the bottom of her hoodie. If only I'd quit going on Chunky Monkey binges, I could look like that. Well, not exactly like that, not without a rigorous exercise regimen, and a top-notch plastic surgeon. And possibly a fairy godmother.

With a sigh, I plopped down on a chaise to wait for the class to end. And as I did so, I noticed a man on a nearby chaise, his face hidden behind a newspaper.

"Hi, Daddy," I called out.

He pretended not to hear me. Daddy liked playing detective.

Meanwhile, across the pool, still sporting his black eye, Doc Wilkins was being coddled by a cluster of mother hens.

"You poor thing!" cooed a gray-haired matron in a daisy-dotted capri set.

"Some people should be banned from the Ping-Pong tables," said another, shooting Daddy's newspaper a dirty look.

Doc Wilkins was clearly loving every minute of this.

"Faker!" Daddy muttered. He was still convinced Doc Wilkins was blackening his eye with make-up in a shameless bid for sympathy.

"Okay, ladies!" Ginny was saying. "That's it for today. Good work!"

The class straggled out of the pool in twos and threes, several of them chatting about blowing their diets and going to the Tampa Vistas Café for bagels and cream cheese.

Ginny started over to a table where she'd left her tote bag, and I hurried to her side.

Still determined to keep news of my investigation from getting back to Mom, I'd come up with what I hoped was a plausible excuse for a conversation.

"Hi, there!" I said, with the perkiest grin I could muster. "I've been watching your class, and I think you're a terrific teacher."

"Thanks," she said perfunctorily, not even bothering to look up from her purse.

Something told me if you weren't male and rich, she wasn't interested.

"Actually, I was wondering if you gave private lessons."

That sure perked her up.

"As a matter of fact, I do." She turned to grace me with a blinding smile.

Lord, what a beauty she was, with velvety skin and eyes as green as Mom's simulated emeralds.

"But," she warned, "I charge a hundred dollars an hour."

"No problem. I really need the individual attention."

"Yes," she agreed, with a none-too-discreet glance at my thighs, "I suppose you do." With lightning speed, she whipped out her day planner from the depths of her tote. "How about tomorrow at two?"

"Oh, tomorrow's no good. I was thinking sometime after Christmas. In January."

Of course, I'd be back in L.A. in January, but she didn't know that.

"Okay, how about the third, at eleven?"

"Perfect!"

"Don't worry," she winked. "We'll have that nasty cellulite under control in no time."

The woman was beginning to get on my nerves.

"By the way," I said, "I just wanted to offer my condolences on the death of your fiancé."

Ginny blinked, puzzled.

"How did you know I was engaged to Dr. McCay?"

"I was there that night at the Chinese restaurant."

She peered at me with those amazing emerald eyes, and recognition set in.

"Was that you, standing behind the others, eating an egg roll?"

"Actually, it was a sparerib. But yes, that was me."

"What an awful scene. Those poor gals were so upset." She tsked in sympathy.

But I remembered how triumphant she'd seemed at the time, basking in the glow of the rock on her finger. There'd been no sign of sympathy then.

"Excuse me for asking, but didn't it bother you when you learned Dr. McCay had been seeing those other women?"

"Oh, no. Preston explained it all to me. Those were just platonic friendships. The poor ladies misinterpreted his kind intentions."

Are you buying any of this? I sure wasn't.

Something told me Ginny knew exactly what she was getting with Preston, and she didn't care. She just wanted to be Mrs. Dr. Preston McCay with a rock on her finger and charge accounts at Neiman's and Saks.

And then it suddenly occurred to me that — in addition to the rock Preston had given her as an engagement present — maybe Ginny got him to leave her money in his will. And that maybe, just maybe, she'd knocked him off before she actually had to marry him.

"I've really got to run," she said, heading for the clubhouse, "or I'll be late for my next class."

"I'll walk you to your car."

"Why would you do that?"

To weasel the truth out of her, that's why.

"Look," I said, following her inside the clubhouse, "I think you should know there are some pretty ugly rumors circulating."

That stopped her in her tracks.

"What ugly rumors?"

Time for a handy dandy fib.

"That Dr. McCay left you all his money, and you killed him to inherit."

I watched her closely for a flash of guilt, a glimmer of fear. But all I saw was righteous indignation.

"That's an outrageous lie!" she sputtered. "All that cheapskate left me was a crummy cameo that belonged to his mother!"

Gone was all pretense of having actually cared for her dead fiancé. Nope, as I'd suspected, Ginny Knight was a gold digger of the highest order.

But a killer? Frankly, I couldn't see it. She seemed to be telling the truth about Preston's will. Which meant Preston was worth far more to her alive than dead. Ginny might have been backstage the night of the murder, but I was having a hard time believing she'd done any wire tampering.

"If anybody did it," Ginny was saying, "it was that ridiculous old tugboat Gloria Di Nardo."

"What makes you say that?"

"When Preston and I were driving back from the restaurant that night, we saw her letting herself into the clubhouse with her key."

Very interesting. So Gloria had paid an advance visit to the scene of the crime.

Ginny Knight may have been a washout as a suspect, but it looked like Gloria Di Nardo had just catapulted to the top of my list.

"You can come out now."

Daddy crept out from behind a nearby potted palm.

"So did you hear what she just said?" I asked.

"Yep," Daddy nodded. "That Preston sure was a cheapskate. Leaving her a two-bit cameo."

"No, the part about Gloria sneaking into the clubhouse the night before the murder."

"Oh, Gloria's the killer, all right." He nodded confidently. "I said so all along."

"You did not say so all along. Just the other day you thought it was Edna."

"Oh, please, Lambchop, you must've misinterpreted me. Anyone can see Gloria has 'killer' written all over her."

"You're not allowed to think she's guilty of murder just because she didn't give you the lead in Edna's play."

"That has nothing to do with it! I've always thought there was something sneaky about that woman. I've seen her put extra rolls in her muumuu at Sunday brunch."

"That'll get her fifteen to life, for sure."

"You know, Lambchop," he said, putting a fatherly arm around my shoulder, "you may have done some investigating before, but your old daddy could give you a lesson or two in the private eye biz."

Oh, dear. Why did I get the feeling that any day now he'd be showing up at the clubhouse in a trench coat and fedora?

Chapter Eleven

Okay, class. Time for a pop quiz.

Name the state bird of Florida.

According to the gang at the *Encyclopedia Britannica,* it's the mockingbird. But what do those guys know? The real state bird, as any true Floridian can tell you, is the Early Bird.

Every day the restaurants are full of them, bargain-conscious diners eager to save money, even if it means eating dinner while most people are still digesting their lunch.

My parents are two prime examples of the species. They have been known to linger over five-course dinners and still be home in time for the six o'clock news.

Which is why the sun was shining brightly late that afternoon when Daddy pulled into the parking lot at Tampa Vistas' most swellegant restaurant, Le Chateaubriand.

"Nothing but the best for my two gals!" Daddy beamed.

He'd taken us here partly as a treat for me, but mainly to score brownie points with Mom, who was still ticked off about those holes he'd drilled in the living room carpet.

"This way, ladies," he said, ushering us into a pale pink faux French chateau, heavily influenced by the Disneyland school of architecture.

A tuxedo-clad maître d' greeted us at the door.

"Austen, party of three," Daddy announced.

"We're here for the Early Bird dinner," Mom chimed in, to lock in our complimentary Early Bird wine and dessert.

"Oui, madame," said our genial host, his French accent as authentic as the architecture.

He led us past a lushly decorated Christmas tree into the main dining room — a cavernous space filled with linen-clad tables and a vast sea of Early Birds. A chandelier about the size of my Corolla hung from the center of the room.

"Omigosh," Mom said as we stepped inside. "Look who's here!"

Straight ahead of us, at a cozy table for three, Doc Wilkins was sandwiched between the same two mother hens who'd been clucking over him at the pool earlier that day.

"Damn!" Daddy muttered as the maître d' led us directly in their path.

"Be nice, Hank," Mom warned.

Daddy, remembering he was there to score brownie points, forced a stiff smile.

"Doc!" Mom called out as we approached their table. "LuAnn! Yolanda! How lovely to see you."

"Lovely to see you, too," Doc replied, avoiding eye contact with Daddy.

"How are you feeling?" Mom asked, eyeing his shiner with concern. Regrettably, it was still a pulsating purple.

"Still a bit sensitive." To prove his point, he touched his owie and winced.

"Oh, dear!" Mom said. "I'm so sorry to hear that."

"It's not *your* fault, Claudia," one of the mother hens said, shooting Daddy a dirty look.

"C'mon, girls," Daddy said, hustling us off. "The maître d' is waiting."

Thank heavens we were seated at a table some distance away from Doc Wilkins and his posse. The way those gals had been glaring at Daddy, I wanted to be out of firing range in case they decided to lob a dinner roll or two.

"Poor Doc," Mom sighed when we were alone with our menus. "His eye still looks terrible."

"Of course it looks terrible," Daddy sniffed. "He's using make-up on it. I'm telling you, Claudia. The guy's a faker. He's playing this thing up for all it's worth so everybody will feel sorry for him."

"That's the silliest thing I ever heard, Hank. Anyone can see it's a real black eye. And it's all your fault. We have to make it up to him somehow."

"Sweetheart," Daddy said, once again remembering his mission, "do we have to talk about his now?" He took her hand in his. "This was supposed to be our fun night out. I just want you to be happy."

"If you want to make me happy, Hank," she said, grabbing her hand back, "you'll go over to Doc's table and invite him over for dinner."

"Forget it, Claudia! I refuse to entertain that faker in our house."

Mom's jaw stiffened in determination.

"Well, if you won't invite him, I will!"

"Wait!" Daddy said as she started to get up from the table. "I've got a better idea!"

"What better idea?" Mom gazed down at him skeptically.

"Why don't we send him a complimentary

dessert?"

"Oh, please, Hank. Desserts are already complimentary with the Early Bird Special."

"But only certain desserts," Daddy pointed out.

It's true. Le Chateaubriand Early Birders were entitled to either ice cream, fresh fruit, or key lime pie. Anything else cost extra.

"We'll send him" — Daddy paused dramatically — "the Chateau."

At the mention of Le Chateaubriand's famed "Chateau," Mom's eyes lit up.

The restaurant's pièce de résistance, known for miles around as the ne plus ultra of desserts, the Chateau was an elaborate ice cream and cake concoction molded in the form of a castle, surrounded by a hot fudge moat. The few times I'd seen it ordered, it had been ushered in on a trolley with the kind of fanfare usually reserved for royal coronations.

"That does sound awfully nice," Mom said, sliding back down into her seat. "I just hope it's enough to make up for Doc's pain and suffering. What do you think, Jaine?"

I looked over at Doc and his entourage. By now the gals were practically cutting his meat for him. I decided right then and there that Mom had enough on her hands, taking care of Edna and waiting on Prozac hand

and foot. She didn't need to be whipping up dinner for Doc Wilkins.

"I think the Chateau sounds like a great idea, Mom."

"Okay, Hank," she said, at last gracing him with a smile. "Let's do it!"

"How about I order one for us, too?" Daddy said, still angling for those brownie points.

"You'll do no such thing!" Mom said, coming back down to earth. "The key lime pie is good enough for us. Right, Jaine?"

I, for one, wouldn't have minded taking a swan dive into that hot fudge moat, but I wasn't about to saddle Daddy with the extra cost.

"Oh, yes," I lied. "I'd much rather have the pie."

Daddy signaled the waiter and put in a special order for a Chateau to be delivered to Doc Wilkins's table. And having assuaged her guilt over Doc's black eye, Mom finally began to relax. As she sipped her complimentary glass of Chablis, the cold shoulder that she'd been giving Daddy slowly started to thaw.

"Oh, Hank!" she blushed, when he told her how pretty she looked in her new "plashmere" (polyester cashmere) beaded sweater.

By the time our salads showed up, the ice had totally melted. She was actually laughing at Daddy's knock-knock jokes. And if that isn't true love, I don't know what is.

I picked my way through my Caesar salad, eager to get to the main event.

Daddy had ordered the prime rib; Mom and I, the petit filet mignon.

When my filet showed up, sizzling on my plate and nestled beside a steaming baked potato, I dug in with gusto. So what if there were toddlers out there eating later than me? A steak was a steak. And this one was darn delicious.

When I'd scarfed down every last morsel, I sat back with a contented sigh. Thank heavens for elastic-waist pants.

Glancing over at Mom's plate, I saw she'd eaten only half of hers.

"Aren't you going to finish your steak?" I asked, prepared to nab a bonus bite or two.

"Oh, no! I promised darling Zoloft I'd save her some."

Darn that cat. I was surprised Mom hadn't put her in a capri set and plunked her down at the table with us.

Our entrée dishes were whisked away with clockwork efficiency, the staff eager to turn our table over to the big spenders who showed up after sunset.

"Hope you gals saved room for dessert!" Daddy said as our key lime pies approached.

Fear not. In my tummy, there's a special wing set aside for desserts.

We were just about to dig into our tart treasures when we saw the unmistakable sight of Le Chateaubriand's famed "Chateau" being wheeled in on a trolley from the kitchen.

Everyone turned to admire the towering confection of cake and ice cream.

Doc Wilkins looked up in surprise when the waiter stopped at his table and nodded in our direction.

With a puzzled expression, Doc turned to look at us. Mom waved and nudged Daddy, who once again forced a wooden smile.

Doc, clearly startled by Daddy's largesse, nodded in thanks from across the room.

Even his posse seemed somewhat mollified. Eagerly they picked up their forks and began eating.

"What a wonderful idea that was, Hank," Mom said. "How clever of you to think of it!"

Yep, that wine had done its job, all right.

Daddy took her hand in his, back in her good graces, brownie points scored.

He got to enjoy his marital bliss for all of about seventeen seconds.

Because suddenly all hell broke loose at Doc Wilkins's table.

"Omigod!" one of the gals cried. "He's choking!"

"Somebody call 911!" shrieked the other.

We got up and raced over to their table, where we discovered Doc Wilkins gasping for air, lips rapidly swelling, his face and arms covered with blotchy red hives.

"Oh, heavens!" Mom wailed. "What on earth happened?"

"Are there peanuts in this?" Doc managed to sputter, pointing to the Chateau.

"Oui, monsieur," the waiter replied. "In the moat."

By now Doc's lips had puffed up to balloon-like proportions.

"Ergic oo enuts!" he gasped.

Which we figured, correctly, meant that he was allergic to peanuts.

Luckily, some quick-thinking soul had called 911 and before long the paramedics came charging into the room.

The next thing we knew, they were wheeling Doc out on a gurney.

"Now look what you've done!" one of the posse snarled at Daddy.

He turned to Mom, a pleading look in his eye.

"Surely you can't blame me for this,

Claudia. I had no idea he was allergic to peanuts."

"No, Hank," Mom said wearily. "I don't blame you. It's just horrible luck, that's all."

Daddy sighed with relief, happy to have evaded a return trip to the doghouse.

"We're so sorry about this," Mom said to the posse as they gathered their purses before heading off to the hospital. "Aren't we, Hank?"

"Of course we are," Daddy said in his most conciliatory tone of voice. "And we want you to know, ladies, that if you're not going to finish your Chateau, we'll be happy to take it off your hands."

The posse gaped at him in disbelief. As did Mom. And everyone else within hearing distance.

Some daddies just can't seem to stay out of the doghouse.

CHAPTER TWELVE

With visions of Mom's breakfasts no doubt dancing in her head, Prozac had taken to clawing me awake each day at the ungodly hour of 5:30 a.m.

That next morning was no exception.

There she was, kneading her claws into my flesh, commanding me to snap to attention.

I'd like Eggs Benedict please. With extra hollandaise.

"You'll get leftovers and like it."

I hauled myself out of bed and staggered to the kitchen, where I was happy to find Mom's doggie bag from Le Chateaubriand.

By now I had given up any and all attempts to feed my pampered princess cat food. I cut her some bite-size chunks of filet mignon, nabbing a few for myself, hoping this would tide her over until Mom woke up.

Instantly she buried her nose in the stuff.

I was about to trot back to bed to catch up on my much-needed beauty rest when I happened to glimpse my reflection in the predawn kitchen window. Was it my imagination, or had I gained about 8,798 pounds since I came to Tampa Vistas?

I'm sure you remember that little vow I'd made to start a vigorous exercise and sensible eating regimen. Well, I'm glad you do, because up till that point, it had pretty much been banished to a dusty corner of my brain reserved for dental appointments and memories of my high school prom.

But that glimpse of myself in the window was a wake-up call. Suddenly all the calories I'd been packing away came back to haunt me — yesterday's humungous chopped steak lunch. The filet mignon dinner with all the trimmings. Not to mention my Chunky Monkey excursion, and the Christmas fudge I'd been munching between binges.

No, there was no doubt about it. This feeding frenzy had to stop. From this moment on, calories would be burned. Instead of returning to the soft cocoon of my bed, I would throw on some sweats and take a vigorous walk around Tampa Vistas. Heck, I'd walk all the way to St. Pete if I had to.

Minutes later I was out on the street, me

and my cellulite brimming with determination.

By now the sun was beginning to come up, and I marched along, feeling about as virtuous as a person can feel without attaining actual sainthood.

As I made my way past lawn Santas still wet with dew, my thoughts drifted back to last night's scene at Le Chateaubriand. Daddy had done a lot of foolish things in his time, but there was no way he could have possibly guessed Doc Wilkins would be allergic to peanuts.

Mom had called the hospital the minute we got home to check on his condition, but was unable to get any answers.

I sure hoped he was okay. The last thing Tampa Vistas needed was another corpse for Christmas.

And then, as if in answer to my wishes, I looked up and saw the good doctor striding toward me in a jog suit, his reedy arms swinging weights as he walked.

"Doctor Wilkins!" I cried. "You're okay."

"Of course I'm okay," he assured me with a grin.

Indeed, aside from his black eye and god-awful toupee, he looked quite well.

"They shot me up with antihistamines and I was home in an hour."

"I'm so happy to hear it. My parents and I feel terrible about what happened."

"No need to feel bad, sweetheart. Accidents happen."

"And Daddy feels awful about your black eye, too," I fibbed in the interests of goodwill.

"He ought to," he snapped, his bonhomie fading just a tad. "How your sweet mother stays married to him I'll never know. But I can see you're just like your mother."

And then he winked at me with his good eye.

Good heavens. Was The Toupee Prince actually flirting with me?

"I see you're a walker, like myself. Nothing like a nice energetic walk to start the day. Keeps you healthy. I'm seventy-five years old," he said, tapping his chest proudly, "and the only pills I take are vitamins."

"That's terrific."

"Yep, underneath this jog suit is the body of a thirty-year-old."

Better give it back, I felt like telling him. *You're getting it wrinkled.*

"Go on," he said, holding out his arm. "Feel my muscle."

I gave his arm a reluctant squeeze. It was surprisingly steely for such a skinny guy.

"Well, nice running into you," I said, determined to be on my way before he asked me to squeeze any other body parts.

But then it occurred to me that Doc Wilkins might be a decent source of info about the murder. After all, he seemed to be quite popular with the ladies. Maybe he'd heard a bit of gossip that would prove helpful.

"Gee," I said, "it sure is terrible about what happened to Dr. McCay."

"Frankly, I'm not all that surprised."

"Oh?"

"I could tell the minute I laid eyes on him that he was an oily character. The kind that attracts trouble. Probably had malpractice suits up his wazoo."

I hadn't considered that angle before. Was it possible, I wondered, that Preston had been killed by an angry ex-patient?

"I never did think much of those plastic surgeons," Doc was saying. "Frivolous, if you know what I mean, with their nose jobs and eye lifts. A heart transplant is surgery. A tummy tuck is a joke!"

"Do you think Preston might have been killed by a disgruntled patient?"

"Anything's possible."

"How about at that medical convention? The one where he heard you speak? What was the word on him there?"

"Haven't a clue," he shrugged.

"What about here at Tampa Vistas? Did Preston have any enemies that you know of?"

"Whoa, there, little lady. Why all the questions?"

Oops. Looks like I'd come on a little too strong.

"Watching too many TV crime shows, I guess. I just can't get over the fact that someone was murdered right here in my parents' retirement community. Everyone I've met so far seems so nice. It's hard to believe one of them might be a killer."

"Don't fret, sweetheart. For all we know, Dr. McCay cut the wire himself."

I blinked in surprise. "Why on earth would he do that?"

"Last year I played Jacob Marley in *A Christmas Carol.* That old battle-axe Gloria Di Nardo directed. What a nightmare. The woman is enough to drive anyone to suicide."

And with one last wink for the road, he left me to resume his constitutional.

I came back from my walk ready to eat the wallpaper. That's the trouble with exercise. It makes you so darn hungry. But luckily for my thighs, I was too exhausted to fix myself something to eat. Instead I tumbled back into bed, where I promptly fell into a deep sleep.

Around eight o'clock I was wakened by the smell of bacon frying. I trundled off to the kitchen, where I found Mom and Daddy at the breakfast nook, Mom staring off into space while Daddy cursed at his crossword puzzle.

Completing the family tableau was Prozac, her pink nose buried in one of Mom's good china dishes, sucking up the remains of last night's steak tidbits.

I could tell by the way Mom was picking at her eggs that she was still worried about Doc.

"Good morning, sweetheart," she said, catching sight of me. "There's some bacon and eggs on the stove. Help yourself. But don't finish the bacon. Zoloft might want some later."

Prozac glanced up at me from her steak.

I like the crispy pieces.

"Would you believe they made another mistake in the puzzle, Lambchop?" Daddy said as I helped myself to a heaping plate of bacon and eggs, my sensible eating plan biting the dust, as you knew it would. "As soon as I finish putting up the tree, I'm going to write a very stern letter to the editor."

"How can you even think about your puzzle," Mom huffed, "when we may very well have sent poor Doc Wilkins to his deathbed last night?"

"Not to worry, Mom," I said, sliding onto the banquette, next to her. "I was out walking earlier this morning and ran into him. He's all better. In the pink of health. Apparently all he needed last night was a shot of antihistamine."

"Omigosh! That's wonderful. I swear, I didn't sleep a wink worrying about the poor man."

"Of course he's all right," Daddy grunted. "I'm telling you, the guy's a faker. He's been fine all along."

"Don't try my patience, Hank." Mom shot him a death-ray glare. "I still haven't forgiven you for asking Yolanda and LuAnn for their dessert."

Reminded of his doghouse status, Daddy dropped his Doc Wilkins theory and went back to cursing the crossword puzzle. And now that she knew Doc was fit as a fiddle, Mom dug into her eggs with gusto.

"We have to do something nice for Doc," she said, buttering a piece of toast, "to make up for all the trouble Daddy caused."

Daddy opened his mouth to object but

quickly clamped it shut again when Mom lobbed him another death-ray glare.

"Maybe I'll order him something from the shopping channel," she mused.

The thought of buying a gift for his Ping-Pong nemesis was too much for Daddy.

"Oh, for Pete's sake," he muttered, clasping his puzzle to his chest and marching out to the living room.

"Have you had enough to eat, sweetheart?" Mom asked "darling Zoloft," who was by now curled up in her lap.

Prozac arched her back, demanding an after-breakfast love scratch.

"You don't mind doing the dishes while I scratch darling Zoloft, do you, Jaine?"

Prozac yawned lazily.

Be sure and rinse before you load.

One of these days, I'm going to put that cat up for adoption.

After doing the dishes, I headed off to shower and dress. By the time I was through, Mom had torn herself away from Prozac and gone next door to check on Edna. In the living room Daddy had resumed work on the Christmas tree from hell, which still refused to rotate if the tree's lights were on.

Scattered about him on the floor were what had to be every tool in his toolbox.

I tiptoed past him out the front door, happy to resume my investigation without Daddy on my tail.

It was time to pay a return visit to Gloria Di Nardo. As those of you taking notes will no doubt recall, Ginny Knight said she'd seen Gloria sneaking into the clubhouse on the eve of the murder.

Had Gloria been paying an after-hours visit to the gym? Taking a midnight dip in the pool? Or had she dropped by to tamper with a cable and send her leading man plummeting to his death?

"Jaine, *ma chérie!*"

Gloria greeted me in another of her flowing caftans, this one splashed with hibiscus flowers the size of baseballs.

"Entrez, entrez!" she said, ushering me into her gold-flocked living room. "I was just signing my Christmas cards."

She trotted over to an ornate puff of a desk, where a bunch of photo cards were splayed out.

"Lovely, aren't they?" she said, handing me one.

I blinked back my surprise to see, under the message *Warmest Holiday Wishes,* a publicity shot of Gloria from her Secaucus Dinner Theater days.

"That's me as Mrs. Bob Cratchit, in a little play I wrote called *A Very Cratchit Christmas.* It's *A Christmas Carol* told from Mrs. Cratchit's point of view. In my version Tiny Tim isn't on crutches, but he does have a most disabling attention deficit disorder."

"Sounds fascinating," I lied.

"Oh, it was," she assured me. "Anyhow, sweetie, as long as you're here, you may as well save me the postage and take a card for your parents."

She quickly inscribed one of her Christmas head shots and handed it to me.

"I'm sure they'll love it," I fibbed, slipping it into my purse.

"So to what do I owe the pleasure?" she asked. Then her face lit up. "I know! You've come to see Volume II of my scrapbook!"

"No!" I cried before I could stop myself. "I mean, I wouldn't dream of taking up your time when you're so busy with your Christmas cards."

And then I trotted out the excuse I'd invented to explain my visit.

"I just stopped by because there's an ugly rumor going around Tampa Vistas that I think you should know about."

This phony rumor ploy had worked so well with Ginny, I figured I'd use it again.

"Oh?" She raised an inquisitive brow.

"Apparently, someone saw you sneaking into the clubhouse on the eve of Preston's murder, and people are saying that you went there to tamper with the cable on his gingerbread man costume."

"What a monstrous lie!" she cried, flushing as pink as the hibiscus on her caftan.

"So you weren't at the clubhouse that night?"

"Well, actually," she said, with a nervous cough, "I did happen to pop by. But I can assure you I went nowhere near that cable."

"What were you doing there?"

"If you must know, *chérie,* I went to get some bourbon."

"Bourbon? I didn't know they sold bourbon at the clubhouse."

"They don't."

I shook my head, puzzled. "I don't understand."

She plopped down with a sigh on her red velvet hooker sofa.

"That scene at the Chinese restaurant with Preston and his aerobics bimbo was most upsetting, and naturally I needed to ease my turmoil with a wee bit of bourbon."

"Naturally." I nodded, oozing sympathy.

"But when I got home, I realized I was out of Jack Daniel's. I didn't feel like driving all the way over to the liquor store. So I went to the clubhouse. I keep a spare bottle backstage. Trust me, darling. I need it, working with these amateurs here at Tampa Vistas."

A stash of backstage bourbon? Yikes. And I was ashamed of the emergency M&M's I keep in my glove compartment.

The question was — was Gloria telling the truth? I'd seen her guzzle her Jack Daniel's, so I could easily picture her zipping over to the clubhouse for a quick nip. But Gloria was an actress. For all I knew, this was just a performance and she was lying through her teeth.

"Exactly where," she now asked, with an indignant heave of her bosom, "did you hear this disgusting rumor?"

Time for some fancy tap dancing.

"Um, at the clubhouse pool. I overheard some ladies talking."

"Well, I'm going over there right now," she said, leaping to her feet, "to shut those biddies up."

Oh, hell. The last thing I needed was World War III breaking out over my trumped-up rumor.

"But they're not there anymore! They left to go Christmas shopping."

Much to my relief, she sat back down again.

"Besides, it was just idle chatter," I said, my tap shoes working overtime. "I should've never even told you about it. In fact, if I see those ladies again, I'll be sure and set them straight."

"You do that."

She forced a faint smile, but I could tell by her furrowed brow that she was still steamed.

"Gee, look at the time," I said. "I've really got to run. But would it be okay if I used your restroom before I go? Too much coffee for breakfast, I'm afraid."

"Of course, hon," she replied with an absent wave of her hand. "It's down the hall to your left."

I scooted down the hall to her bathroom. I did not, however, need to use her facilities. No, I had another mission in mind.

Once inside her guest bathroom (where a framed photo of Gloria as Auntie Mame hung over the commode), I looked around but did not find what I was searching for.

Back out in the hallway, I heard Gloria on the phone, grousing to somebody about the busybody gossips at Tampa Vistas.

"I should've never left New Jersey!" I heard her wail.

Taking a chance that she'd continue her rant for a while longer, I tiptoed down the hallway to her bedroom.

Here, in her private quarters, she'd abandoned her bordello motif for a Turkish harem theme. Gauzy curtains hung from her canopy bed and a small fountain tinkled near the window.

But I didn't care about her decor. The only thing I cared about was what I saw next — right there on Gloria's dresser, next to a bottle of Calvin Klein's Obsession — my thirty-five-dollar natural bristle hairbrush.

If Gloria thought she was going to get away with practically stealing it from under my nose, she had another think coming!

With a triumphant "hah!" I slipped it in my purse and headed down the hallway.

Back in the living room Gloria was still on the phone.

"I pour my heart's blood into these productions," she was moaning, "and what do I get for it? Aggravation!"

At this point in her narrative, I waved good-bye and left, feeling quite proud of myself.

I'd solved the Case of the Stolen Hairbrush. Now all I had to do was solve the pesky little problem of Preston's murder.

Chapter Thirteen

Let's take a stroll down Suspect Lane, shall we?

Both Raymond and Gloria had been seen sneaking into the clubhouse. Raymond claimed to have been fixing a leak in the men's room, while Gloria said she'd popped by for a harmless nip of bourbon. I wasn't quite sure I believed them. But at that point, I had no proof whatsoever that either of them went anywhere near the cable that sent Preston hurtling to his death.

Same with Laurette. True, I had my suspicions that underneath her cool exterior, she was simmering with rage, but that's all I had. My suspicions.

As for Ginny Knight? She may have been a gold digger of the highest order, but she sure wasn't much of a suspect. After all, Preston had been worth far more to her alive than dead.

So there you have it. Suspects: 3 1/2.

Pieces of actual evidence: 0.

Feeling a tad frustrated, I decided to take a break from the case and tackle my Christmas shopping.

For once I would not put it off till the last minute. I would get the whole mess over with eons in advance — five whole days before Christmas.

After assuring Daddy I would not be going anywhere near a murder suspect, I left him cursing his topless Christmas tree and tooled over to the mall in Mom's Camry.

"Don't park next to a white van," Mom had warned me as I set out. "Nine out of ten abductions happen in white vans."

Where she gets these facts, I'll never know.

A half hour later, after parking between two white vans (it was the only spot I could find), I strode into the mall, firm of jaw and spirit, determined not to buy Daddy the same boring sports shirt I buy him year after year, or Mom the same old Youth-Dew perfume.

With five whole days before Christmas, surely I'd have a cornucopia of interesting and unusual gifts from which to choose.

Of course, that was the trouble. Too many choices. I wandered around, picking up atomic alarm clocks, monogrammed mouse pads, Waterford beer steins, hand-painted vases, pashmina shawls, Emeril Lagasse steak knives, and Martha Stewart tea cozies.

Within fifteen minutes I was paralyzed with indecision, plodding glassy-eyed from store to store, reprising my annual role as an extra from *Dawn of the Dead.*

All the while, Frosty, Rudolph, and Alvin and his dratted Chipmunks crooned endless holiday ditties over the PA. Around about the time Mel Tormé was yearning for some chestnuts roasting on an open fire, all I was capable of choosing was a chocolate waffle cone at the Dairy Queen.

You know where this is going, right? After three hours of agony, I wound up buying a sports shirt for Daddy and some Youth-Dew for Mom.

Uncle Ed got a tie (forget the fact that he's retired and hasn't worn one in years); Aunt Clara, the woman who hates to cook, an apron. Cousin Joanie and her husband, Brad, got a garden gnome for their high-rise condo. And little Dexter, their son, got a battery-operated robot, which I was certain he'd destroy before his father even installed the batteries.

For Prozac, I chose a squeaky toy. And for my two best friends back in Los Angeles, my neighbor Lance, and my girlfriend Kandi, I bought the ever-popular gift of the truly desperate, scented candles.

Weighed down with packages and feelings of inadequacy, I started for the parking lot. Trudging along, I happened to pass a cutesie little shop called *How Does Your Garden Grow?* Displayed in the window were exotic plants, wicker baskets, and frilly gardening gloves.

But the window display wasn't what caught my eye.

There, standing on the checkout line, was Laurette Kendall.

Unable to resist the lure of a hot suspect, I made my way inside the shop. Fortunately, it was crowded and Laurette didn't notice as I watched her from behind a display of wicker baskets.

By now it was her turn at the register.

"I'd like to return these," she said to a slack-jawed teenage girl with hair the color of traffic cones.

Laurette handed her a pair of pruning sheers.

"Were they defective in any way?" the teenager asked, barely stifling a yawn.

"No, I tried them out and decided I didn't like them, that's all."

And right away I couldn't help wondering if she'd tried them out — not to prune her bougainvillea — but to fray the cable on

Preston's gingerbread man costume. Yet, why return them to the store? Why not just toss them in the nearest Dumpster, like nine out of ten other murder weapons?

I was mulling over this pivotal question when suddenly I heard a familiar voice shouting:

"Stop! In the name of the law!"

Good heavens, it was Daddy! The sneaky Pete had been tailing me again!

Now he charged over to Laurette.

"Hank Austen! What on earth are you shouting about?"

She shot him a withering glare, but Daddy refused to be withered.

"I'm making a citizen's arrest."

"Of who?"

"Of you."

"Me?!" she gasped.

"Call 911," Daddy instructed the now wide-eyed teen, "and tell them I've got the murder weapon in the Gingerbread Man Murder."

At last awakened from her torpor, the salesgirl reached for the phone.

"I've always suspected you were mentally unstable, Hank," Laurette snapped. "But now I'm sure of it."

Immune to her scorn, Daddy charged ahead in full-tilt District Attorney mode.

"I submit that you used these shears to tamper with the wire on Preston's gingerbread man costume."

"You really have lost your mind." She shook her perfectly coiffed pageboy in disbelief.

"And now, having no more use for it, you're returning it to get your money back."

"Oh, please. If I'd really used these shears to fray that cable, I would've thrown them in the bay and not brought them back to the store with my fingerprints all over them."

"We'll let a jury decide that," Daddy said, arms clamped firmly across chest.

"Besides," Laurette pointed out, "I couldn't have possibly used these shears to tamper with the cable."

"Why not?" Daddy asked.

"Because I just bought them yesterday, and the murder happened four days ago."

Oopsy. Major oopsy.

But Daddy was not about to give up.

"How do I know you bought them yesterday?"

"It says so right here on the receipt, sir," the salesgirl piped up.

"Oh, well," he blustered, clearly desperate to save face. "In that case, you're free to go."

"I'm free to go?" Laurette said. "Of all the colossal nerve!"

By now icicles were dripping from her every syllable.

"See you around the clubhouse," Daddy said in a pathetic attempt to mend the fence he'd just smashed.

He started for the door, but his exit was blocked by two refrigerator-sized security guards.

"What's going on here?" one of them wanted to know.

"This guy is nuts," the salesgirl said. "He tried to arrest this lady."

"I was just exercising my rights as a concerned citizen!"

"He accused her of killing a gingerbread man."

"I made a little mistake, that's all."

"Was he harassing you, ma'am?" one of the refrigerators asked Laurette.

"He most certainly was."

"Would you like to press charges?"

"I most certainly would." That said with a triumphant smirk.

"You'll have to come with us, sir."

The security goons took Daddy by the arms and were about to haul him away.

As much as I was tempted, I couldn't let this happen.

"Wait!" I said, emerging from behind the wicker baskets.

Laurette blinked in surprise.

"Jaine! Have you been hiding behind those baskets all along?"

"Sort of," I confessed.

"The apple doesn't fall far from the tree," she sniffed.

Clearly, I had joined Daddy on her list of Least Admired People.

"Daddy didn't mean any harm, Laurette. He's been under a lot of pressure lately, putting together a rotating Christmas tree. I'm sure he's very sorry, aren't you, Daddy?"

I poked him a sharp one in the ribs.

"Yeah," he said grudgingly, "I'm really sorry."

"So let's let bygones be bygones," I said to Laurette, "and wish each other a Merry Christmas. Please. Take this lavender-scented candle with our very best wishes."

"Oh, all right. But only because I happen to be fond of your mother, and I'm a sucker for lavender."

She instructed the security goons to let Daddy go, and together Daddy and I slunk out of the store, past the small knot of shoppers who'd gathered to catch all the action.

"I told you I was just going Christmas shopping," I grumbled. "Why did you have to follow me?"

"Let me carry your packages," Daddy said, eagerly taking some from my hands. "They must be heavy."

"Don't try to change the subject. Why were you following me?"

"Because I love you, Lambchop, and don't want anything bad happening to you."

I gazed up into his hazel eyes rimmed with crow's-feet, and saw so much love, it was hard to stay angry. It's at times like these that I can see why Mom has put up with him all these years.

"You won't tell Mom about what happened with Laurette, will you?" he asked as we approached the Camry.

"Only if you agree to stop tailing me."

"Okay," he agreed reluctantly. "But I still say Laurette's the killer."

"C'mon, Daddy. First you thought it was Edna. And just the other day you swore it was Gloria."

"This time I know I'm right. Laurette's a natural-born killer if I ever saw one. Maybe those shears in the shop weren't the ones she used to fray the cable. But I've seen her working in her garden. I bet she's got a bunch of pruning shears. Who's to say she didn't use one of those?"

If truth be told, I'd been wondering the exact same thing.

Chapter Fourteen

Mom was in the living room when we got home, tearing open a package from the shopping channel.

"Look what just came!" She held up a tiny pink sweater with what looked like four sleeves.

"Isn't it adorable?"

Daddy squinted at it from where he was stretched out on the recliner, recuperating from his recent run-in with the mall security goons.

"What the heck is it?"

"A cashmere hoodie," Mom beamed, "for darling Zoloft!"

Wait just a cotton-pickin' minute. I get a cotton/poly flamingo T-shirt, and the cat gets cashmere? What's wrong with this picture?

"I saw it the other day," Mom said, "and couldn't resist. I even spent six dollars extra for express delivery." She gazed at the sweater in admiration, fluffing up the tiny hood. "It's just so darn cute, I don't think I'll be able to wait until Christmas to give it to her. Jaine, sweetheart, go find the little angel and I'll try it on her right now."

I found the little angel in the guest bedroom, hard at work clawing my good suede boots.

Up to now, Prozac had Mom fooled with her wide-eyed Adorable Act, but she would soon reveal her true colors. This was a cat who threw a major hissy fit if you so much as put a bell on her collar. Forget about trying to put on a sweater. All hell would break loose. And I, for one, wanted a front row seat when Mom discovered the truth about her "darling Zoloft."

"Let's see how long Mom hand-feeds you steak tidbits now," I muttered, carrying Prozac out into the living room.

"Here she is, Mom!"

"Look what Grandma got you for Christmas," Mom said, waving the sweater.

Prozac sniffed at it much like she sniffs at a vet with a hypodermic needle.

And suddenly I felt a tad guilty. I couldn't let Mom walk blindly into the bloodbath that was sure to follow.

"Mom, she really doesn't like wearing clothing."

"Don't be silly, Jaine. She's going to love her new Christmas sweater."

"Okey doke," I said, handing her the furry ball of dynamite that was about to explode.

Can't say I didn't warn her.

Mom trotted over to the sofa and settled a strangely compliant Prozac on her lap. And then, much to my amazement, Prozac actually let Mom zip her into the hoodie. Nary a peep when she put the hood over her ears. Not only that, she actually looked up at Mom with worshipful kitty eyes.

That calculating devil knew exactly what she was doing. If it had been me trying to zip her into that thing, I would've been halfway to the emergency room by now.

And then — get this — the little ham started prancing around the living room in her pink cashmere hoodie like a runway model in Milan.

"Isn't she just precious?" Mom gushed.

"Just precious," I grumbled through gritted teeth.

At which point Prozac peeked up at me from under her cashmere hood.

I'm hoping she'll leave me money in her will.

Mom raced to get the camera and spent the next five minutes snapping photos of her cashmere-clad angel. When she'd finally shot enough poses to fill an album, she plopped down on the sofa with a contented sigh.

"Guess what I did while you two were gone this afternoon?" she said. "I called Doc Wilkins and invited him to dinner. And please, Hank." She held up her hand to ward off any objections. "No arguments."

"I'm not arguing," he said with a genial smile. After his little incident at the mall, he was obviously unwilling to make waves. "If that's what you think we should do, Claudia, that's what we'll do."

"You promise you'll behave yourself?"

"Of course I'll behave, honey."

She eyed him uncertainly.

"Really? I was sure you'd put up a fight."

"Honey, when you're right, you're right. I sent the poor guy to the hospital. It's the least we can do to have him over for a meal."

"Thanks heavens you're being so sensible!"

"I always try to be sensible, darling."

Man, he was pouring it on.

And apparently it was working. Mom got up and rewarded him with a peck on his check.

But this picture of marital bliss came screeching to a halt just seconds later, when the phone rang.

"I'll get that," Daddy said, jumping up

from the recliner.

I could practically see the wheels spinning in his brain. *Could it possibly be Laurette, calling to blab about what happened at the mall?*

"Don't bother, sweetheart," Mom said, pushing him down again. "Sit back and relax. It's probably Edna. I told her to check in with me."

"It's no problem," Daddy said, racing for the phone.

By now Mom's antennae were up. She smelled trouble. Daddy was a guy who, under normal circumstances, had to be surgically removed from his recliner.

Mom sprinted ahead of him to the kitchen phone and managed to grab the receiver.

"Hello? . . . Oh, hello, Laurette."

Shoulders sagging in defeat, Daddy slinked back to his recliner, a doomed man. I stuck around to listen.

"He what?" Mom gasped. "A citizen's arrest? . . . Accusing you of murder? . . . Jaine? . . . Hiding? . . . Behind the wicker baskets?"

Uh-oh, it looked like Daddy wasn't the only one headed for the guillotine.

After profuse apologies to Laurette, Mom hung up and came storming back to the living room, fire burning in her eyes.

"How on earth could you accuse Laurette Kendall of murder? The woman has been president of the Tampa Vistas gardening club five years in a row."

"She looked guilty to me," Daddy said with a sheepish shrug.

"Hank Austen, I think you've finally gone off the deep end. First thing tomorrow, you're going to see Dr. May and get a thorough examination. I don't care if we have to wait in his office all day for an appointment."

Then it was my turn.

"And what on earth were you doing hiding behind those wicker baskets, Jaine?"

"I wasn't hiding," I lied. "I just happened to be shopping in the store at the time."

She shot me a look positively dripping with skepticism.

"Honestly, you two!"

And with that, she stomped back to the kitchen to crack open the Christmas fudge. By now, she was on box number five.

"Are you sure you don't want to come with us, Lambchop?" Daddy asked.

He and Mom were standing at the front door in their holiday finest (a *Rudolph the Red-Nosed Reindeer* sweater for Mom, and a *Generation Rx* sweatshirt for Daddy), about to take off for a Christmas party down the street.

"The Shusters always have such fun parties!" Mom said.

Only if your idea of fun is playing Pin the Toupee on the Bald Guy and Spin the Bottle of Mylanta.

"That's okay, Mom. I'd really rather stay home. But you guys enjoy yourselves."

"I'll try," Daddy said, "but it'd be a lot easier to enjoy myself if your mom would start speaking to me again."

Mom had been giving him the cold shoulder ever since Laurette's phone call, but I suspected she would quickly thaw after a glass or two of eggnog.

"Good night, my precious angel," she said, blowing a kiss to Prozac, who — still in her cashmere hoodie — was rubbing against Mom's ankles with wild abandon. "There's leftover salmon in the fridge," Mom said to me, "in case she gets hungry. Don't forget to crumble it into tiny pieces. She doesn't like it too chunky."

Prozac swished a bossy tail in my direction.

Yeah, not too chunky.

The minute my parents left, she started clawing impatiently at her hoodie.

Get me out of this stupid sweater, willya?

It's like a sauna in here.

I was sorely tempted to let her stew in her own cashmere, but I knew she'd claw it to shreds and somehow blame me for it, so reluctantly I helped her out of it, sustaining only a few minor wounds in the process.

Fifteen minutes later I was stretched out in the guest bathtub, up to my neck in something called Peach Nectarine Bubble Bath and Body Velvet (only $16.99, plus shipping and handling — and guaranteed to leave my body soft and supple as a newborn babe's).

After that embarrassing confrontation with Laurette, it felt good to unwind.

I intended to spend the rest of the night vegging out and watching corny Christmas movies on TV, a bag of white chocolate macadamia nut cookies at my side.

(Okay, so I stopped off at Mrs. Fields while I was at the mall.)

But alas, that was not to be. Somehow, after changing into my jammies and settling down in the den, I just couldn't get into those movies (although I managed to polish off the white chocolate macadamia nut cookies without any problem).

Even *Christmas in Connecticut,* with Barbara Stanwyck in her glorious black-and-white heyday, failed to enchant. In spite of myself, my mind kept drifting back to the murder. I couldn't help feeling I'd let Edna down.

Poor Edna.

Alive, Preston broke her heart. And dead, he'd made her a murder suspect. So much suffering over such a ghastly guy. And there was no doubt in my mind that Preston McCay had been a slimebucket of the highest order.

I thought about my encounter with Doc Wilkins that morning, how he said he wouldn't be surprised if Preston had been hit with a bunch of malpractice suits.

Was it possible that there was an angry ex-patient of Preston's here at Tampa Vistas? Someone whose surgery he'd botched? Someone eager for revenge?

Just out of curiosity, I decided to check out Preston's medical past on the Internet.

Logging on to my parents' computer, I found one of those doctor rating sites, where patients post medical reviews. I slotted in Preston's name, crossing my fingers that he'd be listed.

Bingo. There he was. And just as Doc Wilkins suspected, he had several clunker reviews. True, there were also some raves (written, I suspected, under duress by members of his own staff), but most of the posts were angry diatribes about what an arrogant, uncaring bastard he'd been and what a mess he'd made of their noses/thighs/crow's-feet.

Unfortunately all the posters were anonymous. So I had no idea if any of them were living here at Tampa Vistas. It was the same way on all the other rate-a-doctor sites. No names, just gripes. And no indication of whether or not he'd been sued for malpractice.

And then it occurred to me that if Preston had been sued, it might have been covered in his local newspaper.

I remembered Preston bragging about how he'd had one of the most successful plastic surgery practices in Cleveland. So I logged on to the *Cleveland Plain Dealer,* and searched for Preston in their archives.

The first headline that popped up was PRESTON MCCAY NAMED PRESIDENT OF THE LOCAL MEDICAL SOCIETY.

For crying out loud. In spite of complaints up his wazoo, Preston had been a honcho in the medical society. Remind me never to get sick in Cleveland.

I scrolled down past a few other innocuous headlines until I got to one, dated back about ten years, that stopped me in my tracks:

LOCAL WOMAN COMMITS SUICIDE OVER PLASTIC SURGERY.

Wasting no time, I clicked on the story.

It turned out the woman who killed herself was a 42-year-old gal named Pam who had been despondent for months over a botched eye lift by Preston. After losing a long, drawn-out malpractice suit, she did the unthinkable and took her own life, leaving behind her husband, Jim, 46.

And her 12-year-old daughter, Ginny.

Oh, yes. One more thing. Their last name was Knight.

Chapter Fifteen

So Ginny had a motive to kill Preston. And a darn good one. The man was responsible for her mother's death. Suddenly my image of her as a gold-digging trophy wife crumbled. Maybe she'd wormed her way into Preston's life not to marry him but to murder him.

The next day I was waiting for her at the pool after her aerobics class.

"Oh, hi there," she beamed, a vision in hot pink spandex. "Do we need to re-sked your appointment?"

"No," I said, handing her a printout of the newspaper story. "We need to talk."

Five minutes later we were seated across from each other in the Tampa Vistas Café — Ginny with a gooey cheese Danish and me with a cup of the café's watery coffee. (Honest. In a moment of rare restraint, that's all I ordered.)

"You some sort of private eye?" she asked,

eyeing me warily.

"Part-time, semiprofessional. Mainly, I'm a writer. Small space ads, brochures, industrial films —"

"Whatever." She tapped the newspaper printout with a hot pink fingernail. "You plan to go to the cops with this?"

"That depends," I said, "on whether you murdered Preston."

"Would you blame me if I had?" she asked, her eyes flashing with anger. "The bastard killed my mother just the same as if he'd stabbed her through the heart."

"You want to tell me about it?"

"Not really. But it looks like I don't have a choice."

For a minute I thought she was going to take a nibble of her Danish to give her strength for the ordeal ahead, but then she decided against it.

"My mom was a beautiful woman, the kind of woman whose whole life revolved around her looks. And when the wrinkles started coming, she panicked. So she foolishly cashed in what little money we had to get an eye lift from Preston. She'd heard from her hairdresser that he was supposed to be good. Well, her hairdresser couldn't have been more wrong. When it was all over, one eye was lower than the other. She looked worse than when she started. Far worse."

I shook my head in sympathy.

"She sued Preston for malpractice, but she'd shot our savings on the surgery, and all she could afford was some low-rent ambulance chaser. Preston's barracuda insurance attorneys ate him for breakfast. The bastard walked away without having to pay a cent."

Ouch.

"My mother was never a very stable woman, and this just destroyed her. She was convinced her looks were shot, and she hung herself.

"Lucky me," she said with a bitter laugh. "I discovered her body."

"Oh, God. How awful."

"It all went downhill from there. Daddy hit the bottle and took a powder. I was put in a series of foster homes that made the gang in *Oliver Twist* look like *The Waltons.* And Preston? He got named president of the medical association. That's justice for you."

By now she had totally forgotten about her Danish. Not me. I'm ashamed to admit I eyed it covetously, yearning to bite into the creamy cheese oozing from the pastry seams.

"Years passed," Ginny was saying, "and then one day I was in the waiting room at a tanning salon when I happened to glance down at an abandoned newspaper. And there was Preston's picture. It had been decades since I'd seen him last, but I'd never forgotten that smug, self-satisfied smile. I read that he was giving up his practice and retiring to Tampa Vistas. My mother was in her grave, and this bum was retiring to Florida."

She shook her head in disgust.

"I knew then what I had to do. I'd saved up quite a bundle working as a stripper, so I bribed the aerobics instructor at Tampa Vistas to quit her job and recommend me for the gig."

"Wait a minute. You're not really an aerobics instructor?"

"Nah. I bought a fake certification and got some exercises off the Internet. These old biddies don't know the difference."

Clearly, Ginny had not majored in scruples in reform school.

"So you moved here to kill Preston."

"Kill him? Hell, no! I'm a bad girl, but not that bad."

I dunno about that. She looked pretty naughty to me.

"I was going to rob him blind and steal

every cent the bastard made. True, I had to sleep with him to put my plan in motion. But the good news is the mattress action was over with in seconds. Then he'd roll over and conk out. And as soon as I heard him snoring, I'd sneak down to his den. It took me a while, but I managed to get my hands on his Social Security number, his mother's maiden name, and the password to all his bank and brokerage accounts."

What a busy little bee she'd been.

"My boyfriend and I were going to clean him out and then run off to the Dominican Republic and start a new life. We had phony identification papers all lined up.

"That's where I made my mistake," she sighed. "If only I'd taken the money then. But no, I stuck around. I wanted to wipe Preston out on our wedding day and leave him stranded at the altar, to destroy him just like he destroyed Mom.

"But as you know, before wedding bells could ring, he took a swan dive onto the clubhouse stage and broke his neck. And now it's too late. All his assets are frozen in probate. And all I'm walking away with is my engagement ring — which turned out to be fake, by the way — and the crummy cameo he left me in his will."

She reached over and picked up the printout still lying on the table between us.

"So rat on me to the cops if you want. But I didn't kill Preston. And this newspaper story doesn't prove that I did."

With that, she ripped the printout in two and sashayed out the door.

And as soon as I finished her Danish, I sashayed out after her.

What do you think? Was Ginny telling the truth? Was she merely a thief and not a killer? Or was she just a very convincing liar? (Bad girls often are, you know.)

Had she tiptoed over to the cable on opening night of *The Gingerbread Cookie That Saved Christmas* and sliced it when nobody was looking?

I needed to pay another visit to Raymond, the genial handyman, to see if he remembered seeing her anywhere near the pulley.

I found him seated behind his battered desk in the maintenance building, making notes on a clipboard.

"*Hola,* Ms. Austen," he said, flashing me an impish smile. "Come to accuse me of murder again? If so, I'm afraid you're going to be disappointed. I'm still not the killer."

Up close I could see he was working out a schedule for the maintenance crew, using one of the prop gingerbread cookies from

Edna's play as a paperweight.

Interesting that he still hadn't thrown out those cookies. Was he keeping them as a happy memento, perhaps, of the night Preston bit the dust?

"Actually I came to ask you a question about Ginny Knight. The aerobics instructor."

"Ah," he nodded. "The hot tamale."

"Apparently she was seen backstage the night of the murder."

"*Sí.* She came to visit Preston in his dressing room."

"Did you notice if she went anywhere near the cable?"

"So now you think she's the killer? What a relief." He mopped his brow with an exaggerated swipe of his hand. "I'm off the hook."

Quite the wise guy, wasn't he?

"Sorry to disappoint you again, Ms. Austen, but I didn't see Ginny near the pulley. That doesn't mean she wasn't there. I was working my tail off and wasn't exactly keeping track of her whereabouts."

A fat lot of help he was.

I was about to bid him a not-so-fond adieu when the door opened and a stocky guy in coveralls came clomping in.

"Qué pasa, Manuel?" Raymond asked.

So this was Manuel, the guy who had given Raymond his alibi the night of the murder.

Raymond picked up one of the prop cookies and began fidgeting with it. Was it my imagination, or did he seem a tad uneasy?

"Guess I'll be going," I said.

With a jaunty wave, I headed outside.

But I was not about to go anywhere. Instead I was careful to leave the door open a crack, the better to engage in one of my favorite activities: eavesdropping.

The bad news is that Raymond and Manuel conducted their conversation in Spanish. The good news is that, having lived in L.A. all my life, I'm practically an honorary Hispanic. So when Manuel happened to mention the word *dinero,* I knew they were talking about money.

Always a topic of interest in a murder investigation.

I hung around, hoping to catch a few more tidbits, but aside from a few *muys* and *por favors,* I heard nothing I could translate.

Then Miguel was saying adios.

My cue to dive behind a nearby shrub.

With yucca fronds up my nose, I watched Manuel step outside the maintenance building with an envelope in his hand. He then reached into the envelope and took out a small wad of money.

Whoa. What was Raymond doing giving Manuel an envelope full of *dinero?*

I had a hard time believing Tampa Vistas paid their employees in cash. Surely they issued checks like every other corporation in the Western world.

I supposed it could've been a Christmas bonus. Or a friendly loan.

Then again, maybe Manuel was collecting his payoff for giving Raymond an alibi for the night of the murder.

Chapter Sixteen

That's the trouble with solving murders. Just when you think you're zeroing in on a hot suspect, another one pops up who seems just as guilty. I started back home, see-sawing between Ginny and Raymond as my Most Likely Suspect.

Periodically I glanced behind me to see if Daddy was on my tail, but it hardly seemed likely.

True to her threat, Mom had frog-marched Daddy to Dr. May's office early that morning without an appointment. Which meant they could be sitting in the waiting room for weeks to come.

But when I opened the front door, I heard them talking in the kitchen.

"How did everything go?" I asked, joining them.

"A total waste of time," Daddy said, helping himself to a V8 from the fridge. "Dr. May said I was perfectly fine."

Mom rolled her eyes.

"His exact words were, 'He's no crazier than usual, Claudia.' "

"That's not how I remember it," Daddy huffed and marched out to the living room to do battle with his topless Christmas tree.

"Oh, well," Mom sighed when he was gone. "I suppose Dr. May is right. Daddy's no worse than usual. And besides, I can't afford to waste one more minute worrying about him. I've got to figure out what I'm going to make Doc Wilkins for dinner tonight."

Soon I was sitting with her at the kitchen table, surrounded by a sea of cookbooks.

After much deliberation, she decided on a menu of chicken cordon bleu, roasted potatoes, and string beans almondine, with split pea soup for a starter and chocolate mousse for dessert.

If this was how Mom made amends, I could see why Daddy was always getting them into trouble.

"You think Doc Wilkins will like it?" she asked, worry lines furrowing her brow.

"Of course he will."

"And what about you, sweetheart?" she asked Prozac, who was napping atop *The Joy of Cooking.* "Do you like chicken cordon bleu?"

"Oh, for crying out loud, Mom, she'll eat anything that isn't nailed to her bowl. Except cat food, of course. I think you've broken her of that habit for good."

"Why do you make her eat that smelly goop, anyway?" Mom said, wrinkling her nose in disgust. "I'm sure it tastes simply vile. Doesn't it, Zoloft, darling?"

Prozac looked up at her with Little Orphan Annie eyes.

You can't imagine how I suffer.

Somehow Mom managed to tear herself away from her suffering angel long enough to write out a grocery list.

"You don't mind going to the market for me, do you, Jaine? I want to do a little housecleaning."

Yeah, right, if by housecleaning she meant spending the next half hour giving Prozac a belly rub.

I headed off to the market, where I dutifully bought everything on Mom's list — plus a carton or two of Chunky Monkey. (Just in case a hurricane should hit, it never hurts to stock up on staples.)

Back home I found Mom in the dining room, in an advanced state of panic.

"Oh, Jaine! Terrible news!"

"You're not making the mousse, after all?"

"Look!" she cried, pointing to a white lace

tablecloth on the dining table (only $59.95, with free shipping and handling). "I could've sworn it was clean when I put it away, but now it's got that ugly stain on it."

I checked out the stain in question, which looked suspiciously like a paw print to me.

At which point I spotted Prozac lurking next to Mom's ficus plant.

"Prozac, did you track dirty paw prints from that plant onto Mom's tablecloth?"

Moi?

Her eyes grew wide as saucers, an Academy Award–winning performance of a Wrongly Accused Cat.

"How could you even say such a thing?" Mom said, swooping her up in her arms. "It's probably an old gravy stain. Now be a dear, and run next door to Edna's and see if she's got a tablecloth she can loan me. And while you're there, ask her to join us for dinner tonight. It'll do her good to get out of the house."

Shooting Prozac a reproving glare (which did no good whatsoever), I left her gloating in Mom's arms and trotted off to Edna's.

Edna came to the door with a nearly completed sweater dangling from her knitting needles.

"Jaine, sweetheart, what perfect timing!

I'm almost finished with this sweater for my daughter-in-law, and I want you to try it on. You're just about her size and I need to check the fit."

I followed her into the living room, where she settled down in her armchair, her wicker knitting basket at her feet. I sat down on the sofa opposite her and watched as she resumed her knitting, needles flashing.

"How lovely," I said, admiring the baby blue cable knit.

"It's a miracle I've been able to work on it at all. I've been so darn upset about this whole murder thing."

"I'm sure you have."

She looked up and stared off into the distance.

"Of course, Latasha did it. Just one look at her, and you can see she's guilty as sin."

"Latasha? Who's Latasha? And why would she want to kill Preston?"

"Oh, Latasha didn't kill Preston. She set fire to her ex-boyfriend's stamp collection."

Huh?

"Judge Judy," she said, pointing behind me. I turned and saw that Edna had her TV on with the sound muted. And, indeed, there on the screen a woman I assumed was Latasha was being browbeaten by Judge Judy.

"Latasha set that fire, all right." Edna nodded sagely. "Just look at her shifty eyes. As for Preston, I have no idea who could have tampered with that wire. All I know is that everybody thinks it was me.

"Oh, honey," she sighed, "it's been so awful. I haven't even bothered to bake Christmas cookies. That's how depressed I've been. All I've got this year are candy canes left over from last Christmas. And chocolates left over from last Easter."

I felt simultaneously guilty for having made so little progress on the case and awed that she still had chocolates left over from Easter.

"Finished!" she said, completing the final stitch on her sweater. Reaching into her knitting basket, she pulled out a pair of scissors and snipped off the yarn.

Then she held up the sweater for my inspection.

"It's beautiful!" I said. "I'm sure your daughter-in-law will love it."

"Now, how about I fix you a nice cup of tea?" Edna asked after I'd tried it on and she'd declared it a perfect fit.

"No, thanks. Actually, I just stopped by to ask if we could borrow a tablecloth. Mom's invited Doc Wilkins over for dinner tonight. She wants you to come, too."

"That's very sweet," she sighed, "but like I told your mom, I'm just not up for socializing right now." Then she forced a bright smile. "But you wait here, and I'll go get my pretty brocade tablecloth from the linen closet."

As she hurried off down the hallway, I glanced over at the TV. Judge Judy had harangued her last harangue and had been replaced by the news.

A pretty-boy anchor, looking quite solemn under a helmet of sprayed hair, was talking earnestly into the camera. Then suddenly a picture of Raymond popped up on the screen behind him.

I raced over to the TV and turned up the volume just in time to hear the anchor say, ". . . was arrested this afternoon in the Gingerbread Man Murder Case. No further details are available at this time."

Holy Moses. It looked like Raymond was the killer, after all.

I stepped back from the TV in a daze, trying to picture the diminutive Cuban hacking away at the cable, when I stumbled over something. Drat. It was Edna's knitting basket. I'd knocked the darn thing over and now its contents were scattered on the carpet.

Cursing myself for being so clumsy, I bent

down to pick up the mess.

And that's when I saw it. There, among the balls of yarn and knitting needles, was a pair of shiny new wire cutters!

What the heck was Edna doing with wire cutters hidden in her knitting basket? Was it possible that sweet little Edna Lindstrom was the killer? Did she have a dark side no one knew about? Hadn't Daddy said he saw a show on TV about a minister who killed his brother-in-law and stuffed his body in the church organ? Was Edna one of those mild-mannered people who'd suddenly gone berserk?

Had she been worried all this time not because she was innocent, but because she was *guilty?*

"Jaine, dear," I heard her calling from down the hall. "So sorry to keep you waiting!"

I hurriedly stuffed her knitting supplies back in the basket and got back on my feet just as she came puffing into the room with a red brocade tablecloth.

"Sorry it took me so long. I could've sworn it was in the linen closet, but for some insane reason I had it stored in the guest bedroom. Oh, well, as long as I found it, that's all that counts. I think red is perfect for a holiday dinner, don't you?"

"Perfect."

I nodded woodenly, wondering if the cops had just arrested the wrong person.

Chapter Seventeen

News travels fast at Tampa Vistas. By the time I got home, one of the local gossips-at-large had already phoned with the news about Raymond's arrest.

"I knew all along it was him," Daddy boasted.

"Oh, please, Hank," Mom sniffed. "At first you thought it was Edna."

I groaned inwardly to think he may have been right.

"It's so hard to believe that dear, sweet Raymond is a killer," Mom sighed. "He's such a wonderful handyman. Why, I'll never forget the time he came over on Thanksgiving Day to fix our garbage disposal. You'd think anyone who'd fix a garbage disposal on Thanksgiving would be incapable of murder. Oh, well. At least, poor Edna's off the hook . . . What's wrong, Jaine? You look upset."

Oh, Lord. I couldn't possibly tell her that

her best friend might be a killer.

"Nothing, Mom."

"Well, then, be a dear and set the table."

I spread out Edna's tablecloth and scattered the silverware in a fog, unable to get rid of the image of Mom's best friend slipping over to the clubhouse in the middle of the night, a trench coat over her granny nightgown, a pair of wire cutters clenched in her stubby fist.

I was just arranging Mom's holly berry centerpiece, with the candle that had not once been lit in fifteen years, when I heard Daddy calling, "C'mere, you two! I've got something to show you!"

Out in the living room Daddy was standing in front of his topless Christmas tree, glowing with pride.

"I fixed it!"

Then, with all the pomp of Tom Edison about to flick the switch on his first lightbulb, he pressed a button on the remote, and the tree started turning — with the fairy lights blinking, to boot.

According to my lightning calculations, Daddy had spent at least twenty hours putting up his "no fuss, no bother" Christmas tree.

"I bet nobody in Tampa Vistas has anything like it," Daddy crowed.

"Nobody on the *planet* has anything like it," Mom said, rolling her eyes. "Oh, well. At least it's working."

Only too well, as we were about to discover.

"Doc!" Mom cried. "How lovely to see you!"

Doc Wilkins was standing on our doorstep in khakis and a windbreaker, his toupee freshly shined for the occasion.

"Come in!" Mom said, ushering him inside.

"Mmmm, something sure smells good," Doc said, with an appreciative sniff.

And, indeed, the house was fragrant with the smell of chicken baking and potatoes roasting. In the background, completing the Kodak moment, Andy Williams was crooning a medley of holiday favorites.

"How lovely you look, Claudia," Doc said to Mom, who was gussied up in her best slacks set and "formal" white organdy apron.

"And you, too, Jaine," he added, with a sly wink.

Oh, for Pete's sake. I was hoping I'd been imagining things when I ran into him yesterday and he'd asked me to feel his muscle. But it looked like the Toupee Prince had the warmies for me.

That's the story of my life, I'm afraid: always irresistible to the highly resistible.

After hanging up his windbreaker in the hall closet, I followed him and Mom into the living room where Daddy stood, preening, next to his topless orange Christmas tree. Which was, miraculously, still revolving.

"What the hell is that?" Doc asked, tossing tact out the window.

"Our Christmas tree," Daddy snapped in reply.

"What happened to the top?"

"It's supposed to be that way."

"It's moments like these," Doc said, "that make me glad I'm an agnostic."

Uh-oh. Batten down the hatches. I smelled a storm brewing.

"And this is Jaine's darling cat, Zoloft," Mom said in a desperate attempt to change the subject. She picked up Prozac, who had been conked out on the sofa, sleeping off the orgy of snacks Mom had been feeding her all afternoon.

Waking with a cavernous yawn, Prozac looked up at Doc Wilkins, zeroing in on his industrial-strength toupee.

Hey, buddy. Did you know you have a dead animal on your head?

Another yawn, and she was out like a light again.

"Jaine, honey," Mom said, "why don't you get Doc Wilkins some eggnog?"

Ah, yes. The old "Get 'Em Tootled and Hope For the Best" Plan.

I scooped up a cupful of Daddy's rum-laden eggnog and handed it to Doc. Needless to say, I was rewarded with another wink.

"Make yourself comfortable, Doc," Mom said, pointing to Daddy's recliner.

Daddy shot her a filthy look, clearly miffed at the thought of giving up his throne.

But Doc Wilkins passed up the recliner in favor of the one chair in the room that faced away from the Christmas tree.

"Nothing personal," he said, "but this way I don't have to look at it."

Daddy muttered something inaudible, which may or may not have involved a colorful four-letter word.

Mom, eager to distract, held out a tray of cheese and crackers.

"Hors d'oeuvre?"

"Don't mind if I do," Doc said, hacking off a slab of cheese.

"So how is your eye feeling?"

"You'll be glad to know the area is no longer sensitive."

"Wonderful!"

"Now it's numb. Can't feel a thing from my eyebrows up."

"Oh, no!"

"I'm sure it's okay. Probably just the meds I'm on."

"I hope it's nothing serious," Mom said, her brow furrowed with concern.

"Don't worry," Doc chuckled. "If it is, I can always sue Hank for assault and battery, ha-ha!"

By now the eggnogs were starting to do their job and Daddy actually laughed at this. Indeed, thanks to the rum he and Doc were swilling, they were soon chuckling and chortling like long-lost buddies. After a while, even Mom began to relax.

And then, just when it looked like fences would be mended and goodwill would triumph, tragedy struck.

The chair Doc had chosen, although facing away from the tree, was directly in front of it. And when he got up out of his seat to grab another slab of cheese, one of the rotating branches got caught on his toupee!

We watched in horror as the errant branch whooshed the wig clear off his head.

Suddenly he was standing there, bald as an eagle, his toupee making a slow orbit around that dratted tree!

And thanks to his numbing painkillers, he didn't even realize it was missing!

"Holy mackerel!" Daddy cried. "Your hair!"

"Looks lovely!" Mom interrupted. "So shiny and healthy! You must give us the name of your shampoo."

And without wasting another millisecond, she grabbed Doc by the elbow and hustled him into the dining room, closing the door on his orbiting hairpiece.

"Now, you sit right here," she said, shoving Doc down into a chair, "while Jaine and Hank help me in the kitchen."

"I'll help, too," Doc said, getting up.

"No, no! I insist." She shoved him back down again. "You're the guest. Just sit back and relax! Soup's almost on!

"Here," she said, tossing him the bread basket. "Have a bread stick."

And off his slightly puzzled smile, Mom hauled me and Daddy off to the kitchen.

"What on earth are we going to do?" Mom whispered as the three of us stood huddled near the refrigerator. "First, Daddy gives him a black eye, then we send him to the hospital, and now we've scalped the poor fellow!"

"You could always move to Boca," was my

helpful suggestion.

"Just give him his stupid toupee," Daddy hissed, "and tell him to use some wig glue."

"Don't be ridiculous, Hank. We can't possibly let him know what happened. He'd be too humiliated. And you heard what he said about suing us."

"I think he was just kidding, Mom."

"We can't be sure of that."

"So what are we going to do?" Daddy asked, beginning to look a tad worried.

"He didn't feel the toupee coming off," Mom said, "so we'll just put it back on his head again. He said his meds were making his scalp numb. Chances are he won't feel a thing."

"But what if he does?" Daddy asked.

"That's a chance you're just going to have to take."

"Me??"

"Yes, you! It was your idiotic rotating tree that caused this mess. Now go get the toupee, and while I'm serving the soup, pretend you need something in the credenza behind him, and then just drop the dratted thing on his head."

"Is everything okay in there?" Doc called out.

"Yes, Doc. We'll be right out!" Mom said, pushing Daddy out the other door toward the living room.

Seconds later he was back, empty-handed.

"I don't understand it," he said. "It's gone!"

"Gone?" Mom gasped. "How could it be gone?"

I knew the answer to that one.

And her name was Prozac.

"Why on earth would darling Zoloft want Doc Wilkins's toupee?"

"I saw the way she was eyeing it, Mom. She thought it was a dead rat."

"Oh, dear," she said, wringing the lace on her apron in dismay. "Well, excuse yourself during dinner and see if you can find it."

At last we returned to the dining room, with fake smiles and a tureen of Mom's split pea soup.

"Just a little soup snafu," Mom chirped, "but everything's okay now."

"What a beautiful table you set, Claudia," said Doc, who by now had made some serious inroads into the bread sticks. "These dishes are so sparkling clean, I bet I could see my face in them."

Before he could put that theory to the test, Mom quickly ladled some soup in his bowl.

Gosh, it looked good. Thick and creamy and studded with leftover ham from the chicken cordon bleu.

I dug into mine with gusto, sopping up the remains with one of Mom's light-as-air popovers.

When I'd slurped up every last morsel, I helped Mom clear away the dishes and brought in the chicken cordon bleu, hungrily eyeing the golden brown bundles of chicken, ham, and cheese.

And I was just about to spear myself a piece when Mom said, "Jaine, dear, didn't you have an important phone call to make?"

"What call?" I said, sniffing the potatoes.

"The important phone call to California. About that writing assignment. For the *hair* care product."

"Oh, right," I said, reluctantly parting company with my fork.

To this day I still can't believe Mom didn't let me stick around for just a bite or two of that chicken.

With stomach growling, I scooted out of the dining room and began casing the house for Prozac and the purloined toupee.

I found the little devil in my parents' bedroom, lolling on their quilt, bits of toupee hair in her whiskers.

"Okay, where is it?"

She gazed up at me in Inscrutable Confucius Mode.

That's for me to know and you to find out.

Then she rolled over and resumed her beauty nap.

Back home I knew all her hiding places, but this was virgin territory. I searched everywhere — under the beds, in the closets, in my boots (always a favorite spot for a cache of Cat Chow). I found dust bunnies and lost socks and thirty-two cents in spare change, but nary a toupee.

From the dining room, I could hear Mom serving the chocolate mousse.

I'd already missed the chicken, and I'd be damned if I was going to miss out on dessert, too.

So I headed back to the dining room to reclaim my rightful calories.

"How did everything go with your phone call?" Doc asked when I returned.

"Oh, I'm afraid I didn't get the job."

"You didn't?" Mom gulped.

"No, I didn't."

"That's too bad," Doc clucked. "I'd hire you in a minute."

"Looks like I'm just in time for dessert," I said, reaching for the mousse.

"Not so fast." Mom grabbed me by the elbow. "I'm going to need you and Daddy to help me with the coffee."

Seconds later the three of us were huddled

in the kitchen again.

"What happened?" Mom hissed.

"Prozac's hidden it somewhere, but I couldn't find it. I swear, I looked everywhere."

"Actually," Daddy whispered, "this may be all for the best."

"How on earth could this be all for the best, Hank?"

"Well, when Doc gets home, he's going to realize that the toupee is missing. But he won't know for sure he lost it here. For all he knows, it flew off in the street."

I had to admit, Daddy had a point.

"And if he ever asks us about it, we'll just deny, deny, deny."

"You think it'll work?"

"It has for several presidential administrations."

"Maybe you're right," Mom said, allowing herself a tentative smile.

"Of course, I'm right," Daddy huffed. "It does happen on occasion, you know."

We trooped back to the dining room, with hope in our hearts. This whole fiasco might turn out well, after all.

The mousse was fantastic, as I knew it would be, and for the first time since she sat down at the table, Mom seemed to enjoy her food.

The rest of the evening passed mercifully without incident, amid silent prayers that Doc Wilkins wouldn't ask to use the bathroom and catch a glimpse of himself in the mirror.

But our prayers were answered, and at last he was ready to leave.

"Such a wonderful meal," he said as we stood in the hallway. "Hank, you're a mighty lucky man to have a wife like Claudia."

"Don't I know it," Daddy said, putting his arm around Mom.

"And a daughter like Jaine," Doc added, with a farewell wink.

I smiled weakly and put my hand on the doorknob to open the front door.

And it was at this exact moment, just when our happy ending was in sight, that Prozac came prancing down the hallway.

She was not, I regret to inform you, alone. There, dangling from her mouth, was Doc Wilkins's toupee.

She dropped the chewed-up mess at his feet, her tail swishing with pride.

Here. I styled it for you.

Chapter Eighteen

"Zoloft, how could you?" Mom said after Doc had stormed off into the night. "Bad kitty!"

I fully intended to savor every moment of this rift between Mom and her pampered princess. But, alas, it lasted only about thirteen seconds. Prozac launched into her impersonation of Little Eva on the Ice Floe, all helpless and needy, and Mom caved like a soufflé in an earthquake.

"Poor thing," she tsked, scooping Prozac up in her arms. "I can tell she feels terrible. Don't you, darling?"

Prozac purred lazily.

Yeah, right. Anybody wanna rub my belly?

"Dammit," Daddy said, taking Doc's windbreaker out of the hall closet. "The darn fool left his jacket here. I'd better return it to him before he accuses me of stealing it."

"Oh, no," Mom said. "You'll just get in

another fight with him. Why don't you do it, Jaine? Doc seems to have taken a shine to you."

After tonight's winkfest, there was no doubt about that.

"And before you go, let me get you some fudge to bring him."

Mom hurried to the kitchen for a box of fudge, which by now she was buying in bulk.

Armed with my peace offering, I headed out into the moonlit night, past the neighbors' houses lit up with Santas, Rudolphs, and the occasional rebel menorah.

Soon I was at the address Mom had scribbled on a Post-it, a tidy one-story affair just past the clubhouse.

Doc had opted to forego any holiday decorations, unless you consider the NO PET POOP sign on his lawn a form of decoration.

I rang the bell, and seconds later Doc threw open the door, irritation oozing from every pore of his bald head.

"You forgot your jacket," I said, holding it out.

"I guess this is my lucky day," he snorted. "Your cat didn't pee on it."

No doubt about it. The flirtatious coot who'd been winking at me all night was gone with the wind.

"I'm so sorry, Doctor Wilkins. We feel

simply awful about what happened to your . . . um . . . hair."

"No worse than I."

"My mom wanted you to have this fudge."

"A box of fudge isn't going to make up for what you people have put me through," he said, grabbing it anyway.

"Needless to say, we're prepared to pay for a new toupee."

"Damn right you will. I was just typing out a bill for your parents.

"Wait here," he said, allowing me to step inside to his foyer. "I'll be right back."

He stomped off down a corridor, leaving me to enjoy a scenic view of his hall closet, across from which was a small occasional table and mirror. I checked myself out in the mirror, dismayed to see a chocolate stain on my DEAR SANTA, I CAN EXPLAIN . . . sweatshirt.

Glancing down at the table, I couldn't resist taking a peek at Doc's mail piled on a tray. There, along with the latest issue of *People,* were what looked like several Christmas cards, all addressed to "Doc" Wilkins.

How odd, I thought. Why would people put "Doc" in quotes? As if "Doc" was his nickname, and not his profession.

And then I noticed a postcard that had dropped behind the table, trapped behind one of the legs. When I bent down to retrieve it, I saw it, too, was addressed to Clyde "Doc" Wilkins. Flipping it over, I saw it was an invitation to the annual Christmas party of the Pipe Fitters Local Union 542.

Hello. What on earth was Doc Wilkins doing with a party invitation from the pipe fitters' union?

At which point, I heard him stomping back down the hall. Quickly, I shoved the postcard back where I'd found it and was staring innocently into space when Doc showed up in the foyer.

"Here," he said, slapping a piece of paper in my hand. "It's an invoice for pain, suffering, and my ruined toupee."

I checked the invoice and saw that he was asking six hundred dollars for the darn thing. Highway robbery, in my humble op. He couldn't have possibly paid more than $29.95 for that polyester monstrosity.

But I uttered not a peep of protest.

Doc Wilkins was one angry bald guy, and I was not about to get him one whit angrier.

I started back home, thinking about that invitation from the pipe fitters' union. Was it possible Doc wasn't really a doctor, but a blue-collar pipe fitter?

But that couldn't be. Hadn't Preston

McCay said he'd seen Doc at a medical convention?

I remembered that day at the clubhouse when Daddy hit Doc in the eye with his Ping-Pong ball and Preston hurried over to help. I could see Preston now, with his unctuous smile and thick mane of silvery hair.

He'd asked Doc if he was Clyde Wilkins, the cardiologist. And when Doc had said yes, Preston replied:

The keynote speaker at the AMA convention back in '92! I never forget a face!

All Preston said was that Dr. Clyde Wilkins had spoken at the convention. But he'd never actually said that the speaker was Doc! What if he remembered another Dr. Clyde Wilkins, a famous cardiologist, and knew that this "Doc" was a phony? And what if his *I never forget a face* crack was his way of letting Doc know he was on to him?

All along Daddy claimed Doc was a faker. Maybe Daddy was right. Maybe Doc was faking — not his black eye, but his past.

A theory began to take shape in my mind:

Supposing Doc Wilkins spent his whole life as a blue-collar worker, but when it was time to retire, he decided to move up in the world. Maybe he wanted respect. Or status. Or just a nicer table at a restaurant. And what better place to reinvent himself than a retirement community? Who was to know that he'd spent his adult life wielding a blowtorch?

So he started living a lie, becoming Doc Wilkins, never dreaming that there was a real Dr. Clyde Wilkins out there, a famous cardiologist. Then Preston showed up at Tampa Vistas and knew instantly that Doc was a fake. I remembered how anxious Doc had been to end the conversation with Preston that day at the Ping-Pong table, how uncomfortable he'd seemed. At the time, I thought it was because he was in pain. Maybe it wasn't pain — but panic. What if he knew he'd just been caught in a trap?

What if Preston had later threatened to tell everyone the truth? Maybe Doc couldn't bear to be exposed as a fraud, and so he slipped into the clubhouse to fray the cable that hooked up to Preston's costume.

Hadn't Doc said he'd been in last year's Christmas play? And hadn't Edna told me that the actors always got a master key to the clubhouse facilities? Which meant Doc could have crept in during the middle of the night and done the dirty deed.

Was I onto something here, I wondered as I approached the clubhouse, or was Doc merely another suspect du jour? Just this afternoon I'd been ready to convict Edna.

But then I remembered that look of rage in Doc's eyes when he handed me the invoice. My gut was telling me he was the killer.

One thing was for sure. The minute I got home, I was going to call the —

If I'd had the chance, I would've said, "Cops."

But I never did get to finish that thought, because just then I felt the cold steel rod of a gun in my back.

"Start walking," Doc's voice hissed in my ear. "Eyes straight ahead."

With the butt of his gun, he began prodding me up the path to the clubhouse.

Could I possibly make a run for it? Surely, he wouldn't risk drawing attention by firing a gun.

"Don't even think about running," he said, his breath hot against my neck. "Or I'll shoot."

Coward that I am, I continued up the path.

"I knew you were nosing around," he said, "asking questions about the murder. Up until now I wasn't worried. But then tonight I saw you looking at that postcard from the union."

"You did?" Unless he had X-ray vision, I didn't see how that was possible.

"You were so caught up in your discovery, you didn't notice me watching you in the hall mirror."

Damn. I remembered the mirror hanging over the table. Why the heck didn't I realize he'd be able to see me snooping as he came down the hallway?

"The minute you saw that postcard, I knew you'd figure out the truth." Another sharp jab to my vertebrae. "Too bad, really. Because now I can't possibly let you live."

Oh, Lord. I had to keep him talking. Maybe somebody out for an evening walk would hear us and realize what was happening.

"I'm still not sure why you lied about being a doctor," I said, speaking as loud as I dared.

"I never planned to. It all just sort of happened. Back home my buddies used to call me Doc, because I was a smooth operator with the ladies."

I thought about all those winks he'd been giving me. He was an operator, all right. Not exactly smooth. But an operator.

"I could never stop myself from flirting with a pretty gal," he added, with a poke to my tush. "Even if her fanny could use a little toning."

How I yearned to turn around and poke him in a few choice places.

"Over here," he said, shoving me onto the narrow path leading to the maintenance building.

"The first day I showed up at the pool," Doc said, picking up his tale, "one of the gals asked me my name. I told her it was Doc Wilkins. You should've seen her eyes light up when she thought I was a real doctor. I was going to tell her the truth, but she was so into the doctor thing, I never got around to it.

"That night she had me over for roast beef and Yorkshire pudding, and I knew I had a good thing going. Why not let everybody think I was a doctor? Before long, I really got into the part."

As Doc blathered on, I kept praying for someone, anyone, to walk by out front. Where the heck were Christmas carolers when you needed them?

"It was all going great," Doc was saying, "until Preston showed up. How was I supposed to know there was a real Dr. Clyde Wilkins, and that Preston had seen him at some stupid medical convention? When he asked me that day if I was Clyde Wilkins, the cardiologist, I should've said no, of course, that I was some other Dr. Wilkins. But thanks to your father practically taking my eye out with that Ping-Pong ball, I didn't know what I was doing.

"As soon as I said yes, I realized what a mistake I'd made. Afterward, Preston took me aside and told me he wasn't going to let some two-bit fraud pass himself off as a professional, that he intended to tell everyone the truth. I begged him not to blow my cover and gave him some cock-and-bull story about how I wanted to be the one to set everyone straight. The guy was stupid enough to believe me.

"The rest is history. I let myself into the clubhouse in the middle of the night and cut the cable. Easy as pie."

By now we'd reached the maintenance building.

"It's a good thing Gloria gave me that master key last Christmas," he said. "It's come in real handy."

I heard a key jingling, and now Doc reached from behind me to open the door.

Inside the tools cast ominous shadows in the moonlight.

With a final poke of his gun, Doc shoved me into the room.

I stumbled over the threshold and turned around, only to see that the "gun" in Doc's hand was nothing more than a piece of pipe.

"A gift from the union when I retired," he explained. "It says, *Lots of luck from your pals at Local 542.*"

Oh, for crying out loud. First, I didn't notice him spying on me in his foyer. And now he'd fooled me with a fake gun. If I'd actually had a P.I. license, it would've been yanked away so fast, my head would be spinning.

Furious at myself for being such a patsy — and at Doc for that crack about my fanny — I shoved him aside and ran for the door.

But all those morning constitutionals had really paid off. For a guy in his Metamucil years, Doc was in pretty darn terrific shape. Before I knew it, he'd whacked me in the legs with his commemorative pipe, sending me staggering backward toward Raymond's desk. I sank to the floor, taking half the papers on the desk with me.

Lying dazed in the moonlight, I noticed for the first time that Doc was wearing gloves, probably the same gloves he'd worn when he'd cut the cable on Preston's gingerbread man costume. As a pipe fitter, he probably owned a whole treasure trove of tools he could have used to do the job.

Now he began rummaging around the machinery in the shop.

"Gotta find myself a nice blunt murder weapon," he said. "Preferably metal, one with Raymond's prints all over it."

"Nobody's going to believe Raymond killed me. He's in jail."

"Not anymore." Doc turned around, a feral grin on his face. "I saw it on the news when I got home. His lawyer got him released on bail."

Ouch.

As he searched for a murder weapon, I somehow managed to raise myself to a sitting position. But when I tried to get up, I felt a shooting pain in my calf.

"Aha!" Doc cried.

With those bulging muscles he was so proud of, he lifted a hunk of metal from the floor and held it out for my inspection.

"This engine will do for a murder weapon, don't you think?"

"You still won't get away with it. My parents know I went to see you."

"But you never showed up. That's what I intend to tell the cops." He looked down at me with a reasonable facsimile of pity in his eyes. "I hate to crush your pretty little skull, sweetie, but you don't give me much choice."

Then he started walking toward me, the engine held high over his head.

I thought about running, but I knew I'd never make it.

And that's when I saw it. One of the prop gingerbread cookies. It had fallen to the floor along with Raymond's papers. It wasn't much of a defense weapon, but it was all I had.

I snatched it up and lobbed it at him.

At which point, my many years of aiming Almond Joy wrappers into the trash finally paid off. Somehow I managed to hit him smack in his bad eye.

With a pained yelp, he dropped the engine, which came crashing to the floor, practically splitting the floorboards.

I took advantage of this lull in the action to scramble to my feet and grab a nearby two-by-four. Now it was Doc's turn to get whacked. Still aching but fueled by adrenaline, I slammed him with every ounce of strength in my body, sending him sprawling to the ground.

As he lay there, moaning, the door burst open and Daddy came rushing in.

"Lambchop!" he cried, wrapping me in his arms. "I was looking all over for you!"

Thank heavens for doting daddies. And prop Christmas cookies.

I gazed down at my little brown defense weapon, my heart welling with gratitude.

As far as I was concerned, it really was the gingerbread cookie that saved Christmas.

After the police had taken a groggy Doc Wilkins into custody, Daddy and I headed back home and told Mom the news.

"My poor darling!" Mom cried. "You could've been killed!"

She instantly began fussing over me, settling me down on the living room sofa and plying me with ice packs and cocoa and fudge.

"First thing tomorrow we're going to Dr. May and have X-rays taken."

"Mom, nothing's wrong with me that another piece of fudge or three won't cure."

"We're going, anyway," she clucked, fluffing a pillow beneath my head. "Comfy, sweetheart?"

Nearby Prozac glared.

She's fine, okay? But I could use a back scratch over here.

"Gosh," Mom said, now massaging my feet with a most soothing lavender oil. "I still can't believe Doc Wilkins is the killer."

"Really?" Daddy replied with a smug smile. "I knew all along it was him."

And over in the corner, his topless tree just kept on spinning.

Epilogue

Criminal justice fans everywhere will be happy to know that "Doc" Wilkins is currently fitting pipes in the geriatric wing of Florida State Prison.

Back at Tampa Vistas, the garbagemen refused to cart away Daddy's hideous topless Christmas tree. Eventually, he had to drop it off at the hazardous waste dump.

Mom's just thrilled to be rid of the darn thing.

Marvelous news about Edna. On New Year's Eve her hot water heater broke and flooded her kitchen. That's not the marvelous part, of course. The marvelous part is that she called Raymond in a panic. And that sweet man drove over from his New Year's Eve party, along with his recently widowed father. Well, Edna and Raymond's dad locked eyeballs over a wet mop, and the bottom line is — the wedding is next month.

(About those wire cutters in Edna's knitting basket, it turns out that hand-knitted wire jewelry is all the rage in the crafts world, and Edna was making me and Mom bracelets for Christmas. I absolutely love mine and plan to wear it to her wedding.)

Last I heard, Laurette Kendall was dating a guy she met at the garden supply store. And Gloria Di Nardo moved back to Secaucus, New Jersey, where she is currently starring in her one-woman tribute to Cole Porter, *It's Delightful! It's De-Lovely! It's Di Nardo!*

And remember that "crummy cameo" Preston left Ginny Knight in his will? Well, it turned out to be a rare doodad that once graced the monumental bosom of Queen Victoria. Ginny sold it at auction for two hundred grand. So in a way, Preston wound up paying for what he did to Ginny's mom, after all.

As for me, I'm back in L.A., writing toilet bowl ads and working on my relationship with my significant other (Prozac). After months of pleading, groveling, and back scratching, I finally broke her of her ridiculous filet mignon habit.

(Now she prefers top sirloin.)

Well, gotta go now. The princess wants a belly rub.

■ ■ ■ ■

P.S. If you're reading this during the holiday season, have yourself a very merry Christmahannakwanzaa. (And a piece of fudge for me.)

■ ■ ■ ■

Gingerbread Cookies and Gunshots
Leslie Meier

■ ■ ■ ■

Chapter One

It was Christmas . . . again.

Lucy Stone knew that some women loved Christmas. Her friend Sue Finch was one of them. Sue put up a Christmas tree in every room of her house, she baked dozens of cookies that she distributed to everyone, from her manicurist to the mailman, and she kept her husband, Sid, busy for a week wrapping every tree in their front yard with twinkly white lights. She also shopped all year, snapping up bargains, which she stored in her Christmas closet and which, when elaborately and imaginatively wrapped and presented to the lucky recipients, were the absolute best, most perfect gifts imaginable.

Lucy admired Sue's Christmas spirit, but she preferred Thanksgiving, a relaxed holiday requiring only a turkey dinner and football, or Halloween, simpler still with a mask and a couple of bags of candy. As

Lucy was a busy wife and mother, as well as a part-time reporter and feature writer for the town's weekly newspaper, the *Pennysaver,* her schedule was already jam-packed without the shopping and baking and wrapping that Christmas required. So today she'd brought her son, Toby, and twenty-one-month-old grandson, Patrick, along, as well as her reporter's notebook and camera, to cover the annual arrival of Santa Claus at the town pier.

Unfortunately, it was one of those bone-chilling, drizzly gray days, and she was shivering as she looked out over the slate-colored water, hoping to spot Santa's bright red boat. A few inches of snow lingered from last week's storm, and they were rapidly turning to slush, which was seeping into her left boot, which must have sprung a leak.

"He'll be here soon!" she told Patrick, who was tucked snugly into a backpack worn by Toby. She stepped closer and nuzzled his plump pink cheek with her nose.

"An-a!" Patrick knew who Santa was; a colorful version of "The Night Before Christmas" was his favorite book. Lucy enjoyed reading it to him, too. In fact, it was because of Patrick that she was almost looking forward to Christmas. Last year he was just a baby and too little to understand what all the excitement was about, but this year he was old enough to enjoy the surprise of Christmas morning, with its bulging stockings and piles of presents under the tree.

"Christmas is going to be wonderful this year," she told Toby, who was bouncing up and down to amuse his son. "I can't wait to see Patrick's face on Christmas morning."

Toby stopped jiggling and bit his lip. "Uh, Mom, there's something I've been meaning to tell you."

A foghorn blasted, and the crowd on the pier began cheering as the little red boat rounded Quisset Point and began chugging across the harbor.

"He's coming!" exclaimed Lucy, grabbing Patrick's mittened hand. "Santa's coming!"

Patrick's eyes lit up and he gave a bounce in the backpack, nearly knocking Toby off balance.

"You know Molly's folks?" Toby asked, referring to his wife's parents.

"Sure," said Lucy. She knew that Molly's family would also want to spend time with Patrick; in fact, she was planning to invite them for a special Christmas Eve dinner. She was even thinking of making that Mexican Christmas salad with oranges and pomegranate that was such a hit at Sue's open house last year.

"Uh, well, they've invited us on one of those Disney cruises for Christmas."

The boat was halfway across the harbor now, and they could clearly see the lighted Christmas tree on its bow, and the plump figure of Santa, standing beside it.

"That's nice," said Lucy, snapping a picture of Patrick's smiling face. Adorable. It was cute enough to run on page one. "When are you leaving?"

The boat was slowing as it approached the dock, and everybody was cheering and clapping. Lucy got another good photo, a shot of Santa waving.

"That's the thing, Mom," said Toby. "We're leaving a couple of days before Christmas."

Lucy missed her chance to shoot Santa jumping onto the dock with his bulging bag of presents on his back. "You mean you won't be here for Christmas?"

"That's right, Mom."

Santa, actually Lucy's friend Officer Barney Culpepper, was making his way down the dock, toward the seat that had been arranged for him out of a pile of lobster pots. He was reaching out to the children, clasping their hands as he passed, and when he reached Patrick, he stopped. "Ho-ho-ho!" he roared in a deep Santa voice.

Startled, Patrick burst into tears.

Lucy knew exactly how he felt.

A few days later, on Wednesday afternoon, Lucy was at the supermarket. She liked to do her big grocery shopping then, after the noon deadline at the *Pennysaver.* It was too early to start working on the next week's edition, so she had a free afternoon.

If only the groceries were free, she thought, wincing at the price sticker on a jar of mincemeat. Almost seven dollars! What was in the stuff, anyway? And did she really need to make mincemeat cookies? She was already well over her weekly budget thanks to the holiday extras she'd put in her cart: chocolate chips for Santa's thumbprints, almonds for sand tarts, a couple of tubs of candied fruit and a box of currants for plum pudding, extra eggs, and a bag of sugar.

She started to replace the mincemeat on the shelf, then changed her mind and placed it in her cart. Her husband, Bill, loved mincemeat cookies, and he hadn't taken the news about Patrick's Disney cruise very well. "No wonder he can afford to take them on a cruise. He's in insurance. He's making out like a bandit," he'd declared, referring to Molly's father, who owned an insurance agency. "It doesn't matter what the economy's doing. You've gotta have insurance."

The economy hadn't been doing well for Bill, who was a restoration carpenter. The recession had hit the building trades especially hard, and Bill had lost his big job renovating an old barn when the owner lost his job on Wall Street. Bill had managed to pick up some small handyman jobs installing replacement windows and insulation, but he wasn't making the kind of money he had during the boom years.

Lucy knew he was worried about the family's finances, but she didn't think Christmas was the place to cut corners. She'd make him his mincemeat cookies and economize someplace else. They could have a meatless meal one night a week, or she'd put the thermostat down when he wasn't home.

The girls, her daughters Sara and Zoe, could also do a better job turning off lights, she thought, rounding the corner of the baking goods aisle and practically bumping into a little boy in a too-small orange parka.

"Nemo!" she exclaimed, recognizing the child she'd driven home from a Halloween party when his parents had car trouble.

"Sorry," muttered his mother, grabbing him by the hand. "How many times do I have to tell you not to wander off like that?"

"No problem," said Lucy, smiling at the young mother. "It's nice to see Nemo again. I don't know if you remember, but I drove him home on Halloween night. I'm Lucy Stone."

The girl was holding tight to Nemo, who was squirming. "Oh, right," she said.

Her tone was vague and Lucy was sure she didn't remember. Judging from her shaved head and numerous facial piercings, Lucy suspected Nemo's upbringing was, to use a polite term, unconventional.

"I'm Ocean," she added, "Ocean Anderson."

Lucy couldn't help smiling. It was too cute. Ocean and Nemo, she knew, lived in an abandoned aquarium on Route 1. It had been a flourishing tourist trap in its prime but was now a derelict collection of buildings with a broken neon sign. "Nice to meet you in the daylight." She turned to Nemo. "Did you see Santa when he came to the town pier?"

Nemo frowned. "Did he have reindeer?"

"No. He came by boat."

"That's wrong. Santa doesn't have a boat. He has a sleigh and eight tiny reindeer."

Nemo, a typical four-year-old, was a stickler for detail.

"I think he can have both a boat and a sleigh. I'm not sure reindeer can swim."

Nemo's little face was set in a determined expression. "If they can fly, they can swim."

"Come on, Nemo. Don't argue with the lady," said his mother, tugging at his hand. "We've got to go."

Nemo wasn't about to knuckle under parental authority without a struggle. "I want a cookie," he declared, pointing to a basket full of decorated gingerbread men wrapped in cellophane that was displayed on top of the bakery counter.

Ocean gave Lucy an apologetic smile, then gave her cart a push toward the canned goods. "Come on, Nemo. Rick's waiting for us."

"No! I want a cookie." Nemo had placed himself in front of the glass case and wasn't budging.

Lucy went in the opposite direction, toward the cereal aisle, thinking it was best to let Ocean handle her son without an audience.

"Nemo," she heard her say, followed by a big sigh. "You know we can't afford extras right now. Look, I've got a piece of gum. How about some gum?"

"Is it sugarless?" he asked in a doubtful tone, which made Lucy smile. She remembered having the same discussions with her kids when they were small and stubborn.

"No. It's Juicy Fruit."

There was a long silence, but Nemo apparently knew when he was defeated. "Okay," he finally said.

Lucy picked up a box of Raisin Bran, then turned back toward the bakery counter. The gingerbread men were oversized cookies, decorated with white icing and chocolate chip eyes and buttons. No wonder Nemo had wanted one, she thought, impulsively choosing a cookie. If she hurried, she could catch them at the checkout; she just had to pick up some ice cream first.

But when Lucy wheeled her cart up to the checkout, there was no sign of Nemo or his mother. Looking through the plate-glass window, she saw them crossing the parking lot, so she asked Dot, the cashier, to scan the cookie first and ran outside, leaving her to finish ringing up the order.

When she caught up to them, Ocean was loading the groceries into the trunk of their very small, low-slung sports car and Rick was bent over double, strapping Nemo into a booster seat.

"Excuse me," she said, tapping Rick's

shoulder. "I got this for Nemo. Is it okay if I give it to him?"

Rick straightened up; he was tall with a shaved head and a fashionable two days' growth of beard. Like Ocean, he had numerous rings and studs sprouting on his face, as well as a barbed-wire tattoo around his neck. He grinned at her, revealing a gold tooth. "I guess that's okay," he said, taking the cookie, which he passed to Nemo. "Merry Christmas, kid."

"Merry Christmas," she said, with a little wave. She hadn't exactly expected a handwritten note, but a simple "thanks" would have been nice, she thought as she hurried back inside to pay for her groceries.

Dot was already busy bagging her order. "That'll be one-sixty-seven and forty-one cents."

Lucy had a hundred and fifty dollars in her wallet; she'd have to write a check. She was opening her checkbook when there was a squeal of tires, and she looked up to see the low-slung black sports car speeding through the parking lot.

"Idiot," said Dot. "That's no way to drive." She was a strong law-and-order type; her son was the town's police chief.

"They're young and careless," said Lucy, signing her name. And, she might have added but bit her lip, they had their priorities all wrong. How come they could afford a Porsche, but they couldn't afford a dollar forty-nine cookie for their kid?

"If you ask me, it's drugs," said Dot, taking her check. "It's a bigger problem than you'd think."

As she wheeled the loaded cart out to her car, Lucy wondered if Dot was right and Rick and Ocean were on drugs. They looked as if they might be, with their shaved heads and assorted piercings, but she remembered how upset her parents had been when she had declared herself a feminist and refused to wear a bra and even gave up shaving her legs — briefly. For all she knew, Rick and Ocean were making a political statement, or a fashion statement. And when it came to that, who was she to assume they were irresponsible parents? She didn't know anything about them, really. It wasn't her business to make assumptions or pass judgment on people. In her years working as a reporter, she'd learned there were always at least two sides to a story, usually more, and things were rarely what they seemed.

Tossing the last bag into the Subaru, she slammed the rear door, pushed the empty cart into the corral, and hopped into the car. When she started the engine, the radio came on. It was the song about the little drummer boy. She sang along, thinking about the poor child who had nothing to offer baby Jesus except his drumming, as she headed for home.

Just as Lucy usually did her grocery shopping on Wednesdays, she had a standing date with three friends for breakfast on Thursday morning, followed by a stop at the post office on her way to work to mail her bills. The girls teased her about her refusal to pay by computer, but she felt more in control when she wrote checks, even if it meant buying stamps and sticking them on the envelopes. This week, when she got to the envelope with the oil company's logo on front, she paused, shaking her head. She'd just gotten the first big winter bill, and it was a doozy. The amount due had wiped out her checking account, and it was only December. It was going to be a long, cold winter and not only for her family. A lot of people in Tinker's Cove were struggling to make ends meet this year; some had even lost their houses in foreclosures.

She slipped the bills into the slot for outgoing mail and paused to admire the little Christmas tree the postal workers had set up by a display of holiday-themed packing materials. It was decorated with twinkly white lights and paper angels. Looking closer, she realized the angels had descriptions of the local children that patrons could "adopt" for Christmas. Phil, age three, needed warm winter clothes and hoped Santa would give him a Transformer; Heidi, age eight, needed a size ten parka, preferably pink, and wanted a Barbie.

Suddenly, Lucy felt ashamed for fretting about the oil bill. She had enough money to pay the bill. So what if she had to dip into her savings account to get through the winter? There were people in town who couldn't even afford to buy warm clothes, much less Christmas presents, for their kids.

She was studying the angels, trying to decide which one to take, when she remembered Nemo. He was such a cute kid. He'd dressed as the fish character in the Disney movie for the Halloween party, and she'd been confused when he announced his name was Nemo; she thought he was referring to his costume, especially when he told her he lived in an aquarium. But he was right. His name was Nemo, and he did live in an aquarium, albeit a rather squalid one.

There was something very appealing about Nemo, the way he was so definite about things. He seemed more mature than the average four-year-old. Maybe he was very bright, or maybe, she thought, biting her lip, he'd had to grow up fast because his parents weren't especially nurturing. Thinking back to that Halloween party, she remembered that Nemo hadn't been at all upset when his parents failed to show up to take him home. A lot of kids would have been in tears, but not Nemo. He was quite casual about the whole thing, as if it happened fairly frequently.

Lucy turned away from the Christmas tree and headed for the door. Instead of adopting a stranger, she decided, she'd adopt Nemo. It would be easy to shop for him: she knew his winter coat was too small, and he seemed to like anything connected with the *Finding Nemo* movie.

Stepping outside into the nippy morning, where sparkling flakes from a passing snow shower were dancing in the sunlight, she decided it would be good for the girls to share their holiday with someone less fortunate. Sara, in high school, and Zoe, in middle school, had complained loudly when Lucy told them their back-to-school shopping would be limited to new shoes and school supplies this year; the new clothes purchases would have to wait until the end-of-season sales. They'd been resentful when

Lucy explained their clothing allowance was needed to pay the new fees the school department was charging for activities like field hockey and cheerleading.

Lucy hadn't liked their attitude, the way they felt entitled to new clothes and cell phones and the way Sara, who now had her driver's license, just expected the gas tank to always be full. She thought it would be a good lesson for them to learn firsthand that many families were struggling and they could help. And besides, it would be fun to surprise Nemo.

She was smiling to herself when she slid behind the wheel and started the car. It was true, she decided, that the joy of the season came from giving, not getting. She shifted into drive and eased up on the brake, rolling slowly across the parking lot. The radio was producing static, so she leaned over and turned the knob. She was thinking there ought to be a way for car heaters to work faster when an AMBER Alert was announced.

"Nemo Anderson, age four, was snatched from his front yard, where he was playing. . . ."

Chapter Two

"He is described as forty pounds, about forty-one inches tall, with red hair. The public is asked to look out for a gray Honda CR-V with Massachusetts license plates. The driver is described as a large African American woman wearing a quilted maroon coat. If you see anyone matching this description, or the vehicle — again that's a gray Honda CR-V with Massachusetts plates — call nine-one-one immediately."

She had stopped in the middle of the road, Lucy realized, hearing a friendly toot from a Mini Cooper stopped behind her. The driver, a young woman with long legs, wearing a Navajo blanket jacket, was now approaching with a concerned look on her face. "Is everything okay?" she asked as Lucy lowered the window. "Do you want me to call for a tow?"

"No, no. The car's fine."

The woman leaned closer. "Are you all right?"

"I just heard some bad news on the radio. . . ."

"The AMBER Alert? Do you know that little boy?"

"I do," said Lucy, remembering Nemo's certainty that reindeer could swim.

"It's terrible. Who does something like that?"

"They said it was a black woman in a maroon coat," said Lucy. "Maybe she's one of those people who couldn't have a child and always wanted one. He's awfully cute." She was desperately hoping the kidnapper wasn't one of those perverted monsters who preyed on young children.

By now a pickup truck had stopped behind the Mini, and a woman in a big black Volvo wagon was stopped on the other side of the road. She was sticking her head out the window.

"I better move along," said Lucy. "Thanks for stopping."

"Are you sure you're all right?" the woman asked again.

"I'm fine," said Lucy, lifting her foot off the brake, where it had landed apparently of its own accord. "It was just the shock." She gave a little wave with her hand as the

Subaru began rolling down the road toward home.

Reaching the stop sign at Red Top Road, she automatically flipped the turn signal lever up, to go right, then impulsively changed her mind and switched it down to left as she steered the car in a wide turn. She had an hour or so before she had to cook dinner; she had a full gas tank. She might as well take the long way round along back roads on the off chance she might see that gray Honda CR-V.

Next morning Lucy was down half a tank and Nemo was still missing, according to the morning news on the car radio. Lucy had heard the story a million times, she could have recited it word for word, but she listened again, hoping it would be different this time. Maybe there was a new development; maybe someone had seen the CR-V; maybe a clue of some kind had turned up.

No such luck. Nemo was still gone, snatched while playing outside his house, which was described as "a former tourist attraction known as the Aquarizoo." This morning a new detail was added. "The child was taken while his horrified mother watched from inside her home. Ocean Anderson told investigators she immediately ran outside but was too late to stop the abductor, described as a large black woman in a quilted maroon coat."

Lucy could picture the whole scene: the struggling child, the dark abductor in her swirling coat, the frantic mother. It was so clear in her mind that she could have been there. She had that déjà vu feeling, as if she'd actually seen the abduction, but she hadn't. It was probably just that she identified so strongly with Ocean, she decided as she followed the familiar route to work. She was a mother, too, and she knew what it was like when you lost sight of your child for just a moment in a crowded store. She'd probably dreamt it or seen it on TV. It was funny how those images could stay with you. They were powerful and tapped into some subconscious pool of fears and anxieties that came along with parenthood. Rachel, her friend who was a psych major in college, could probably explain it.

When she walked through the door at the *Pennysaver* office, she didn't even notice the little jangling bell that announced her arrival. Neither did her boss, Ted, or Phyllis, the receptionist. They were staring at a small TV tuned to the regional cable station, watching an amateur home video of Nemo blowing out the four candles on his birthday cake.

Lucy joined them. "He is such an adorable kid," she said.

"Yeah." Ted muted the TV and nodded to Phyllis. "Let me know if there are any new developments."

His voice sounded old, something she'd never noticed before, and she looked at him. It was funny, she thought, how you could work with someone, even live with them, without really seeing them. But now that she took a good look, she realized Ted was looking old. The boyish shock of hair that fell across his brow was gray, and he'd developed a bit of a tummy. When had this happened? Was it part of the natural aging process? She'd recently noticed the lines between her brows were deepening, and even though she weighed the same, her jeans were tighter. This was something different, though. It was as if Ted had suddenly lost a certain spark, she decided, wondering if he was coming down with something.

She quickly glanced at Phyllis, reassured to find she looked the same as always, with her dyed red hair and harlequin glasses. She'd recently gained some weight back after dieting for over a year, and it became her; her recent marriage to mail carrier Wilf Lundgren seemed to agree with her.

"Lucy!" Ted was talking to her. "I want you to come along to Gilead with me. The DA's holding a press conference in thirty minutes."

"We're both going?" This was surprising. Ted, who was publisher, editor, and chief reporter, usually covered press conferences himself.

"This is a big story. I don't want to miss anything." He attempted a grin, but it came out crooked. "I know I'll get in trouble for saying this, but I want the benefit of your feminine intuition."

Lucy knew that Pam, Ted's wife, was a staunch feminist who believed most characteristics attributed to gender were actually cultural. "I won't tell Pam," she promised, returning the smile.

Ted disappeared into the morgue, the oversized closet where the old issues of the paper were stored, bound in oversized volumes, and Lucy sat down at her desk and booted up the computer. She scrolled through her e-mails, automatically deleting the ads that flooded in every day and thinking about Ted. That bit about female intuition simply didn't ring true; something else was going on. He'd said he was afraid he might miss something — was he having trouble remembering things? Could it be early onset Alzheimer's — perish the thought — or maybe he was worried about something? That seemed more likely, especially considering the poor economy and the recent rash of newspaper closures. Spotting a message from the town assessor, Lucy turned her mind to the recent revaluation. Property values were down, she noted, reaching for the phone.

When they arrived at the state police barracks in Shiloh, the basement room used for press conferences was packed. Kidnappings always attracted a lot of media attention, and all the local TV stations, as well as the regional cable channel, had sent reporters and cameramen. There were no seats left, and Lucy and Ted had to push their way into the crowd of standees in the back of the room. It was so crowded that Lucy could barely manage to retrieve her reporter's notebook from her bag, and when she found it, she had to hold it next to her chest.

It seemed they were standing there a long time, staring at a blown-up photo of Nemo that was propped on an easel, before the DA, Phil Aucoin, took the podium. He was flanked by various law enforcement officials, including Lucy's sometime friend state police detective Horowitz and Tinker's Cove police chief Jim Kirwan. They all looked grim, standing with clasped hands and clenched jaws. Aucoin didn't have anything new to report, except to say that every effort was being made to find the child, which was greeted with a show of hands and shouted questions from the reporters.

Calling for silence, he announced that Nemo's parents, Ocean Anderson and Rick Juergens, would make a joint statement, and Lucy was practically knocked off her feet as the pack of reporters surged forward to get better vantage points. The people seated in the chairs all stood up, and Lucy couldn't see a thing until Ted helped her climb onto one of the vacant chairs and handed her his camera.

Looking through the viewfinder and snapping a photo, Lucy found Ocean was every bit as pale and wan as you would expect, and had dark circles under her eyes. She seemed very small and thin, dressed for the press conference in a short gray sweater dress, black tights, and ankle boots, with a lumpy knitted beret pulled over her shaved head. Rick, standing next to her, seemed slighter than Lucy remembered, and was fidgety. He kept jiggling from one denim-clad leg to the other and repeatedly shrugged his shoulders in his oversized plaid flannel shirt while Ocean read from a small slip of paper.

"We just want to say to whoever took our little boy that we love him very much and want him back. Please, please take good care of him and . . ."

Ocean was unable to continue, and Rick wrapped her in his arms for a long moment. He then took the paper from her and continued reading in a thin, reedy voice.

"Please take good care of Nemo and take him to the nearest police station. Christmas is coming, and getting Nemo back is the best present we could have. Thank you very much." When he finished, he folded the paper, reducing it to a tiny rectangle in his large hands. Then he raised his head and quickly brushed tears from his eyes.

He wasn't the only one who was crying. Lucy was blinking furiously as she rummaged in her pocket for a tissue, and many others were in the same predicament. It was quite amazing, she thought, to see these hardened reporters reduced to tears. Even tough old Ted's eyes were glistening.

The questioning that followed was somewhat subdued, even respectful, but Aucoin had little to say. "Every effort is being made to find the boy," he repeated each time. "That's all I can say right now." This went on for about ten minutes before he ended the conference.

"Well, what do you think?" Ted asked as they joined the stream of reporters leaving the building.

Lucy was thinking about Ocean, imagining the desperate fear that must be gripping her heart, and Rick's unexpected display of emotion. She couldn't forget the awkward way he'd brushed away his tears.

"It's so horrible," she blurted out. "I can't think about anything else. I'm terrified for Nemo, and I have a dreadful feeling in the pit of my stomach all the time. I used up half a tank of gas yesterday driving around looking for that Honda CR-V. I'm literally sick with worry that this story won't have a happy ending."

Ted's head was bowed; he was studying the camera display. He stared at it for a long time, then swallowed hard. "You got a great shot. I'm going to run it on the front page."

Lucy shook her head. It was only Friday, and the paper wouldn't come out until next Thursday. "Let's hope we'll have a photo of Nemo, safe and sound, being reunited with his parents," she said, privately vowing to do everything she could to find the boy.

When they got back to the office, Ted disappeared once again into the morgue, shutting the door behind him. Lucy exchanged a puzzled glance with Phyllis, then settled down at her desk to tackle the events listings. It was a struggle to concentrate on the flood of holiday events, like church bazaars, cookie sales, and *Nutcracker* performances, and she was relieved when she typed up the last press release, announcing the Little Theatre's performance of Dickens's *A Christmas Carol.* She logged off her computer, deciding to start her search for Nemo with her friend Sue Finch. She knew that Nemo was enrolled at Little Prodigies Preschool, which was owned in part by Sue.

When Lucy arrived at the bright and cheery preschool, she found Sue helping a group of four-year-olds make Christmas ornaments. She was seated at a very low table where the kids were painting pinecones with glue and dipping them into trays of colored glitter. It was a messy project, and Sue seemed happy to hand it over to one of her assistants.

"Let's go into the kitchen," she told Lucy, brushing a shower of glitter off her black flannel slacks. The pants were rumpled, which Lucy thought must be a first for the usually meticulous Sue, and she needed a manicure. "It's almost snack time."

When they were inside the little efficiency kitchen, she closed the door behind them. “I’m sure you’re here to talk about Nemo, and I don’t want to upset the kids,” she said as she washed her hands.

“I was at the press conference this morning. Ocean and Rick made a statement. . . .”

Sue was counting out small paper cups on a tray. Her head was bowed, and Lucy was startled to see she’d skipped putting on her usual eye make-up. “How are they doing?”

“Ocean looked devastated, dark circles under her eyes. Rick was the big surprise. He broke down.”

Sue stopped in mid-count. “Rick broke down?”

“Yeah. He teared up.”

Sue resumed setting the cups into neat rows. “I never thought he was that involved with Nemo.”

Lucy’s interest was piqued. “Why do you say that?”

Sue began filling the cups with apple juice. “I never saw him. It was always Ocean who dropped Nemo off in the morning and picked him up in the afternoon. She was the one who enrolled him. I wouldn’t know Rick if I saw him.”

“Oh, I think you would,” said Lucy. “He’s got the same shaved head, and they have matching tattoos on their necks."

Sue was opening a second bottle of juice. "That is so sweet," she said sarcastically, tucking a limp lock of hair behind her ear. "True love."

Lucy shrugged. "It takes all kinds, I guess." She paused. "I was hoping you could tell me about them. Background stuff."

Sue capped the bottle and put it in the fridge. Turning back to Lucy, she crossed her arms across her chest. "My impression is that life at the Aquarizoo is pretty unorganized when it comes to meals and bedtimes and stuff like that. Ocean seems more like a kid herself. She's more like a big sister than a mother. That said, Nemo is a darling kid. He's smart and funny and . . ." Sue paused to brush away a tear. "He's not a whiner or a complainer. He's very independent, very resilient." She let out a long, quavery sigh. "If any kid can come through something like this, it's Nemo."

Lucy thought of the large black woman in the maroon coat. "It doesn't seem like he was snatched by one of those sickos — it was a woman. Maybe she just wants a child of her own."

Sue nodded. "I hope that's the case. The real weirdos seem to be men."

Lucy had a horrible thought. "They say it

was a large person — it could have been a man in disguise."

"Let's not go there," said Sue, reaching for a box of graham crackers.

"Right." Lucy watched as Sue arranged the crackers on a plate. "Something's been bothering me about Rick. Did you know he has a Porsche?"

Sue's eyebrows shot up. "Really?"

"Yeah. I saw them all at the IGA. Nemo wanted a gingerbread man, and Ocean said they couldn't afford any extras. So I bought the cookie and gave it to him in the parking lot. Rick was strapping him into a booster seat in a Porsche."

Sue put the plate of crackers on the tray. "I've seen this sort of thing before. A lot of men really resent having to cough up money for family expenses. You should hear the song and dance I get sometimes about our fees here. They think that since they're the big earners, they should have more for themselves."

"Do you know what Rick does for a living?"

"No, but I'm surprised money's a problem for them. Nemo's fees are always paid on the dot." Sue shook her head. "I do know that Ocean drives an old heap of a truck. Not a club cab, mind you, just an old model with a bench seat. She puts Nemo in a booster next to her, but it's not safe, and I've told her so numerous times."

"A Porsche isn't much better. I mean, it's not exactly a family car."

Sue picked up the tray. "I know I shouldn't say this, but I never had the feeling they were much of a family."

Lucy watched her carry the snacks out to the classroom.

"Time to finish up our project and wash our hands," Sue said, using her teacher voice. "Then we'll have our snack and a story."

Lucy caught her eye and gave a little wave as she headed for the door. *That's how childhood ought to be,* she thought, thinking back to the days when her own kids were small. Each day followed a reassuring pattern of activities punctuated with meals and naps, storybooks and puzzles. They were wrapped up in warm clothes and hats and mittens when they went outside; they were tucked into cozy beds at night along with their teddy bears. Maybe they didn't have a lot of extras, maybe some of their toys and clothes were picked up at yard sales, but they had the security of a well-ordered home.

Lucy wasn't convinced that Nemo had those same advantages at the Aquarizoo.

Chapter Three

Even if Lucy had wanted to forget about Nemo for a while, it wasn't possible. The story was everywhere: there were constant updates on the radio, TV channels ran a crawl along the bottom of the screen with his description, and his face was on the front of every newspaper. When she got home from work and clicked on the TV to the regional cable channel to check the weather, she found they were running an interview with Ocean at the Aquarizoo.

"So this is the spot where Nemo was playing when he was abducted?" asked the reporter, a stocky man wearing a Windbreaker with the NECN logo. He was standing with Ocean in the abandoned parking lot that served as a front yard. It was covered with a couple of inches of ice and gray snow, crisscrossed with tire tracks.

"Yes." She had a knit cap pulled over her shaved head and was wearing a warm coat with the collar turned up, but she still looked as if she was freezing. She pointed with a bare hand to a window in the ramshackle building that had once housed tanks of colorful tropical fish. "I was watching him from there. I saw the car pull up, and I didn't recognize it. . . ."

"It was a gray Honda CR-V?"

"That's right. I don't know anybody who has a car like that, so I started to go out but . . ." Her voice broke and she wiped away tears with her raw, chapped hand, then swallowed hard and looked straight at the camera. "It was all over so quickly. I barely got out the door when the car speeded away with . . . with . . ."

"With little Nemo," said the reporter, finishing for her. "And you saw the abductor? A large black woman in a maroon coat."

"That's right." Ocean pressed her lips together and nodded. "It was one of those puffy, quilted coats." She looked off toward the road, as if picturing the whole thing all over again, and blinked. "I just hope she takes good care of my little boy."

"Absolutely." The camera closed in on the reporter. "And once again we're asking our viewers if they have any information about little Nemo to please call this number. One-eight-hundred-five-five-five-zero-one-two-

two. And now, I understand, you're going to show us Nemo's room."

"That's right," said Ocean. "Follow me."

The camera followed them through a creaky door into a neat, basic kitchen where a spider plant hung in the window over the sink, down a dark hall, and into a brightly lit child's room. Lucy found herself watching, fascinated, even though she felt like a voyeur.

The room was painted blue and looked to be something right out of a Pottery Barn Kids catalog. Lucy knew that stuff wasn't cheap — she'd often seen things she thought would be perfect for Patrick, only to be deterred from ordering by the price. But there was the bedding with colorful trucks, the matching rug, the sturdy white-painted furniture. Toys were neatly arranged in baskets and bins on white shelves, there were plenty of books, and a stuffed orange and white Nemo fish was propped against the pillow.

"This is the chair I use when I read stories to him," said Ocean, pointing with a shaky finger at a roomy armchair upholstered in blue and white stripes. "He was beginning to recognize words."

Lucy nodded. She could believe that. She was confident that Nemo was a smart kid who probably was beginning to figure out how to read. But the rest? The room with its expensive fittings? Somehow that just didn't fit in with what she knew about the Anderson-Juergens family. What was going on? They could afford a Porsche and a Pottery Barn bedroom for Nemo, but money was too tight to buy him a cheap gingerbread cookie?

She was still pondering this incongruity when she got up and went into the kitchen to make herself a cup of tea. She was putting the kettle on the stove when the phone rang, and she automatically picked it up.

"Mom?"

It was Elizabeth, her older daughter, and Lucy immediately perked up. Elizabeth was calling from Palm Beach, where she was working in the posh Cavendish Hotel. It was her first job — she'd graduated from Chamberlain College in Boston in the spring — and Lucy was eager to have a nice chat. Elizabeth's job entailed odd hours — she sometimes worked the night shift — so Lucy didn't get to talk with her that often.

"Elizabeth! How are you?"

"I'm fine, Mom."

"How's the job?"

"Well, that's kind of what I'm calling about."

Lucy felt that familiar tightening of her stomach that preceded bad news. What had Elizabeth done? Had she gotten herself fired? Or laid off? Times were tight, after all, and unemployment was high among twentysomethings. "Is everything okay?" she asked, preparing herself for the worst.

"Oh, yeah. I just had my thirty-day review and they love me. It was all good. I even got a raise."

Lucy felt a huge sense of relief. "That's terrific."

"Yeah, well, working the front desk isn't really all that challenging. I heard a rumor that the assistant manager is going to be transferred to Cabo, lucky her, and I'm hoping they'll promote me."

Lucy didn't think that was likely, since Elizabeth had been on the job for only a month, following a two-month training period, but she didn't want to dampen her hopes. "Well, you never know. . . ."

"That's one reason why I volunteered to work Christmas."

It hit Lucy like a sucker punch. She didn't see it coming. "What?"

"I looked into flights home, but it's already too late and I couldn't get anything except first class so when they said they needed somebody to cover during Christmas I said

I'd do it."

"I'll pay," said Lucy in a moment of maternal madness, completely forgetting her growing credit card balance.

"That's crazy, Mom. Christmas is just one day, like any other."

Lucy's jaw dropped. Here she'd been knocking herself out for twenty-odd years to make Christmas memorable for her family, and this was what she got for her trouble? "I can't believe what I'm hearing."

"Well, you know Patrick and Toby and Molly aren't going to be there, either. So I figured I'd work Christmas and get a whole lotta Brownie points and then I'd come home for New Year's. Don't you think that's smart? We can have a sort of second Christmas. Like Twelfth Night or something."

Lucy watched as Zoe, her youngest, wandered into the kitchen. A middle-schooler, she had suddenly shot up an inch or two and was always hungry. She was peering into the refrigerator, looking for something to eat.

"I guess it's okay," said Lucy in a resigned voice. "It will have to be, won't it? We'll miss you, of course." Zoe was giving her a questioning look.

"And I'll miss you, too. But I'll be busy at work, and then I'll be home a week later."

"Right," said Lucy. "Zoe's right here. Want to talk to her?"

"Sure."

Lucy handed over the phone and went into the powder room, where tears began to flow. She put the lid on the seat down and sat with a box of tissues in her lap, pulling them out one by one. First Patrick and his fickle parents and now Elizabeth, the selfish little witch. This was no way to celebrate Christmas. Families were supposed to get together for Christmas, not go wandering off to Florida and the Caribbean. What kind of Christmas did they have there, anyway? It was not like it snowed or anything. It was just wrong — imagine celebrating Christmas in a swimsuit!

There was a little knock on the door. "Mom?"

Lucy's voice was thick. "Come on in."

Zoe leaned against the sink, her shoulders slumping. "I can't believe it."

"Me neither."

"This is going to be a crummy Christmas with just you and me and Sara and Dad."

Lucy knew she had to rally the troops. "Well, it'll be different." She paused, thinking. "Maybe we need to rethink our priorities."

"We always go to church. It's not like we

leave Christ out of Christmas."

"We could do more, though. We could help others."

"Like in *Little Women?* Where they take breakfast to the starving family and poor Beth catches scarlet fever?"

Lucy found herself laughing in spite of herself. "We'll skip the scarlet fever part."

"What's so funny?" Sara, a willowy high school senior, was standing at the door.

"Elizabeth's not coming home for Christmas," said Zoe.

"What's funny about that?"

"Nothing at all," said Lucy. "We were just trying to cheer ourselves up. And you know what Sue says. 'When the going gets tough, the tough go shopping!' Let's go out to the outlet mall and do some Christmas shopping! It'll put us in the Christmas spirit, and we can pick up a pizza for supper on the way home."

What she didn't say, but thought to herself, was that half the family seemed not to have any Christmas spirit at all.

When they got in the car, Lucy switched from the news station to the classical music station. They were playing a medley of Christmas carols, and they all sang along. A light snow was falling, and the houses they passed were decorated for the holiday with lights and wreaths. Some people had even put out illuminated plastic figures of Santa and his reindeer, or Frosty the Snowman. But fa-la-la as she might, Lucy was only going through the motions in hopes of summoning up some Christmas spirit for Sara and Zoe.

Even worse, Lucy hated the gigantic Toys 'n' More store. The place was huge and filled with overpriced toys she didn't quite approve of: techno-robots and superheroes and sexually precocious dolls. Everything binged and buzzed and blinked and required at least four AA batteries, conveniently located at the checkout and sold at the manufacturer's suggested retail price.

But this wasn't about her, she reminded herself as she pulled a shopping cart out of the rank by the entrance. These were the sorts of toys kids wanted, they didn't want wooden blocks and baby dolls, and she was determined to find something that would make a big hit with Patrick. But what?

"Toys for toddlers are down this aisle," said Sara, pointing the way.

"How about one of those benches you pound with a little hammer?" suggested Lucy.

"Look at this!" exclaimed Zoe. "It's a toy chain saw. It goes." She held up a miniature version of the real thing, which buzzed as a chain of beads ran around the blade. "They have drills and saws. So cute, just like Dad's."

They were cute, but Lucy didn't think Patrick had the coordination to operate them. "Maybe when he's a bit older."

"Take a look at this!" Sara had found a bright orange Tigger figure that did somersaults. Battery operated, of course.

"Kind of a one-trick tiger." Lucy was studying a large yellow cement mixer.

"Mom. That's a sandbox toy. Patrick's sandbox is full of snow," said Zoe.

Reluctantly, Lucy put it back. "How about a sled? A little one with a rope that we could pull him around on."

The girls thought that was a good idea and a search was launched, but no such sled could be found. When Lucy finally confronted a sales associate, after tracking the elusive figure down just in front of a door marked PERSONNEL ONLY, she discovered Toys 'n' More didn't carry sleds. "That's sporting equipment," the pimply youth informed her.

Back in the toddler section they passed shelf after shelf of colorful boxes. A xylophone? Too noisy. Dinosaurs? Too scary. Shape sorters? Too boring. Then, rounding the corner, they came upon a section of go-carts. And right in the middle, dwarfing all the others, was a bright yellow kid-size front-end loader with a clawlike shovel. Lucy knew Patrick would love it.

"That's cool," said Sara.

"The shovel works," said Zoe, who was examining the toy. One lever raised and lowered the toy's plastic jaws; another opened and shut them. Patrick might not be old enough to manage the levers, but he would enjoy sitting in the seat behind the litle steering wheel and zooming around the house.

"How much is it?" Lucy was afraid she couldn't afford it.

"It's on sale," said Zoe. "Fifty-nine ninety-nine."

Lucy was tempted but hesitated. "It seems like an awful lot for a chunk of plastic."

"It's a lot of plastic," said Zoe.

"His other grandparents are taking him on a Disney cruise," said Sara.

Lucy was convinced. "We'll take it," she said, feeling a glimmer of Christmas spirit. It was truly the perfect present for Patrick.

"This is a floor model. You take the ticket to the service desk," explained Zoe.

"Figures," sighed Lucy, spotting the line

at the counter. So much for Christmas spirit.

Forty-five minutes later they were once again in line, this time at the checkout, with a huge box precariously balanced on their cart. The line was slow: a lot of toys were mis-marked, and customers were arguing with the cashier. The store manager was frequently summoned and stubbornly maintained the price produced by the scanner was the correct price, even when confronted with evidence to the contrary in the colorful flyers provided at the door. "We're not responsible for misprints," he insisted, pointing to a printed sign.

Lucy was vowing not to pay a penny more than $59.99 when her eye was caught by a bin full of marked-down toys, including a fishing pole and colorful magnetized fishes. She immediately thought of Nemo. Digging through it, she found a fish puzzle and a snorkel set, perfect for dress-up play. Impulsively, she grabbed them all and threw them into the cart.

"For Patrick?" asked Sara, puzzled.

"No. For Nemo."

The girls looked at each other, and from their expressions Lucy was pretty sure they'd concluded she'd lost her mind.

"For when they find him," she said, wheeling the cart up to the counter.

"That'll be one-oh-nine forty-six," announced the cashier.

Lucy handed over her charge card without a word of protest.

"They charged you too much," said Sara as they headed for the door.

Lucy thought of Patrick, who would be far away on the high seas on Christmas Day, and she thought of Nemo, wherever he was, and an enormous sense of desolation swept over her. It was a big world out there, and a dangerous one. All she could do was hope they were safe and, in Patrick's case, let him know he was loved. "I don't care," she said.

Sara and Zoe were shaking their heads.

"What?" she demanded, struggling to push the cart through the slushy snow that covered the parking lot.

"Nothing. It's just not like you to let something like that go," said Zoe.

Lucy popped the rear door of the car and began loading the toys. "You gotta choose your fights," she said, slamming it shut. It wasn't worth wasting her energy arguing with the idiotic store manager for a few dollars. Not when she had far weightier matters on her mind.

Chapter Four

When Lucy got a phone call that evening from her daughter-in-law, Molly, she figured the word had gone out on the grapevine that she wasn't her usual, cheerful self and was taking her family's defections hard.

"We're going to make gingerbread cookies tomorrow, and we're hoping you can join us," said Molly. "I could use some help with Patrick."

Lucy jumped at the invitation. "I wouldn't miss it for the world."

When Lucy arrived around three on Saturday afternoon, Patrick was just waking up from his afternoon nap. Toby was carrying him downstairs, and he was rubbing his eyes and looking absolutely adorable with his pink cheeks and wispy blond hair. Lucy loved the way he was dressed in a tiny flannel shirt and contractor's jeans — just like his father and grandfather wore. He was even wearing a tiny pair of tan work boots.

"I could eat you up," cooed Lucy, plucking the toddler from his father's arms and burying her nose in his warm, soft neck.

Patrick didn't giggle, but he didn't protest, either, as Lucy followed Toby into the kitchen. Molly was already rolling out the gingerbread dough on the center island. Lucy seated herself on a stool and bounced Patrick in her lap. She picked up one of the cookie cutters and tapped it on the counter, reciting: "Run, run, as fast as you can. You can't catch me. I'm the Gingerbread Man."

Patrick reached for the bright red plastic cookie cutter, and Lucy gave it to him. He promptly put it in his mouth.

"Everything goes in his mouth," said Molly, deftly taking the cookie cutter away and substituting a wooden spoon.

Patrick was squirming, so Lucy set him down, and he toddled over to the pot cupboard. Opening the door, he pulled out a pot and sat down on the floor, banging it with the wooden spoon.

"He's the next Ringo Starr," said Lucy.

"And we're going to be deaf," said Molly, rinsing off the cookie cutter.

Toby scooped up his son and flew him through the air like an airplane, much to Patrick's delight. The little fellow stretched out his arms and giggled merrily.

"Don't get him overexcited," warned Molly.

"Give him to me," said Lucy, holding out her arms.

Toby handed over his son, and Lucy sat him in her lap. Holding him tight, she gave him the cookie cutter once again and guided his plump little hand, pressing the cookie cutter into the dough. "There! Look what you did! You made a gingerbread man!"

Patrick quickly smashed his fist down, pressing the cutter crosswise on the gingerbread man.

"No, no, no," cooed Lucy. "We have to try again."

The next attempt was more successful, and soon a sheet of cookies was baking in the oven, filling the kitchen with the delicious scent of molasses and spices. Molly was busy rolling out another batch of dough, and Toby was unloading the dishwasher. Patrick was sitting in Lucy's lap, eating raisins.

"I didn't hear the news this morning," said Lucy, smoothing Patrick's silky hair. "Was there anything about Nemo?"

"No." Molly lifted the rolling pin and shook her head. "It's so awful. I never thought something like that would happen here in Tinker's Cove. My friends are all terrified. They're afraid to let their kids out of sight for even a second."

"That's natural," said Lucy, giving Patrick a hug.

Toby paused in front of the glass cupboard, holding a tumbler in his hand. "I'd like to get my hands on that kidnapper!"

"They say it's a woman." Molly was laying a cookie on the baking pan.

"I don't care," growled Toby.

"A big woman," said Lucy. "Maybe it was a man in disguise."

"Whoever it is, it's a terrible thing to do," said Molly. "Although I do think Ocean was a bit irresponsible letting him play outside there, so close to the road."

Lucy had already heard similar sentiments expressed by other people around town. It was inevitable, she supposed, that people would begin to blame the parents. Especially since Ocean and Rick were so unconventional. "It's not like you have to pass a test to be a parent," said Lucy. "I think they were doing the best they knew how."

Toby shut the dishwasher door and whirled around. "Rick? Are you kidding me?"

"What do you mean? I saw him at the IGA parking lot. He was strapping Nemo into a car seat." Patrick was squirming and Lucy set him down; he made a beeline for his father, demanding "ups" and more airplane.

Toby grabbed him under the armpits and swung him back and forth. "He's no good. He's a drug dealer."

Lucy thought she knew what was going on in town, but this was news to her. "He is?"

Toby shrugged. "That's what they say."

Molly was lifting cookies off the pan and setting them on a wire rack to cool. "I've heard that, too, and I think he's a user. Just look at him."

Lucy switched on the mixer, creaming a stick of butter with confectioners' sugar to make icing. It made sense, she thought. Rick didn't have a job and neither did Ocean, but they had money, at least some of the time. That would explain the expensive furnishings in Nemo's room, and the fast car. And it would also explain why the family occasionally ran out of money, in between shipments. And if he used, it would explain his extreme thinness and his nervous twitching.

"I think that's mixed enough," said Molly, breaking into her thoughts. "Let me add a drop of vanilla."

Lucy clicked off the mixer and removed

the beaters, giving one each to Patrick and Toby.

Molly clucked her tongue in disapproval. "The sugar will make them crazy — especially Toby!"

Back at work on Monday, Lucy found time dragged as she followed her regular weekly round, covering the meetings of various committees that conducted the town's business and interviewing the manager of the local food pantry, where supplies were running low in the face of unprecedented demand. There were no new developments in the kidnapping, and the story was already getting a lot less coverage. It was old news, just a tag at the end of the report, a couple of inches in the back of the daily paper.

Ted wasn't about to let it go, however. His jaw set, he doggedly pursued local officials, demanding updates. When they had nothing new to report, he'd slam down the receiver and head for the morgue, where Lucy and Phyllis could hear him slapping the heavy volumes of bound old papers onto the table and muttering as he flipped through them.

"What's with him?" Lucy asked Phyllis.

Phyllis shrugged. "Maybe he's looking up old cases, looking for similarities?"

Lucy understood his frustration — she was frustrated, too, at the lack of progress in the case. Her thoughts constantly turned to Nemo and the approaching holiday in what had become a mantra. *Please, please bring Nemo home for Christmas.* It ran through her mind constantly, a silent little prayer.

Lucy wasn't the only one upset by Nemo's disappearance. When Lucy arrived at Jake's Donut Shack on Thursday morning for her weekly breakfast with her friends, she was shocked at Sue's appearance. Sue was known for her fashionable outfits and impeccable grooming, but today her usually sleek pageboy hairdo was frizzy and she'd skipped her usual make-up, applying only a smear of red lipstick. A fresh copy of the *Pennysaver,* which came out on Thursday morning, was on the table in front of her. Lucy recognized the photo she'd taken of Rick and Ocean at the press conference. There it was, taking up most of the first page, and she remembered how she'd hoped they'd have a photo of a happy family reunion instead.

"He's been gone for a whole week," said Sue as Lucy slid into the booth beside her. Pam Stillings, Ted's wife, and Rachel Goodman were sitting on the other side.

Rachel's expression was sad and her brown eyes seemed enormous. "It's not good. The longer these things go on, the more likely it is that the victim is . . ."

"Dead." Sue finished the sentence. "I know."

"That's not always the case," said Pam, ever the optimist. She had been a cheerleader in high school and still had that rah-rah spirit. "Look at Elizabeth Smart. She turned up okay. And that poor girl who was locked in a backyard and had two kids. She was a captive for twenty-odd years."

Lucy nodded. "It was a woman, after all. Maybe she couldn't have kids of her own and saw Nemo and just had to have him." She sighed, thinking of the toys she'd bought for Nemo. "That's what I cling to."

"I feel so bad for Ocean. She may not be the Mother of the Year, but she loves Nemo." Sue was fiddling with her coffee cup. "I can't imagine the pain, can you? I mean, not knowing what's happened to your child."

Lucy nodded thoughtfully, watching as Norine, the waitress, approached with a coffeepot in each hand. "You girls ready to order?" she asked as she poured. "The usual?"

"I'll have French toast," said Sue, causing a little stir. Sue always limited herself to black coffee.

"Comfort food?" asked Rachel in a sympathetic tone.

Sue stared at her, stunned. "I can't believe I'm doing this."

"It's okay," said Pam. "You're not going to turn into a blimp just because you ate a plate of French toast."

"In fact," said Lucy, making an executive decision, "make it French toast for all of us." She looked round the table for agreement. "Okay?"

It was unanimous.

The French toast was delicious — made with thick slices of multigrain bread and topped with real maple syrup. There was an unspoken agreement to avoid talking about the kidnapping, and conversation turned to the upcoming holiday.

"Is Elizabeth coming home?" asked Pam.

Lucy cut an extra big piece of French toast and popped it in her mouth. "Nnnoo," she said, shaking her head.

"How come?" Rachel took a sip of coffee.

"She thinks she might get a shot at a promotion if she works Christmas. And since Patrick won't be there, anyway, she said we might as well celebrate a week later." Lucy snorted. "It's like the domino effect — one goes and then they all go."

"She sounds smart to me," said Sue, cutting herself a miniscule bite. "Most kids today aren't that ambitious. I wish the girls at the day-care center would take their jobs a little more seriously. They call in sick all the time — especially on Mondays and Fridays. I call it Weekend Flu."

"I guess we've all been guilty of that at one time or other," said Pam as they all chuckled. "But that Cavendish chain is supposed to be one of the best places to work. Terrific benefits and training programs."

"The owner is a psychiatrist," said Rachel. "I read about him in *Modern Psychology.* He's done tons of research on retaining employees, and customers, too. They keep an enormous database on all their guests' preferences, so the front-desk people can greet return guests like VIPs. They know if you're happy with a shower or want a full bath, if you eat eggs for breakfast or just want coffee, a hard pillow or a soft one. He's got a slogan like 'Every guest is a VIP at Cavendish,' something like that."

"Sounds divine," sighed Sue, pushing away the plate of French toast, which she'd barely touched. "I wish I were spending Christmas at a place like that instead of on

Sidra's lumpy old sleep sofa." Sue's married daughter lived in a tiny apartment in New York City. "We call it 'The Rack.' "

"At least you get to see your daughter," grumbled Lucy, polishing off the last bit of French toast. "Since I won't have the kids this year, I'm thinking of having an open house on Christmas Eve. Can you all come?"

"Sorry, sweetie," said Sue. "Sid wants to leave on the twenty-third, to avoid traffic."

Lucy turned to Pam and Rachel.

"Since Richie's so far away — I mean, there's no chance he can get home from Greece — we've decided to spend Christmas in Florida," said Rachel apologetically. "Bob's been working so hard lately, trying to help people avoid these foreclosures. He really needs a break."

"We decided to go down to New Orleans to see Tim," said Pam. "Believe me, I'd much rather stay here and come to your open house, but Ted's . . ." Her voice trailed off.

"Ted's what?" asked Lucy.

"He's not quite himself. I think it's this Nemo thing. He's really taking it hard. It's not like him to get emotionally involved. I think he really needs to get away from it all for a bit, and I was able to get last-minute seats on a Christmas Eve flight." She ran her fork around her plate, catching the last of the maple syrup, and licked it off. "And the rebuilding after Hurricane Katrina is so hopeful and positive. People doing something good for a change."

"I think you're right," said Lucy, remembering how emotional he'd been at the press conference. She ran her fork around her plate, too, to get the last of the maple syrup. To tell the truth, she'd like to get away herself, but she didn't think distance was the cure she needed. No matter where she went, she'd be thinking about Nemo.

Jake's was perched on a steep hill above the harbor, where a large patch of asphalt provided parking for the stores on Main Street as well as the fishermen. Soon the cove would ice up completely, so only a few boats remained, waiting to be hauled out by their owners. Lucy looked at the bleak scene: gray water, gray asphalt, gray sky. She shivered, sliding behind the steering wheel and starting the car. The radio came on; it was that song about the little drummer boy. She was really beginning to hate that song, she thought, twirling the knob in search of a news station. Sometimes when conditions were just right, she could pick up a Boston station, but today all she got was static. *No wonder,* she thought, studying the heavy gray clouds that hung low in the sky.

She clicked the radio off and drove slowly toward the exit, flipping the heater to high. It was a bitter cold day, and the heater didn't seem to be making much difference in the cold car. Lucy thought of Nemo and hoped he was someplace dry and warm, drinking hot cocoa with marshmallows.

It was only a short drive to the *Pennysaver* office, and the car didn't have time to warm up. Lucy was seriously chilled when she stepped inside; the little bell on the door jangled as she hung up her coat and rubbed her hands together.

"I hate this damp, bone-chilling weather," she complained to Phyllis, who was stuffing bills into envelopes.

"I'd almost rather have a real cold snap," agreed Phyllis. "I don't mind the cold if the sun is shining."

"Yeah," agreed Lucy. A stack of freshly printed papers was on the reception counter, and she glanced once again at the photo of Rick and Ocean holding Nemo's picture. "Any news?" she asked.

Phyllis lifted the gadget she used to moisten the glue on the envelope flaps and shook her head. "Honestly, it's like the poor little fellow just dropped off the face of the earth. You'd think somebody would have seen him, what with that AMBER Alert and everything. It went out minutes after he was snatched, and the Aquarizoo is out there on a well-traveled road, quite a distance from anything. There's no cover for miles — you'd think somebody would have seen that CR-V."

"I suppose the kidnapper could have taken back roads, worked her way to the interstate. Say it took fifteen minutes to get the AMBER Alert on the air . . ."

"That's what I mean," said Phyllis, with a nod that slid her harlequin readers down her nose. "There's no way she could have gotten to the interstate in fifteen minutes, and once she was on the highway, she would have been spotted."

The more Lucy thought about it, the more she thought Phyllis was right. "Maybe she slipped through the cracks somehow."

Phyllis pounded her fist on a loose bit of envelope flap that wasn't sticking. "I don't see how."

"Maybe she's holed up someplace around here. There are a lot of empty houses — summer places, foreclosures."

Phyllis shrugged and snapped a rubber

band around her stack of envelopes. "It just doesn't make sense to me. It's winter in Maine. There's not a lot of people around. We all know each other. We know each other's cars and trucks. I don't know any black woman who drives a CR-V. And if I did see somebody like that, a stranger, I'd notice. It's been a week, after all. She'd have to come out eventually for food and gas."

It was true, thought Lucy. The town's population doubled in July and August, when summer people and vacationers arrived, and autumn brought a substantial number of leaf peepers, but once the leaves fell, the tourists scattered to the four winds. Come winter, the snowy, windblown streets were largely deserted as people clung to their warm homes, emerging only to shop at the IGA or gather at the post office and Jake's.

Lucy looked up as a white TV satellite truck trundled past the plate-glass window, rattling the wooden blinds. "Even the media people are leaving," she said.

"They're off after other stories," said Phyllis.

"We can't drop it," said Lucy, with a fierce expression. "We can't let Nemo become yesterday's news."

"No, no." Phyllis's tone was reassuring.

"The police won't give up. In fact, Ted's off interviewing the police chief right now. Ted will keep him on the hot seat."

Lucy thought of Dot, over at the IGA. "And if Ted doesn't, Dot will," she said, causing Phyllis to chuckle.

"That reminds me — I got next week's ad. Turkeys are on sale, forty-nine cents a pound. You ought to pick one up if you're having a crowd for Christmas."

Not much of a crowd, thought Lucy, remembering her plan to hold an open house. "That reminds me. I'm going to mix up a big batch of wassail and invite everybody to come on Christmas Eve. I hope you and Wilf can make it."

Phyllis's face fell, but only for a moment. "I'm sorry. We're going away this year, kind of a late honeymoon. Wilf has booked us on a Caribbean cruise."

"Lucky you," said Lucy.

"Yeah. We're going to cha-cha under the palm trees this Christmas."

Lucy sighed and switched on her computer. It seemed like nobody was dreaming of a white Christmas these days.

Chapter Five

As she usually did on Thursdays, Lucy got started on the events listings. She took the accordion file of press releases over to her desk and pulled out the stack for next Friday, sorting them by category before entering them into the computer. The week between Christmas and New Year's was generally pretty quiet, but there were a few special events. The theater group's production of *A Christmas Carol* was continuing, and there were some special school vacation story hours at the public library. The historical society was hosting an open house at the Josiah Hopkins House: a harpist was going to play and refreshments would be served.

It didn't take long to go through them. With nothing else to do for the moment, Lucy went over to the watercooler and got herself a drink, then wandered into the morgue. She wasn't exactly snooping, she told herself, just kind of checking to see what Ted was finding so absorbing in there. It didn't take long to figure it out: the volume for the summer before last was sticking out a couple of inches.

Lucy didn't have to open it to figure out what he'd been reading. That was the summer Corinne Appleton was kidnapped. The teen, who had lived in Shiloh, had had a summer job in the town's recreation program. Her mother had dropped her off at the park, where the program took place, and had gone on to her job at a nearby bank. That was the last she ever saw of her daughter. Sometime later a hiker found human remains in the woods, along with scraps of cloth that were identified as Corinne's underpants.

Shiloh was one town over from Gilead.

Lucy pulled down the big volume, and it fell open as she laid it on the table; Corinne's pretty face was looking up at her.

"Hey, Lucy, the court clerk just faxed over the court report." Phyllis was standing in the doorway. "What are you looking at?"

"I think Ted's been fixating on the Corinne Appleton case."

Phyllis's face was thoughtful. "They caught that guy, didn't they?"

"Yeah. It was an open-and-shut case."

"Maybe not so open and shut."

"He confessed. Besides, he had duct tape and rope in his van."

"He might've been faking." Seeing Lucy's doubtful expression, Phyllis continued. "Don't scoff. I saw a TV show about it. This guy had all these guilty feelings stemming from his childhood, so he confessed to crimes he didn't commit and even manufactured phony evidence so he'd be convicted. He wanted to be punished."

Lucy shook her head. "That's not the case here. There was DNA." She replaced the heavy volume on the shelf. "I wonder if it's because of Nemo. You know, another kidnapping. I think it's really bothering him."

Phyllis snorted. "It's bothering all of us."

"Yeah, but it's really upsetting Ted. Pam even mentioned it. That's why they're going to New Orleans."

"A change of scene will do him good," said Phyllis, handing her the stack of papers the fax had delivered.

"Whoa," said Lucy, flipping through the pages. "Crime seems to be up."

Phyllis shrugged. "Christmas."

It was true, thought Lucy, returning to her desk. Christmas did tend to produce an uptick in crime, and this year's poor economy certainly wasn't helping. Domestic assaults, predictably, accounted for most of the increase. The cold weather kept people cooped up in their houses, and small disagreements could escalate into violence. And there was the added stress of financial pressure and frustration over high holiday expectations. DUIs also accounted for a lot of arraignments, but Lucy was shocked to see that Howard Higgins, aged seventy-eight, had attempted to rob the Seaman's Bank in Gilead.

"Ohmigosh!" she exclaimed. "Did you see this about Howard Higgins?"

"The bird-watcher you wrote about? Didn't he discover some rare bird?"

"That's the guy. He had a hummingbird at his feeder around Thanksgiving."

"That's not a crime."

"Robbing a bank is, though."

"Maybe he couldn't afford the hummingbird food."

"Not funny, Phyllis. And besides, the bird died. But I do feel bad for Howard. He's really a nice old guy. He must've been drunk or something."

Lucy was typing away, shaking her head. Mira Carter, shoplifting and improper use of a credit card, obviously a Christmas crime. Shaun Bumpus, assault and battery with a dangerous weapon (shod foot) and unarmed robbery. Richard Smythe, assault and battery with a dangerous weapon (kitchen plates). Sylvester Milley, possession of OxyContin with intention to distribute, malicious destruction of property, breaking and entering in the daytime.

When she was nearing the end of the dispositions and arraignments, Lucy voiced her thoughts. "I wonder if this is a story. It really seems like a significant increase," she said when the phone rang.

"It's me," said Sue.

"Hi, you," said Lucy, ready to take a break. She leaned back in her chair and stretched her hands over her head. "What's up?"

"I was making out this month's bank deposit," said Sue.

"Lucky you." Lucy hadn't made a deposit in quite a while; the trend was definitely in the other direction. "Isn't it kind of late in the month?"

"Yeah. A lot of people are slow to pay these days."

It figured, thought Lucy. "They say the economy is improving."

"Maybe it is for 'they,' whoever they are."

Lucy laughed. "Good point."

"Speaking of which, I came across something I thought might interest you. Nemo's account is all paid up."

"Really?"

"Yeah. I have a check here from his grandparents. Ralph and Clementine Anderson of Bridle Path Road in Dover, Massachusetts."

"Ocean's parents?"

"Yeah."

"What nice grandparents. Are they wealthy?" Lucy was thinking of the Pottery Barn furniture and the plentiful toys and books she'd seen in the video clip of Nemo's room.

"Dover is one of the wealthiest towns in Massachusetts," said Sue. "Even the check looks rich."

Lucy was busy Googling Ralph Anderson. "He's CEO of something called Wilberforce Industries."

"Never heard of it."

Lucy scrolled down. "That's because 'Wilberforce is discreet, professional, and effective.' That's their slogan." Lucy was scanning the screen. "Profits are up. Their stock is up. Looks like Ralph is doing a heck of a job — whatever it is they're so discreet about."

"I bet they do something with security — like Blackwater, or maybe Halliburton." Sue paused. "What about Clementine? Can't you just picture her? Cashmere sweater set, pearls, tweed slacks, Ferragamo flats, and a short clip for a hairdo. With highlights."

Lucy was clicking away, typing in her name. "Ah. How do you do it?" she asked as a photo appeared, matching Sue's description. "You could be wrong about the shoes and slacks — it's a head shot."

"Trust me," insisted Sue. "That type always wear Ferragamos."

"Well, whatever she wears, she keeps busy with the Winter Antiques Show, which raises money for Ellis Memorial." Faces of smiling children filled the screen. "I'm guessing it helps underprivileged kids in Boston."

"Hmmm," said Sue, and Lucy could practically hear the wheels turning. "Maybe she'd be interested in helping kids here in Tinker's Cove."

And maybe, thought Lucy, Rick had the same idea. Only instead of a scholarship for some disadvantaged child, he wanted the cash for himself.

She replaced the receiver and sat at her desk, staring at the long catalog of crime she'd been typing. The more she thought about it, the more likely it seemed that Nemo's kidnapping was a hoax designed to extort a handsome ransom from Ocean's parents.

To begin with, there was the mysterious

black woman in the maroon coat, driving the gray Honda CR-V. As Phyllis had pointed out, it didn't seem possible that nobody had seen such a car after the AMBER Alert went out. The truth was, with African Americans accounting for something like 2 percent of Maine's population, a black woman with a white child would have been noticed.

It wasn't the first time a fictitious black person had been accused of a crime. Lucy remembered Boston's notorious Charles Stuart, who'd shot his wife and then blamed a black man. And there was that woman somewhere in the South who'd driven her car, with her two young children inside, into a lake but claimed she was a victim of a carjacking by a black man. In both cases police had circulated crude drawings of the alleged perpetrators; an innocent man had even been arrested in the Stuart case.

The more she thought about it, the more convinced Lucy became that nobody had seen the kidnapper because there wasn't any kidnapper. Nemo had probably been secreted away somewhere by Rick, while Ocean's parents received a totally fictitious ransom demand.

Come to think of it, she realized, Rick did seem to have disappeared. Tinker's Cove was a small town, and you saw people from day to day. She'd seen Ocean a few times since the press conference: picking up mail at the post office, getting gas, waiting for a prescription at the drugstore. But she hadn't seen Rick; she hadn't even seen his car anywhere.

"Are you all right?" It was Phyllis, peering over her shoulder. "The shoplifter is M-I-R-A, not Myra with a *Y*."

Lucy blinked and focused on the fax. "Oh, thanks."

"At this rate you won't finish by next Wednesday's deadline. And you know what Ted says. . . ."

Lucy grinned. "It's not a guideline. It's a deadline." She also knew that suspicions weren't enough for a story; she needed confirmation. But how could she get it? The most obvious tactic was to simply give Clementine and Ralph a call. It was easy enough to get the number of Wilberforce's corporate headquarters, but the operator demanded identification and, when she admitted she was a reporter, refused to put her call through. A search on Google for the Andersons' home phone number came up empty, and it occurred to Lucy that the Andersons probably paid some computer whiz a handsome sum to preserve their privacy.

She decided to shelve the matter for a while and returned to the court report, deciding to let her subconscious work on the problem. It wasn't until she got a call from Elfrida, Phyllis's cousin who was working as a dispatcher at the fire department, that it came to her.

"Lucy," came Elfrida's rather breathy voice. "I know this is last minute, but it would be really great if you could run something in the *Pennysaver* about the silent auction to benefit the firefighters' fund."

Lucy sighed. Elfrida marched to a different drummer; she was a complete individualist who seldom thought beyond the present moment.

"Well, when is the auction?" asked Lucy.

"New Year's Eve. There's going to be a band and hors d'oeuvres, and we're going to lower a lighted dalmatian at midnight. Not a real one, of course. It's made of papier-mâché." She paused. "And I'm going to pole dance. I've been taking a course."

Lucy couldn't help rolling her eyes. Elfrida already had a well-deserved reputation for being free and easy with her favors. "You know it's after deadline, and we're only putting out an abbreviated holiday issue, anyway, because Ted's going on vacation."

"Oh, Lucy, please." Elfrida's voice took on a frantic tone. "The chief will kill me. I was supposed to do this two weeks ago."

Lucy sighed. "You know how Ted is. He's really strict about deadlines."

Ted chose that moment to walk in, head lowered and throwing his hat and gloves in the direction of the old-fashioned steam radiator and missing. He stood, still in his jacket, and demanded, "What's going on?"

Lucy put her hand over the mouthpiece. "It's Elfrida. She's got a late press release. . . ."

"Run it," barked Ted, tossing his jacket on his chair and marching into the morgue, slamming the door after him.

Lucy's eyes met those of Phyllis, who replied with a shrug.

"Ted says it's okay," said Lucy. "Do you want to fax it over?"

"How about I read it to you?" suggested Elfrida.

"Faxing would be better," said Lucy, who'd learned the hard way that errors tended to slip into announcements delivered over the phone. "Or an e-mail."

"I haven't exactly written it out," said Elfrida. "I figured that's what you do. It's your job, really."

Lucy felt her back stiffen. First Ted had failed to back her up on a policy that had been in place since Hector was a pup, and now scatty Elfrida, of all people, was telling her how to do her job.

"Maybe you should talk to Phyllis," suggested Lucy. Phyllis, however, was shaking her head vehemently and heading for the lavatory. "Never mind," said Lucy, deciding to get it over with. "Shoot."

"Well, the gala — be sure you get that word, *gala* — is on New Year's Eve at the firehouse, beginning at eight clock. Admission is fifteen dollars per person, which includes dancing to a DJ, hors d'oeuvres, and nonalcoholic drinks. Guests can BYOB, but the chief reminds everyone to please drink responsibly. It's all to raise money for the firefighters' fund, which helps with medical expenses not covered by insurance. And there's all these wonderful prizes, including a three-night stay at a luxury hotel in Orlando. . . ."

"That's enough," said Lucy, who had suddenly remembered the Cavendish hotel chain was known for keeping an enormous database of information about its well-heeled clients and her daughter had access to that database.

"But there's lots more prizes," protested Elfrida.

"Just fax that list to me," said Lucy. "I'll take it from there."

"Okay. And thanks, Lucy. Or maybe I should thank your boss."

If she'd been in striking distance, she would have strangled Elfrida. As it was, she had to content herself with hanging up and dialing Elizabeth's cell phone.

"Mom!" protested Elizabeth when she answered. "I can't give you information like that! Preserving guest confidentiality is number one in the job description here. For everyone! Chambermaids, electricians, cooks. Leaking any of that information is grounds for immediate dismissal."

"Can't you just check and see if Clementine and Ralph Anderson of Dover, Massachusetts, are in the file?"

"No! No! No! There are people who monitor the computers. If you get caught browsing, say Madonna or Kevin Bacon, they will find out and . . ."

"Has Madonna stayed there?"

"I don't know, Mom. That's the point. I'm not supposed to know. I'm only supposed to access the files of people who check in, and even then it's supposed to be very discreet. A quick glance . . . just so I can bring up some chatty little item. Like how's the dog? Something like that. Then, once they've gone to their room, I send their info to the head concierge, who takes it from there."

Lucy couldn't believe this was her daughter. Since when had Elizabeth turned into such a little Goody Two-shoes? "Couldn't you make a mistake accidentally on purpose? For your mom?"

"Not even for you. No! I'm trying to get ahead here and some guests are coming and I have to go."

Lucy sat at her desk, screwing up her face and twiddling her thumbs. This was very disappointing. What was the point of going through labor and breast-feeding and paying college tuition if your children turned against you and wouldn't even do a little favor for you? Blood was supposed to be thicker than water, but here it was turning out to be pretty thin stuff, at least as far as Elizabeth was concerned. And she wasn't even coming home for Christmas! And then there was Molly and Toby carrying little Patrick off onto the high seas for the holiday!

"Lucy?" It was Phyllis. "What's got into you?"

Lucy turned to look at her. "It's my family," she said, staring at the photos on her desk. "They're all a bunch of ungrateful wretches."

"So what's new? Why do you think Wilf and I are going on that cruise? It's so we can avoid Christmas with his folks. All that Swedish food — lutefisk and *korv* — it's enough to make you sick, and if you don't eat it, his mother has a fit."

"I don't serve lutefisk, whatever that is," said Lucy as the phone rang.

She picked it up, surprised to hear Elizabeth's voice. At least she thought it was Elizabeth. Whoever was calling was speaking very softly.

"Can't you speak up?" she asked.

"No, Mom. I can't. But you're in luck. I got the phone number. It's 508-555-0135."

Lucy scribbled it down. "How'd you manage it?"

"Must be divine intervention. Honestly, I don't know how you do it, Mom, but the people who were checking in were named Andersen, with an *e*. Like you said, anybody can make a mistake. And they didn't think anything about it when I pulled up the Andersons with an *o*, because it happens all the time." Elizabeth paused. "But don't ask me to do this again, okay?"

"I promise." Lucy hung up, with warm feelings toward her enormously clever daughter. It was all worth it when you produced a gem like Elizabeth. *What a kid!* She wasted no time punching in the numbers.

The call was quickly answered by a woman with a slight Spanish accent. "Anderson residence."

"May I please speak to Mrs. Anderson?" Lucy used her most polite voice.

The person on the other end was equally polite. "May I ask who's calling?"

Lucy decided to switch to a more informal tone, implying she was a friend of the family. "It's Lucy."

It didn't work. "I'm sorry but I need your last name."

"My goodness, you'd think you'd recognize me by now. It's Lucy Stone."

"My apologies."

That sounded good, thought Lucy.

"And what is the call in reference to?"

Not so good. Journalistic ethics required she identify herself.

"I'm with the *Pennysaver* newspaper in Tinker's Cove."

The voice was firm. "I'm sorry, but Mrs. Anderson is not taking calls from the media."

Lucy had gotten this far; she wasn't about to give up. "But Muffy Witherspoon asked me to call — I'm doing PR for the Winter Antiques Show."

There was a pause and Lucy's hopes rose, only to be dashed. "I'm surprised they didn't tell you the show has been canceled this year due to the poor economy." Then the line went dead.

Lucy was back to square one, sitting at her desk, staring at the computer screen and not seeing a thing.

"Lucy!" It was Ted, peering over her shoulder. "There's no *w* in auction."

"Oh, thanks." She shook her head to clear out the cobwebs and turned back to the court report. There had to be a way to find out if the Andersons had received a ransom demand. But how?

Chapter Six

A few strokes on her keypad took her to Google and an aerial view of Bridle Path Road; she even got a video tour of the neighborhood. Very nice. A few more clicks and she discovered it was about two hundred miles from Tinker's Cove to Dover, and if she managed to miss rush hour in Boston, she could be there in four hours. Of course, she'd have to go on her own time — Ted would never allow her to go while on the clock at the paper. And with Christmas only a few days away, when would she find the time?

It was something to think about as she finished up the court report and turned to the town calendar. Not much there. The usual meeting of the board of selectmen on Tuesday and the finance committee on Thursday. None of it really registered. While she was typing with one part of her brain, another part was busy thinking about Rick and Nemo. How come, she wondered, Rick's last name was Juergens and Nemo's was Anderson? Kids usually were given their father's name, even when the parents weren't married. She thought of Phyllis's cousin, Elfrida, who was pregnant once again. She had married some of her kids' fathers, but not all. The kids all had different last names. It had become a bit of a joke in town. "Now, who are you?" people would tease when the kids sold Girl Scout cookies or stood outside the IGA with football helmets to collect donations. "Are you a Norman or a Moskowitz?"

The kids were all cool about it. Their most frequent answer was, "I'm a hot ticket, that's who I am," and people would chuckle as they bought a box of Thin Mints or tucked a dollar bill in the helmet.

She was wondering if perhaps Rick wasn't really Nemo's father, and if he wasn't, who was, when Ted broke into her thoughts.

"Lucy, are you all right?" It was Ted, scowling at her.

"Sure. Why?"

"You've been sitting there for fifteen minutes, staring at the wall." His tone was accusatory.

"No, no, I'm working," she said, checking the computer screen and seeing row after row filled with *I*'s.

He shook his head and pursed his lips. "No, you're not. You're daydreaming."

Desperate times called for desperate measures, decided Lucy, sighing and hanging her head. "You know, you're right. I don't feel well," she said, pressing her hand against her forehead and sinking a little lower in her chair. "I think I'm coming down with something."

"Maybe it's that flu that's going around," said Phyllis. "Did you get the shot?"

"I didn't," confessed Lucy, propping her head on her hand. "I went to the drugstore, but the line was right out the door."

Phyllis gave a prim little nod. "Everyone was supposed to get the shot."

"That's right, Lucy," added Ted, who had editorialized at length about the importance of flu shots. "Did you at least get the kids immunized?"

"They got shots at school," she said, rubbing her eyes. "Oh, gosh, I hope I'm not coming down with it."

"You better go right home," said Ted in a peevish tone. "I don't want you spreading the infection, especially after my editorials on the subject."

"Okay," said Lucy, feigning reluctance as

she logged off. "That's probably the best thing."

"And don't come back until you get a clean bill of health from Doc Ryder," instructed Ted.

Phyllis was covering her nose and mouth with a tissue and reaching for the Lysol. "Get that Tamiflu. It's supposed to work."

"Good idea." Lucy pulled on her coat and picked up her handbag with effort, as if she barely had enough strength to lift it. "If I don't see you before you leave, have a good trip," she said, making her way slowly to the door.

"Just what I need," complained Ted as the door closed behind her.

Once outside she straightened up and took a deep breath of fresh, cool air. It was too late to head for Dover today, but she had tomorrow, Friday, all to herself. If she didn't come down with the flu, that is.

Lucy had printed out driving directions to the Andersons' house on Bridle Path Road in Dover, and it seemed easy enough: get to the Maine Turnpike, pick up Route I-95 and stick with it until it became Route 128, the infamous highway that circled Boston, and take the Dover exit. Easy-peasy. If she left by 6:00 a.m., she could make Dover by ten, allow half an hour for an interview, and be home by two thirty, well before the girls got home from school.

Except, of course, that she wasn't used to highway driving, at least not the way they did it in Boston. For one thing, the signs were confusing. Sometimes Route 128 was marked 128; sometimes it was Route I-95. Sometimes it was north, and sometimes the signs said south. And the printed directions were difficult to read without her reading glasses, not to mention while she was speeding along at eighty miles per hour. That was way above the speed limit but seemed to be her only option if she wanted to keep up with traffic and not become a dangerous obstacle.

"Can't you see I'm a stranger around here? I've got Maine plates," she muttered as a Saab honked loudly before zooming past on the right. She wanted to get over to the right lane — she knew her exit must be coming up — but there were two lanes of traffic to get through and nobody seemed to want to let her in. She saw the sign for the exit as she sailed past, stuck in the wrong lane. It took a couple more exits before she could finally get off the highway, and then she found herself on a deserted country road. She turned left off the ramp, thinking to cross the highway and get back on on the other side, but there seemed to be no signs at all for Route 128 or I-95 or anything except quaint little roads: Uncle Ernie's Way, Stage Coach Road, Elm Street. Even Main Street, when she found it, didn't seem to lead anywhere. Thoroughly confused, she turned into a gas station and asked for directions. The clerk, however, was rapidly speaking a foreign language into the cell phone he had glued to his ear and didn't seem to understand her question. If he did, he certainly wasn't interested in answering.

Back in the car she studied the directions once again and even consulted a map before deciding she had no option but to retrace her path. Traveling from the other direction, she finally spotted the sign for Route 128, half covered by a low-hanging evergreen bough, and casting her fate in the hands of Providence, launched herself once again into the oncoming rush of traffic. Horns blared but nobody hit her, and she stuck to the right lane, dodging merging cars, until she finally regained the Dover exit. There, once again, she found herself on a country road, passing white-fenced pastures where blanketed horses grazed on the brown winter grass.

The houses that she could see were mansions, much larger than anything in Tinker's Cove. They stood far apart from each other on attractively landscaped lawns, spaced well back from the road, and were reached by long, curving drives. But those were the exceptions; most were hidden by tall hedges or surrounded by stone walls. Some even had gates across the driveways, and that was the case when she finally found the Anderson estate on Bridle Path Road.

Why hadn't she thought of this? she asked herself, braking in front of a decorative wrought-iron barrier that incorporated an elaborate *A* in its design. Decorative, but sturdy. The gate was operated by a keypad, but you had to know the code. There was also a telecom system, but she doubted the gate would be opened for her. The trip seemed a huge waste of time and gas; all she'd learned was that the Andersons were much richer than she'd imagined. They existed in a privileged parallel universe to her ordinary middle-class life. These were people who lived in a small, secure orbit, insulated and protected by chauffeurs and maids and cooks and gardeners, and probably private security guards. Maybe even dogs. She'd never really encountered anybody this inaccessible before, she realized, shifting into reverse.

It made her wonder what business Wilberforce Industries was actually in that the Andersons felt the need for such extreme security. Was Sue correct that it was some sort of security company? Oil came to mind, even computers. Weapons? Or maybe he was simply paranoid, and rich enough to indulge his fears.

She had just backed into the road, intending to start for home, when she saw the gate begin to open for a Volvo station wagon. She drove slowly in the opposite direction but turned into the first driveway she encountered and turned around, keeping a respectful distance between her car and the Volvo. It proceeded at a leisurely pace, eventually reaching a tony shopping plaza with a large grocery store. She parked as close as she could and watched as a young woman with coffee-colored skin and wavy black hair climbed out, clutching a number of reusable green grocery bags to her chest. She then went around to the back of the Volvo and opened the rear hatch, revealing more of the reusable green bags, all filled with returnable bottles.

Seizing the opportunity to strike up an acquaintance, Lucy quickly jumped out of her car and seized an abandoned grocery cart, which she wheeled over to the Volvo.

"Looks as if you could use this," she said, with a smile.

"Thank you," said the woman, with a Hispanic accent.

"It's nice to see somebody who recycles," said Lucy. "Lots of people just throw the bottles away."

"Not Mrs. Anderson. She's my boss." The woman was unloading the bags into the cart. "Everything gets recycled, even the newspapers. She has me take the old magazines to the library, too." She paused, wrinkling her nose. "She wants me to put kitchen scraps on a big pile near the garden, but I'm afraid of rats."

Lucy had struggled with this issue herself. "Or raccoons."

"Yeah." The woman shuddered, giving the cart a push. "Do you work around here?"

"Yes, as a matter of fact, I do," said Lucy. She wasn't lying; she was working. She was working on a story for the paper, investigating Nemo's kidnapping.

"I'm Sylvia Gonzalez," said the woman.

Lucy hesitated, tempted to give a false name in case Sylvia had answered the phone the day before, when she had called the house and tried to speak to Mrs. Anderson. The pause was going on too long, it was getting awkward, and she finally blurted out her real name. "Lucy Stone."

Fortunately, it didn't ring any bells with Sylvia, who smiled. "Nice to meet you." Sylvia was taking her time; she was pushing the cart slowly toward the entrance. Lucy guessed she was enjoying this bit of freedom and was in no hurry to get back to the Andersons' house. "These people are very rich, and their houses are very . . . I don't know the word. . . ."

"Isolated."

"*Sí.* It's not like my home in Honduras, where people are friendly."

"Not like my home, either," said Lucy. "I come from a small town in Maine where I know everybody."

Sylvia nodded. "Do you miss it?"

"I sure do. I don't like the traffic here. That Route one-twenty-eight . . ."

"Dios mío." The woman crossed herself. "I only drive on the little roads. That's what I told Mrs. Anderson. I cannot drive on the highway."

"Are you the cook?"

"No. They have a chef. They call me a girl Friday. I do errands, mostly. Shopping, getting the dry cleaning, going to the post office. And I help out, whatever is needed. Laundry. Cutting vegetables."

By now they were in the store lobby, which was filled with a lavish display of poinsettias and Norfolk pines, and Sylvia was feeding bottles into the discreetly screened recycling machines. When she finished, she was careful to take the slips totaling the cash due back.

"Mrs. Anderson watches her pennies?" asked Lucy.

"She gives it to charity, at least that's what she says," said Sylvia, lowering her voice. "These rich people, they give to charity, but they won't spend . . ." She stopped suddenly, catching herself and shrugging her shoulders.

"She makes you buy store brands?" prompted Lucy.

"Si!" Sylvia laughed, pushing her now empty cart toward the produce department. "That's true, and a lot worse, too." Her flashing eyes grew dark and she pursed her generous lips.

Lucy sensed something was troubling her and she wanted to talk about it but was afraid of getting in trouble. Or maybe this wasn't the place — the bustling, brightly lit store with its relentless sound track of Christmas carols. She offered some bait, something Sylvia could top. "A lot of rich people are like that. My employer makes her children wear hand-me-downs, and they aren't allowed to watch TV."

"This one," said Sylvia, leaning close and whispering in her ear, "believe it or not, her grandson was kidnapped and she won't pay the ransom."

Lucy widened her eyes. "Kidnapped? Really?"

Sylvia nodded. "He's cute. He visited last summer. He's a funny little boy."

"That's terrible." Lucy paused. "Do the kidnappers want a lot of money?"

"To you and me, yes. Half a million dollars. But to the Andersons? It's nothing. And he's their only grandson."

"They won't pay?"

Sylvia shook her head. "In my country rich people get kidnapped all the time, and they pay. They don't hesitate. They know the kidnappers will . . ."

Lucy grabbed her hand. "I know."

"These Andersons, they don't seem to care. I heard them talking. 'I won't be bullied,' he said. 'Not one penny. He'll come round when they realize I'm not giving in.' That's what he said."

"It almost sounds like they know who the kidnapper is," suggested Lucy.

Sylvia's eyebrows rose. "Maybe you're right. They talk all the time about the daughter and her boyfriend. Mr. Anderson is . . ." She shook her head. "He hates him."

"What about Mrs. Anderson? The grandmother."

"I don't know, but I think she's upset. She used a whole box of tissues in one day." Sylvia shook her head. "And it's Christmas, too."

Lucy nodded. "I'm going to pray for that little boy."

"Me, too," said Sylvia. "I pray to Santa Maria all day long."

Lucy sighed. "Well, I have to find the laundry detergent."

Sylvia was putting oranges into a plastic bag. "Aisle ten."

"Thanks. I hope we meet again."

"Me, too." Sylvia paused, then fumbled in her purse. "Let me give you my number. Maybe we can have coffee sometime. My day off is Tuesday."

"That's too bad." Lucy didn't have to fake the disappointed tone; she really liked Sylvia and hated lying to her. "I only get Thursday afternoons — they're very strict."

"Take it, anyway," said Sylvia. "Maybe I can switch."

"That would be nice," said Lucy, jotting down the number and thinking it might be good to have a contact in the house.

Back in the car on Route 128, Lucy couldn't escape the cloud of guilt that enveloped her. She'd taken advantage of that poor lonely woman who was so far from home and friends and family. She was never going to call her for a coffee klatsch, and she hoped Sylvia wouldn't think she didn't like her. She hoped the young woman's feelings wouldn't be hurt, and she was grateful for the information she had shared.

Her suspicions were true, it seemed. The Andersons' reaction to the ransom demand seemed to provide clear evidence that the kidnapping was a hoax, perpetrated by Rick. Ocean was probably in on it, too, no doubt pressured by Rick.

From what Sylvia had said about the Andersons, Lucy got the impression they were rigid and tight with their money. It didn't seem like much of a stretch to assume that Ocean's father wouldn't approve of Rick or their freewheeling lifestyle. Ocean probably figured this was the only way she could get money out of them, money that didn't come with strings like the child-care payments, money that she felt entitled to. What was the harm? They had more than they needed; some people might say more even than was decent. And there was no danger to Nemo. They'd probably convinced him it was some sort of game and he had to hide for a while.

Lucy figured it wasn't all that hard for Rick and Ocean to rationalize their behavior. She'd found the ever-so-discreet display of wealth in Dover a bit unnerving, considering the toll the recession was taking on so many people. The *Pennysaver* always ran a charity drive at Christmas for the local food pantry, but donations had been slow in coming, well below last year's total. Lucy knew that people were really struggling to make ends meet in Tinker's Cove; she saw the evidence every day. Houses with FOR SALE — BANK OWNED signs, kids in winter jackets that were too small, people lining up at the Community Church's Free Store for cast-off clothing and household items. She suspected a lot of those items would end up under the Christmas tree as gifts.

The blare of a horn startled her, and she realized she had slowed to something approaching the speed limit, which Boston drivers seemed to regard with the same casual attitude they had toward using their directional signals. She'd better pay attention to the road, she decided, if she wanted to get home in one piece.

CHAPTER SEVEN

Lucy was approaching Tinker's Cove when her cell phone rang. It was Zoe, checking in to let her know that she and Sara were home from school. "I let the dog out and we're making popcorn for a snack," she reported.

Lucy could hear the microwave humming in the background. "There's cider in the fridge."

"Super. See you later."

The popcorn was beginning to pop as she ended the call, and Lucy felt a comfortable sense of reassurance. Everything was okay on the home front. She could stop in at the office and report to Ted.

"How are you feeling?" he asked suspiciously when she stepped inside.

"Fine. It never amounted to anything. I guess I was just tired."

"That's a relief," said Phyllis, replacing the cap on the can of Lysol she had ready. "Did you hear the entire Gilead football team is sick?"

"No. I was out of town. I went to Dover to track down Nemo's grandparents."

"You did?" Ted leaned forward eagerly. "What did you find out?"

"Well, for starters, I discovered they're enormously wealthy. He's CEO of Wilberforce Industries. They live in a huge mansion behind a stone wall and a sturdy gate. I didn't get to talk to them . . . ," said Lucy.

"Big surprise." Phyllis's tone was sarcastic and Lucy gave her a sharp look.

"But I did talk to an employee. A girl named Sylvia Gonzalez."

Ted was skeptical. "You checked her ID? You know she's really on the inside?"

Lucy glared at him. "Uh, no Ted. I didn't ask for an ID. And I didn't identify myself as a reporter. As it happened, I was in the neighborhood and saw her drive away from the Andersons' house. I followed her to the supermarket and struck up a conversation, during which the subject of the kidnapping came up."

"And what did this unconfirmed source divulge to you?"

Lucy sighed. She hated it when Ted got picky. "She said the Andersons got a ransom demand for half a million dollars but they're refusing to pay."

"Can you imagine?" Phyllis was indignant.

"According to Sylvia, it's pretty much in character. They're tight with the money."

"That's what my mother used to say," declared Phyllis. "How do you think rich people get rich? They hang on to their money."

Ted's face was white; he looked as if he'd been slapped. "The chief didn't tell me anything about this. . . ."

"He may not know. I have a feeling Ralph Anderson is a very private guy. But Sylvia overheard them talking. She was quite clear about the amount. Half a million dollars." Lucy paused. "I really think she's telling the truth." She swallowed hard. "And I think the Andersons believe the kidnapper is Rick Juergens, and I think they're right. I think he staged a fake kidnapping to get money out of them."

"How can a father kidnap his own kid?" asked Phyllis.

Ted sat down in his swivel chair, causing it to creak. "A hoax to extort money from the wealthy grandparents," said Ted thoughtfully. "It does make sense. The mysterious black woman in the CR-V that nobody saw . . ."

Lucy nodded. "I think she was a figment of Rick's imagination."

Ted was suddenly energized: he had regained the color in his cheeks and was already reaching for his phone. "We need confirmation on this. But Lucy, that was really inspired. Good work."

"So I can put in for the time and the gas?" she asked.

He waved a hand. "Sure."

"I'm going to head home," said Lucy. Tomorrow was Christmas Eve, and she had a million things to do to get ready. "Call me if you need me."

"Yeah," said Ted, beaming at her. "Wouldn't it be great if Nemo was home for Christmas?"

Lucy smiled and headed for the door, pulling on her gloves. Great? She wasn't so sure. What sort of parents contrived a fake kidnap plot to extort money from their relatives? Poor Nemo! What sort of people were Ocean and Rick? And those grandparents didn't sound very nice, either. Wouldn't Nemo be better off with, well, anybody? *Sylvia would be a better mother,* she thought as she stepped outside, discovering a light snow had started to fall. She drove home carefully, mindful of the slippery roads, hardly noticing the Christmas carols on the radio. That little drummer boy song was playing when she pulled into the driveway, and she was humming the tune in spite of herself when she stepped into the kitchen and smelled the popcorn.

"Sorry, we didn't save you any," said Sara, who was putting the empty bowl into the dishwasher.

"That's okay," said Lucy. "I'm not hungry." She stood there, looking at the jug of holly sitting in the middle of the round golden oak table, next to the cute little Mr. and Mrs. Santa Claus salt and pepper shakers. It was so warm and homey, she didn't think she could stand it. "You know, I think I'll take the dog for a walk. Want to come?"

Sara looked at her as if she was crazy. "No, Mom. Haven't you heard? We're supposed to get quite a storm."

Lucy looked out the window and wasn't impressed. The snow had barely started to stick. "They always exaggerate these storms, like a little snow is some sort of tragedy. Besides, I like the way the woods look when it snows." She called Libby, who lumbered in lazily from the family room. "Come on, girl. We're going for a walk."

The dog sighed; she obviously would have preferred to continue snoozing on the couch. When Lucy opened the door, she made a big production of stretching before stepping out onto the porch and sniffing the air.

It was still daylight, the sky was milky white, but darkness was gathering in the woods, where snow was beginning to frost the trees. There was no wind to speak of, just the gentle drifting of the snow. She glanced at her watch. It was three thirty. She had time to walk to Blueberry Pond and get back before dark, if she didn't dillydally. But that was fine with her. She wasn't in the mood to dawdle. She wanted to move her arms and legs and get the blood flowing. She needed to lift her spirits.

The snow tickled her nose, and the air was damp and cool on her face; it felt refreshing as she tramped along the old dirt logging road, making fresh tracks in the inch or so of new-fallen snow that lay on the ground. Libby was loping along, sticking her nose in the snow here and there, then snorting noisily when she lifted her head. Twigs and dried-up leaves poked through the fresh snow, along with pine needles; they were all bits of black punctuating the clean whiteness. There were also tracks from rabbits and raccoons, and the four-pointed stars left by birds. It was very quiet, except for the occasional raucous calls of the crows, announcing the presence of these intruders to the woodland creatures.

She'd been walking for about fifteen minutes when the road widened, joining the well-traveled road to the pond. Here the snow was only beginning to fill the deep ruts worn by constant traffic, as the pond was a popular destination even in winter. Lots of people came here to ice fish or walk in the daytime. At night it was a popular hideaway for lovers. She was heading for her favorite spot, a big rock where she liked to stand and take in the view, when she noticed Rick's sporty car in the parking area. Oddly enough, the door was hanging open.

She called Libby and fastened her leash before approaching. She didn't have a good feeling about this — who would leave a car door open in the middle of winter? Advancing slowly, she looked around, half expecting to see him returning to the car, along with Nemo.

But when she looked inside, she saw Rick sitting behind the wheel. At first she thought he was asleep, but then she noticed his eyes were open, and spotted the neat round hole above his left ear. Instinctively stepping backward, she saw a spray of red on the passenger-side window, the globs of brain and flesh, all illuminated by the glowing canopy light.

Lucy backed away, dragging the dog with her. Libby didn't want to go: she scented blood and every bit of doggy DNA she possessed was telling her this was something worth investigating. Lucy, on the other hand, was trying very hard not to throw up, and it was taking all her concentration. When she'd gotten a fair distance between herself and the car, she steadied herself against a big old tree and pulled out her cell phone and dialed 911.

It was getting cold, the light was dimming, and the snow was coming faster now. The flakes were larger and a stiff breeze blew up while she waited for help to arrive. It didn't take long before she heard sirens, but even so, her teeth were chattering and she was doing a little stamping dance to keep warm when the first patrol car barreled into the parking area. The cop took one look at Rick's body, then suggested Lucy and the dog sit inside his car, where it was warm. It was actually overheated, and Libby was soon panting, but Lucy couldn't stop shivering. Eventually Lieutenant Horowitz stuck his head inside, and she scrunched over, settling the dog in her lap to make room for him. Libby's warmth felt good, and her hands stroked the dog's thick fur, finding comfort in her muscular neck and silky ears.

"This is what we call a new development in the case," he said grimly.

Lucy gave him a little half smile. He was the state cop usually assigned to investigate serious crimes in the area. Their relationship was uneasy, however, because Lucy's job meant she had to ask questions he didn't want to answer.

"I didn't expect this," said Horowitz, stroking his chin. His face was pale in the strong lights that were now illuminating the crime scene. The lights picked up the blood stains in Rick's car, the windows glowed like red stained glass, and Lucy looked away. "He was shot in the head. The exit wound is pretty messy."

"I think Rick was playing with fire," said Lucy. "He staged the kidnapping."

Horowitz raised a thin, graying eyebrow. "How'd you come up with that theory?"

"A hunch. There was no sign of the black woman in the CR-V, and Ocean's parents are filthy rich."

Horowitz nodded. "I was on my way to the Aquarizoo with a warrant to search the place when I got the call." He sighed. "I can't believe this happened now, when we're so shorthanded."

"What about Nemo?" asked Lucy. "Where is he?"

Horowitz sighed. "It looks like he was with him in the car." He opened his hand, revealing the remains of a half-eaten gingerbread cookie.

The same cookie she'd bought for him at the IGA. "I gave him that cookie the day before he disappeared. It's probably been there ever since." She didn't want to think that Nemo witnessed the shooting.

Horowitz shook his head. "There was a half-drunk cup of hot chocolate, still warm."

Lucy's heart skipped a beat. "You think whoever shot Rick took Nemo?"

Horowitz nodded.

Lucy squeezed the dog's loose skin, and Libby growled gently in protest. "So it's not a hoax anymore."

Horowitz opened the door. "Nope, now it's the real thing."

"But who . . . ?"

"Probably an accomplice. He couldn't pull this off alone. He had to have help. Somebody to watch the kid while he was making his tearful plea for the TV cameras."

"And the accomplice got impatient when the grandparents didn't fork over the money?"

"It could've been anything. Something

about the kid, his mother, money, drugs. Your guess is as good as mine." Horowitz slumped. He was a man who had seen too much. He got out but turned, leaning his hand on the roof of the car. His face grew serious. "One more thing. Leave the investigating to us. Whoever did this, and there's no guarantee it's just one person — and this is all off the record, by the way — well, whoever it is, they're dangerous."

Lucy glanced at Rick's car, where the crime-scene technician's high-powered lamps illuminated the gory scene. "Can I go?" she asked.

"Yeah. I know where to find you." He nodded. "Do you want a ride?"

Lucy shook her head. "It's not far. I'll walk."

"Be careful," he said.

Lucy got out of the car and gave the leash a tug. Libby reluctantly gave up her comfy seat in the police car but picked up speed when she realized they were heading for home. Lucy shared her eagerness and walked briskly through the snowy woods, finding the ringed moon gave just enough light. Still, she felt uneasy, alone with no protection except the dog, who was clearly thinking only of dinner and her usual spot on the couch.

If only she had a one-track mind like the dog, she thought, trying to sort out the images and thoughts that were flitting through her mind — and to quell the sickening feeling in her stomach. She was terrified for Nemo, who was now at the mercy of a cold-blooded killer — or killers. Bill and the girls would have to fend for themselves, she realized, looking ahead to a long night. This was news and she had to call Ted.

Flipping open her cell phone, she tried to organize her thoughts while she waited for him to answer. "Listen," she began. "I found Rick Juergens's body, he was shot, his car's all bloody, it looks like Nemo was with him, but he's gone now. . . ."

"Hold on, Lucy. What are you saying?"

"Rick Juergens. Shot to death. At Blueberry Pond. Police are there."

There was a long silence. "You said Nemo was with him?"

"It looks that way. There was food in the backseat. The cookie . . ." Lucy's voice broke and she stopped in her tracks, causing the dog to regard her with concern. "There were bits of cookie and a still-warm cup of hot cocoa."

"Oh my God."

Lucy brushed away her tears with her woolly mitten and swallowed hard. "Yeah."

"It looks like your theory about the hoax was right."

She nodded. "Horowitz said that's the theory they're working on. Rick was probably shot by an accomplice."

"And the accomplice took Nemo?"

"Yeah. Horowitz said, 'It's the real thing now.' That's a quote." Lucy let out a big sigh. "He also said everything he said was off the record. I guess he'll be putting out a statement. Until then we can use the stuff I saw, right?"

There was a long silence, and Lucy started walking again, trying to get warm. Finally, Ted spoke. "You know, Lucy, tomorrow's Christmas Eve and I've got to catch a plane to New Orleans."

Lucy was shocked; she knew Ted picked up extra money as a stringer, selling big stories to the *Boston Globe* and *Portland Press Herald.* He had plenty of time before he had to go to the airport. "This is huge, Ted. . . ."

"Get real," he said in a resigned voice. "*Inside Edition* is probably already on their way. CNN's probably running it now. What a Christmas present for them."

"But we're local. We've got inside information."

"Go home, Lucy. Trim your tree. Cook

your turkey. Try to forget about it and enjoy your family."

Lucy had stopped again, not believing what she was hearing. "Ted, this doesn't sound like you. What's the matter?"

She heard him let out a sharp breath. "Let's just say I've been here before and I'm not going down this path again."

"But we can help. Get the word out, get people looking."

"Stop it. This story isn't going to have a happy ending. Let it go."

Lucy shook her head. "You don't know that. We have evidence, finally, that Nemo's alive and probably in the area."

"He's dead."

Lucy's back straightened. "Don't say that," she snapped as Libby whined and nudged her leg with her snout. Suddenly Ted's attitude began to make sense and her voice softened. "This isn't about Nemo, is it, Ted? It's about Corinne."

"Yeah. Corinne and all the other kids, the Jasons and Megans and Etans, but especially Billy Poole. He was my best friend in first grade and all of a sudden he wasn't around and my mom said he'd moved away. But one day — I was older, old enough to be home alone — I found a newspaper clipping tucked in a book, and it said Billy's naked body had been found in a Dumpster."

Lucy felt a surge of sympathy. "That must have been a terrible shock."

"Yeah."

Lucy was suddenly cold. "I've got to get inside," she said. "I'm going home."

"Stay there," said Ted. "Enjoy the holiday as much as you can."

"You, too," she said, but it was nothing more than an automatic response.

Christmas was the last thing on her mind as she let the dog inside the brightly lit kitchen, where Sara was browning hamburger in the frying pan. She stripped off her gloves and rubbed her hands together to warm them. "I have to go to work for a little while. Go ahead with supper. I'll be back as soon as I can."

Sara was used to this sort of thing; Lucy often had to dash off to follow a story. "Okay, Mom."

Then Lucy pulled her beret down over her ears, tightened her scarf, pulled her gloves back on, and went back outside, into the snowy night. Climbing into the Subaru, she cranked the heat up as high as it would go and flipped on the radio. The story wasn't on the airwaves yet, but she knew she didn't have much time. She wanted to get to Ocean before the police, or the networks.

When she arrived at the Aquarizoo, however, it was eerily peaceful. The only light came from the green *Q, U,* and *R* that still flashed in the broken neon sign, and when Ocean answered the door, she was composed but wary. "What do you want?"

"I have some news. Can I come in?"

"Have they found Nemo?" she asked.

Lucy looked at her; she wasn't finding the act convincing anymore. "No, it's about Rick."

Ocean stepped back, opening the door wide so Lucy could enter the kitchen. Spotting a table and chairs in the corner, Lucy suggested they sit down.

"So what about Rick?" demanded Ocean as soon as her bottom hit the chair.

"He's been shot," began Lucy in a gentle voice. "He's dead. His body was found in his car in Blueberry Pond."

Ocean's eyes widened. "Was he alone?"

"There's evidence Nemo was with him recently," said Lucy. "The police are probably on their way, and I suggest you level with them."

Ocean gave her a sharp look. "What do you mean?"

"It's obvious this kidnapping was a hoax

to extort money from your parents. . . ."

"That's ridiculous!"

Lucy was losing patience. "Cut it out, Ocean. Things are out of control now. Nemo's in real danger."

Ocean was on her feet. "Don't you think I know that?"

Lucy rose and faced her. "You need to come clean with the police, tell them the whole story. That's the only way you're going to get Nemo back."

"The police!" snorted Ocean. "I don't think so. This thing you've cooked up is just fantasy. I would never do anything to put Nemo in danger, and neither would Rick." She glared at Lucy. "And what's your part in this? You're acting like you care, but you just want a story!"

Lucy felt like slapping the girl. "Ocean, this isn't about me. You stood there in front of the TV cameras, lying through your teeth, begging people to help you find your little boy, who wasn't lost at all. Now he's really in danger. It's time to get serious. You've got to come clean and tell the police everything." She paused, remembering the gruesome scene in the woods. "Rick was shot in the head. I saw his body. There was blood all over. It's not a game anymore, Ocean."

Ocean's face went white and she set her

jaw. “This is none of your business. Get out!”

“Okay.” Lucy was on her feet, zipping up. “I hope you’ve got a plan.”

Ocean was already at the door, pulling it open. “Don’t you worry about me — or Nemo. I’m going home to Daddy. He’ll take care of this.”

Chapter Eight

Ted was right, thought Lucy, driving home. It was time to drop this story and concentrate on her own family and their Christmas. There was nothing she could do to help Nemo. Face it, she told herself. The poor kid never had a chance. His father was a drug dealer, and his mother was immature and irresponsible. They were greedy and selfish, and the people they associated with were even worse.

Maybe, she told herself, clinging to a slender thread of hope, maybe Ocean could actually save her son. Maybe she could convince her parents to cough up the ransom money — her father wouldn't be the first man who capitulated to a remorseful and tearful daughter. Or maybe she actually knew who killed Rick and had a little leverage of her own. *Maybe, maybe, maybe,* thought Lucy, pulling into her driveway. Maybe it would all work out. She hoped so.

But now there was absolutely nothing she could do but hope and pray and try to pull together a merry Christmas for her family.

"Here she is!" exclaimed Bill when she stepped inside the kitchen. "Ho, ho, ho!" he bellowed, handing her a cup of eggnog. "It's Christmas! Where did you hide those cookies?"

In spite of herself, Lucy smiled. "I'll get them," she said. "But they're for dessert."

Lucy always took part in a cookie exchange early in December. Fearing that the cookies would be eaten before Christmas, she hid them away, making sure to change the spot from year to year. This year she had tucked the tins away in the bottom of a blanket chest in the attic and was greeted with cheers when she emerged with the goodies.

"Just one?" begged Bill. "Those spritz are really good with eggnog."

"Okay," she relented, with a smile. "It's Christmas. But don't spoil your dinner."

After dinner Bill brought in the balsam fir Christmas tree while Lucy loaded the dishwasher. He was stringing the lights when she joined him in the family room, where the girls were opening the boxes of ornaments.

"That's a really nice tree," she said, admiring the fir's classic shape and lush branches. "I love the smell of a Christmas tree."

"Yeah." Bill stood back to admire it. "I've had my eye on it for quite a few years now. It was growing behind that old apple tree."

"Oh, look!" exclaimed Zoe, holding up a bit of cardboard decorated with macaroni and glitter that encircled a photo of six-year-old Elizabeth. "It's the ornament Elizabeth made in first grade."

Sara held up a similar, somewhat cruder example of the same ornament, with Toby's photo. "Toby was so cute!" exclaimed Sara. "I wonder where mine is."

"They're all here somewhere," said Lucy. Mrs. Barlow's first-grade class made the sparkly macaroni ornaments every year, and the Stone family had a complete set.

There was also a cotton-ball snowman, which Lucy remembered having the cub scouts make when she was a den leader, and numerous rather squashed but still colorful paper cranes Elizabeth had made during her origami phase. "They're a symbol of peace!" she had exclaimed angrily when Toby made fun of them.

Every ornament seemed to prompt a memory, and Lucy was thoughtful as they trimmed the tree. There were the heavy glass kugels shaped like bunches of grapes that had been in Bill's family for generations, the somewhat crushed paper chains that had decorated the scrawny tree they'd put up that first Christmas in Tinker's Cove, and the perky elves her mother had loved so much. A sudden bleat announced Bill had found the plastic trumpet he'd put on the tree every year since his childhood.

Celebrating Christmas was easier than she thought, concluded Lucy, humming along to the Christmas carols playing on the stereo and sipping a bit more eggnog, better than the before-dinner eggnog. Bill had served it to her with a naughty wink, announcing he'd added a "wee bit of rum."

"Yum, rum," giggled Lucy, watching as the girls danced around the room, exclaiming over each discovery as the ornaments were stripped of crumpled tissue paper and added to the tree. "Oh!" she exclaimed, remembering the cookies she'd baked with Patrick. "We mustn't forget the gingerbread men!"

And that was when she couldn't pretend everything was all right anymore and had to scurry into the powder room, hiding her tears as Bill switched on the lights and the girls oohed and aahed over the beautiful Christmas tree.

■ ■ ■ ■

The little gingerbread man was running as fast as he could, but the woman in the maroon coat was chasing him, gun in hand. His little legs were so short and he was running as fast as he could, but when he got to the brook, he knew he was trapped. If he tried to swim across, he would melt. That was when the fox appeared and offered to let him ride on his back. The gingerbread man gratefully hopped on, but when the fox reached the middle of the brook, he gave a shake and the gingerbread man flew up into the air. He flailed his little arms and legs, trying desperately to avoid the fox's sharp white fangs. . . .

"Lucy!" Bill was shaking her. "Wake up. It's only a dream."

"Wha?" Lucy didn't want to leave the dream. She was with that little gingerbread man, hoping somehow to escape the fox. But it was too late. Morning sunshine was streaming through the windows, the covers were all in a tangle, and she was freezing cold.

"Merry Christmas Eve," said Bill, tossing her warm red fleece robe to her.

"Merry Christmas Eve to you." Lucy was

sitting up, sticking her arms in the sleeves and drawing the robe around her. She glanced at the clock, surprised to discover it was already eight. "Oh my gosh, I've got a million things to do. How much snow did we get?

"Only about ten inches — the road's already been plowed. But you can't go anywhere until I clear the driveway with the snowblower."

She reviewed her list of errands while she brushed her teeth. She had some last-minute presents to wrap, she had to deliver the cranberry bread she'd made to the neighbors on Prudence Path, she had to pick up some last-minute groceries and make a stop at the liquor store, and there was that chocolate mousse cake to bake for Christmas dinner. *Don't forget to buy some whipping cream,* she reminded herself as she descended the stairs to the kitchen, fragrant with the scent of coffee.

Pouring herself a mugful, she sat at the table, sipping and waiting for the coffee to clear her head. Rick was just like the gingerbread man, she thought, idly watching the chickadees fluttering around the bird feeder. He wasn't as smart as he thought, and he'd got himself killed. But who was the fox?

Sara broke into her thoughts. "Mom, is it

okay if I go to the movies with Jenn and Renee this afternoon?"

"Are you all set for tomorrow?"

"Yup. All my presents are wrapped and ready."

"I guess you can go then," agreed Lucy, remembering how her mother used to say Christmas Eve was the longest day of the year. It would be good for Sara to have something to do. "What about Zoe?"

"She's helping out at the Friends of Animals shelter today." Sara laughed. "She says they're bringing Christmas cheer to the puppies and kittens. Like they know it's Christmas."

"They'll know now," said Lucy, getting up and popping an English muffin into the toaster.

While it toasted, she decided to get started on the mousse cake and dug the springform pan out of a cabinet. The cake was quick to assemble, and it could bake while she got dressed and wrapped those presents. Besides, she couldn't go anywhere until Bill cleared the driveway.

Lucy always made chocolate mousse cake for Christmas. It was a family tradition. She assembled the ingredients, eggs, chocolate bits, butter, pausing now and then to take bites of her English muffin.

"Ooh, mousse cake," cooed Zoe, spotting the springform pan as she passed through the kitchen on her way to the family room.

"Did I hear somebody say mousse cake?" asked Bill, pulling on his boots before heading outside.

"Wouldn't be Christmas without it," said Lucy, starting to whip the whites of seven eggs.

After she tucked the cake into the oven, she retrieved the loaves of cranberry bread she'd made on the weekend and tied red ribbon around the foil she'd already wrapped them in. They still looked a bit plain, so she clipped bits of balsam from the back of the tree and added them before calling the girls and sending them off to deliver them.

Now that the house was empty, if only for a short while, she quickly set about wrapping those last few presents. Bill's was the largest, a new chain saw, so she tackled it first. But even after it was wrapped, the oddly shaped box was unmistakably a chain saw, so she decided she would have to hide it. That meant wrapping up a note: *If you can find it, you can keep it!* That done, she was faced with a couple of bags of pesky little stocking presents for the girls: lip gloss, mascara, pens, mini soaps shaped like snowmen. They seemed to take forever, but she finally finished just as the oven timer dinged.

Hurrying downstairs, she inhaled the heady, rich scent of chocolate. It was wonderful — and she hadn't thought about Nemo all morning. Until now. *There's no sense dwelling on things you can't change,* she reminded herself, carefully removing the cake from the oven. It had puffed up like a soufflé, but she knew it would soon settle into a wonderfully dense but ethereally light concoction. Leaving it on the counter to cool, she checked to see how Bill was progressing with the driveway and discovered he was almost done. He'd probably be finished by the time she got dressed.

Lucy quickly washed her face and gave her hair a quick one hundred brush strokes before putting on the Christmas sweatshirt the girls had given her years ago. It was bright red and had an appliquéd Christmas tree on the front, lavishly trimmed with beads and sparkly rickrack. Sue always laughed at Lucy for wearing it, but she didn't care. She was going to wear it until it wore out, which wasn't going to happen anytime soon, because it was 100 percent polyester.

Checking her reflection in the mirror, Lucy thought she certainly looked festive. If only she felt that way, she sighed before clumping downstairs. She was perched on a kitchen chair, pulling on her boots, when Bill came in.

"I started the car for you," he said, pulling off his watch cap. His face was red from the cold, and he looked a bit like Santa in his red hunting jacket.

"Thanks, Santa." She smiled. "Anything you need from town?"

He poured himself a cup of coffee and sat down at the table. "You know what would be nice for Christmas breakfast? Some of that sausage from the smokehouse out in Gilead."

"I've got bacon, and stollen," said Lucy.

"Never mind, then. It's kind of far."

"Yeah," said Lucy, standing up and pulling on her jacket. "I don't know how good the roads are."

Bill took a big slurp of coffee. "Take it slow. Drive carefully."

"You bet."

Despite the snow, the IGA was busy and Lucy had to wheel her cart slowly through the crowded aisles as she picked up those last-minute items. The list seemed to keep growing, too, as she added a box of eggs and a carton of eggnog. You never knew. You certainly didn't want to run out. Did she have enough coffee? *Better safe than sorry,* she decided, tossing a can in her cart. And so it went, until she finally wheeled her overloaded cart to the checkout.

When she'd loaded all the groceries in the car and started the engine, she noticed the gas tank was low, so she headed to the Quik-Stop for a fill-up. She was pretty sure you weren't supposed to let the gas tank get to low in cold weather; sometimes it made the car hard to start. She poured in a little bottle of Drygas, too. Something she remembered her father advising her to do.

The liquor store was also doing a brisk business and she had to wait in a long line with her bottle of Christmas champagne. A display of port was temptingly located near the register, and she added a bottle, remembering how Bill enjoyed it.

She was ready for lunch when she finally got home, but there were groceries to unload first and put away.

"What is all this stuff, anyway?" asked Bill, hoisting a couple of bags out of the car.

"I'm not quite sure myself," admitted Lucy. "But we sure don't want to run out of anything on Christmas."

"Like the cupboard is bare? You have been cooking for weeks, Lucy."

It was true, she realized, with a shrug.

"Chalk it up to the season. Christmas makes me act weird."

Bill laughed and shook his head. "You said it, not me."

But when lunch was over and the girls went their separate ways and Bill went outside to split wood, Lucy found herself at loose ends. Everything was done; there wasn't anything more to do except wait. She grabbed a magazine and sat on the couch, putting her feet up, but her mind was miles away as she flipped on the brightly colored pages. Where was Nemo? Was he alive? Or was he dead, like poor Billy Poole, who was found lying cold and naked in a Dumpster? She thought of Nemo's spirit, his stubborn streak, and remembered how her own children had been forces to reckon with even when they were very small. She recalled telling Bill when Toby was a terrible two that he started out the day quite small but seemed to grow like Jack's bean stalk into a towering and completely irrational creature in the afternoon. Of course, when Bill returned at the end of the day, Toby shrank right down to his actual size again.

But that was the reaction of a loving, if somewhat overwhelmed young mother.

Lucy knew that Nemo was no match for his kidnapper, who hadn't thought twice before shooting Rick. What sort of person could do something like that? How did it happen? A quarrel? A surge of anger? Or was it a calculated move to get rid of a rival? A nuisance?

Suddenly restless, Lucy got up and moved a few ornaments on the tree. She stalked through the house, straightening cushions, tidying things, emptying the dishwasher. Finally, unable to think of anything else to do, she popped a movie into the DVD player. The townsfolk were arriving at Jimmy Stewart's house with bags of money when Bill came in with an armful of firewood and started laying it in the fireplace. Then the girls returned and it was time to start thinking about supper.

Lucy was scrubbing potatoes when Elizabeth called.

"Merry Christmas!" she exclaimed. "I wanted to call today because I might not get a chance tomorrow."

"Merry Christmas to you," said Lucy, pleased that her daughter had remembered to call home. "Is it odd having Christmas in Florida?"

"Don't you know it! Palm trees and flowers and no snow — I really miss the snow."

"We've got plenty," said Lucy, watching out the window, as Bill filled his arms with another load of firewood. "Maybe I should send you some."

"I wish you could." Elizabeth sounded wistful. "But the time's going to fly. You wouldn't believe how busy we are. The hotel is full. I guess a lot of people like to spend Christmas down here." She lowered her voice. "In fact, remember those people you asked me about?"

"The Andersons?"

"They're here. They checked in yesterday."

"Are you sure?" Lucy was struggling to understand how the Andersons could take a trip to Florida when their grandson was missing.

"Absolutely, I noticed because their names are a bit odd. Clementine and Ralph."

"Is their daughter with them? Her name is Ocean."

"No. Just them. And they've got our most deluxe suite. I guess they come here a lot, because the concierge and the manager and the chambermaids were greeting them like long-lost relatives."

"Wow," was all Lucy could think to say.

"Is Dad there? And Zoe and Sara? I'd like to talk to them."

"Okay," said Lucy, taking the handset into the family room and handing it to Bill, who was now on his knees in front of the fireplace, crumbling up newspaper. "It's Elizabeth."

Lucy went in search of Sara and Zoe, her thoughts in a whirl. Ocean had said she was going home to her parents, but her parents weren't home. Was she all alone out there in Dover? What was going on? Had the Andersons coughed up the ransom money? Or had they washed their hands of their troublesome daughter? Was Ocean in on the kidnapping — or had the kidnapper threatened her?

Practically bumping into Sara on the upstairs landing, Lucy delivered a terse message. "Elizabeth's on the phone, and I have to go out. You can get supper ready, right?

Sara gave her a funny look. "Are you okay, Mom?"

"I'm fine. There's just something last minute I have to do. And," she added, remembering not to make assumptions about her children's competence, "don't forget to put the potatoes in the oven with the ham."

"Okay," said Sara, shaking her head as she bounced down the stairs.

"Elizabeth's on the phone," Lucy told Zoe, who was emerging from the bathroom. "Dad's talking to her in the family room."

"Great." Zoe followed Sara down the stairs, leaving Lucy alone on the landing.

She stood for a moment, running through her Christmas checklist one last time. Then, certain that everything was ready, she went down to the kitchen. Bill was there, with a puzzled look on his face. "Sara says you're going out?"

Lucy wasn't about to admit the true nature of her errand. "I think you were right about the sausage," she said.

"All the way to Gilead?" he asked.

"It won't take me long. I'll be back in time for dinner," she said. "I promise."

Bill shook his head. "We don't really need it — you said we've got bacon. I don't think you should go. The temperature's dropping and the roads are going to get slippery."

Lucy didn't have a choice; she'd have to play her trump card. She gave him an exasperated look. "It's Christmas, Bill. Maybe Santa needs a bit of help."

He nodded, with sudden comprehension. "Ohhh. Careful on the roads."

"I will," she said, reaching for her coat.

Chapter Nine

The road to Gilead seemed endless, a long gray ribbon already lined with filthy, blackened snowbanks. The trunks of the leafless trees were gray, the pointy fir trees were black against the blank gray sky, and the air itself was heavy, as if more snow was on the way. When Lucy turned into the Aquarizoo parking lot, it seemed more forlorn and derelict than she remembered. It hadn't been plowed, but the snow was scarred with tire tracks. Ocean's battered pickup was parked next to the main building, where booted feet had carved a slippery path through the drifted snow. Lucy negotiated it carefully and, pausing on the icy stoop, took a deep breath before knocking.

There was no answer.

The truck was there, she reminded herself. That meant Ocean was probably home. She banged louder. "Ocean, it's me, Lucy Stone. Answer the door!"

Again there was no answer, but Lucy thought she saw a tattered plastic mini-blind move slightly.

"Ocean! I know you're there. Don't be stupid. I can help!"

This time the door opened, but only a few inches. Lucy could see only part of Ocean's face, but one red-rimmed eye seemed proof that she had been crying.

"Why do you keep coming around?" she asked. "Don't you get it? I don't want to talk to you. Go away!"

"Look," began Lucy, speaking softly, "this is not for the newspaper. I'm here because I care about Nemo, that's all."

Ocean's eyes narrowed suspiciously. "Why should I believe you?"

Lucy's patience was exhausted. She was standing out in the freezing cold, knee-deep in snow, pleading with this stupid girl to accept her help. "Why should you believe me? Because it's Christmas Eve, and instead of being home in my cozy house, drinking eggnog with my family, I'm here, trying to help you get your kid back, that's why."

"Oh." There was a long pause, but the door finally opened and Ocean stepped back. "Come on in."

Lucy didn't need to be asked twice. She moved so quickly that she almost lost her balance on the ice and had to grab the doorjamb to keep from falling. Once the door closed behind her, she discovered it wasn't much warmer inside the house than outside, but at least she was out of the wind. "Do you have a cup of tea or something?" she asked, rubbing her frozen hands together.

Ocean quickly brushed at her eyes. "Uh, sure," she said, filling the kettle and setting it on the gas stove, which she had to light with a match.

Lucy took a seat at the kitchen table. "I think this has gone on long enough. The only way you're going to get Nemo back is if you cooperate with the police."

"They came here, earlier," said Ocean. "I had to let them in. They had a warrant. They searched the whole place. It was horrible."

"You didn't tell them what you know?" asked Lucy.

"I didn't tell them anything. I don't have to. It's my right. I have the right to remain silent."

Lucy took a deep breath. "If they find out you're withholding evidence, they can arrest you."

Ocean's tone was uncertain. "Are you sure about that?"

"Oh, yes." Lucy stared at the refrigerator door, which was covered with Nemo's artwork. A snowman made of cotton balls glued onto construction paper caught her eye. "You obviously love Nemo. You're a good mom. How did you ever agree to this?"

Ocean sat down at the table, her shoulders slumped. "I don't know. I must have been crazy. It was Rick's idea. He said Mom and Dad are so rich, and here we are, living in this dump. He said they didn't care about me. They only gave us money for things for Nemo, like his school and presents and stuff. It was like we didn't exist, he said. But if we pretended Nemo was kidnapped, they'd pay the ransom real quick." The kettle shrieked, and she got up to turn the stove off. Taking two mugs out of the dish drainer, she put a tea bag in each and filled it with steaming water. "He said it would serve Dad right, that he was part of what's going on. You know, globalization, grabbing natural resources from indigenous cultures, generally screwing everybody everywhere, supporting repressive military regimes. All that stuff. It wasn't fair that they had so much and we had nothing, and they owed us enough to give us a fresh start."

Ocean set the steaming mug in front of her, and Lucy wrapped her hands around it. She didn't quite follow Rick's argument that extorting money from the Andersons would balance the inequities in the world economy, but it had apparently been enough to convince Ocean. Maybe it was the part about her parents not really caring about her that did the trick. "So what happened?"

Ocean sat down. "Dad's pretty smart. He hired a private investigator, who figured out the kidnapping was fake. He said he wouldn't pay and he was going to cut me completely out of his will, too." She paused. "And then he and Mom went off to Florida for Christmas, just like they always do."

This was a new twist. Sylvia was wrong about Ralph. He wasn't coldhearted like she thought; he'd been actively involved in recovering his grandson. He'd discovered the hoax and refused to play along.

"Rick must've been pretty upset," said Lucy, taking a sip of tea.

"Yeah. Plus he had to figure out how we could stage Nemo's return. Rick's idea was that he'd been found in a highway rest stop, like the kidnapper dropped him off there. But we needed somebody to keep an eye on Nemo, you know, make sure he'd be safe." She straightened her back. "I mean there are all sorts of people in those places. It wasn't safe for a little guy like Nemo."

Caught unawares by Ocean's attitude, Lucy choked on a swallow of tea and began coughing, but Ocean continued. "That's when Slash got involved."

"Slash?"

"Nemo's father."

"I wondered. . . ."

"Yeah. Nemo doesn't look at all like Rick. I was in a relationship before Rick, with Slash Milley. He's Nemo's father."

Lucy stared into her tea. The name was familiar. She'd seen it somewhere recently. And then it came to her. The court report. Sylvester Milley had been arraigned earlier that month for what? Assault? Breaking and entering? Drugs? She didn't remember the details, but she remembered the name. "You mean Sylvester?"

Ocean was staring at the tabletop. "He hates that name. Everybody calls him Slash."

Everybody except the courts, thought Lucy. "Let me guess. He wanted part of the ransom?"

Ocean pressed her lips together. "Yeah. Rick went to meet him, to explain. . . ."

Lucy held up her hand. "Stop. You're telling me he took Nemo along to meet this guy?"

"He said Nemo was his life insurance.

That Slash wouldn't do anything to him if his kid was there." She sighed. "You know, I don't think Rick was really too smart."

That might be the understatement of the year, thought Lucy. "Well, you have to tell all this to the police. Slash is obviously a dangerous person. . . ."

"No!" Ocean slammed her fist down on the table, making the mugs jump. "He called me and said he'll kill Nemo, just like he killed Rick, if I go to the police."

"He wants the ransom money?"

Ocean looked down at the table and shook her head.

"What does he want?"

"Me. He wants us to get back together."

Lucy drank some more tea, wishing it was something a bit stronger. "That doesn't seem so hard. Isn't there some way you could trick him into thinking you would get back together?"

"That's what I've been trying to figure out," said Ocean, rolling up her sleeve and showing Lucy the white skin on the inside of her arm, dotted with circular scars. "He did this to me, with a cigarette," she said.

Lucy swallowed hard. "We'll figure something out," she said, taking Ocean's hand in hers. "We can do this."

"You know, Rick wasn't so bad. He was

real nice to me, not like Slash." She shook her head. "I don't know what I was thinking, but I was wild about Slash. I met him when I was in college, at Winchester, you know, and he used to pick me up and take me for rides on his motorcycle. I thought he was so cool, much cooler than the college guys, who were always worried about their biochemistry and stuff like that."

"Good girls love bad boys," said Lucy.

"I sure did. And when he said he didn't want to use condoms or any kind of birth control, he told me it was because he loved me so much, he didn't want anything coming between us. I was really dumb. And then, when I got pregnant, well, all of a sudden there was no more Slash. He was gone." She opened her hand. "Poof."

"Did you consider terminating . . . ?"

"No! That's what my parents wanted me to do, but I knew that was wrong. That's when I met Rick, and he didn't mind. He said pregnant women are sexy and he always wanted a kid and that's what happened. He was terrific, didn't beat me or yell at me, and he was cool with Nemo. Not exactly the Father of the Year, but he was never mean to him. The only thing was we didn't have much money. He always had these deals going, but somehow things would go wrong and the bank was gonna foreclose and we were gonna be homeless. That's when he thought up the kidnapping thing."

"Okay. You know who took Nemo. This isn't hard. We go to the police, you tell them the whole story, and they'll arrest Slash."

They'll also bring in social services, thought Lucy, but she didn't mention that.

"No. I told you. Slash will kill him the moment he feels threatened. I know him. He will."

"So you're just going to let him keep Nemo until he gets tired of him?"

"No!" exclaimed Ocean. "I have a plan. I think I know where he is. There's this old house in the woods behind the college where he used to take me. I bet he's there."

Lucy couldn't believe where this was leading. "And you want to confront him?"

Ocean nodded. "I was afraid, but now that you're here . . ."

Lucy had a sudden vision of Rick's lifeless body and the bloody car. "You should be afraid! He's a monster. We've got to go to the police. They're experts. They have SWAT teams, professional hostage negotiators. They know how to handle these situations."

Ocean stood up and walked over to the kitchen counter, where she opened a drawer.

"Rick left me this," she said, pulling out a bulky object wrapped in a greasy bandana.

"No way," said Lucy, watching with horrified eyes as Ocean unwrapped a black automatic.

"I know how to use it," she said, pulling a clip out of the drawer. "Rick showed me."

Lucy bowed her head and put her hands flat on the table. "No," she said, raising her chin and making eye contact. "I won't be part of this."

"Well, I'm going with or without you," said Ocean.

Damn, damn, damn, thought Lucy. This was crazy. She had to find a way to stop the girl. But how? "Okay," she finally said, letting out a long sigh, "but first I've got to use the bathroom."

As soon as the ill-fitting door was closed behind her, Lucy pulled her cell phone out of her jeans pocket. Perching on the wobbly toilet, she realized she didn't dare speak, or Ocean would likely hear her. Instead, she pecked out a quick text and, after a moment's thought, sent it to Horowitz. He was the one she trusted, she realized, the one who would know how to handle the situation. But, she acknowledged to herself, it would be a miracle if the text went through, considering the region's spotty cell coverage. Then, tucking the phone back in her pocket, she washed her hands and studied her image in the spotty mirror, hoping this wasn't the last time she'd see her own reflection.

When she was a little girl, Lucy had an illustrated version of the Hansel and Gretel story that pictured the brother and sister following a winding path through the woods to the witch's gingerbread house. She'd always hated the story; she found the notion that parents would desert their children absolutely terrifying, she felt like screaming whenever she thought of the witch baking the children in the oven. Most disturbing of all was the fact that her mother had insisted on reading the story over and over when it upset her so.

Even though she hadn't thought of that awful book with its graphic illustrations in years, that was what she was thinking about as she and Ocean followed the tire tracks that wound through the woods to a snow-covered farmhouse. The dilapidated house had a pointed roof just like the witch's house, and its broken gingerbread trim was coated in ice that sparkled like spun sugar in the setting sun, which had broken through the clouds. Most terrifying of all, just like in the book, a thick column of gray smoke rising from the crooked chimney gave proof that a fire hot enough to cook a child was burning inside.

As she drew closer, she made out two sets of footprints leading from a parked car to the porch: one large and one small. No tracks led out, indicating that Slash and Nemo were inside. Lucy grabbed Ocean's hand and pulled her aside, ducking behind a tree. "I don't like the looks of this," she whispered. "There's a ton of snow on the roof. He's got a big fire going. I'm afraid the whole thing is going to collapse and burn up."

"That's why we have to get Nemo out," hissed Ocean, waving the gun. "Come on."

Lucy shook her head. "Let's call for help."

Ocean was already moving. "I'm going in," she said.

Lucy tried to send off a quick text, but her gloved hands were clumsy and Ocean was already climbing onto the porch. She hit SEND and shoved the cell phone into her pocket, hurrying to catch up. She grabbed a post to haul herself onto the porch, and it shifted under her hand, making a loud groan.

Ocean turned and waved a finger in front of her lips, signaling silence. Lucy crept to her side and peered through the filthy, cracked window into the derelict living room, where the tattered remains of furnishings were strewn about in front of a soot-blackened brick fireplace. Nemo was crouched in front of the fire, holding a stick with a marshmallow on the end. The only sign of Slash was a lumped black shape on the torn sofa, which was spilling discolored stuffing and missing a leg.

Lucy had no sooner taken this all in when Ocean crashed through the door, causing the building to emit an even louder groan and sending a shower of snow off the roof.

Nemo turned, his marshmallow plopped off the stick into the fire, and he ran to Ocean, wrapping his arms around her hips. "Mom!"

Lucy was holding the door open, waving her arms frantically. "Get out! Let's go! Move it!" she was screaming. The house seemed to be shifting around her, the fire gave a loud pop, and a big glowing ember landed on the wood floor. Ocean saw and was going over to stamp it out, dragging Nemo with her, when the black shape on the sofa suddenly rose with a roar.

That was when something hissed past Lucy's head and exploded, filling the air with smoke and noxious fumes. Her vision was mysteriously narrowing, growing dark around the edges, but she had to get Ocean and Nemo out, she took a step inside, and then her legs gave out beneath her and everything went black.

Chapter Ten

When Lucy came to, she was upside down, apparently on a fireman's shoulder. Her rescuer was running, and she was bouncing about like a rag doll. All she could see was the snowy ground and a pair of black-clad legs. *Not a fireman,* she concluded. He wasn't wearing fireman's boots or the rubber coats issued by the Tinker's Cove Fire Department.

She wanted to know what was going on, but all she managed to say was, "Whuh?"

"Hang on," said a male voice. "You're gonna be fine."

"Uh," replied Lucy as she was heaved forward and deposited on the snowy ground, her back against a tree. Hearing a loud boom, she turned her head and that was when she saw the orange glow in the windows and realized the gingerbread house was on fire.

"Is everybody out?" she cried, but her

black-clad rescuer had already vanished between the trees.

Confused and somewhat disorientated, Lucy scrambled clumsily to her feet, unsure what to do or where to go. She was trying to extricate her cell phone from her pocket when she saw Ocean coming toward her, carrying Nemo.

"Let's get out of here," Ocean screamed.

Lucy shook her head, trying to figure out what had happened. The air was filling with smoke and cinders, and it was hard to breathe. "What about Slash? Did they get him out?"

Ocean was holding tight to Nemo. "Forget about him. We have to get out of here."

She was right. The blaze was huge and likely to spread to the trees surrounding the house. The noise of the fire was enormous, a relentless roar punctuated with explosions.

"But we can't . . . what if he's . . . ?"

"Get a move on," screamed Ocean, screaming over the roar of the fire. "Or give me the keys."

She had them in her hand, Lucy realized, extending her arm toward Ocean. She grabbed them and ran to the car, pulling the backseat door open and shoving Nemo inside. Then she was starting the engine and the car began moving. Lucy had to run alongside, yanking the door open and jumped awkwardly inside. Lucy managed to snap the seat belt and found her cell phone. She was dialing 911 when she heard sirens approaching; somebody must have spotted the blaze and called the fire department. Ocean was maneuvering the all-wheel-drive car as fast as she could down the snowy road, gunning the engine whenever it began to lose traction, and they soon reached the highway, where they could see the fire trucks approaching, red lights flashing.

"We have to tell them about Slash," insisted Lucy, grabbing Ocean's arm.

"No way . . . Besides, it's too late for him."

"Maybe not. Maybe they can get him out."

"Don't be stupid," snapped Ocean. "He's dead."

Lucy pressed her lips together, trying to remember what had just happened. All she remembered was standing in the doorway as something whizzed past her. "There was a bang," she said. "That's all I remember."

"Well, forget it," snapped Ocean. "All you need to know is we found Nemo. Slash was passed out, and the fire started after we left."

Lucy remembered the dark shape rising from the decrepit sofa. "He wasn't passed out." She waited for Ocean to say something, but she remained silent. "Who were those guys? The guy who rescued me?"

"I didn't see anybody."

"Ocean, I didn't get out of there on my own and neither did you." She remembered the ease with which the guy had carried her, his dark clothing, the way he melted into the forest. "There must've been some commandos or something."

"Will you shut up?"

"No. Not till you tell me what really happened."

"I don't know much myself," admitted Ocean. "But I'm pretty sure they were Wilberforce operatives sent by Daddy."

"Your dad has a private army?"

"Not just him. The company. They're international. They do business in dangerous places. They have a security department to protect their workers."

Lucy pictured the chubby security guard at the bank, who smiled at everybody and gave lollipops to little kids. "Must be one hell of a security department," she said.

"Hey!" It was a little voice, piping up in the backseat. "There's some toys back here."

Lucy remembered the little fishing rod and other toys she'd bought for Nemo. "They're for you," she said. "Santa must've put them there. He must've known we were going to find you."

"Wow! First ninjas and now toys!" exclaimed Nemo, scrambling over the seat back and settling in the cargo area to examine his presents. "This is the best Christmas ever!" he declared, waving the fishing rod around. "Say, where's Rick?"

That was when Ocean's steely resolve broke. "He's gone, baby. He's gone for good." She paused, brushing tears from her eyes. "He's in heaven now."

Nemo's tone was serious. "I don't think so, Mom. Pretending to kidnap me was a bad thing, and he used a lot of bad words when that guy came and took me away." There was a long silence. "He said Rick was sleeping, but I think he killed him."

"We're home and you're safe," said Ocean, turning into the parking lot and braking beneath the sputtering neon sign. "That's all that matters." She turned to Lucy. "Can you manage from here?"

Lucy nodded.

"Good. C'mon, kid," Ocean said, opening the rear hatch and gathering up the toys. "Let's make some hot chocolate."

"I wouldn't mind some myself," said Lucy as Ocean slammed the hatch shut.

Then she and Nemo were gone, walking hand in hand through a haze of dancing green snowflakes, illuminated by the neon sign. Lucy got out of the car and stood for a minute, watching as they opened the door and disappeared inside. She didn't know what she expected, but it certainly wasn't this. It was all over. Nemo was home safe. She should feel relieved and happy, but all she felt was emptiness and confusion. She was dazed, as if the earth had shifted under her feet, a seven-pointer on the Richter scale. Moving slowly, she stood, looking up at the glowing green, *Q, U,* and *R.* A light snow had started to fall, the neon sign hissed and the *Q* gave up the ghost. She walked around to the driver's side and slid behind the wheel. She couldn't wait to get home.

The old antique farmhouse on Red Top Road had never looked so welcoming. It was ablaze with lights when Lucy turned into the driveway: all the windows were glowing and colorful Christmas lights had been strung on the porch. The neat path Bill had shoveled earlier in the day was now lined with glowing luminarias that had been set in the snow; Lucy suspected it was a holiday surprise cooked up by Sara and Zoe. When she went inside, the air was fragrant with the scent of cloves and ham, and Christmas carols were playing on the stereo. The girls were putting the final touches on the dining room table; they had used the good silver and china and had lighted the red candle centerpiece. It was all a bit surreal to Lucy, who was beginning to wonder if the last two hours were nothing more than a nightmare or a hallucination.

Sara and Zoe were in high spirits as they all sat at the table, continuing a family tradition of teasing about presents on Christmas Eve. "Oh, Sara, I hope you like brown. It's your favorite color, isn't it?" asked Zoe as she ladled some bourbon sauce on her ham.

"Brown — I hear it's the new black," replied Sara, helping herself to a baked potato. "I know how much you love to play games, Zoe. I don't think checkers is too hard for you, is it?"

Even Bill joined in. "I wish somebody had told me tomorrow is Christmas," he grumbled as he sliced the ham. "I guess I shouldn't have left my shopping to the last minute. Are you sure the stores are all closed?"

Lucy wanted to join in, but try as she might, she couldn't get the image of the burning house out of her mind. Libby, in her usual place under the table, seemed to sense her disequilibrium and rested her chin on Lucy's knees. Or maybe, thought Lucy, she was just hoping a bit of ham might come her way

"You're very quiet," said Bill, laying down the carving knife and taking his seat. "Are you missing Patrick and Elizabeth?"

"I guess that's it," said Lucy, forcing herself to smile. "But we're going to have a wonderful Christmas, anyway. Let's have a toast, to Christmas," she declared, raising her glass of cider.

"To Christmas," they all said, clinking glasses.

After dinner they all climbed in the car and headed for the carol service at the Community Church. It was crowded, of course, but they were able to squeeze into a pew in the choir loft. Lucy tried to concentrate on the service, hearing once again the familiar story of Christ's birth in a stable. At the end of the service the lights were always dimmed and candles were lighted, the flame passed from one person to another until the whole building was illuminated and everyone was holding a candle. Then they held them aloft and sang "Silent Night."

The beauty of the moment always caused Lucy to tear up, but not this time. It wasn't a silent night, it wasn't a holy night, and she couldn't pretend it was. Of course she was glad Nemo had been reunited with his mother, but she couldn't forget that two people had died violent deaths. Rick and Slash weren't nice people, they weren't good, but they were human beings made in God's image. Who knows? They might have redeemed themselves, but now they would never have the opportunity. Even the line from the Lord's Prayer, "and deliver us from evil," seemed like a tall order tonight when there was so much evil afoot in the world — and not just Tinker's Cove. She thought of war in Iraq and Afghanistan, massacres in Africa, earthquake in China.

"Come on, Lucy. It's time to go," said Bill, breaking into her thoughts.

"Oh, right." She blew out her candle and placed it in the rack that held hymnals.

Back at the house they hung their stockings on the mantel in the family room and put a glass of milk and a plate of cookies on the hearth for Santa. The girls opened one package — new pajamas — which they would wear to bed. Once they'd gone upstairs, Lucy and Bill arranged the presents under the tree and filled the stockings; Libby found the cookies on the hearth and polished them off in two gulps. Lucy barely had time to save the glass of milk.

"We should've put it on the mantel," said

Bill, scratching the dog behind her ears. That set her tail to wagging, which sent a few ornaments flying off the tree and breaking into smithereens as they crashed on the new hardwood floor.

"I'll clean it up," offered Lucy. "You go on to bed."

"Thanks," he said. "I'm beat."

When she'd finished sweeping up, Lucy checked that everything was ready for tomorrow morning. The chain saw was a particular concern. She wanted to make sure Bill could find it, but didn't want it to be too obvious either. She finally decided to prop it in a corner of the living room, behind an armchair. Then she went upstairs, washed her face, brushed her teeth, and put on her long flannel nightgown. Nemo's ninja rescuers and the fire might all have been a dream, she thought, except for the faint whiff of smoke she scented when she stuffed her clothes into the laundry hamper.

Bill woke up when she slipped into bed, curling her body against his. "Where were you?" he asked sleepily.

"Just tying up a few loose ends," she whispered, nestling into the warm bed.

"Did you get the sausage?" he asked.

For a moment Lucy was stumped. "No," she finally said. "It sold out."

"Mmm," responded Bill.

Next morning Lucy was up before the sun. Bill was snoring gently; the girls were sound asleep in their beds. She tiptoed downstairs in bare feet and made coffee, then padded into the family room to switch on the tree lights. She clicked on the TV, checking the news while waiting for the coffee to brew, and saw Nemo's smiling face.

"In what's being called a Christmas Eve miracle, a missing Gilead boy has been returned to his family. According to a statement released by Nemo Anderson's grandfather, Wilberforce CEO Ralph Anderson, the child, who had been missing since last Thursday, was returned to his mother yesterday evening. Anderson says no ransom was paid. No other details were offered except that the child was unharmed.

"In other news, the body of the child's stepfather, Rick Juergens, was discovered in his car in Tinker's Cove, the apparent victim of a homicide. It is not clear if Juergens's death is related to the return of the child, but police are investigating.

"And finally, a twilight fire destroyed an abandoned house near Gilead and took the life of a Shiloh man," reported the anchor. "Sylvester Milley's body was discovered by firefighters who responded to the blaze, which investigators believe was ignited when Milley fell asleep, leaving a fire he had lighted for warmth untended."

Well, that's that, thought Lucy. Things couldn't have gone better for Ralph Anderson from a PR standpoint. Nemo's rescue was a feel-good story for the holiday, and nobody was going to ask any difficult questions. As for the promised investigation, Lucy doubted it would get very far, considering the state's budget constraints. No DA was going to take on Ralph Anderson, not when he could afford to hire the very best lawyers and had friends in high places. This was the last they would hear of the kidnapping. She was willing to bet on it, she thought as Libby made an appearance. The dog sat herself rather pointedly in front of the door and looked up at her with mournful brown eyes. "Do you want to go out?" she asked.

The dog wagged her tail, so Lucy got up and opened the kitchen door for her. A few inches of fresh snow had fallen during the night and the sun was rising, turning the backyard into a crystalline fairyland. It was a white Christmas, the best kind, she thought, missing Elizabeth.

"Merry Christmas!" Bill had come downstairs and was standing behind her, slipping his arms around her waist. Lucy leaned against him, enjoying his strength and the way his beard tickled the back of her neck.

"Merry Christmas to you," she said, turning and raising her face for a kiss. He obliged and they were standing like that, kissing, when Sara and Zoe bounced down the stairs.

"It's Christmas! Can we open our presents?" demanded Zoe.

Sara was opening the door for the dog, who bounded in and shook snow all over the floor. "Bad dog!" she scolded.

Lucy was unwrapping the stollen and setting it on the table while Bill was looking for the breakfast sausage. "Where's the smokehouse sausage?" he asked.

"I told you last night. They were sold out. We'll have to have bacon instead." She smiled at Zoe. "Why don't you bring in the stockings? Sara, you can set the table."

Soon they were all gathered at the old round oak table in front of the kitchen windows, eating breakfast and pulling little gifts out of their stockings.

"You shouldn't have," protested Lucy, discovering a small box containing a beautiful watch trimmed with crystals. "It's gorgeous." She was leaning toward Bill, intending to kiss him, when Libby suddenly began barking like crazy. Looking out the window, they saw a long black limousine pulling into the driveway.

"What the . . . ," began Bill, watching as the chauffeur opened a rear door and Elizabeth popped out.

It was all hugs and exclamations as she bounded through the door. Another place was set at the table, a plate was filled with eggs and bacon and stollen, and juice and coffee were poured.

"I thought you had to work," said Lucy, beaming at her daughter.

"I did, but when the Andersons decided to head back east to spend Christmas with their daughter and grandson in Gilead, I mentioned that I had family in Tinker's Cove and they insisted I come with them. In their private jet! It was unbelievable. Big, comfortable seats, their own stewardess who gave you anything you wanted. And then they had the chauffeur bring me home."

"What about your job?" asked Bill.

Elizabeth hunched her shoulders in a shrug. "Mr. Anderson talked to my supervisor and fixed it all up. I'm on vacation until January second. It's like he's Santa Claus or something."

Lucy nodded. "It's amazing what money can do," she said. "I hope you remembered to say thank you."

"Are you kidding? I must've thanked them a million times." She paused. "I still can't believe I'm here."

"Neither can I," said Lucy, giving her a hug.

The day passed in a happy whirl as presents were opened and a turkey dinner was cooked and served and eaten. Toby called from the cruise ship, and Patrick said something that sounded a little bit like "Merry Christmas." Then, as evening fell, the whole family gathered in the family room to watch *A Christmas Carol* on TV.

As Lucy watched the familiar tale replay once again, she thought how very fortunate she was. She had terrific kids, an adorable grandchild, a loving husband — not to mention a beautiful new watch, as well as a new flannel nightie, a couple of books, bubble bath, and lots of other wonderful presents. They might not have as much money as the Andersons, but she thought that was probably a good thing. In truth, she didn't envy them one teeny bit. Well, maybe just a tiny bit — it was natural — but she certainly wouldn't trade her daughters for Ocean. Her girls all had a healthy sense of right and wrong, and she hoped they were sure enough of themselves to say no and wouldn't let love — or lust — override their common sense.

She was congratulating herself on raising such nice children when her gaze happened to fall on the Christmas tree, where a red ribbon had lost its ornament. She got up to investigate, hoping it hadn't rolled onto the floor, where somebody could step on it, and discovered a small bit of gingerbread was still attached to the ribbon. All that was left of the gingerbread man was this little crumb and a bit of ribbon. In fact, she realized, looking closer, only two gingerbread men were still on the tree and they were hanging close to the very top.

"Somebody ate the gingerbread men!" she exclaimed.

"It wasn't me," said Zoe.

"Not me," declared Sara.

"Don't look at me," said Bill.

They all turned toward Libby, who skulked from the room, a bit of red ribbon dangling from her mouth. "God bless us, everyone," declared Tiny Tim from the TV screen, and they all laughed.

"God bless us, everyone," whispered Lucy, squeezing Bill's hand.

Mexican Christmas Salad

1 20-ounce can pineapple chunks, with juice
1 cup canned beets, with juice
2 cups peeled, sliced jicama
1 tablespoon lemon juice
1 head lettuce
3 oranges, peeled and sectioned
1 apple, cored and diced
2 firm bananas, sliced
Seeds of 1 pomegranate
1/2 cup roasted peanuts, chopped
French dressing

Combine undrained pineapple, undrained beets, jicama, and lemon juice in a large bowl. Chill for several hours.

Drain the beet mixture. Line a serving platter with lettuce and arrange the beet mixture, oranges, apple, and banana on top. Sprinkle with pomegranate seeds and peanuts. Serve with French dressing, or make a dressing by reserving 2 tablespoons of juice from beet mixture and mixing it with 1/2 cup mayonnaise.

Linda Kemp's Chocolate Mousse Cake

1 stick unsalted butter
7 ounces semisweet chocolate chips
7 eggs, separated

1 cup sugar, divided
1 teaspoon vanilla
1/8 teaspoon cream of tartar

Preheat oven to 325 degrees F.

Melt butter and chocolate chips.

Beat egg yolks with 3/4 cup of the sugar in a large bowl for about 5 minutes, until light and frothy. Gradually add chocolate mixture and vanilla.

Beat egg whites with cream of tartar in a large bowl, gradually adding remaining 1/4 cup of sugar one teaspoon at a time until peaks form.

Fold egg whites into chocolate mixture.

Bake in an ungreased springform pan at 325 degrees for 35 minutes.

Cool cake on wire rack before removing from pan.

Serve with whipped cream.

ABOUT THE AUTHOR

Like Hannah Swensen, **Joanne Fluke** was born and raised in a small town in rural Minnesota, but now lives in sunny Southern California. She is currently working on her next Hannah Swensen mystery and readers are welcome to contact her at Gr8Clues@aol.com, or by visiting her website, murdershebaked.com.

Laura Levine is a former sitcom writer whose credits include *The Bob Newhart Show, Laverne & Shirley, The Jeffersons, The Love Boat, Three's Company,* and *Mary Hartman, Mary Hartman.* As an advertising copywriter, she created Count Chocula and Frankenberry cereals for General Mills. Her work has been published in *The Washington Post* and the *Los Angeles Times.* In her latest (and favorite) incarnation as a mystery novelist, she has been an IMBA paperback bestseller and winner of the Romantic Times' Toby Bromberg award for Most Humorous Mystery. When not writing mysteries, she contributes comedy material to Garrison Keillor's *A Prairie Home Companion.* She lives in Los Angeles with her husband and her cat.

Leslie Meier is the acclaimed author of twelve Lucy Stone mysteries and has also written for *Ellery Queen's Mystery Magazine.* She lives in Rhode Island with her husband, where she is currently at work on the next Lucy Stone mystery.

The employees of Thorndike Press hope you have enjoyed this Large Print book. All our Thorndike, Wheeler, and Kennebec Large Print titles are designed for easy reading, and all our books are made to last. Other Thorndike Press Large Print books are available at your library, through selected bookstores, or directly from us.

For information about titles, please call:

(800) 223-1244

or visit our Web site at:

http://gale.cengage.com/thorndike

To share your comments, please write:

Publisher
Thorndike Press
295 Kennedy Memorial Drive
Waterville, ME 04901